<u>**ADVANCED PRAISE FOR DEINCEPTION:**</u>

"DeInception is a fast-paced sequel that will keep you on your toes and wanting more. Straus is a master of futuristic Sci-fi!"
—Charleigh Frederick, author of *Rule 25: Don't Fall for the Target*

"A mesmerizing sequel to an amazing debut novel. DeInception picks up immediately where ReInception left off. Leandra and Ward are both thrown back into a world that will test their newfound feelings for each other and their ability to resist a world trying to (re)program their very lives. Along the way, they meet some new friends and old enemies. All the characters have clear motivations and Straus does an amazing job continuing to craft a well-thought-out world. The book moved at a great pace that had me flying to the pages to get to the ending. I need book 3 like yesterday."
—Alexander Nader, author of *Absolution Blues*

<u>**PRAISE FOR REINCEPTION.**</u>

WINNER OF MORE THAN TEN AWARDS INCLUDING:
The 2023 Independent Book Awards Benjamin Franklin Award for Best Audiobook, Fiction
First Place CIBA Cygnus Award for Science Fiction
2023 Independent Press Awards Distinguished Favorite
2023 Pencraft Award – First Place for Science Fiction
2023 Eric Hoffer Awards: Category Finalist
Winner: 2023 Literary Titan Gold Award
Finalist for the 2022 American Writing Awards for ScienceFiction
2023 Finalist for the IAN Book Awards

"A richly detailed world full of thought-provoking tech. Straus's imagination and deft story telling shine in this impressive debut!"
—Jason M. Hough, *New York Times* Best-Selling author of *The Darwin Elevator*

"This is a remarkable book. Brilliant, gripping, endlessly creative. "
—Roger Canaff, Amazon Best-Selling Author of *City Dark*

"*ReInception* is an excellent science fiction novel with a focus on genetic engineering. The adventure readers go on as they follow the characters in the battle for humanity's free will is engaging and thrilling. With the moral question of what is right or wrong and what is the benefit for society asa whole at the forefront of this novel, it will be hard to put down once you start."
—Literary Titan Gold Award

"A riveting read that will have a special resonance with readers with an interest in post-apocalyptic and dystopian science fiction, "ReInception by Sarena Straus is original, compelling, thought-provoking, deftly crafted storytelling and a truly memorable read that will linger in the mind of the reader long after the book itself has been finished and set back upon the shelf. Especially and unreservedly recommended for community and college/university library ScienceFiction collections."
—Midwest Book Review

"A smartly plotted, futuristic thriller packed full of twists, turns—and suspense. A FINALIST and highly recommended!"
—Wishingshelf Book Awards

"ReInception is a thrilling, exciting, and dark look at a future where people can reprogram their minds to eliminate undesirable habits. In a vividly realized world of haves and have nots, where corporations control and spy on citizens, Leandra isa college student who accidentally gets caught up in a resistance movement led by the underclass, known as the Proles... She meets and falls for a Prole, Ward, and they work together to uncover dangerous secrets that can bring down the system. I thoroughly enjoyed the fast-paced plot, the swoony romance, and the technological dystopian themes. Highly recommend it!"
—Sylvia Liu, Multi-Award-Winning Author of *Hannah Shu and The Ghost Crab Nation*

"This is. the true nature of our collective Speculative Futures, and we hope to see more from this author."
    —Savage Planets

"This is a truly futuristic and intriguing story that will have the reader wondering if the future could be like this…The story is one that will keep you reading and get you thinking."
    —LitPick Five Star Book Review

"*ReInception* felt incredibly nostalgic tome. It brought back that Science Fiction dystopia mood which I've been craving."
    —Utopia State of Mind

"This was an absolutely incredible read! ReInception is a book with an incredible premise…this was gloriously done."
    —Functionally Fictional

"This was an amazing sci-fi novel, that gives the reader a chilling glance into an all-too-possible future…I do have to warn you—set aside a few hours before you start reading, Straus's unique style will hold you captive for quite awhile."
    —The Faerie Review

DeINCEPTION

DeINCEPTION

SARENA STRAUS

NEW YORK | LOS ANGELES

Jacket design by Rejenne Pavon

Jacket Copyright © 2024 by Winding Road Stories

Interior Design by Winding Road Stories

ISBN#:   978-1-960724-42-7 (pbk)

ISBN#:   978-1-960724-43-4 (ebook)

Published by Winding Road Stories

www.windingroadstories.com

To My Father—Marc Joshua Straus—poet, author, physician, gallerist, entrepreneur, real estate developer, amateur architect, globe trotter, torah scholar, Yankees fan, poacher of foods in the microwave, writer of unintelligible emails, and dragger of children to art studios. You are a true Renaissance Man and it is a joy to watch you reinvent yourself again and again.
As Robert Heinlein said, "Specialization is for insects."

"What we do now echoes in eternity."

— MARCUS AURELIUS

Author's Note:
A glossary of terms appears at the end of this book
for the reader's convenience.

CHAPTER ONE

"Inventions are like children. We birth them, but eventually they grow up. They change and become products of their environment. They evolve. Arlo Genesis may claim that the invention of ReInception was about eliminating addiction and nothing else, but even he had to admit that anyone, especially someone with an exceptional mind like his, could foresee its broader application. ReInception doesn't just eliminate addiction, it can rid humankind of all unwanted behaviors. Progress means that we can't stop with just this one application when ReInception can make the world a better, safer place for everyone."

— CONGRESSMAN RAN CHOWDRY,
THE CONGRESSIONAL HEARINGS ON REINCEPTION, 2032

Day - 27: November 11, 2126: Columbia University, New York City
Ward

T he Ward waited in the utility closet. It was the third time that month. He kept his back to the hallway, anticipating the quiet *shush* of the door across the way sliding open. He tried to look busy in case any Unis walking by actually paid attention to him. They never did. In his blue jumpsuit, he was all but invisible.

Still, he couldn't linger. His movements would be logged and monitored. Even with his hacks, there was only so much idle time he could conceal before someone would start asking questions.

If he didn't find a reason to engage with Andromeda soon, he'd have to sabotage her comm system so she'd order tech support. That would be risky. Any link he created between them would be a breadcrumb later. It had taken him two years to land this job just so he'd have access to her. If he blew it now, just when he was finally close to making contact, it would all be for nothing. He needed a little more patience...

He was about to give up for the day when he heard voices and the soft pad of boots on the glass walkway. Stepping further into the closet, keeping his face in shadow, he glanced through the screen of his shoulder-length hair toward the sound.

Like many Wards, this one kept his hair long. In a world of limited, environmentally conscious, color-coded jumpsuit wardrobes, the upper caste took every measure to make themselves look distinct by manipulating their hair, eyes, and skin. Wards did everything possible to look alike. The less conspicuous you were, the better. This one in particular had reasons to want to go unnoticed.

Squinting, he waited for the approaching Unis to come into focus. The sloppy eye mods that ReInception had forced on him as a child to hide his identity had damaged his vision, and he couldn't afford a transplant. They had to get closer than he would have liked before he could be sure who they were.

Yes. It was two of Andromeda's friends—a guy and a girl he'd frequently seen her with in the cafeteria. Missing was the little redhead who was the Ward's beacon. The four of them were always together, so she was probably lurking somewhere nearby. Andromeda changed her hair, eye, and skin color so frequently that she was often hard to identify.

With that thick, bright, curly hair and fair skin that she never altered, the redhead he could spot.

The guy, the Ward heard him called Hallyn on past reconnaissance missions, stopped in front of Andromeda's door, talking into the comm port.

"Oi. Andy! Lea's waiting in the Cats. Ya'la."

Resisting the urge to turn around and look at them, the Ward instead reached into the closet, rattling things about as if searching for something. What was the redhead doing waiting in the Catacombs alone? Not that it was dangerous; no Prole would risk harming a Uni. It was just that Uni's were frightened anyhow; too many fairytales featuring Prole as ogre or boogeyman. It was fine by the Prole; they preferred it that way. It was the only place they had any peace. So why was she there?

"Can't we just go to Bar in the Sky?" The girl asked. Her voice was on the deep side, yet still, somehow, whiney.

Hallyn gave a frustrated groan. "This again? If you don't want to go, then don't."

Ward heard the *shush* of a door opening.

"Ya'la!"

He recognized Andromeda's voice, bubbly and high pitched.

"Gold, really?" Hallyn asked.

Ward risked a glance.

Andromeda had a complex, multi-colored skin pattern looping over her shoulder, up her neck, and hooking around an ear. Ward couldn't make out the details of it, just tones and patterns, but enough to tell that it was expensive. Her hair and eyes were gold—a way of showing alignment with ReInception. The metallic finish combined with her silver Uni jumpsuit made her look more award trophy than human. He wondered where they were going that she'd mod her appearance to make a political statement. If they were going to meet the redhead, looking that way in the Catacombs would be offensive to Prole. Not that she'd care; not with who she was.

The Ward waited until he heard them moving away before stepping out of the closet, closing the door, and following the trio down the hall.

The top of the glass walkway was covered in a thin veneer of sparkling snow, big flakes falling all around. It was like being inside one of the snow globes his mother had inherited from her grandparents. His favorite had been one of New York City. Crowded together, as if all in one place, were the Statue of Liberty, the Brooklyn Bridge and Times Square—a city in a dome before there were domes, like this one, all over the city.

It was surreal in The Above, so bright, clean, and quiet. The Catacombs could be quiet, too, but where The Above was the silence of insulated glass, soft felted boots and the distant thrum of the monorail speeding past far below, The Catacombs had a different kind of silence; hushed and wary. It was the silence of fear and stealth; of trying to go through life unnoticed. It was something the Ward had never adjusted to after he'd Fallen—this need to be small, even when he was the biggest person in the room; this expectation that he appear meek when, inside, he was exploding with energetic rage.

The Ward rounded the corner just as the pod doors closed behind the friends. He watched as they descended all the way to the ground, spilling out the doors and into ankle-deep snow, greeting their red-haired friend. From up here, she was just a tiny dot, like the lit tip of a match. Despite the biting cold, they'd be warm in their temperature-controlled Uni jumpsuits and boots. He'd be cold in his Prole blue.

Grabbing his lead-impregnated cloak, he wrapped it around himself and called for the pod, hoping it would come quickly enough so that he wouldn't lose them in the white-blurred world.

⸺◆⸺

By the time the Ward exited into The Catacombs, Andromeda and her friends were already a couple blocks away. He followed at a distance, wondering where they were going, grateful, for once, for the electric rationing that kept The Catacombs in shadow.

They stopped at the door of one of the few establishments that was lit up at this time of day and then stepped inside. Ward sucked in a breath. What were they doing at the West End? It was a simple Prole bar to most, but to him, it was far more. It was his secret gateway to the underground and to The Origins. It was where two of the people he loved most in the world pretended to be like every other Prole. Unis coming here meant trouble.

After waiting a few more minutes, the Ward stepped inside the building, pushing through the crowd of inebriated Prole and stepping up to the bar. The place thrummed with retro electronic music and smelled of sweat and hops. All the barstools were full, but Sebbe shooed a Crim off of one so the Ward could take it.

The orange jumpsuited Crim scowled, but stood anyhow, taking his beer and shoulder-checking the Ward as he passed. The Ward noted his designation: Crim 188,233 Rikers. ARSON. That the man was out and still wearing the orange meant that he'd been reprogrammed so he could complete his sentence at liberty, but was still on parole. It was the type of mod the Ward wondered about most. If the desire to light fires was a choice, the mod made sense, but if it was a compulsion, how could the mind reconcile the reprogramming? People whispered that misuse of ReInception was the reason so many crims went non-comp. Of course, ReInception denied the connection.

Sebbe ran a damp rag across the bar in front of the Ward. "Uzhe?"

"Lah." The Ward nodded, glancing over his shoulder to see where the Unis had gone.

Across the crowd, the Ward spied the neat, shiny helmet of Vella's purple hair. Shooing a group of Crims from a booth, they ushered Andromeda and her friends into the dark corner. Unis were bad for business and Vella had no poker face. The Ward hoped they'd keep their mouth shut, and that the Unis would fail to notice the disdainful sneer. He didn't need Vella scaring them off. Better if they weren't here, but now that they were, maybe this was finally his opportunity...

Sebbe filled a glass with beer, sliding it toward the Ward. He aimed his chin toward Andromeda and her friends. "What dat bout?"

The Ward shrugged. "Siao s."

Sebbe shook his head. "Uni here like dat bring down storm, no need."

The Ward nodded. He knew he should tell Sebbe who Andromeda was. But that would lead to questions about why the Ward knew; questions the Ward couldn't afford.

Vella carried a tray of drinks over to the Unis—something neon green and pretentious. The Ward snorted—it figured they'd come to a Prole bar and still order a Uni drink. He downed his beer, tapping the empty mug on the bar, signaling for another.

Sebbe raised an eyebrow. The Ward rarely drank much, and for good reason. He tended to say whatever he was thinking when he drank. And he wasn't a very nice drunk.

"Yeh sure?"

Holding up his thumb and index finger parallel to the bar, Ward pinched them together, squinting his eyes. "Skootch a beatha."

"Lah." Sebbe laughed, pouring amber liquid into a tall cup. "Jes er skootch, sure." He pushed it over to the Ward. "Nay be clady."

The Ward pointed an index finger at his own chest, raising his brows and widening his eyes. "Yo? Nicht." Sebbe laughed again as the Ward spun his stool, turning so that he faced out toward the crowd. He sipped his drink. It was some kind of synthetic Scotch produced by Scottish Prole—something affordable for their downtrodden brethren to dull the pain. It wasn't half bad. Would have been better if the Ward could have afforded some ice, though. He had no idea how it compared to the real stuff, but it warmed his belly and muted the aches and pains. It was surprising that the government allowed its import; Prole were permitted so few luxuries. But alcohol had always been a balm for the poor. Keep 'em drunk and maybe they'd be a little less unhappy.

Toasting no one, the Ward raised his glass. "Sköl!"

No one toasted him in return.

Squinting to see them better, the Ward watched the Unis. They were laughing together at their table, the grouchy dark girl curling her lips and pulling her sleeves over her hands; coughing when she tried the drink. Probably modified, so she couldn't tolerate the sauce. He felt his own lip curl, mirroring hers, his gut going warm, heat rising up his esophagus and spreading through his brain, synapses firing off in angry bursts. If she was so disgusted by the place, why the floods had she come?

He couldn't quite understand this group of friends. Not that he needed to, but watch people long enough, you start to form impressions. The boy, Hallyn, was lean and handsome by upper caste standards; one of those anti-ReInception zealots modified within an inch of his life. Ward couldn't decide if it was hypocritical—it wasn't his fault his parents had modded him. But what business did he have telling people they shouldn't do something he'd done? Then again, the Ward had felt the same way before he Fell and became a Prole—back when he was Kallum Gordon and had tried to stop his mother from modifying his sister.

In his more charitable moments, he thought that, had his life stayed on the intended track, he might've been friends with Hallyn—idealistic, intelligent, easy to laugh. But as the liquor flowed, the Ward's charitability ebbed, leaving his impression of Hallyn as spoiled, entitled, delusional and, most of all, self-righteous.

Then there was the grumpy one, Kallilloo or Kassio or something like that. She said little. She didn't smile much. Vocally pro-ReInception, like Andromeda. Unlike Andromeda, she was utterly forgettable. Much as he despised her and everything she stood for, he had to admit that Andromeda was hard to ignore. In her element, Andromeda's behavior might signal confidence or, perhaps, overcompensating. With a father like Kelvin, she must be. But here, her boisterousness signaled arrogance—an utter lack of awareness or care for her situation.

The Ward felt his tongue loosening with desire to say things he'd regret. His limbs itched, urging him to rise from his seat, walk over to the table, and tell the Unis they had no place in a Prole bar, especially the daughter of their greatest enemy. He needed to stop drinking. Leave before he did something lowQ. What was he accomplishing sitting here, anyhow? It's not like Andromeda was going to talk to him or he would talk to her. He turned his back toward the group, torn between having a third drink and leaving while he was still half in possession of his faculties. Of course, he could also take a sobriety pill, but pakshet...he wanted to be inebriated.

Then, in his peripheral vision, he saw that hair. Andromeda's friend was standing right next to him. Close up, it was less the color of a match tip and more like the deep orange of a sunrise. Keeping his body facing the bar, he watched her out of the corner of his eye. What was her name? He couldn't remember if he'd heard it before or not. Her face flushed red as Sebbe ignored all the Prole who'd been standing there, waiting to be served, to take her order. What did she think he'd do? Make her wait?

"What's your poison?" Sebbe asked her.

"My...why would I want poison?" She shook her head.

The Ward watched Sebbe shrink, knowing it was only half act. Unis here could be a disaster for the operation they ran through this bar. Sebs'd want to get the group out of here as quickly as possible. Leave 'em happy enough to have nothing bad to say, but disappointed enough that they'd never return.

As Sebbe mixed drinks for the Uni, the Ward caught the other bartender's eye and pointed to the tap. She poured him another beer, sliding it in front of him and walking away.

He turned his attention back to the girl. It was his first chance to examine her up close and to see her as more than just a pale blur. She was pretty in her own way, with high cheekbones and a small, full mouth. Looking her up and down, he tried to figure out her mods. She was shorter than average, even for an upper caste. Small-breasted. Fit, but not particularly. Slim, but not particularly. It appeared as if she didn't have any physical mods, which probably meant she couldn't afford them. It was rare these days to see a person in their native form. How human she looked tugged at something deep inside of him.

He didn't believe she was completely unmodified—no upper caste was. So, if not physical mods, ones he couldn't see. If she went to the Uni, surely she had academic mods; probably ones for things like appetite control. But nothing obvious. Floods. She was so small. With her fair skin and freckles, she looked like she'd stepped into the room, not from The Above, but from another century. From a time before there were Prole.

So, Creationist, he decided, nodding to himself. They believed God made them perfect and ReInception was sacrilege. They were the worst. So sanctimonious, like ignoring progress was some kind of badge of honor.

He didn't know why simply looking at this girl made him so angry. He didn't remotely resemble the person he would have looked like if he hadn't had all the physical mods. And he hadn't asked for those; they'd been forced on him. He had no academic mods—he'd been too young for them when his life went sideways—yet he could run mental rings around most Unis. For that matter, most anyone he'd ever met. Did that do him any good? He could be the smartest person on the planet. All that mattered was that he was Prole. And here was this girl—ordinary, unexceptional, obnoxiously modest and polite, yet associating herself with Andromeda, a girl who'd forcibly reprogram every Prole in the bar given half a chance.

Ward stood, like he was being pulled from his seat by invisible strings attached to his shoulders and elbows; the nape of his neck. Anger prickled there, right in his brain stem, his guts wriggling like fish, hot blood pumping into his muscles, pulling them taught. A little voice in the back of his mind warned him, *Don't do this*; he ignored it.

"Fly home canary."

She turned to face him. "Beg ya?"

"Y'aren't welcome here."

Her eyes flicked up toward his left breast, looking at his designation: Ward 17,362 Bedford. In the last fifty years, over 40,000 Wards had been raised in the massive orphanage that had been a women's penitentiary over a hundred years earlier, before ReInception cut crime by more than fifty percent. Before the civil war and the creation of the caste system cut it by yet another twenty-five percent. The upper caste called it progress. They called it humane. The Ward called it trading one prison for another.

She lifted her chin. "I didn't ask your opinion."

He clenched his hands into fists. "Up there, I've to be polite. I've to do what you birds say. Down here is my domain. Go play in your own cage."

Sucking in a breath, she straightened her spine, face going red. Lifting her chin, she tried to stare him down from far below. It made him want to laugh. Like she stood a chance against him if he actually dared raise a hand to her. Like he stood a chance against her simply because of her status relative to his.

"I don't believe in the castes."

Snorting, he told her she was self-righteous. Sebbe warned him to back down, but Sebbe didn't understand what a threat this girl was. It was these little innocent looking ones who you had to look out for. She thought she was better than him, better than her friends because she was against the system, but hadn't she brought them here? The enemy was behind the gate and the Ward didn't want to waste his time with this pious hypocrite. He wanted Andromeda. This girl was getting in his way; risking everything he'd been waiting for.

He barely knew what was coming out of his mouth—taunting her with knowledge he'd gleaned from stolen history books. Books that told stories forbidden by the U.S. government since the war. Books she didn't have access to, and that he shouldn't have. He didn't know why he felt the need to prove he was just as smart as she was, smarter even, but he couldn't stop himself. It was dangerous and LowQ of him to bait her like that, but he couldn't stop himself.

Turning away from him, she stomped back to her table, climbing into her boyfriend's lap and making a show of it.

Keeping his back to the bar so he could watch her, he called over his shoulder to Sebbe. "Give me another."

"Yev had enough."

The Ward glanced at him. "Ken sai."

"Yeh tink yer grandfather own this place?"

"Nay. But you think me dah does."

"If I were yer dah, I'd pune yer cara."

The Ward laughed. "Jes give et."

Instead of handing him a drink, Sebbe slid a small blue pill across the table. "Dry out."

"Sobriety tab?"

Sebbe stared at him for another moment, pushing the pill closer and then walking away.

The Ward pushed air out of his nose. Sebbe was always playing Da to him. He liked the feeling of the alcohol, the way it made his brain lighter in his head and loosened his always-sore muscles, including his tongue, which he spent most of the time biting. He knew Sebs was right to be angry with him. He'd said too much to the redhead. But it was his place, not hers. She should have stayed away.

"Gondu," the Ward muttered, unsure if he meant Sebbe, the redhead, or himself.

The redhead was kissing Hallyn, but as she pulled away from him, she looked toward Ward.

"Fly home canary," he mouthed, flapping his hands, feeling mean. Hating himself for it.

That's when Andromeda rose to her feet. She smirked at him, saying something to the redhead that the Ward couldn't hear. The redhead's eyes widened, and her mouth dropped open. The friends argued. The Ward narrowed his eyes, turning his ear toward them, trying to catch what the quarrel was about. Over the noise of the bar and the band warming up from its break in the background, it was impossible.

And then Andromeda was coming toward him, a half grin on her face. The look was full of hunger.

He froze, sitting up straighter in his chair, hands squeezing into fists, and heart thumping hard in the chest.

Reaching behind him, he felt across the bar until his fingers palpated the sobriety pill. Grabbing it, he slipped it into his mouth.

Tucking his hair behind his ear, he returned Andromeda's smile.

Finally.

Ward floated in that space between dreams and waking, remembering that night almost a month ago when he'd first met Lea. Why had he doled out bits and pieces of his story and not told her everything? She'd earned his trust—the right to know all of it. He thought he'd told her his biggest secrets, yet still, he'd held back.

"Tomorrow," he promised himself, the medication ebbing and flowing through him, numbing the pain, making his memories go fuzzy around the edges, like his vision, like her face in his memories, blurry and beautiful and his.

"I'll tell her everything tomorrow."

CHAPTER TWO

Seasteading...is predicated on the idea that government regulation stifles innovation, and therefore the route to a better world can only be found by unleashing a new generation of start-up societies that are forced to compete for citizens in a free market of ideologies. Don't like the rules of your current micro-nation? Simply move to another one. "We will give people the freedom to choose the government they want," said Friedman, "instead of being stuck with the government they get."

—SEASTEADING: A VANITY PROJECT FOR
THE RICH OR THE FUTURE OF HUMANITY?
THE GUARDIAN, JUNE 24, 2020

Day 0: December 8, 2126: The Marshes
Leandrea

T he tiny box shook in Leandrea's hand. She almost dropped it. Somehow, Officer Aisling was transmitting through the chip that had just been removed from Ward's back. It shouldn't have been possible. Comms were powered by the nervous system. Once removed, it should have been nothing more than data files. But this comm chip wasn't like the one she and others of the upper caste had. It was something that had been implanted into the Prole to track them, to control them. Or had something different been put into Ward's back? He thought no one knew who he really was, but what if someone—the person who'd put this in his back—had?

The box crackled and hissed.

"Please. Ward. There's no more time."

Aisling's voice was hushed, like she was trying not to be overheard. She sounded desperate. Pleading. Sincere. But Lea knew how deceptive this woman could be.

Lea glanced at Ward, unconscious in the cot nearby. His back was covered in gauze, small spots of red spreading through the fibers like blooming flowers. She'd never seen him so still, his face so serene. It was impossible to believe that she'd once found that face harsh and frightening. He had seemed so strong. So certain of himself. Now that she knew who he was, what he'd been through, she saw him differently. She'd never let anyone hurt him again.

She moved further away, afraid that the sounds would wake him. Blowing at the tiny speaker, she cleared it of the last of Ward's dried blood.

"Ward. Kallum."

She froze.

"Kitty sent me."

Leandrea felt the blood drain from her face. She went cold. Her body trembled. How did Aisling know? The only people besides her who knew were Izabelle and Ferryman and Ferryman was dead. She'd killed him escaping from Aisling. And now, here Aisling was again, and she knew Ward was Kallum Gordon.

"Meet me in the stairwell between the fourth and fifth floors. I'll explain everything. Please. Kallum. There's no time to wait."

What kind of trick was she playing this time? The only thing that made sense was that Izabelle had been captured and undergone ReInception. She'd given up Ward's identity. Otherwise, there was no way she would have told anyone who Ward was. Her entire plan had been to wait for just the right moment to reveal his identity. To use Kallum Gordon to spark a Prole uprising. But the information that Ward and Lea had almost died sneaking to the Origins hadn't yet been smuggled to the Mod-Free zone, which meant Izabelle was not yet ready to reveal Ward to the world. The only copy of the information was on the chips that Ward had concealed in a tiny incision in Lea's side. Who could possibly know other than Iza?

As if to reassure herself that the data was still safe, Lea touched the spot where, just yesterday, Ward had secreted the files back inside of her. Her "lifeline," he'd called them as he'd cut her with the fine blade.

"I'm armed, but only to defend myself from capture." Aisling continued whispering through the box. "They'll know soon enough that I was a spy, and I can't let them take me. I'm alone. You can bring a weapon. You can do whatever you need to feel safe from me, but please, hurry. There's going to be a raid any—"

Aisling stopped mid-sentence. Lea heard the distant *Thwomp Thwomp* of Authority hovercraft.

And then it hit her. That nickname—Kitty. Only Ward had ever called his sister Kitty, and Lea was the only person Ward had told. The only other person in the world who knew was Kitty herself.

Lea started to run, keeping the small device to her ear.

"Floods, they're coming. Please, hurry. With or without you, I have to leave before they get here. You know what they'll do to you if they find out who you are."

Lea was about to burst through the fire door and into the stairwell, but she couldn't confront Aisling with only a knife to defend herself. Not when Aisling would have a stun gun. Or a real one. Guns were illegal in the United States, but that didn't mean she didn't have one. There were hundreds of millions of them floating around the country from the time before the War of Coastal Incursion. It wasn't hard to get one if you knew who to ask.

But if Kitty really had sent Aisling...If she really was from somewhere else...Lea couldn't let the chance, no matter how slim, slip away.

"Your sister sent me to find you. I couldn't tell you who I was. Couldn't risk exposing myself until I was sure it was you. I'm still not sure, but I'm out of time so Ward, Kallum, please, if it's you…"

The thrumming of the hovercraft grew louder. Lea ran into the computer lab, the heart of The Origins. It was chaos. People darted around the room, shouting to each other. Blue-clad figures stood in front of computers, barking out commands, erasing data, forwarding information. Setting things on fire.

Lea's heart pounded in her chest. Her throat squeezed so that she could barely breathe. She raced around the corner, unlocking a closet with a code that Ward had given to her in case she needed to defend herself. Opening the door, she scanned the shelves of neatly organized weapons. Ward had demonstrated the basics of loading a gun, holding it, firing, taking off the safety, but she'd never actually used one. She didn't know one from the other. She grabbed the one closest to her, along with the small magazine next to it. Turning back toward the exit, she slammed the magazine home.

Leandrea paused outside the exit stairwell door, gasping for air, trying to slow her breathing. She was on the second floor. The third floor was where, two nights ago, she and Ward had held each other and talked about a future together. She'd imagined the two of them escaping to the Mod-Free zone, exposing ReInception's lies and plots to the world. She'd imagined a peaceful future with him. How could she have been so naïve?

Above the third floor, the building was empty. Aisling said she was between the fourth and fifth.

Voices echoed in the stairwell and doors opened and slammed. Orders were shouted, and on the landing below her, a woman sobbed and shook. Lea looked up, but the stairs above her were dark. She couldn't see anything.

She held the box to her ear. "…leave in two minutes. The crafts are landing. They'll be in the building. I've already waited too long."

Inching her way up the stairs, Leandrea kept her back to the wall so that if Aisling was where she said she was, if she peered over the side, she wouldn't see Lea approaching.

Aisling stopped talking, but Lea could still hear her, breathing hard. She sounded frightened.

Could the woman be trusted? Could she possibly be telling the truth?

Lea thought back to that first time she'd seen the officer. Aisling had interviewed her about what she'd been doing at the anti-ReInception rally she'd gone to the night she met Ward. It was a bombing at that rally that prompted Hallyn's parents to forcibly reprogram him. Those events lead her down the path to Ward and The Origins; to the truth.

During that interview, Aisling kept looking off to the side and then abruptly stopped her questioning. The behavior had puzzled Lea. Then, when Ward and Lea had fled Ward's apartment during a raid, Aisling broke off, coming down the alleyway and entering the building alone. Leandrea had thought it was about having all the glory when she caught The Origins, but what if it was about something else? What if it had been about trying to identify Ward so she could get him out?

"Please, Kallum, please." Aisling was barely audible, now simultaneously coming from above her in the stairwell and through the device. "I have to go. I've already waited too long. Please, I don't want to leave without you."

When Aisling had pursued them into The Floods, she again separated herself from the other Authority. When one of them came after her, she was angry. She didn't want to believe this woman. Everything Aisling had ever said to her had been a manipulation. But maybe this was why. None of it had ever made sense, but this...this did.

The screams and shouts grew more distant as Lea approached the fourth-floor landing. She slid the small device into her pocket so that if Aisling started speaking again, she wouldn't hear her own voice as Lea approached.

"Gondu, Ward. I can't wait anymore."

Leandrea heard a thump as Aisling hit the bar on the exit door.

Lea swung around the corner, gun held out in front of her, just as Ward had shown her.

"Don't move!" She shouted.

Aisling froze. Lifting her hands, she turned slowly to face Leandrea. She wasn't in her red uniform. Her hair was no longer a swirl of fire, dyed to match her Authority jumpsuit. Her eyes were no longer that disconcerting blood-rust color. Now, she wore citizen black. Her hair was cropped short and dyed black, too. Her eyes, a generic dark blue—a basic, inexpensive shade selected by millions of other people. Her skin was monochromatic and slightly lighter than before. But it was her, Leandrea had no doubt.

"Where's Kallum?" Aisling demanded.

"I'm asking the questions."

"Floods, Lea, there's no time. I have to get him out of here."

The gun shook in Lea's hand. She was afraid she'd drop it. Aisling looked at the weapon and then back at Lea. "Have you ever even held one of those things before?"

"Does it matter? Hard to miss when you're two feet away."

Fast, so fast that Lea didn't even see it coming, Aisling stepped forward, grabbing Lea by the wrist and twisting her hand so that the gun clattered to the floor. Stepping back, she stared at Lea, leaving the gun on the floor between them.

"See? Now we know I can hurt you. And now we know I'm not going to. Why are you here and not Ward? I know he wouldn't have sent you instead of him, which means you heard the message and not him. How is that possible?"

Leandrea held Aisling's gaze, resisting the urge to look away.

"Floods. He did it already, didn't he? Gondu! Is he in the hospital? Where—"

There was a loud crash below them and screams.

"Authority! On the ground!"

Lea heard the familiar tinny crash, pop, and hiss of smoke bombs.

"Pakshet!" Aisling cursed. "Let's go!"

Aisling crashed through the exit door. Lea had no choice but to follow.

Aisling's breaths came in small, sharp bursts. Looking left and right down the hallway, her eyes widened, and her hands shook. "We're trapped! You've been here. Is there another exit?"

Leandrea shook her head. "I'm not sure. I don't think so." Then she thought of her night with Ward, of something she'd seen as she stared out the window, looking at the full moon. "Wait. I have an idea."

Leandrea burst through one of the doors into an abandoned, rotting office. Chairs encircled a conference table, sitting where they'd been left decades earlier. Dust so thick you couldn't even tell what color they'd been coated the surfaces.

Racing toward the window, Lea heaved, trying to push it open. It creaked and crackled in its frame until, finally, it inched up just high enough for her to squeeze through. Ward wouldn't have stood a chance getting through the space, but Aisling was small, like Lea.

"Here. There's a ledge."

Leaning out the window, Lea gasped. Below her, Ward was being carted away toward a waiting Authority hovercraft. Amie raced along beside him, holding aloft an IV bag. Ward's back was bloody, and he wasn't moving. The Authority holding his gurney hit uneven ground and the cot tipped sideways, spilling Ward to the dirt. Lea's breath caught.

"It's Ward," she called over her shoulder to Aisling. "They're taking him away!"

"Gondu! Get back inside!" Aisling grabbed her shoulder, trying to pull her back in, but Lea shook the woman off.

"I have to get him. I have to help."

Eyes wide, bile rising up her throat, Leandrea watched as Ward was lifted back onto the gurney and they started moving forward again.

Leandrea was halfway out the window. She didn't know what she'd do when she got outside. She couldn't think clearly. She had to do something, had to get to Ward. She couldn't let them take him.

Amie glanced up. Eyes meeting Lea's, she mouthed the words, *Run! Run!*

Wards arms hung over the sides of the cot, heavy and unmoving. Blood soaked through the gauze on his back, running down his sides and arms, dripping off the ends of his fingers.

Lea's heart pounded. Her breath came in short bursts. She swung a leg over the side. She was almost all the way out of the window when Ward lifted his head. Twisting it to the side, he looked over his shoulder, eyes meeting Leandrea's. They were watery, pleading.

Aisling grabbed Lea by the waist, dragging her back inside.

"No!" Ward screamed. "No!"

Aisling pulled Lea in all the way, throwing her to the floor and slamming the window shut. Cutting off Ward's screams.

CHAPTER THREE

Under Part II of the Prole Reassignment Act of 2075, certain children of the Fallen are recast as Prole. While post-pubescent minors can no longer benefit from the genetic modifications that are endemic to the Prole, we have determined that pre-pubescent minors can receive certain treatments to make them Prole. Which process is used should be determined based on the stage of the child's growth, with infants and very young children receiving the same DNA modifications as Prole-born. Older children, for whom DNA modification is no longer viable, can be reassigned as Prole through a series of treatments designed to stimulate physical and muscle growth. This will have similar outcomes to treatment with DNA modification.

—FROM THE FILES OF DENNISON KELVIN

Day 0: December 8, 2126: The Marshes
Ward

T he screaming roused Ward from his drug induced sleep. And pain. So much pain. Like someone pouring liquid hot metal across his spine and shoulder blades. He was face down on a cot, back on fire, new skin tearing at the seams as he was jostled from side to side. The *thwomp thwomp* of Authority hovercraft pounded in his ears. Close. So close. He lifted his head, trying to get his bearings. Trying to understand what was happening. It was like lifting an anvil. Shapes moved past him, blue and red blurs. Gray smoke was everywhere. His mind was foggy. He shook his head, trying to clear it, his brain like a boulder crashing against the sides of his skull. He was supposed to be in the infirmary. Lea was supposed to be by his side. There was nothing but noise, shapes, and movement. The cold of the outside world was flames on his bare skin.

His head dropped back down.

Everything went black.

Back in that half state between dreaming and waking. Back in The Catacombs, inside his sparse room. It was dark save for a candle flickering on the dresser. He curled up on his thin cot, his back to the wall, Lea facing him, pressed up close against him. There couldn't have been room for both of them on that narrow mattress, yet, somehow, they fit, like irregular pieces of a puzzle that, when clicked together, match perfectly. Her hair pooled in large soft waves all around them, a pale, smooth shoulder glowed in the dim light. A furnace behind him scorched his back, the pain almost unbearable, but Lea smiled at him, her tiny, pale hand caressing his cheek; he didn't dare move. If he moved, she'd disappear, and he'd be alone again. Lonely again. It'd been so long since he hadn't felt alone. So long since he'd felt hopeful. He slid his hand around the back of her neck, pulling her forward, his lips almost touching hers...

His body hit the ground hard.

Ward moaned, unable to move, face against dirt. Hot blood trickled down his cheeks and sides; fire ants crawling across his back.

The pain was worse than he thought possible. Worse than the torture that had given him his scars; the pain of electrodes implanted into every muscle in his body to stimulate his growth. The torture that turned him from Kallum Gordon into the Prole, "Ward 17,362 Bedford."

"Gondu! You'll kill him!" A female voice screamed.

Lea? No, not Lea. There was a heavy accent. Familiar. He couldn't place it in the fog of pain.

Hands and knees came into view and then a face, chestnut skin, long black hair hanging to the side.

"Ward? Ward! Are you okay?" A small hand on his cheek, soothing, like warm honey. He leaned into it. "Amie," he tried to whisper; nothing came out but a moan.

Two large hands reached down, yanking Amie to her feet.

"Keep moving!"

"I'm his doctor."

"Keep moving."

"I won't leave him!"

Rough hands gripped Ward by his ankles and under his armpits, hauling him into the air.

"Careful!" Amie shrieked.

There was more screaming. Screaming so loud that it felt like it was crushing his skull. His screaming.

He was dropped onto the gurney, and his back exploded.

Everything went black.

⸻⬥⸻

He was moving again. He could hear the wheels of the cot scraping through gravel. Each bump felt like his back was being marked with a thousand brands all at once. He didn't think he could survive the pain much longer.

"What's happening?" His words were garbled, his mouth a scorching-hot desert full of cotton. He lifted his head just enough to see in front of him. A large body, clad in red—Authority carrying his cot toward a hovercraft. He turned his head to the side. Members of

The Origins, hands bound behind them, were being herded into waiting vehicles. He turned his head the other way: Amie holding his IV aloft.

She tapped the shoulder of the Authority in front of her, the one guiding the head of Ward's gurney. "Please, let me give him his antibiotics and something for the pain. He'll die."

The man laughed. "As if I care."

A voice from behind him said: "Boss says to keep them all alive, or it'll be our heads."

The first man grunted. "Fine. Go ahead."

They lowered him to the ground with a thud. Another scream escaped him. Amie bent over him, putting her hand to his forehead.

"He has a fever."

"Just hurry."

"He shouldn't have been moved in his condition!"

The Authority laughed. "Guess he shouldn't have been a terrorist either."

"What's happening?" Ward's words sounded like they were being dragged through mud. They were coming from someone else.

Amie put a needle into a tube attached to the IV bag. "A raid," she whispered.

"Lea. Where's Lea?"

She pressed the plunger on the syringe. "I don't know. She wasn't in the infirmary when it happened."

A hand grabbed Amie by the back of her jumpsuit, yanking her away.

"No talking!"

She vanished from sight, and he was moving again.

He wanted to be glad Lea hadn't been there. Wanted it to mean there was hope she'd escaped.

But she'd promised never to leave his side.

He was in an abandoned subway tunnel waiting for Kitty to return. He shivered in the damp cold, and his stomach cramped and ached. Someone was coming, their footsteps heavy and slow. With each step, the person emitted a low, deep moan. Kallum moved further back into the darkness. Kitty was supposed to find them some food and come right back for him, but it had been days now. The footsteps were getting closer. Kallum let out a whimper. A hand shot out into the darkness, grabbing his arm...

———◇———

The cot banged against the side of the hovercraft, and Ward's eyes flew open. Amie looked up, mouthing something to someone. *Run! Run!*

He followed her gaze, looking toward the building. Lea was climbing out of a window. Her face, a vague white orb, turned toward his—the red haze of hair, her mouth a black pit. She must have been coming for him, trying to save him. She hadn't left him. Not his Lea. So brave. So strong. He should have known she wouldn't have. But there was no saving him, there was only saving herself.

No! He willed her with his mind. *No! Go back!*

A figure leaned out of the window behind Lea. She was dressed all in black with black hair; Ward couldn't make out the features or the face. The person grabbed Lea around the waist, dragging her back inside. Lea reached for him, arms outstretched.

Ward tried to stop himself, but the cry escaped. "NO!!!" Craning his neck, he watched as the person pulled Lea back through the window and out of sight. "No!"

Lea disappeared, the window slamming shut behind her.

"What are you shouting about?" The Authority at his feet looked behind him and then up at the building, scanning the windows.

"There's nothing there," said Amie. "Ignore him. He's delusional."

"Amie." Ward reached out, grabbing her arm.

Amie looked at him, shaking her head. "There's nothing we can do."

The pain killers kicked in, a fog rolling in through his mind. He didn't want them to. He needed to stay awake. He needed to help Lea. Shaking his head, he tried to fight it, but everything grew heavier and heavier.

His back prickled as the medication sped through his bloodstream. The pain receded like water pulling back from shore.

No. He thought. *Please, no.* He wished for the pain to come back so he could stay awake.

His eyelids were so heavy.

No. Please.

Everything went black.

CHAPTER FOUR

WHEREAS, *pursuant to the Prole Reassignment Act of 2075, upon criminal conviction, members of the upper caste are designated Fallen and recast as Prole, and*

WHEREAS, *a determination must be made as to the caste of the children of the Fallen*

NOW, THEREFORE, *the government of the United States has determined that the following rules will apply to minor children of the Fallen:*

(1) If the child of a Fallen member of the upper caste has two parents and only one is convicted of a felony, that child shall remain a member of the upper caste, in the custody of its upper caste parent

(2) If the child of a Fallen member of the upper caste has only one parent and that parent Falls, or the child has two parents and both parents Fall, that child shall, too, be designated Fallen and recast as Prole.

(3) Fallen minors will be Wards of the state for so long as their parent(s) remain incarcerated or until they reach the age of majority, whichever comes first.

—THE PROLE REASSIGNMENT ACT OF 2075, PART II: PERTAINING TO THE CHILDREN OF THE FALLEN

Day 0: December 8, 2126: The Marshes
Leandrea

"Let me go!" Lea twisted out of Aisling's grasp. "They're taking Ward! We have to do something."

"Get your head on straight! He's surrounded."

"I have to go with him. I promised."

There was a loud crash and thumping on the stairs.

"Authority! Freeze!"

"Hands where I can see them!"

"On the floor!"

People screamed. Smoke bombs hissed and there was the thudding of bodies falling to the ground.

Aisling cursed. "The only way you even have a chance to help him is by getting out of here and not getting us both caught."

She cracked open the door, peeking down the hallway and then closed it with a quiet *click*. "We're trapped." Scanning the room, she said, "Deuce! Think, Lea! There has to be a way out!"

Leandrea shook her head, looking around the room. But wait. Was there? This office was directly above the room she'd shared with Ward. If the layout was the same…

"Not an exit, but…."

She ran across the room to a bookcase filled with matching sets of thick, crumbling tomes with titles like "New York Civil Procedure," and "Rules of Court." The shelves were like time capsules with dusty photographs and decorative glass birds, sitting right where they'd been left decades ago. Ordinarily, Leandrea would have been fascinated, wanting to examine all of it, trying to learn more about the room's former occupant. But at that moment, the bookcase blocked what might be their only means of escape.

"Help me with this!" she called to Aisling.

Without asking questions, Aisling grabbed one end of the bookcase and pulled while Leandrea pushed from the other side. Slowly, it slid sideways, revealing a pocket door.

"Utility closet!" Lea pulled at the pocket door. It stuck. She smacked it with her hand and rust fell from the track and onto the floor. She pulled again, putting her weight into it. Slowly, she slid it over. "We can leave the door open and move the shelving back in front of it. Hopefully, they'll be too busy—"

"Got it."

Aisling pushed Leandrea into the tight space, stepping in after her. Breaths coming in quick gasps, they grabbed onto supports on the back of the shelves, sliding it in front of the opening just as the door to the room flew open.

"Check under the desk!" a voice shouted. There was the sound of footsteps moving across the room and scuffling noises.

The steps came closer. Leandrea was still breathing hard from the exertion. The room was tiny and hot, Aisling pressed close against her. Her lungs felt like cement; she could barely pull in enough air. Switches from a long dead electric panel poked into her back. She covered her mouth with both hands, praying that the person outside couldn't hear her panting.

Items rattled on the shelf. "What a bunch of bruto junk," the person on the other side mumbled. She listened as small glass birds and picture frames fell to the floor, shattering.

"Anything?" A voice from further away called.

"Empty!"

"Then stop playing with that old trash and get moving. We got a whole deucing building to get through."

Something clanked back onto the shelf and a man mumbled something incoherent. There was the sound of footsteps retreating, and then silence.

Their breathing seemed deafening in the tiny space. Leandrea clasped her hands together, trying to still her shaking.

"We'll have to stay here until they leave," Aisling whispered.

"That could be hours."

"We don't have hours. Once they've cleared the place, they'll start doing thermal scans to look for anyone who's hiding. Then they send in a swarm of nanobots."

"The building is lead impregnated. They can't see into it. That's why The Origins used this building in the first place."

"The floors The Origins used were lead-protected, but these upper floors aren't. Besides, even if they can't find us with thermal scans, the nanobots will find us."

Leandrea swallowed. The tiny space grew hotter by the moment. Sweat pooled between her breasts, trickling down her belly, tickling like tiny spiders. She started to sway.

"It's too hot in here. I can't breathe."

"Well, you'll be wishing for heat in a moment."

Aisling began heaving the bookcase aside.

Lea grabbed her arm. "What are you doing?"

"We don't have much time. I have coolsuits. They block thermal tech and if you don't move or breathe, the nanobots can't scan you."

As soon as there was enough space, Aisling slipped out of the closet, pulling her bag out after her. She unzipped it, removing two black suits and two sets of goggles.

She threw one of the suits toward Lea. "Quick. Put this on."

Lea unzipped the blue jumpsuit she wore and handed it to Aisling to put in the pack. She stepped into the black suit. It was made of stretchy, smooth material impregnated with a mesh.

"The hood, too," Aisling said as she pulled her own hood up and over her short bob.

Leandrea struggled to get her huge swarm of hair under the fabric. Curls kept escaping out the sides. Aisling came over, helping her tuck her hair in.

"We'll have to cut this. It makes you too identifiable."

"So I've been told," Lea said. But the idea made her want to clutch at her head. Holding onto her hair felt like holding onto the last vestiges of her old self.

"Okay then." Aisling stood back, admiring her success in containing Lea's tresses.

She tapped something on Lea's shoulder and Lea suddenly felt her body start to cool.

She gasped. "What is this?"

"It's a coolsuit. Old technology. Used to be used by people who did hot jobs. Side benefit? It fools the thermal scans."

Lea shivered. "It's freezing."

"You want to be warm or alive? Besides, once we're back in the closet, you'll be thankful for it."

Aisling handed Lea a slim pair of glasses and Lea slid them on. Suddenly, she could see everything in the room—purple outlines in clear relief against black. She gasped, taking them off.

"What are these?"

Aisling slid on a similar pair, but hers didn't go over the ears. Rather, Aisling pressed the sides of hers against her temples and they adhered.

"My goggles have a neural interface. There are implants at my temples that are dormant until the goggles are engaged. They help me see clearly no matter what the lighting or conditions. They also help me auto-target my weapons. Well, they do a lot of things that I can tell you about later, but for now, you need to put yours on and get back in the closet before the bots show up."

Lea hesitated. She'd gone through a lot to divorce her body from technology. She was reluctant to introduce it back into her life, especially from an unknown source.

Aisling sighed. "It's safe. Just tech goggles but paired to mine. You'll be able to see better, and it has some basic functionality that your comm had, like mapping. You'll only be able to communicate with me through them, but I can share data from mine with you, like images. More important, they'll stop the nanobots from doing a retinal scan on you. They can't identify you with these on."

Lea didn't like it, but she put the glasses on.

Aisling tucked everything back into her pack and threw it in the closet. "Time to get back inside."

She stepped in and Lea came in after her.

It was just in time because right at that moment, they heard the swarm making its way down the hall.

"Okay," Aisling whispered. "We're going to take some deep breaths. When you hear them come into the room, hold your breath, and don't move. With the suit and the goggles, they can't see you, but you must stay still."

The humming grew louder, and they heard the bots swoop through the door. It was like the buzzing of a thousand bees. Tiny surveillance robots no bigger than flies spread around the room, investigating every crevice. Lea took a deep breath and held it just as two of the bots slipped through the crack between their door and the wall.

She froze as one of the bots hovered right in front of face, thrumming and scanning. It felt like it was there forever. She was sure it had identified her. Her guts quivered; she was afraid the shaking would spread to her hands. Her lungs burned. Any second and she would have no choice but to take a breath.

The bot reversed course and exited, followed by its counterpart.

"You can breathe now but stay as still as you can."

Lea startled at Aisling's voice. It sounded like it was inside her head.

"They could come back," Aisling finished.

Lea wanted to ask what the floods was going on. It was like Aisling was using telepathy. But she bit her lip, keeping as still as she could and waiting until the buzzing subsided and moved away.

Aisling exhaled. "I think it's okay now, but we should stay in here, at least for a while, just to be sure."

"How are you talking to me?" Lea asked. "Is it reading your brain waves or something?"

Aisling laughed softly. "There is tech like that—BCIs record neurons in the brain as they fire and translate that to speech. But that requires netting, which people here don't have. This tech is much simpler. In the suit, there's a vocal dampener. It mutes the audible tones of our voices and transmits the sounds to the goggles. It's stealth tech, so we can communicate without being heard."

"Right. Simple." She had so many questions—where had this tech come from? What was netting? If it was so safe, why didn't the U.S. have it?

"What else can these things do?"

"They can communicate for about a hundred-mile range. Navigate. Mine can do a lot more than that, but those are the basic functions of a paired set like this. The best part—the neurals are only active when the external device is engaged. Unlike your comms, we can choose when to be plugged in and when to disconnect. The benefits of tech without the loss of privacy."

"Or at least that's what they tell you," Lea said.

Aisling didn't respond to that.

She wondered if, once she got to the outside world—if she got there—she'd elect to have such an implant or stay unplugged.

They waited for what seemed like an eternity, the space growing hotter by the minute. Aisling was right. Lea was thankful for the suit. Her mouth and lips were dry. Her stomach, churning. She hadn't eaten anything since late the night before, and then, only a small dinner that Amalie had been kind enough to bring her as she sat by Ward's side.

She yearned for the emergency packs that Ward had stowed in their room for when they left or in the event something just like this happened. He'd told her to always keep one with her. Why hadn't she listened? They had integrated converters that removed water from the atmosphere and made it available for drinking. There were Prole ration bars. One of the heavy, greasy bars would be enough to last her for days. The first time she'd tasted one, she thought it was like compacted sawdust. Now, her mouth watered thinking about it.

Ward. Where was he, and what were they doing to him? Did he think she'd abandoned him? She knew worrying was useless—it wouldn't answer questions or solve anything. Ward would have wanted her to do exactly what she was doing right now—hide and then escape. But still, her stomach felt like an empty pit each time she thought about the way he'd looked on that cot, helpless and bloodied. She kept thinking about her promise not to leave his side while he recovered—and now he was alone in the hands of his enemies.

Her stomach growled again. Aisling must have something in her pack, but Leandrea didn't want to ask. Surely, if the woman was holding off, she either didn't have it or was rationing. Lea didn't want to seem weak by admitting that she needed even more than she'd already been given.

Lea thought of how Aisling only had two of everything. She was giving Lea everything she'd brought, planning to smuggle Ward out of the country—not her. What would have happened if they'd both been there? Three of them and only two sets of gear. Lea knew exactly what Ward would have done. She was pretty sure she knew what Aisling would have done, too. But what would she have done, and would she have had the power to enforce her will against these two strong people? She thought no but, she'd been surprising herself a lot lately.

"We need help getting out of the city." Aisling interrupted her train of thought. "Did you and Kallum have a plan?"

Lea shook her head. "Ward had a plan, but I don't know what it was."

Aisling exhaled. Her back was pressed against Lea's front. The room felt too close. Her face was hot, but her body was freezing. She wished for her Uni jumpsuit with its temperature regulated fabric. But they'd destroyed it when she and Ward had fled from Aisling just a few days earlier. "No tech," Sebbe had told her as he melted the jumpsuit with chemicals and washed it down the drain.

No tech.

Her heart jumped into her throat, her stomach flipping.

"Your comm! Can't they trace it?" Aisling would have had to have one implanted to work for the Authority.

"I pulled it out."

Lea sucked in air through her teeth. "By yourself?"

"It wasn't so bad."

"They put me under to remove mine. They were afraid suddenly having none of the communication chips I'd had implanted in me for my entire life would be too jarring. Weren't you concerned?"

"I'm not from here, Lea. Mine was never attached to my nervous system. It was just chips."

Questions flooded her mind. Not from here? Where was she from? Is that where she got all this tech? How was she part of the Authority if she wasn't from here? She picked the question that mattered right now. "Doesn't that leave gaps in the data they could detect about you?"

"The neurals transmitted any information that would signal a gap to people monitoring me."

"Oh." Lea understood nothing Aisling was saying. She worried at the webbing in her cool suit. Her legs cramped from standing in one place for too long. She tried shifting her position, but there was hardly any space to move.

Aisling seemed to have an answer for everything, but would she have an answer for the one question that had been burning in her throat from the moment Aisling's voice came through the small transmitter that had been in Ward's back?

"How did you know?"

Aisling cleared her throat and shifted her weight. "That he was Kallum Gordon?"

"Yes."

"I didn't—not for sure. He's the eighth person I've pursued since Kitty sent me here five years ago."

"Five years?"

"Mm hmm. I was inserted as a cadet with The Authority."

"How? Only citizens can be Authority."

"It's complicated, but suffice it to say we have far more advanced tech than the U.S. and people on the inside that are loyal to Katherine."

"So she sent you to find Ward?"

"Yes."

"How did you know where to look?"

"She assumed if Kallum was alive, he'd be a Ward and that, if he'd escaped, he'd have stayed in New York. It was a place he knew well. We were looking in the right place and for the right designation, but for the wrong appearance. Kallum was too old for DNA mods when he fell, so we were looking for a Ward who looked upper caste and not a Prole. And someone with blue eyes.

"Then, we started to hear rumors about a genius in The Origins—a tech wiz. Kallum had always been brilliant, and it would have made sense that he'd end up with rebels. Kitty sent me to investigate. Once I saw the scars, I knew he'd been modified through muscle stims, which meant he was older when he fell. His age was right. The circumstances. The brilliance. Kitty was certain it was him."

"But you weren't."

"Kitty pushed me to act sooner, but I couldn't risk exposing myself without being positive. I only had one shot to get the right person before I was wrecked."

"So, you went after me instead of him?"

"I figured he would have told you and that it'd be easier to pressure you into telling me than him."

"Thanks a lot."

"Well, if it makes you feel better, you were tougher to break than just about anyone I interrogated in all my years as an Authority. Most Unis would have folded within five minutes. It showed real tapang."

"If it makes *you* feel better, I didn't know who he was until two nights ago."

"Really? Then why did you think I was looking for him?"

"I thought you wanted the glory of catching one of The Origins all to yourself or something."

"Huh. Why did you care to protect him so much?"

Lea pinched the bridge of her nose, shaking her head and inhaling deeply. The last few weeks were such a blur. They'd been through so much that she felt like she'd known Ward her whole life, but really, she'd just met him.

"I'd gone to the West End with Hallyn, Kammeo, and Andromeda.

Hallyn and I were trying to convince Andy and Kam that ReInception was bad, and Prole were misunderstood. We figured we'd stop at a Prole bar before heading to the protest. Kam and Andy figured that a little time "slummin' wit de buhay" would teach us a thing or two. I guess we were both right.

"That was where I first met him. He was sitting at the bar and, to be honest, he was a real arschloch—telling me off. That I didn't belong there."

Aisling gave a small laugh. "Sounds like his sister."

"At the bar, I was scared of him. But after the bombing, I got separated from my friends. The comms were blocked for emergency transmissions only. Without my comm to guide me home, I was completely lost. I followed the Prole, figuring they'd know what to do and where to go. I found my way back to the Catacombs, but I couldn't find my way home. I was hiding in an alleyway and that's when Ward found me. He hid me until it was safe to go home. Like you said that first time you interrogated me, it was a long time. Yeah. A long time."

She thought again of being in the dark with him. In his warm room with only candlelight and silence. How the flame had flickered across his face, softening the harshness that had been there earlier. It was the most peaceful she remembered ever feeling. "We learned a lot about each other in those hours."

"So you felt loyal to him after just that night?"

Lea shrugged, even though Aisling couldn't see it.

"I don't know that I completely trusted him after just one night, but what he said made sense. He told me that The Origins weren't responsible for the bombing. That it was a setup to make an enemy out of the Prole so the government could justify a campaign of forced ReInception."

"And you simply believed him?"

"I thought about it a lot. What he said. Whether and why he'd lie. That night, if he'd wanted to hurt me, he could have. No one was around. The comms were down. I was lost and afraid. But he helped me. He risked himself to hide me. What he said made a flooding lot more sense than the Prole having done it. Why would the Prole kill people who were anti-ReInception?"

Aisling gave a small grunt. "Okay. But how did Ward even find you after the bombing? Didn't that make you suspicious?"

"He'd followed us after we left the bar. Andromeda got drunk. She was bragging about who her dad was. Ward overheard it. He was trying to get to Andromeda when the place was raided, so he followed us."

"Huh."

They were quiet for a little while. Leandrea wondered how much time had passed. If she had her comm, she could have just asked it, but she didn't. It felt like they'd been in there forever. She wondered if she could ask her goggles, but Aisling would have heard, and she didn't want to seem lowQ.

"Maybe we can at least get out of this closet? I'm sure that if they're still here, they're focusing on recovery on the lower floors."

"We can check but be ready to get back in on a moment's notice."

They pushed the bookcase back, only partially exposing the opening, leaving just enough space for them to squeeze through.

Lea took a deep breath of the cool air and stretched, trying to bring the feeling back into her hands and shake the charley-horse out of her legs.

They stood still, listening for any sounds. There was nothing. Aisling eased the entrance door open, poking her head out into the hallway.

"Nothing."

She walked over to the window and, with her back to the wall, peered around the window frame.

"There's still hovercraft out there," she whispered. "Three of them. Authority going back and forth to load things up. They don't seem to be in any rush about it, so they must think they got everyone. We can stay out here, but we need to keep the suits and goggles on. Be ready to get back into the closet if we hear anything. We'll wait until dark and then go. But we need a plan to get out of here."

Lea raised her eyebrows. "You don't have a plan?"

Aisling's mouth turned down, her eyes drooping with exhaustion. "I hadn't planned for the raid and for this place to be swarming with Authority. I can get us out of the building, but from there, my plan is...well, screwed."

Lea thought for a moment and then smiled. "I may have an idea."

CHAPTER FIVE

<u>MISSING! Where is Kallum Gordon?</u>

Two weeks after his testimony lead to the conviction of his parents for murder and conspiracy to commit murder, Kallum Gordon and his sister, Katherine Vega, are missing. The siblings were to be assigned to Wardomes in facilities for children of incarcerated upper caste, being redesigned Fallen. Due to the age gap between the siblings, they were to be separated, Kallum into a facility for youth, and Katherine to one for teens. Sources tell us they were still together and that the WAD (Ward Assignment Department) were in the process of placing them when the siblings vanished. In the wake of his testimony against his parents, public opinion and sentiment about young Kallum has been split with some people considering his testimony against his parents a symptom of what's wrong with our society. Others, who consider him a hero to causes that decry reprogramming children, especially for such things as sexual orientation, fear that his disappearance may not have been voluntary. "We assure you we are doing everything in our power to locate the siblings," says Chief of Police for New York City, Natalie Morales. "No stone will remain unturned until they are safe in our custody."

—NEW YORK TIMES, APRIL 7, 2115

W ard woke to the sound of two men arguing.

"I want him in that machine. Now!"

"Nanites can't do miracles. Your men tossing him around tore all the grafted skin off his back. We'll be lucky if he doesn't die from infection, even with the tiny doctors at work."

"I don't care if he dies, as long as we find out what he knows first."

"You know the magnetic pulses of the machine kill nanites. Put him in now and you'll have no answers. All you'll have is a dead Prole bleeding all over your equipment."

There was a groan of frustration and the sound of something being slammed down onto a metal surface. "Do what you have to, but I'm not waiting long. The Origins wouldn't have gone through such drastic measures to remove the device from his back if he wasn't important."

"If he was so important, they wouldn't have sent him into your home in the first place. They trusted him just enough to do the dirty work and to take a fall. That means they weren't worried about what you'd find out if you caught him."

The other man grunted.

"I get that you're angry. He violated your space and took advantage of your daughter, but don't let anger cloud your judgment. If you want to know what he knows, you need to give him a few days."

There was silence and clicking. Nails drumming on a table? Ward couldn't see.

"Dennison. He's just the scapegoat. Let me do my job."

Ward's skin prickled, and the hair on his arms stood. His muscles tensed, ready to spring, but willed himself not to move.

"You're probably right. But I won't wait long."

There was another pause and then retreating footsteps.

It was quiet for a moment.

Ward heard rustling and things being moved around. And then the person was next to his bed, his breathing slightly labored. A warm hand rested on Ward's shoulder.

"I'm sorry. This is going to hurt."

The Med tried to remove the old bandages from his back gently, but the pain was searing. Ward winced and gritted his teeth, tried not to cry out, but failed. Tears seeped from the corners of his eyes. They felt like an admission.

Gently, the Med lowered new bandages onto him. They were covered in a cool salve that eased the burning and dulled the pain. Ward kept his sigh inside. The Med may have sounded like he was defending him, but the man had just been doing his job. Abiding by an ancient oath that doctors had been taking for millennia, and that many still believed. That didn't make the Med his friend, even if Ward wanted it to. He had to remember that.

Once, Ward had read about something called "Stockholm Syndrome." It was a condition where hostages formed a bond with their imprisoners—a coping mechanism to deal with captive or abusive situations where people developed positive feelings toward their captors or abusers over time. One would think that Ward would be too grown up, too wary, to be susceptible to such things. But he knew himself better than that. When you'd been alone so long, fighting for so long, hurt for so long, you were vulnerable. He had to keep his guard up against this man's kindness. He had to remember that it could be part of a ploy—a classic good cop, bad cop routine.

The salve stopped the pain, but Ward's back itched like hell. The bandage must have been nanite impregnated. The "tiny doctors" healing him. He wanted to scream. All that work to make sure there were no machines in his body—nothing to trace or control him with—and now he was riddled with them. His muscles felt like lead, and his head, like it was filled with waterlogged seaweed. It no longer felt like someone was pouring lava over his back, but the itching was almost worse.

"I can't protect you for long, kiddo."

The voice was right next to him.

Ward's eyes slid back open.

He hadn't realized he'd fallen asleep.

He was still lying face down and all he could see from this vantage was the Med's waist—the white med jumpsuit.

"He really doesn't care if you die. You'd be best off just telling him what he wants to know. He's going to force it out of you anyhow. One way or the other, you're going in the machine. Start talking, at least it might buy you enough time to survive."

Ward tried opening his mouth to speak, but it felt like it was full of glue.

The figure retreated. Everything was blurry. Ward blinked a few times, trying to clear his vision, but the world stayed fuzzy, like viewed through a veil.

"Drink."

The Med put a straw in his mouth, and Ward took a sip. It was something cold and sweet. It went down his throat, dousing the fire. Sucking hard, he grabbed for the cup, but the Med pushed his hand down and pulled the cup away.

"Woah there. Slow down or you'll heave it all up."

The Med walked away, putting the drink down and then coming back toward Ward's cot.

"That was some seriously prehistoric medical care you were getting back there. It shuts down the body. You need to reboot slowly, or you'll crash the whole system."

Ward laughed lightly at the technical explanation of his medical condition, but he appreciated his circumstances being explained to him in terms that made sense. Licking his lips, he swallowed. It still felt like he'd been in a desert for a month, but it was better.

"Where am I?" His voice was raspy and foreign to his own ears. He hadn't felt so weak and vulnerable since he'd been a young boy, alone in the abandoned subway tunnels and running for his life.

"You're at a ReInception outpost."

"Where?"

The Med didn't respond.

"The rest of us?"

"Some here. Some at other facilities. I'm sorry to say that this one's off the grid. If you were expecting anyone to come for you, don't."

Ward wondered why the Med would share this with him, but of course, it didn't matter if he did. What was Ward going to do with the information? By the time he was capable of even standing up, he'd no longer be himself. Ward was about to ask the Med if he'd seen a girl with long, curly red hair—an upper caste, but in a Prole jumpsuit at least two sizes too large. He stopped himself just in time. The pain meds were clouding his thinking. He had to be careful what he said. He was certainly being monitored, everything he said and did, recorded. If Lea had somehow escaped, he didn't want to tip them off that they'd missed someone important. Then again, did it matter? Kelvin knew Ward had conspired with her to get into the apartment. That she'd worked with him to gain access through Andromeda. Still, he didn't have to let them know Lea was important to him personally. Andromeda suspected it, but that was about her insecurity, not about anything based in fact. He didn't have to give them any proof that her suspicions were founded. He couldn't give them more leverage than they already had.

But Amie—she'd been captured with him. They knew she was his doctor. It couldn't hurt to ask where she was.

"The woman they brought me in with? My doctor?"

The Med dragged something across the floor. It came into focus. A chair. He lowered himself into it. His torso came into view and Ward was able to twist his head enough to look at the man's face. His skin was dark, with a lighter, checkered pattern along his neck and under his jaw. He had high cheekbones and a wide nose that suited him. His face was clear of designs and his eyes, a warm, wide, natural brown. Ward wondered if it was something they suggested in medical school: "Pick something that looked trustworthy. Maybe a nice warm shade of brown. Something you could actually be born with."

He put a cool hand against Ward's forehead and then drew it away.

"You still have a fever." He shook his head. "I don't know how you survived with that ancient equipment and medicine."

"Amie?" Ward repeated. "My doctor."

"She's okay. They let her tell me what she'd been giving you and then took her to…well, wherever they're taking everyone." He shook his head, grinning slightly. "Her knowledge of pre-nanite medical treatment is remarkable. I'll give her that."

Ward could tell from the man's face that Amie had impressed him. She had that effect on people. Smart. Endearing. Disarming. He hoped it would be enough to keep her safe until…Until what? He was thinking until he could get to her. Until he could save her. But who was he kidding? He couldn't even save himself.

"What are you treating me with?"

The Med shook his head. "Given how badly damaged your grafts are, other than the nanites, nothing all that much better. But a lot more sanitary than that makeshift hospital you were in when they found you."

"Amie's hospital was pristine."

"I'm sure she did the best she could given her resources, but how do you think the Delhi Superbug started?"

He was referring to the MDR bacteria that had wiped out more than half of India in the mid twenty-first century. It had evolved to resist the sanitization of a hundred years ago—the very technology he believed Amie had been using to keep her medical facilities sterile for The Origins. But there were things that this doctor didn't know about Amie and why she'd been brought to the United States from India. Why she, too, had been on the run, and why she, a part of the upper caste, had allied herself with The Origins.

It was all too much, too exhausting. It was too hard to remember what to say and what not to say. Who to trust and who not to.

Lowering his head back down, Ward closed his eyes. It had taken all his energy just to look at the man. Thinking was beyond his capability right now. His head throbbed and his back stung despite whatever he'd been pumped full of.

"How bad is it?"

"Well, all that new skin they grew for you tore. Your back looks like a blind granny quilted it."

Ward gave a small laugh at this.

"We'll be able to keep it from getting infected here. Beyond that, we have to wait. It'll take time. Skin doesn't like growing over open wounds. I patched it with Synth Derm as best I could. The nanites will knit it all together, but your back'll never be pretty again unless you can afford scar treatment or a new graft, which somehow, I think you can't, and probably don't care about. Then again, if you cooperate, you'd be able to negotiate for a lot."

Ward snorted but didn't comment on that. One way or another, they'd get his cooperation eventually. He didn't intend to make it easy for them.

"You said they can't put me in the ReInception machine for a while. Why?"

"Nanites don't like open wounds either. They can do a lot, but they can't grow skin after open wounds have already started to heal. They have to rebuild your back at a cellular level. If we put you in the machine now, the magnetic pulses will kill the nanites and you'll be further damaged. It's my job to make sure you are healthy enough to survive the process before they put you through it. Not that I really care, but Hippocratic Oath and all. Right?"

"Right." Ward closed his eyes. "Although I guess if you don't care, you shouldn't be a doctor."

He heard the Med lean forward, adjusting something near Ward's side.

"Maybe don't ask so many questions," the man whispered, then sat back up.

Which of course made Ward want to ask more, like why was this man helping him and was he on the side of The Origins? Or was he just trying to gain Ward's trust so Ward would talk to him? One never knew until it was too late.

Plenty of the upper caste didn't support the Prole system. Some didn't even approve of ReInception. You'd think a Med working for ReInception would, but you never knew. Sometimes people saw and did things in life that change their viewpoints. Look at how much Leandrea had changed in just a month. And Ward? He had no idea who he was or what he stood for anymore. He thought that being with Lea had given him a rudder again, but did it really? Or was it more about who he cared about than what he cared about?

The Med lifted something off a metal table next to Ward's bed.

"What you need is time, sleep and antibiotics."

Ward heard a click and opened his eyes. The Med was drawing a clear liquid into a tube.

"Wait," Ward mumbled. He wanted to stay awake. He needed to know more. But the Med was already pressing the NFiT against his shoulder. There was a slight tingle that quickly moved along his arm and spread across the rest of his body, his back and mind going numb.

Ward started to drift off. "Thank you," he said, his eyelids growing heavy and starting to close. Oblivion may have been cowardly, but it was so peaceful.

"Just doing my job," the Med said. "And shutting you up for your own good," he mumbled.

Everything went black.

CHAPTER SIX

SKYBERG INVENTION REVOLUTIONIZES CLIMATE CONTROL

In a groundbreaking advancement for climate change mitigation, scientists have unveiled the "Skyberg" a revolutionary invention designed to deflect the sun's rays back into space. This innovative technology aims to combat global warming by replicating the natural cooling effects of icebergs and glaciers, which have all but vanished due to rising temperatures.

The Skyberg comprises massive, lightweight structures equipped with reflective surfaces. These structures form a shield that reflects sunlight, thereby reducing the heat absorbed by the planet. Initial tests show promising results, with significant drops in local temperatures and a reduction in the overall warming trend.

Environmentalists and policymakers worldwide laud the Skyberg as a potential game-changer. Dr. Serafin Justus, the lead scientist on the project, stated, "This technology represents a beacon of hope. By mimicking the natural processes of our polar ice, we can buy critical time to implement more sustainable solutions."

—CLIMATE CURRENT VIDZIN JUNE 7, 2100

L ea sat in the dark, staring at the pitch-black nothingness of The Floods at night while Aisling slept in a corner. They'd been waiting for hours, taking turns keeping watch while the other tried to get some rest. They waited for the complete silence that would indicate that The Authority had finally vacated the building.

Without her comm, Leandrea had no sense of time—what hour it was, how long she'd slept or been awake. How long they'd been waiting. Her only cue was that it had gotten dark quite some time ago. Again, she lamented her twenty years of complete dependance on her comm for everything from how to get places, to how to contact people, to what time of day it was. She hadn't realized how little she'd learned to navigate the world without technology until it was gone. In moments, like when she was alone in the room with Ward, sharing about their lives, it felt so peaceful. At other times, like now, she felt helpless and unmoored.

She'd do anything to be able to call her parents right now. She hadn't spoken to them in over a week and not since her face had been plastered all over the news vids as a wanted woman. How terrified they must be.

Lea pulled her legs in close to her body. Wrapping her arms around her knees, she rested her head against the wall, trying to warm herself inside the cool suit. If they didn't go somewhere or do something soon, she'd go non-comp. Other than one scare, when they heard voices in the hallway and had to race back into their hiding spot behind the bookcase, there had been no more activity on the floors above the fourth. As the sun set, the hovercraft finally departed. Leandrea had wanted to leave then, but Aisling said they needed to wait a while longer, just to be sure. Leandrea was certain she wouldn't be able to sleep while she was freezing, but a fitful, exhausted slumber had taken her until it was her turn to watch.

She felt edgy and jittery, her thoughts racing, unsure about her decisions to ally herself with Aisling. She was certain now that Aisling had been telling the truth about looking for Ward and having defected from the Authority, but that didn't mean that she was trustworthy. It didn't mean that she hadn't meant Ward harm.

On their last night together before his surgery, Ward had told Lea,

"If something happens, you go to Sebbe and Vella for help. I trust them with my life." That's where she had to go. To the West End. Vella and Sebbe would know how to sneak them out. It's what Sebbe did as head of the underground. He'd gotten Lea and Ward to The Origins headquarters using the flooded subway tunnels that Prole used to move around unmolested. But the Authority tracked them down there during their escape; that route was burnt. They couldn't go back that way. So how? Then again, it was thousands of miles of tunnels. The Authority couldn't monitor all of it. Or could they? Couldn't they use nanobots? And, if so, why hadn't they used nanobots when they were tracking Ward and Lea in the first place? Lea added it to the long list of questions to ask Aisling. She was so naïve.

Leandrea weighed the pros and cons of trying to ditch Aisling. She could leave the woman behind and try to make her way back to Sebbe and Vella on her own. But every time Lea started to rise to her feet, that feeling in her gut punched at her again. When Lea had first entrusted herself to Ward and The Origins, it had been about her quest for the truth—her desire to make a difference. Now, she was certain; she had to do the same with Aisling. This woman was the next step on her journey and Lea's only chance of saving Ward.

It was too late to turn back, and there was no other path forward. Aisling already knew everything Lea knew—or at least, most of it. If this was a ruse, Aisling could have—would have—given her up already. Time to trust her gut again.

Lea heard more than saw Aisling stir in the corner, just a shadow separating itself from other shadows in the darkness. Sitting up, she rubbed at her eyes. "What time is—never mind."

Standing, Aisling stretched, then walked to the window, looking out for a while and then coming back toward Lea. "Anything?"

"Not a sound."

Lea planned to find the Prole Underground—the people who'd helped Ward and her escape when they were being pursued by the Authority through The Floods. Even with announcements blaring from hovercraft and holographic images of her and Ward projected everywhere, the Prole of The Floods had risked themselves to get Ward and Lea out undetected.

That was how they had to get back. She wasn't entirely sure how they'd find the help again, but it was the only way Leandrea could think to escape. That's what Leandrea had told Aisling. But she still hadn't told the woman about Vella and Sebbe. The idea of giving up their identities when it was so critical to The Origins to keep them a secret caused her stomach to plummet like she'd taken a sudden dip on an amusement park ride. But she could think of no other options. The data chips secreted under her skin contained the most important documents in the world. They didn't know exactly what was on there yet, but they knew that at least some of it was explosive. The chance that it was far more—enough to take down ReInception—was worth the risk. The chips, Ward said to tell no one about, not even Sebbe and Vella. Not even her parents. He said she should use them to buy her safety. But she would do better than that. She'd use them to free the entire Prole population, even if it was at her own expense. *Sorry, Ward,* she thought. *Some things are more important than me.*

She took a deep breath. "You were right about The West End. The bartender is the head of the underground."

Aisling pounded a fist on her thigh. "I knew it! The guy with the beard."

Lea nodded. "If we can get to him, do you have a plan for how to get out of the country?"

Aisling nodded. "If you can get us to the West End, I can get us out."

The two women watched each other a while longer. Aisling was an expert liar. If what she said was true, she'd spent the last four years as a part of the government under a ruse. In a society with multiple ways to gauge and validate veracity, Aisling had remained undetected. And if she was lying, then without resorting to a single piece of technology, Aisling had persuaded Leandrea to give up secrets that might mean the difference not just between the life and death of her, Ward and the rest of The Origins, but of all Prole. Now, she had only two paths left—continue to trust Aisling and pray that she was right, or end the woman the way she had ended Ferryman, something she didn't even know if she was capable of with forethought, when not under immediate threat to her life or to Ward's.

As Aisling stood still, staring at her, Lea was sure the woman was performing the same mental calculations about her. Leandrea had already told her who to go to in order to escape the country. Did she need Lea anymore, or was Lea a liability?

Aisling nodded. "Well, I guess it's decided then."

Lea nodded back. "I guess it is."

Aisling eased the door open, looking up and down the hall, and then walked to the end of the hallway, slowly pushing open the fire door and standing there for a while, unmoving. She came back into the room, walking toward the corner where she'd been sleeping and grabbing her pack.

She lifted it onto her shoulders. "Should we do this thing?"

"Floods, yes."

"You know the plan?"

Lea nodded. They'd gone over it at least a dozen times.

"Any questions?"

She shook her head.

Aisling took two harnesses out of her pack. Lea stepped into hers, the way Aisling had showed her, and tightened it. After checking her own harness, Aisling checked Lea's, pulling at the straps and nodding with satisfaction. She clipped carabiners on metal hooks at the front of both their harnesses and then handed Lea a rope, which Lea slipped over her head and under an arm. The coils hung crosswise, leaving her arms free.

Aisling handed a crowbar to Lea and then removed a sidearm from a concealed pocket in her black jumpsuit, extending it out in front of her.

Even though she knew Aisling carried a weapon, it was shocking to see it. Yes, The Origins had an illegal stockpile, but they were a resistance movement, and one that had restrained their use to self-defense. To know indiviuals like Aisling had them too...

"It really is the Wild West out there, isn't it?"

"What do you mean?"

"I mean, we hear about all the guns and shooting outside the U.S. and how dangerous it is..."

Aisling laughed. "You don't think there are bullets in here, do you?"

Leandrea stared at Aisling, head cocked. "I mean, it's a gun."

"Look." Aisling opened the gun to display the insides. There were discs with tiny, glowing pellets inside. "These are intellipellets. They're synced with my neural implants. They can either discharge a fast-acting paralytic neurotoxin or emit an EMP, depending on need."

"Really? How many are in there?"

Aisling shrugged. "At least a thousand."

"So the neurotoxin paralyzes people?"

"Temporarily. It wears off within an hour or so. Gives the shooter plenty of time to escape."

"It won't kill them?"

Aisling laughed again. "No. We don't do that outside the wall. We leave that to the U.S. government."

"So why didn't you just EMP the nanobots?"

"Don't you think the Authority would have noticed if a swarm of their bots suddenly went dark?"

Lea grimaced. She felt so lowQ. She had so much to learn.

"Look, you can ask all the questions you want later. Right now, we need to get out of here. You ready?"

"Ready," Lea said.

"Okay. Let's go."

Following close behind Aisling, Lea ran down the hall. They turned a corner, sprinting a few more yards until they reached a vestibule where there was an elevator. It probably hadn't run in seventy-five years. As they'd planned, Lea put the crowbar into the slim space between the hoistway doors and pushed. The doors were stuck hard, and Lea grunted, straining to separate the panels until there was enough space for both women to get their hands in.

"Okay," Aisling whispered. "Be really careful. We don't know where that car is and if you fall in before we're tethered—"

"I know," Lea said.

"Ready?"

Lea nodded again.

Aisling slipped her weapon into its pocket. Each woman grabbed at one of the hoistway doors. They put all their weight into sliding the doors apart until there was enough room for them to see into the shaft.

Taking the rope from Lea, Aisling tied one end onto Lea's harness and another, a few feet up the rope, into her own.

"You sure you got this?"

Leandrea nodded. "I'm sure."

"Okay. My life is literally in your hands, so I hope we're past the part where you still want to kill me for everything I did before."

Leandrea gave a small laugh. "Mostly."

"Okay. Because I said I was sorry, right?"

Lea laughed again, appreciating the slight relief it gave her from panic.

"You did."

Aisling paused for a moment and then took a deep breath and nodded. "Go."

Lea sat on the ground, holding the rope in her hands and bracing her feet against the partially opened hoistway doors. Aisling stepped between her legs and leaned in, pointing a light into the shaft and looking up and down.

She stood back up. "Okay. Good news. The car is just a few floors down, somewhere around the first floor. Not that we'd survive a fall, but we don't have too far to repel before we get a break. Given where it appears to be, it's probably partly submerged."

"And you're sure when we come out on the first floor, it's not going to be completely under water."

"Yes. We're going to get wet. Might even need to swim. But there's enough of a gap to get some air. You'll follow me to the end of the hall. The windows on that floor are already broken out. We'll find one on the side facing The Marshes. From there, it's up to you."

Lea nodded.

Aisling took a black bar out of her pack. She pulled at the ends, and the bar lengthened. She flipped back the tips, revealing a black, tacky substance.

Placing the bar across the shaft opening, Aishling tugged at it, ensuring it was secure. Puting a clamp on the rope, she handed it to Lea.

"Okay. You're going to lower yourself down until you reach the top of the car. Slow and steady, sliding the clamp like I showed you. Don't worry if you slip, I've got you on this end and the bar is a secure back up. Once you are at the bottom, hang on to the free end of the rope. That way, if I slip, you'll be able to slow me down. Got it?"

Leandrea nodded.

"Okay, go."

Aisling moved herself into the position Lea had been in—sitting on the floor, legs braced against the doors.

Leandrea's heart raced. Her breath came in short, fast gasps. She knew she was safe—three different backups in the simple setup would prevent her from plummeting to her death. Still, she didn't enjoy having her back to a yawning, water-filled pit. And what if this was a setup for Aisling to get rid of her? Now that Aisling knew about the people who'd helped her escape through The Floods and about Sebbe and Vella, what did she need Lea for? She'd only be a liability.

Leandrea shook her head, trying to stop the thoughts. If Aisling wanted to get rid of her, she'd had plenty of opportunities. She could have killed her in the closet. Used one of her paralytic pellets to take her down. She didn't need to bother with this elaborate, risky ruse.

"Waiting only makes it worse," Aisling said.

"Right." Nodding, Leandrea took a deep breath, turned her back toward the opening, and leaned out into the void.

CHAPTER SEVEN

On May 15, 2115, Kallum Gordon was located by the Authority and delivered to the custody of ReInception. Upon arrival at ReInception, Kallum was grossly undernourished and dehydrated. He reported having been living in the subway tunnels with his sister for several weeks. At some point several days ago, his sister left to get food and water and never returned. We have been unable to locate her or to determine if she is dead or alive. Kallum was uncertain how long he was in the tunnels alone before dehydration and near starvation forced him to seek help. His identity as a politicizing force makes releasing Kallum back into society, even to a Warddome, too risky. However, keeping him in ReInception custody and the risk that such information leaks to the public poses its own risks. I have a proposal...

—FROM THE FILES OF DENNISON KELVIN

Day 1: December 9, 2126: Unknown Location
Ward

*K*allum is small. Not only upper caste small, but also young-small. He's in a service tunnel near the subways. Prole use the flooded subway tunnels to boat around the city undetected. He didn't know that before he Fell. Like most upper caste, he'd supposed the subways were abandoned long ago, when the city gave up trying to repair them when flood after flood of brackish water kept destroying the infrastructure. Now, he sits on the platform ledge, legs dangling over what used to be the tracks, watching boats move past. Prole row and use long sticks to navigate around poles and debris. It's hushed down here—always. There is the whisper of people on boats and the clacking of sticks on poles. There is the dull thud of debris hitting the sides of the tunnel and smells...so many smells. Unwashed bodies, decay, and brackish water. But also wonderful smells, like when it rains and the old stagnant water is flushed away and new water rolls in. Or the smell of food cooking over small fires that makes his stomach growl and cramp.

Prole live in the subway tunnels now, too. Some of them want to help him, but most want something in return, especially when they realize he isn't one of them—or at least that he wasn't one of them until recently. They want him to do things for them in The Above, where he can still pass for something that he's not anymore. They want him to steal things or sell them. They want other things, too, mostly from his sister, but sometimes from him. He's not sure what, but once, someone offered Kitty credits for something from him. When she said no, the man got angry and grabbed at Kallum. Kitty stabbed the man in the hand, and they ran.

Kallum doesn't know where Kitty got the knife, but she scrapes it on stone to keep it sharp. He has a knife, too, but he doesn't think he could ever hurt someone with it. Kitty says if he ever really needs it, he'll not be afraid to use it anymore. He thinks she's wrong, but he keeps it sharp just in case.

Kitty says they have to hide. That they're too recognizable after the trial. That everyone is looking for them and that ReInception would pay a Prole a lot of creds to turn them in. She tries to change their appearance, cutting and coloring their hair. Smearing dirt on their faces. If they had any creds, they could have easily changed their hair and skin color, even their eyes, but their accounts were emptied when their parents went to the grid and *anyhow, they don't have comms anymore.*

Not too many upper caste kids are hiding amongst the Prole, especially a teenage sister and a little brother together. They keep being recognized. They kept having to run. A couple of times, when Kitty told Ward to run and he did, when she found him again, there were cuts on her face and arms and blood on her knife. Kallum told himself maybe she'd just tripped or had to kill a rat.

Kallum found this service tunnel a few days ago. It had been covered in debris, hidden from plain sight. Now, he and Kitty are using it to hide, emerging only when they're out of food. She said if they wait long enough, eventually people will stop looking for them and they'll find a way to the Mod Free zone. She says that there, people will help them. She tells him they are heroes to the anti-ReInception movement. He doesn't feel like a hero. Heroes don't get their parents put in the grid. Or maybe heroes don't let their parents kill people in the first place. And heroes certainly don't run and hide.

It would be a long time before The Authority gave up looking for them, he knew that. Kallum was tired of being cold and hungry and scared. He missed his school and his friends. He missed warm meals and his Prole nanny. He missed mom and dad, but he especially missed Dillon, which is why he testified against his parents in the first place. He wondered how Kitty felt about what he'd done. He'd done it for her and for Dillon, but sometimes he caught her staring at him, her eyes blank and dark. He couldn't tell what she was thinking.

He'd been in the service tunnel alone for a long time now. Kitty had gone to get food, but that was—he didn't know how long ago. All he knew was the food had been finished for long enough that his tummy was rumbling hard, and he had a deep, empty pit in his belly. When he stood up too fast, his head spun, and his legs felt wobbly. The fat rats that ran across him any time he fell asleep were starting to look tempting. Even worse, he thought he was starting to look tempting to them.

The water ran out. He knows he can't live too long without water. Two days, maybe three? He didn't know how long he'd been in that tunnel. Kitty had pulled out his comm weeks ago, right before they ran. She dug it out with a knife that she'd burned over a flame to kill the bacteria. It had hurt, and he'd been frightened with it gone. It was his last connection to the world he'd grown up in. His life had seemed normal, but now he knew it was a life of comfort and privilege. You could hardly even see the scar where the comm had been. And he could hardly remember what it was like to be able to ask questions and get answers on the spot. If he could ask his comm anything right now, he would ask it where Kitty was. It would show him the way.

He wishes Kitty would come back. If she doesn't return soon, he'll have to go foraging without her. What if something happened to her? What if she got caught or worse?

He hears scuffling and the sound of feet. Kitty?

He peers between the wires and debris, and out into the larger passageway. A man, thin and covered with sores from saltwater exposure, shambles down the hall and past him, moaning and sobbing. Kallum moves the wires back into place, retreating into darkness.

⸻ ◆ ⸻

Ward woke with a start. The room was dark. Soft voices came from nearby, and there was the scraping of equipment being moved around the room. A gurney rolled past him, the person on it, still. The body was covered with a translucent resin that spread up the neck and over the face as Ward watched—suspension epoxy used to hold people still during delicate surgical procedures. Procedures like those that had been performed on him when he was turned Prole. If you were lucky, they numbed or knocked you out while they were doing it. If you weren't, you were trapped in there, your screams silenced for the benefit of your tormentors. The epoxy moved over the person's face, covering his mouth, leaving just his eyes and nose exposed. His eyes shifted to the side, meeting Ward's, wide with terror.

Ward shuddered. There was nothing he could do about it. He was so drugged and dull that he may as well have been coated in epoxy, too. The pain and itching were creeping in again—enough to clear his head a bit, but not so much that he couldn't tolerate it. He tried to take advantage of the moment to focus on his situation before the pain overtook him again.

He turned his head to the other side and saw a man sitting there, scrolling through documents and images on a flexipad. His features were blurry, and Ward squinted, trying to bring them into focus.

"Ah. Well, there you are." The man rested the device on his chair arm, leaning forward and putting his elbows on his knees.

The voice was familiar, but his face, still just a fuzzy orb.

"How are you feeling, my friend?"

The Med? He thought not. The jumpsuit was gold for ReInception, not white for a medic. The skin was lighter than the Med's, although that could be changed in a matter of minutes with a tone pill.

Ward blinked again, trying to lift his hand toward his face to rub his eyes clear. Even that slight movement of his arm sent pain shooting down his back. A moan escaped him.

"Careful now."

The man moved Ward's arm back into its place, hanging it over the side of the cot. "We don't want you injuring that back of yours any more than you've already done. I need you healthy enough to survive modification. Unless, of course, you'd be willing to just talk."

Ward rolled his eyes, his back throbbing hard—more painful, but bringing yet more clarity with it. He blinked again, shaking his head. The face slowly came into focus, like someone adjusting the lens on a camera.

The man crossed his legs, the gold-booted foot hanging over his knee, jiggling slightly with nervous energy. Tucked in close to the chair leg, nearly blending in with the dull, gray metal, a tiny mouse hunkered down, nose wiggling and scratching at its face. The boot swung, but the mouse didn't move.

"Not that you talking would stop me from modifying you anyhow. How else will I know I can trust what you tell me? But it might at least postpone the inevitable for a while. And maybe, if you are really good, I'll leave more of the real you intact."

He leaned forward, bringing his face closer to Ward's, coming into full focus.

Ward's eyes went wide.

"Ah." Dennison Kelvin smiled. "I see you've finally recognized me."

The pain was gone. The fog was gone. Everything was crystal clear. The man Ward had been waiting to confront for years sat in strangling distance, and Ward couldn't even lift his arm.

"It puts me at an unfair disadvantage, doesn't it? I mean, you know me. Isn't it polite for you to tell me who you are?"

Ward stared at the man—possibly the most powerful man in the world if his position was what The Origins believed, rather than what he claimed. Not an underling reporting to Lucia Genesis, the head of ReInception, but the actual head of ReInception and Lucia's puppeteer.

Ward licked his lips. He had to be careful what he said. They may not have modified him yet, but he was pumped full of all kinds of drugs that dulled his thoughts and did who-knows-what else.

"Don't you have better things to do?"

Kelvin laughed, sitting back in his chair. He seemed so casual and relaxed. The posture of the arrogant. "I guess that depends on who you are."

What to say? How to keep the conversation going?

"Ward," said Ward. Telling Kelvin something that Kelvin already knew because just days ago, Ward and Leandrea's faces had been plastered all over the vids and holoscreens: *Wanted by the Authority.*

"That's cute." Kelvin reached over, pinching Ward's cheek a little too hard.

"You aren't simply *a* Ward. You are *the* Ward. The one who broke into my apartment with the help of someone who was supposed to be my daughter's best friend. The one who was trying to hack into my files when my daughter caught you."

Ward said nothing. The pain was coming on harder now. The nanites were microscopic, but still, it seemed like he could feel each one of the millions of them knitting him back together.

Keep it together, Ward.

"Nothing to say now? Well, that's disappointing, but not surprising. If you were able to get that far into your plan, you can't be a complete fleshhead. Which makes me wonder—how did you know how to hack into my systems? Wards aren't supposed to have that kind of training. I mean, you also aren't supposed to be very smart, but that's just what we tell the upper caste so they won't feel threatened. You and I both know it's a lie. Prole can be as smart or as stupid as anyone else. So tell me, Ward. Which one are you? I mean, I know you're book smart, but are you street smart, too? Smart enough to have an ounce of self-preservation? Smart enough to know how much easier or harder I can make your life?"

Kelvin leaned forward, elbows on knees, eyes inches away from Ward's.

"See, I bet you think you're smarter than me. Maybe you are. But if you have any sense at all, if you don't want to suffer, if maybe you don't want your friends to suffer, you'll tell me where your little friend, Leandrea, is."

Ward froze, trying his hardest not to react, but reflexively pulling in just the smallest gasp of air. That meant that Lea wasn't here. It meant that they hadn't caught her.

"What was that?"

Ward shook his head, not trusting himself to speak.

Kelvin leaned in, cocking his head. "You don't know?"

Ward shook his head again.

Kelvin showed Ward his index finger. "You sure about that?" He reached across Ward's back, digging a finger into a spot right below his shoulder blade.

Ward screamed. It was like a lightning bolt piercing him.

"Want to rethink that position?" Dennison hissed.

Something clattered, and the Med came running across the room.

"What are you doing!" He shouted.

Kelvin removed his finger and sat back in his chair again, grinning.

"Just trying to encourage my friend here to have a chat."

Ward's eyes rolled back. He almost blacked out.

"You swore you wouldn't touch him. You said you just wanted to talk."

Kelvin shrugged. "Lo sento. Guess I got a little carried away."

"That wound needs to be sterile!"

"Don't be dramatic. It's not like he's in that prehistoric torture chamber where they did this to him in the first place. He'll be fine."

The Med turned his back on Kelvin, lifting something off a tray. Another NFiT. He pressed it against Ward's arm. The medicine prickled as it entered his skin and then stung and numbed as it moved through him.

The Med's face turned a dark purple. "It's in places like this that bacteria like the DSB form. We can beat a lot, but Mother Nature always has her way in the end. I don't need you helping her along." The Med kept his back to Kelvin. "I'm going to have to ask you to leave."

Kelvin stood, blurring as Ward started to slip away again. "I was just going anyhow. But don't worry." He patted Ward's hand. "I'll be back soon."

"Gondu," the Med muttered as Kelvin retreated. He lifted something else off the tray—a liquid in a brown bottle, which he shook onto gauze. "This is going to hurt."

He pressed the gauze against Ward's back, just where Kelvin had touched him. Ward screamed again.

Everything went black.

The soft whirring of a machine roused Ward. His eyes slipped open, and he saw a cleaning robot rolling past beneath him, leaving the pale, gray floors a shiny mirror. As it circled below him, his back began to itch like the time he and Kitty had been running through the woods and he'd gotten poison oak all over his legs. His back itched so terribly that it made him want to scratch his skin off. For a moment, it was so excruciating that he lifted his arms, ready for the consequences of tearing his new skin just to make it stop. Then, as suddenly as it started, the itching stopped, the same way that it had when his mother had put the medicine on his legs and the poison oak receded, the blisters flattening and vanishing, like they'd never been there at all.

A light gray powder fell to the floor around him. The robot came back around again, whisking the dust away. Ward fell back to sleep. When he woke again, he'd forgotten that it had happened at all.

CHAPTER EIGHT

After more than a century of service, the New York City subway system has been officially declared defunct, a casualty of relentless climate change impacts. Rising sea levels, increased storm frequency, and aging infrastructure rendered the once-iconic transit system inoperable. The decision to shut down the subway marks the end of an era for New York City. For years, the MTA struggled to cope with severe flooding. Despite extensive efforts to fortify the infrastructure, including the installation of pumps, flood barriers, and waterproofing measures, the relentless onslaught of climate-induced challenges proved insurmountable. MTA Chairperson, Lisa Rodriguez, announced the closure with a mixture of nostalgia and resolve. "The subway has been the lifeblood of our city, connecting millions of people to their destinations every day. However, the realities of climate change have forced us to make this difficult decision. It's time to look forward and embrace new, sustainable solutions for urban mobility."

—THE NEW YORK TIMES, 2041

Leandrea lowered herself to the top of the elevator car, smashing down into frigid, fetid water up to her mid-thigh. All around her, in the darkness, was squeaking and scampering. She shuddered. As the water seeped through the fabric of her jumpsuit and pooled in her boots, she wished again that there had been a way to keep her Uni jumpsuit. It would have kept her dry and warm, something she hadn't fully appreciated until the last few days when she'd been perpetually too hot, too cold and often, soaked to the bone.

"Hold the line," Aisling called down the shaft in a raspy whisper that echoed against the cement walls. "I'm coming down."

As they'd practiced, Lea bent her knees and leaned back, gripping the rope and preparing to halt Aisling's fall if anything went wrong. The equipment held, and seconds later, Aisling splashed down next to her, causing the elevator car to drop a few inches and rock. Submerged as it was, Lea had the sense of being on an ice float in the middle of the ocean. Trying to keep her balance and not get dumped in, where she feared she'd end up pinned between the bobbing elevator car and the wall, Leandrea started to unclip the harness, but Aisling grabbed her hand.

"Stay clipped in. This thing hasn't been in use for decades and it's been submerged for just as long. It could break loose at any moment."

Just as she said it, the car groaned, dropping another few inches. Stifling a shriek, Lea grabbed the rope, Aisling doing the same, the whites of her eyes glowing faintly in the darkness.

"Let's get the floods out of here," Aisling whispered, taking a light out of her belt and shining it around the shaft. The hoistway doors were just in front of them, mostly blocked by the car and mostly below water, but elevated just enough that they should be able to slip through the space between the top of the car and the top of the hoistway door.

"Gondu," Aisling cursed. "We'll have to swim down that hall if we can even get these doors open."

"Will this thing hold us long enough for us to get through?"

"We have to try. If we go up a flight, we risk running into some Reds. Less risk they'll be monitoring a flooded hallway that you'd have to be completely LowQ to attempt to navigate."

"Right. That's encouraging."

Aisling ignored her. "Crowbar?"

Lea reached into a pocket on the side of her pack and pulled out the piece of bent metal. Repeating what they'd done above, Aisling wedged the metal between the hoistway doors, heaving on it, sending the elevator car bobbing and swaying below them. The doors wouldn't budge. She changed her position, trying again. Nothing.

Aisling cursed. "I can't get any leverage in all this water. You'll have to come around to this side and put your weight into it with me."

Cautiously, Lea moved toward Aisling's side of the car. The elevator car tipped, slanting at an angle, and Aisling squeaked in surprise, grabbing at the cables. "Deuce! Careful!"

"What do you want me to do? It's physics!" Lea hissed, then muttered, "Arschloch."

"Let's just get the Floods out of here. Come on."

The two women grabbed the bar, pushing against it, the elevator car bobbing and tilting below them. There was a creaking, and the doors slid open a few inches. Stale, fetid water stinking of rotten eggs sloshed in through the opening and Lea retched. They pushed again and the doors inched open more.

"Okay, slowly, move back across and grab the doors, just like we did upstairs."

Lea moved back, the elevator car bobbing but leveling out. Each of them grabbed a side and they pulled until the opening was wide enough for them to slip through.

"Come on." Aisling put her light between her teeth and slowly removed her backpack, pushing it through the opening ahead of them. Lea did the same.

Aisling looked at her. "Ready?"

Lea's heart rate sped up and her body shook, whether from cold or fear, she didn't know. Probably both. She wasn't ready, but she nodded her head anyhow.

"Okay. You can swim, right?"

Lea nodded again. "Probably a little late for that question." She neglected to add that it had been over a decade since she'd done so.

Aisling gave a nervous laugh. "Yeah, well, details."

"Right. Details."

"Okay. We are going to unclip, and you go through first. If the car drops, don't panic. We'll swim through the space. Once we're in the hall, we'll make our way to the back side of the building and out to The Marshes, just like we planned. Right?"

Leandrea nodded. "What if there isn't enough space between the water and the ceiling to get air?"

"There will be. Look." She shone her light through the space between the elevator doors. "The ceiling is a few feet higher than the top of the doors. It'll be cold, but we'll be okay."

Leandrea nodded again, teeth chattering and arms crossed over her chest, trying and failing not to think about that day she'd almost drowned and someone else had died to save her. Since then, water had been her greatest fear, but for days now, she'd been surrounded by it; immersed in it. The water had now saved her life more than once. The fear wasn't gone, but it had muted to a dull thud. Still, jumping right in like this was further than she'd ever pushed herself to face her fear. And this dark, frigid water would give pause to even the bravest swimmer.

Aisling touched her on the shoulder, giving a gentle nudge.

"It's okay. You first. I'll be right behind."

Lea unclipped and moved toward the elevator doors, pausing at the opening. The elevator car groaned, dropping another couple of inches, about to drop out from under them. Here in this shaft or out there in the hallway, one way or the other, she was swimming. There was no going back.

Turning sideways, she pulled herself through. As soon as she stepped off the elevator car, she found herself treading the surface of dark, frigid water, her head barely below the ceiling. As promised, there was enough room to breathe.

Her heart rate picked up and her breath came in short bursts. Milling her hands and feet in fast circles, she looked around, but it was too dark to see anything. Something bumped against her and she almost screamed, imagining creatures grabbing her from below and dragging her down. It was one of the backpacks. Grabbing it, she wrapped her arms around it, thankful that it was waterproof and buoyant. Aisling had planned for everything.

Holding the pack close to her chest, she kept her legs churning. Even with the movement and the spike of fear-fueled adrenaline, her legs cramped up with cold, her teeth chattering harder, the rapid clicking noises reverberating in her skull.

The small flashlight blinded Leandrea as Aisling pulled through the space. "Let's go before we freeze."

Aisling fumbled around until she found the second pack. Then, turning her back to Lea, she swam down the hall. Debris floated around them, bumping into arms and wrapping around limbs. Leandrea wondered, all these years later, what kinds of creatures these buildings had become habitats for. Shuddering, she swam faster, trying to stay close to Aisling.

Reaching the end of a hall, Aisling and Lea turned the corner into another hallway lined with mostly submerged doors. To the left, the doors were progressively more deeply under the water, the building beginning to list from years of decay.

"We'll have to go right," Aisling said. "Any deeper and I'm afraid the windows will be completely under water. If they aren't already broken, we'll be stuck."

Turning right, they swam until they found a door that was slightly ajar. Aisling pushed on it, and something on the other side clattered and banged against the door.

"Gondu! It's blocked. Try the next one."

Leandrea turned, swimming toward the next door. Her legs cramped, and she could no longer feel her body. Much longer and she was afraid they'd get hypothermic. They had to get out.

She pushed on the next door. It was locked.

"Deuce!" Aisling's teeth chattered so hard she barely got the words out. She had also given up her smart suit so there wouldn't be a risk of the technology being tracked. None of those precautions would matter if they froze to death. More importantly, if Lea died in these watery tunnels, the truth would die with her.

"Keep moving," Lea urged.

They tried two more doors, the water getting higher inch by inch as they moved back up the hall. They were almost to the end when they finally found one that they were able to push open. Behind the door, a metal desk floated, bobbing and banging. They tried to move it aside, but the current pushed it toward them, blocking their way in.

"We'll have to go under," Leandrea said.

Aisling nodded. "Hold my pack. I'll go first with the light, then you can push the packs through. I'll shine the light back so you can see."

Aisling stripped her pack off, handing it to Lea. Taking a deep breath, she dove.

For a moment, Leandrea could see Aisling's light moving below the surface of the water, and then she cleared the door and everything went completely black.

There was a steady dripping of water. Sounds echoed in the darkness and the building creaked and moaned. Something brushed against her wrist. She gasped at the sudden, sharp, stinging pain. She breathed in short, gasping bursts. She couldn't get enough air. She couldn't see anything! Something brushed her again and she shrieked. Treading water faster, she tried to warm her body, to scare away anything that might be down there, but the blackness engulfed her. Her arms slowed. Everything went numb.

She closed her eyes, and there was a light in the distance, small and flickering. It moved closer and she could see that flame. The one Ward had lit for her in the darkness. From the shadows, his face came into view. That wide, unexpected smile on a once-harsh face.

"Little Bird," he whispered, putting his hand to her cheek. "Lea." Then, louder, "Lea!"

Her eyes snapped open as a light shone through the crack in the door and into her face. "Lea! I'm through! Push the bags towards me!"

Shaking her head, she tried to clear the fog. Her limbs felt lethargic and heavy as she pushed Aisling's pack through the opening in the door.

"Come on," Aisling urged. "There's a window in here. Hang in there a few more minutes and we'll be out."

"A few more minutes," she repeated to herself. She forced herself to remember the dark water and sinking below the surface. Her lungs on fire. A hand, reaching down and pulling her to safety. A forgotten woman who died, saving her life. She could not let her story end here. She could not let that woman die saving her, only to drown again all these years later, taking with her the only chance at truly making that sacrifice worthwhile.

Taking a steeling breath, Lea pushed her pack through the opening. She moved her limbs faster to get the circulation going, afraid that if she didn't, she wouldn't make it even the short distance to the other side.

"Okay. I'll shine the light under the water so you can see. You'll have to swim almost along the floor to clear the desk. I got a nasty cut from one of the legs, so go as low as you can. But it's not far. Take a deep breath. On the count of three."

Lea counted to three, took a deep breath, and dove.

The water was murky and green. There was a whole habitat under there, with small fish darting away from her and mollusks encrusting an old planter. A corroded chair lay on its side and the desk hovered above, its legs reaching down like tentacles. A clear Moon Jelly, a flower deep in its belly, pulsed past her, reminding her of Bar In The Sky back at her College with its beautiful, improbable illusions of being under the sea. She couldn't believe that, less than a month earlier, she'd sat at the table with Andromeda, lying to her friend to get her access to her father's files. It was the deception that had led to all of this. To Ward's capture. To her fleeing for her life.

The jellyfish undulated toward her. That must have been what hit her arm earlier. She remembered something about the tops of the creatures not having toxins and she poked it away, careful not to touch the trailing stingers.

And then she was clear of the desk and could see Aisling's legs pedaling in the water, the light in her hand. Breaking the surface, she gasped for air.

"Let's get the Floods out of here!"

Aisling smiled. "Amen to that."

Dim light from the bright, full moon streamed through submerged windows at the far end of the room. Earlier, they'd wished for the cover of more darkness, but now, Leandrea was grateful for the comfort of some illumination. The windows were already broken out, jagged-edged glass threatening their escape, but Lea didn't care. Seeing a path out of the frigid water injected Lea with a burst of adrenaline. She swam past Aisling, kicking out the remaining shards of glass, dove and emerged into the dense grass of The Marshes. Seconds later, Aisling appeared beside her, extinguishing her light.

The frogs, whose nearly deafening chirrup Lea hadn't even noticed, suddenly went silent. Looking around, all Lea could see were tall, green stalks. The only sound was the susurrant breeze through the dense blades of grass.

"Which way?" Aisling asked.

Leandrea wasn't sure. Spread out before them in the impenetrable green of the marsh, watery pathways cut through it in every direction. She'd hoped that the underground would be watching the building, especially after the raid. That someone sympathetic would spot them exiting the building. Then again, all the Authority activity might have caused them to flee the area.

For her entire life, Lea had depended on her comm to tell her which way to go. Without it, she was lost—literally and figuratively. Indecision paralyzed her. Moving was dangerous, but so was staying put. Plus, if they didn't get out of the frigid water, they'd soon die of hypothermia.

"I guess toward The Floods. Do you know which way that is?"

Aisling raised an eyebrow. "You don't know where we're going?"

Leandrea's face went hot. She shook her head.

"Yeah. The comm. Right."

Aisling turned, peering around. "You're going to have to learn how to navigate without that thing, you know?"

"Yeah, well, I've been a little busy since they ripped it out of me. Mostly hiding from you."

"Fair enough." Aisling shrugged. "Ok. So, let's start now. They are more precise ways to navigate, like using the direction of sunrise and sunset, or even the stars, but the basics? Start paying attention to your surroundings because nothing else is doing it for you anymore. Look around. Which way do you think The Floods are?"

Leandrea looked. Ahead was nothing but green all the way to the horizon. Same to the sides. The Floods were filled with tall, partially submerged structures, the water ran in canals between what had once been office buildings and apartments but were now home to the Prole.

"I don't see any buildings, so it must be behind us. Behind this building."

"See?" Aisling smiled. "Now that wasn't so hard, was it?"

Leandrea shook her head. "But even if I did have a sense of direction, I was under a tarp when they navigated us from The Floods, through The Marshes. I'm not sure where we were let off. I just have to hope they're watching, the way they were watching before. They'll have seen the building get raided. Maybe they'll be watching for—"

A grass-shaped form separated itself from the green behind it.

"Yell be wantin' to come with me."

CHAPTER NINE

<u>**Manhattan Celebrates Completion of Cutting-Edge Flood Defense System**</u>

Today marks a monumental achievement in the history of urban engineering and climate resilience as Manhattan celebrates the completion of its state-of-the-art system of dikes and gates, the "New Amsterdam Resilience Initiative" (NARI). The project has been in development for over two decades and represents a fusion of Dutch expertise and American innovation. This innovative infrastructure, designed to protect the iconic island from the increasingly severe impacts of climate change, is a testament to human ingenuity and international collaboration. Inspired by the Netherlands' renowned flood management systems, Manhattan's new defenses incorporate the latest advancements in climate science and engineering. A Modern Marvel, NARI is composed of an intricate network of dikes, storm surge barriers, and adaptive flood gates that collectively create a formidable barrier against rising sea levels and storm surges. Unlike the traditional static structures of the past, these new defenses are dynamic and responsive, capable of adjusting to real-time data on weather patterns, tidal movements, and sea level changes.

—DUTCHNEWS, JUNE 9, 2050

"Raise bed."

Ward felt himself lifting into the air. He tried to open his eyes, but his lids were heavy, his brain stuffed too tight in his skull.

"Higher."

He rose again.

"This is awkward. Can't we turn him over?"

A woman's voice. Familiar.

"Does he look like I can turn him over?"

A male voice. Also familiar.

A grunt. "Fine. Then get me a pillow so I don't have to sit on the deucing floor."

The sounds of feet retreating.

Ward drifted back into that hypnogogic space between sleep and wakefulness. Less dream and more hallucination of that time, back in the tunnels with his sister, running from the authority.

"Hide here. I'll be back soon." But she'd never come back.

"Hey."

There was a poke on his arm. He opened his eyes. The world was smudged, like he was looking at it through rain-covered glass. He was so tired. His eyes started to slide shut again.

"Hey!" Another poke. "Can't you do something to wake him up?" The woman's voice again. Still familiar, but he couldn't quite place it. He couldn't quite care.

"Not if we want him to heal." The male voice again. The Med, maybe?

"I don't care about that."

"Well, your father does, so unless you want to face that wrath—"

A huff and then more persistent poking on his arm, something sharp and annoying.

"Gondu! Wake up."

He opened his eyes again, focusing on the repeated tapping on his forearm. A long fingernail, painted with a holographic swirling pattern that moved away in a spiral. He wanted to slip toward it, fall down inside, like Alice in Wonderland. He loved that book. Kitty's father had given it to him when he was a boy.

"Who in the world am I? Ah, that's the great puzzle."

That one made Ward laugh. Good one.

"What the floods is he laughing about? Has he gone totally non-comp?"

Poke. Poke. Poke.

Like a gnat circling his head. Annoying. He tried brushing it away, but missed, his arms dropping again, heavy and useless. The dreams of Kitty's father, Dillon, were always the best ones. They had books and smiles, "green eyes, like Lea's, bright and flecked with gold. And...."

"Floods. How drugged up is he?"

"Very."

"Is that really necessary?"

"You tell me," the male voice said, "since you seem to know what's best for him."

Ward felt a heavy cloth being lifted from his back and then cold air across raw skin—ice on a burn. His eyes flew open.

"Yikes. What did those butchers do to him?"

"It's more about what the Authority did to him when they dragged him out of a hospital room when he'd just had a massive skin graft put on, but, you know, details."

"Careful, doctor. You're starting to sound like a sympathizer."

"I sympathize with all of my patients."

"I'm sure you do."

A hiss of air through teeth. A face came into view, close enough to be clear. To smell breath. Pale. Green eyes. Long red hair, but not a sunrise, like Leandrea's. More like rusted iron. He didn't recognize her. Or did he? There was something familiar.

She put a hand on his cheek, patting just a little too hard. "Shame. You were so pretty."

"Please don't harass my patient."

"Please get out of my flooding face."

"I think you should go."

"I think *you* should go." A pause. "Like now."

"I'm not allowed to—"

"Leave."

"But your father said not to let anyone—"

"Leave!"

"If something happens, it's on you."

"Whatever."

"Gondu."

There was the sound of footsteps retreating again. Ward wanted to call to the Med. To tell him to come back; not to leave him with this predator. But his mouth was full of glue, his eyes covered in paste.

"There now. Where were we?"

Fingers on his eyelids, prying them apart. His eyes rolled in his head. Tried to focus.

There was a pillow on the ground in front of him. A shape lowered itself down, hazy and ghostly, shimmering as if seen through heat on pavement.

"Recognize me?"

Ward blinked, shaking his head slowly.

"I thought you might like this look. Pale. Green eyes. Red hair. Boooorrrring."

Ward's eyes began to close, the image of the woman in front of him blurring into a memory of him and Lea alone in a room. A mattress on the floor. Sunlight sparkling in her hair. Her telling him, "I told you it mattered."

"Uh uh uh." Sharp poking on his arm. He opened his eyes again.

"Let me give you a hint. Last time you saw me, you drugged me. How the tables have turned."

Ward's eyes opened wider. He blinked several times, trying to shake the gauzy film from his brain. High cheekbones and a narrow nose. Inhuman curves. Now he recognized her. She changed her appearance with such frequency that it always took him a moment. It was even harder, slogging through this mud in his skull. But now he knew. Last time he'd seen her, she was naked, her skin dark with a swirling pattern that wrapped around large, round breasts. Her hair had been...He couldn't remember what it had looked like that day. She changed it so much. It was brown. And then it was gold…

She stood and walked away, returning a moment later with a cup and a straw.

"Drink."

Narrowing his eyes, he pinched his lips shut.

"Don't be ridiculous. I'm not going to poison you. Not that I don't want to, it's just that my father has some plans for you first, and I'm not sure I want to face the consequences of putting my revenge above his. He's not particularly pleased with me right now. You want to guess why?"

She patted him on the face again, too hard.

"So drink."

His mouth was a desert, cracked and parched. He was so thirsty.

He turned his face away.

"Ugh. Fine. See?"

She leaned down so she was eye level with him and took a long pull at the straw. Clear liquid rose into her mouth. She smacked her lips. "Num, num, num." She rattled the cup. Ice. When was the last time he'd had ice? Not since he was small. Not since he was Kallum Gordon.

"Drink."

Putting his lips around the straw, he took a drink, the icy water extinguishing the fire in his throat. He drank until the cup was empty and wished for more. Wished for it more than anything. But he said nothing. He would not give her the satisfaction of asking her for anything, even if it meant hurting himself.

"Okay. Now, let's try again. Do you know who I am?"

He licked his lips. "Andromeda."

His throat was sandpaper.

"Good job! Now, Andromeda what?"

Ward said nothing. He didn't understand what she wanted from him. The interaction was taking everything he had and all he wanted was to drift back off, to dream about being somewhere else, with someone else. But somewhere in the fog, he knew this could be important. Maybe Andromeda could tell him where everyone else was—where Lea was. Angry as she was, maybe she at least still cared about her friend.

"No? Okay. I'll give you a hint. How about 'Andromeda. I'm so sorry that I pitted your best friend against you. Andromeda, I'm sorry I drugged you and stole your father's files. Any of those would be a good start, really.'"

Ward blinked. He couldn't think straight. He wished for the pain of the cold on his back again. The icy water pouring down his throat. Something to clear his head.

"Still no? Well, how about you tell me what you found when you stole those files?"

Ward tried lifting his arms to rub his eyes, but moving them pulled at his back. His skin felt hot and tight. It burned, and he groaned at the pain. But it was good. It made him more alert. Just a little.

"Okay. Then how about you tell me where Leandrea went?"

Ward froze. He looked at her.

She narrowed her eyes, taking a deep breath. "Well deuce. You don't know either, do you?"

He said nothing.

"Hmm. Daddy's not going to like that. You'd better think of something else to share or he might not wait to put you in the machine, whether it kills you or not."

Ward licked his lips. "He sent you?"

"No. I just enjoy talking to people who lie to me and drug me." She rolled her eyes. "Of course he sent me."

"What makes him think I'd talk to you?" His words were slow and slurred, like he was speaking through the big pink bubbles of the gum Kitty used to buy for him—before. He hated himself for being weak in front of her.

"I don't know. Guilt? A modicum of intelligence? Or maybe he figured since I was dumb enough to let you in his home in the first place, I'd be pretty motivated to get the truth out of you, to lessen my own consequences. Besides, it's him or me and trust me, you'd rather have me."

Ward turned his head to the side, laying it down. Holding it up was like lifting a boulder. "I'm not so sure that's true."

"Ouch! That's not very nice," Andromeda tsked. "Seeing you like this almost makes me feel bad. So weak. So vulnerable." She ran her nails along his arm. "Almost." She pinched, and he gritted his teeth, but at least it roused him again.

"Where's everyone else?" he rasped.

"Here and there. Being prepped for ReInception if they haven't already gone through it. Soon, we'll know everything anyhow. If you volunteer the information, things might go easier for you. Maybe they'll even leave your core personality intact. It would be a shame if another one of Lea's lovers suddenly puked every time he saw her."

Ward winced at that. It was the forced modification of Lea's ex-boyfriend, Hallyn, that had, at first, motivated her to find out more about ReInception. Hallyn had been over twenty when it happened, so the modification without his consent was illegal. They took away his beliefs that ReInception and the caste system were bad. They had also done something to him that made Lea repellant to him, but exactly what wasn't clear.

He wouldn't wish what had happened to Hallyn on his worst enemy—having who you are taken from you—and now it was probably happening to all the Origins. To all his friends. To the people who'd saved him. Soon, it would happen to him. His only solace was that they didn't have Lea or Iza. They were two of the few people left in this world who he loved. But they were also the only two people who knew who he really was. He didn't want them in the machine for selfish reasons, true. But also for the sake of The Origins. He was leverage, and he knew it. He had been leverage since the day he took the witness stand against his parents. The truth about his identity would come out eventually, but he'd wanted to do it in his time, on his terms. Given his current circumstances, that was unlikely. The best he could do now was delay as long as possible.

"So, you want to tell me what you found in those files? How much got out?"

He debated telling her that none of it had gotten out. It was true—at least in the sense that she was asking. They hadn't transmitted anything to the outside world before they were captured. The only copies were on Lea's body, but he wouldn't tell anyone that—at least not of his own free will. When it finally came out, when they put him in the machine, he could only hope that, by then, Lea would be long gone, and the files would be out of her. He'd put them in her to protect her—so that she would have a bargaining chip if something like this happened. But those files would make her a wanted woman if anyone knew about them. She'd have no rest until they were in the right hands. Whose hands those were, he wasn't sure.

"None of it got out."

"None of what? How much did you learn?"

"Not much. The file transfer was interrupted when you—"

"When I came out of the drug induced stupor that you'd put me in and caught you in the act."

Turning his head, he looked at her again. Her stare was unblinking. The green of her eyes was not like the warm forest of Leandrea's, or the mica-flecked dappled grass of Dillon's, but a harsh, artificial green, like too-bright light on the turf at wakeball tournaments.

"Yes."

"So you learned nothing? I find that hard to believe."

He'd learned a lot. Most importantly, that the thing they'd removed from his back was a device that could remotely trigger ReInception in all those who had it implanted—about a third of the Prole population. He wouldn't tell her that, not until he had no choice. But there were other things...One thing in particular. Should he tell her? Would it matter? It seemed like something to save for the right moment. He didn't think that was now.

"Why should I tell you anything?" His words were slow and smudged, spoken through murky water. He was so tired. He lay his head back down and closed his eyes.

Andromeda was quiet for a while, but as he drifted in and out of consciousness, he could hear the rustling of her jumpsuit fabric, the rasping of her scratching her hair.

"Lie to me."

The voice was right in his ear. He jumped, his heart beating fast in his throat. She was squatting right in front of him, her turf-green eyes inches from his.

"What?"

"Lie to me. Any little lie. Like...tell me your name is Stephano or something."

"I don't..."

"Just do it!"

"My name is Stephano!"

She squinted, staring at him, unblinking. His heart beat faster and he started to sweat.

"Lie again."

"I don't know what you're—"

"Lie again."

"And say what?"

"Tell me you hate Lea."

Ward scowled.

"Okay. Then say you love me. Say it like you mean it, *Ward*." She twisted his name in her mouth.

"*Siao*," Ward muttered. Turning away.

"I mean it, Ward. Lie." She dug a nail into his back and he screamed. She pulled it away and his breath came in hard gasps. "Lie."

He glared at her. "You learn that little trick from your da?"

She watched him like a cat watches a mouse. Neither of them moved. Sweat beaded on his forehead. He waited for the nail in his back again.

"Fine. I love you Andromeda. Feel better?"

She pursed her lips, crossing her arms over her chest and sat back.

"How are you doing it?"

"Doing what?"

"Did you know when I'm in my parents' apartment, I can't lie?"

Ward's head was pounding. "I don't understand."

"You think that the security you bypassed to get into his files is the only system someone like my dad would have in his home?"

Ward looked up at her.

"From the minute you walked into that apartment there are sensors reading your heart rate, perspiration, pupil dilation. When you live like that, you become a pro at knowing what other people are up to."

"I don't understand."

"See, from the moment Lea told me she wanted to come to the apartment, I knew she was up to something. I could see it in her eyes, her jitters, her sweat. Then, once we were in the apartment, the security picked it up. I watched the whole time you two were in that room. Her pulse was elevated. You were whispering to each other. At first, I thought she was trying to protect you, then I realized that she was falling for you. But you..."

Ward didn't move. He breathed in and out, slowly.

"But you. Nothing moved. Your heart rate didn't increase. You didn't sweat. I asked you all kinds of questions when we were alone in that room, including whether you had a thing for my little friend and you lied right to my face. You fooled me. You fooled the whole system. How?"

Ward wasn't sure, but he had an idea.

He shook his head.

"Even right now, you aren't breathing hard. Your pupils aren't moving. If you were anyone else, I'd believe you didn't know. But you know, don't you?"

He shook his head again.

Andromeda gave a small laugh. "I actually felt bad for you. I know it didn't seem like it, but Lea's little speeches sometimes did make me think—her lecture about you, especially. Maybe you justify what you did to me by thinking that I'm the bad guy. That I would have hurt or used you. I told Lea I'm not like that, and I meant it. I wouldn't have hurt you. Not if you hadn't hurt me first."

Ward put his head back down, turning away and closing his eyes. With her false eyes and her icy stare, her plastic imitation of Lea, he didn't want to look at Andromeda anymore. He was just so tired.

"So you say."

"Well, I guess we'll never know, will we? Because before, the choice was mine; now it's not."

"It's still your choice," Ward said, keeping his eyes closed.

Andromeda ran her nails through his hair. Scratching them against his scalp, like he was a small child she was trying to soothe. He heard the sound deep in his skull, like waves rasping across sand.

"You think that, but it's not. It's no more my choice than if they'd put me through ReInception."

Ward felt hot tears in his eyes, and he wasn't even sure who they were for. This girl seemed so confident, so strong. But her father had broken her. Maybe they had more in common than either of them would have believed.

"I wasn't trying to hurt you, either. You were collateral damage, and I'm sorry for that. But you are wrong about what you can and can't do. I used to think I was powerless, too. That my position in life meant I was doomed to be the pawn of others. But if a pawn reaches the other side of the board, it can promote to another piece. It can become a Bishop, Rook, Knight, even a Queen."

She laughed lightly, slipping her fingers through his hair one last time. "Maybe. But maybe, sometimes, a pawn is just a pawn. There's only so many battles one person can fight. Some of them are bigger than any one of us. Some of them can't be won without all of us. And sometimes, the chance to fight is taken away from us. Soon, your people are going to turn on you and they'll have no more choice in that than you or me. And then where will we be? Ward."

"Andy. Your dad wants you. We have to go." Ward's eyes slipped open. It was the other girl who Andromeda hung out with. Kammeo. Ward hadn't even heard her come in. She was forgettable, slipping in and out of Andromeda's story like a quiet shadow.

His back hurt so much now that he couldn't string together coherent thoughts.

There was pressure on his arm, and Ward's eyes slipped to the left. The Med stood there, pressing the NFiT against his shoulder.

"That's enough for today."

Numbness flowed from Ward's shoulder down his limbs and across his back, flowing up his neck, warm and viscous, like suspension epoxy.

With Andromeda standing there, watching him, the room closed in around him, and he knew no more.

CHAPTER TEN

<u>Key Features of the NARI System:</u> *1. Adaptive Flood Gates: These gates can automatically adjust their height and opening based on predictive models of storm surges, ensuring optimal protection without disrupting maritime traffic. 2. Smart Dikes: Equipped with sensors and AI-driven monitoring systems, these dikes detect structural weaknesses, water seepage, and pressure changes, allowing for proactive maintenance and repair. 3. Eco-friendly Design: The system integrates green infrastructure, such as artificial wetlands and oyster reefs, which provide additional flood protection while promoting biodiversity and improving water quality. 4. Renewable Energy Integration: Solar panels and tidal energy generators are embedded within the structures, providing sustainable energy sources.*

Dutch water management expert, Dr. Annelies van Rijn, who led the design team, remarked, "The NARI system is not just a protective measure; it's a blueprint for resilient urban living in the face of climate change."

—DUTCHNEWS, JUNE 9, 2050

Aisling drew her EMG and aimed. Two grass-covered arms shot up into the air.

"Dun fire. She right—we been watchin', sure, sure. I'm here to help."

Aisling adjusted her weapon, taking sharper aim and backing the man toward the water. "How do we know? How can we trust you?"

The man's arms shook, the grass camouflage waving back and forth with his movement. It would have been comical were it not for the circumstances. The Electromagnetic Gun would only paralyze the man on the ground, but in the water, it could cause him to arrest.

"Lah! I'm de one brought de clady wee salvation here."

Recognizing the voice, Leandrea's mouth spread into a wide grin. That's what he'd called her when he'd helped her and Ward escape. "Ya best be salvation," he'd said. And Ward had promised that she was. She hadn't believed it then, and she didn't believe it now. But the chips under the skin on her side might be, which meant that, at least for the moment, she was, too.

She put her hand on the EMG, pushing it down. "It's okay."

The man lowered his arms. "Lah. We been taking turns at watch. Making sure nothing malo happened. Sure. Sure. It did."

"Yes, really bad," Leandrea agreed. "Can you get us out of here?"

"Depends where yeh need get. Authority crawlin' all over Floods like minnow."

Lea hesitated. *If something happens, go to Sebbe and Vella, I trust them with my life,* Ward had told her. But did she trust Aisling enough to expose them? No, she didn't. But all of Aisling's exits were burned. She had no choice.

"We need to get to the Cats."

The green-painted brows rose. "Yeh sure 'bout dat?"

Aisling turned toward Lea, her expression mirroring the man's. "Yeah, you sure about that?"

Leandrea nodded. "Your escape route is compromised, and I only know one other person who might be able to get us out of here. Besides, Authority know Ward and I fled to the Floods. They are focusing the search here. They'd never think we'd go back north."

Aisling crossed her arms over her chest. "Right, because that would be completely LowQ."

"It's the last place they think we'll go, and it's the only option we have."

"And who is it you think will help us?"

"You'll see when we get there."

Aisling's mouth turned down and her brows pulled together. "And how are we going to get to the Cats? Authority will be watching the tunnels."

The man in green nodded his agreement. "Sure, sure. Tunnels swarmin' wit Authority. You canna' go back how you came."

Leandrea thought for a moment. She and Ward had traveled to the Floods by the tunnels, but they'd evaded the Authority utilizing what was not on the maps.

"Maybe we can." Lea walked toward the man in green, taking his hands. "Is there a place down here where information about the subways was stored? Somewhere we can find maps or plans?"

"I dunna' think so." He paused a few moments scratching at his chin, green paint flaking and falling to the ground, revealing dark skin and a black beard. Then his hand froze, and his eyes widened. "Might a museum help though?"

"A museum?" Leandrea's heartbeat sped up.

"There was a museum bout the train, somewhere in Old Brooklyn, methinks. I ha' na' been there, but I know others who can get yeh there."

Aisling shook her head. "We'd still have to go through the tunnels to get there."

The man laughed. "Yeh canna' get to Brooklyn in the tunnels. They below water."

"Then how?" Lea asked.

"You canna," the man repeated. "They'll catch yeh, sure, sure. But tell me what yer need and we get it for yeh."

Leandrea hated to give away Ward's secret. How he and Kitty had evaded capture by using abandoned tunnels, stations, and service entrances. But it was how they'd avoided detection by Aisling to get to The Origins, and it was the only way Lea could think of to get back. It was the only place the Authority wouldn't be looking because they didn't know it existed.

December 13, 2126:
The Marshes, The Floods, Midtown, The Catacombs

Staring across the street toward the West End, Lea rubbed her hands together, blowing on them and wishing again for the comfort of her Uni jumpsuit. Its smart fabric would have kept her warm, unlike the heavy material of the Prole blue she now wore again.

Lea and Aisling had moved back through the Marshes and the Floods in the reverse of way that Lea and Ward had arrived: First, secreted in the boat of the man covered in marsh grasses and then, through the half-submerged buildings of the Floods by a network of people in the Underground. They were taken to an apartment on a high floor to wait for someone to return with old blueprints for the subway system—the ones that would show all the tunnels and entrances that weren't on the maps the Authority or ReInception would be looking at. It took another two days for Lea and Aisling, using the blueprints and often having to wait in the wet and cold as Authority passed nearby, to navigate back north to The Catacombs. The West End had also been compromised, so they waited across the street in a vacant building.

"It's been three days since we escaped the Floods and no Authority for over twenty-four hours. They got The Origins. I doubt they're even looking for me anymore. Don't you think it's safe yet?"

Aisling shook her head. "They'll have left remote surveillance."

"But you won't be recognized."

"They might not know my appearance or have me in the records, but they'll know I'm not Prole. They'll be looking for anything out of the ordinary."

"So, how are we supposed to contact them?"

Aisling shook her head. "We wait for the right moment."

Which meant that Aisling didn't have a good plan. Neither did Lea, but Aisling didn't know about the other clock that was running. The one where they put Ward in the machine and he disclosed the fact that she had the files on her. Lea's stomach churned just thinking about it. Ward would want her to escape, and that was her only chance of helping him. But she couldn't help feeling like she'd abandoned him. And once they reprogrammed him, then what? Would he even be her Ward anymore, or would they make him hate her, the way they'd done with Hallyn? Here she was again, trying to honor a promise for the sake of someone she loved who probably didn't love her anymore. Part of her wished she could go back a month, to the day they went to the protest—take it all back and live in ignorance.

"We can't keep waiting, Ash."

Leandrea now knew that Aishling's first name was Sirkka, but Lea was so used to calling her Officer Aisling that she couldn't wrap her mouth around something new or the friendship that using her given name implied. Aisling was eager to put her cover as an Authority behind her. It "made her skin crawl," she'd said. So they'd arrived at Ash. Ash and Lea. Lea and Ash. The enemies to friends trope of novels, except that Aisling was not her friend and Lea still didn't trust her as far as she could throw a weighted wake-ball.

From their third-floor window, Lea saw Vella coming down the street. Their face was in shadow under their cloak hood, but Lea recognized the tall, thin form and the long, sure strides. The deep purple hair peeking out around the edges. She had to take the risk. If she hadn't already run out of time, she would soon. Before Aisling could object, she made for the stairs.

"What are you doing?"

"It's Vella. I'm getting them."

Aisling hissed, racing to catch up with Lea. She caught up with her near the exit, grabbing her arm. "Fine. But at least let me do it. You'll be recognized from a mile away."

Lea grabbed at her short hair, tucking it behind her ears. Her hair had always been her defining characteristic. She couldn't get used to the feel of it ending below her ears. Aisling had hacked it off with a knife two days and miles of subway service tunnels ago, hiding the evidence in a bag that they sunk to the bottom of some flooded tracks. They'd planned to color it as soon as they could safely get some dye tabs. The minor change wouldn't fool anyone or anything looking for her carefully. It wouldn't trick the scanners. But at least it would slow down her identification from afar.

"Fine." Lea crossed her arms over her chest.

"If Authority shows up, you run. Got it?"

Lea nodded. It was what they'd agreed to. Aisling would put herself out in front because it was most important that Lea get out of the country so she could tell someone what she knew. There was no plan for how she'd do that without Vella and Sebbe, or knowing that, if Aisling was caught, even her trick of using the service tunnels would be burned. She also still didn't know if it was a trick Aisling was using to get Lea to trust her, but it was the only plan she had.

Aisling leaned out the entryway, peering left and right, up and down the street, and then stepped out the door. She was still shielded from view by the overhang, but she'd be visible to Vella as they passed.

"Vella!" she stage-whispered.

Vella froze, looking around.

"Vella!" They turned, looking toward Aisling. Their face was in shadow, and Lea couldn't see their expression, but she could tell from the stiff posture that Vella was on guard.

"Who's there?" Vella whispered back.

Aisling took a few steps forward, hands up, palms faced out and hands open.

Vella slid their hood down, squinting toward the door. "Who are you?"

Aisling looped a hand toward her body. "Not here. Inside."

Vella squinted again. "I don't think so." They turned and started toward The West End.

"Vella!" Leandrea took the risk of calling out to The Server who Ward trusted with his life. She stepped forward, still behind Aisling and in shadow, but enough for Vella to see.

Vella turned, eyes going wide, and then crossed the span in five quick, long strides. She shoved Aisling and Lea into the building, closing the door behind them.

"Gondu! Siao! Everyone looking for you!"

Lea grabbed Vella by the cloak, pulling them further back into the building.

"We had nowhere else to go."

"Well, you shouldn't'a come to me. You know they're watching the place. That Officer..." Vella's eyes went wide, turning back toward Aisling. "You!"

Aisling put her hands back up. "I'm not who you think."

Vella's arm flew out, quick, eyes narrow, their hand wrapping around the fabric at Aisling's throat and twisting. "I know who you are," Vella growled. Vella lifted, biceps flexing. Aisling was small and light. Vella was at least a foot taller and Prole strong.

"Vella! Stop!" Lea grabbed their arm, trying to pull them off of Aisling. It was like trying to stop a speeding mag train.

Vella kept lifting until Aisling's feet were off the ground. Aisling grabbed at her throat, peddling her feet.

"Vella! Vella!" Lea kept snatching at her arm. "She's trying to help us."

"Fleshhead," Vella hissed. "Yeh bring down storm!"

Leandrea couldn't stop Vella—they were too strong; too angry. She had no choice. Ward trusted Vella with his life—he'd told Lea so. To save it, Lea had to trust Vella with everything. "Vella! She knows where Katherine Vega is. Ward is her brother. He's Kallum Gordon. Ward is Kallum Gordon."

Vella turned their head toward Lea, face a deep, angry red. Eyes blank and veins popped out of their forearm and throbbing at their temples. Aisling was gasping for air, her feet slowing.

"Liar," Vella hissed, spit flying from their mouth.

"Vella, think about it. His secrets. How Izabelle always hinted at how important Ward would be to the cause. She knew. It's what she was saving him for—to be the poster boy for The Origins."

Vella shook their head. "No. Kallum Gordon had blue eyes." But the grip on Aisling loosened enough for Aisling to take a deep breath.

"ReInception did that to him. They changed his eyes. That's why his vision is so bad, from all the scarring so he couldn't be ID'ed on retinal scans."

Vella shook their head again. "I don't believe it. He would've told me."

But they were starting to—Lea could see it happening—Vella putting together the pieces just as she had when Ward told her.

Vella hesitated, eyes darting back and forth. "But Kallum Gordon weren't Prole. Ward is Prole."

"The scars all over his body are from muscle stims. He was too old for DNA mods. But he was young enough for them to use machinery. They changed everything that would identify him as Kallum Gordon and then they threw him away. And now they have him, Vella. We have to help."

Vella dropped Aisling. She fell to the ground, gasping for air and holding her throat.

Vella's eyes were wide. They shook their head. "It can't be."

"But you know it is. Just like I did."

Tears welled up in Vella's eyes. "Why dinna' he tell me?"

Leandrea put her hand on Vella's arm. "Vella. I know how you feel. I felt the same way. He didn't tell anyone. Not being Kallum Gordon was how he's survived the last twelve years. Iza figured it out on her own, and Katherine sent Aisling to look for him, but they knew what to look for. They knew what had been done to him. We don't have time for our feelings to be hurt about his choices. ReInception has him. They have all The Origins. Amie. Everyone. We need your help."

Vella was breathing hard, hands shaking. "All of them? Iza?"

"I don't know. Iza wasn't there. At least not that I saw."

"And you? How'd you escape?"

"Aisling was looking for Ward—for Kallum—all along. Officer Aisling was a cover. She was trying to confirm his identity when the raid happened. But Ward was in recovery from having the code removed from his back. Aisling got me instead. When they started loading everyone into the hovercraft, we escaped."

Vella shook their head. "How could I not have seen it?"

Aisling stood, still wheezing, wiping the dirt from her pants. It was a futile gesture. They were covered in dirt—both of them. They hadn't bathed in three days and all they'd eaten were the rations in their packs. Lea was exhausted and hungry. All she wanted to do was bathe, sleep in a warm bed, and eat a hot meal. But they had to keep moving.

"Vella." She touched their shoulder. "Ward said he trusted you with his life. He told me that if anything happened, I was to come to you and Sebbe. No one else. He trusted you with *my* life. There's evidence against ReInception that Ward and I found out. I have to get out of here. It's my only chance of helping him. Of helping any of them. Can you help me?"

Vella looked up, meeting Leandrea's eyes. Tears poured down their face, but their jaw was set and confident.

"I can. But only if you take me with you."

CHAPTER ELEVEN

The United States, long a beacon of democracy and stability, has descended into civil war. After years of escalating political tensions, economic disparities, and social unrest, the conflict has finally reached a boiling point. The country is now fractured into two major factions, each representing divergent ideologies and regional interests. The war is being fought on multiple fronts, with urban warfare, guerrilla tactics, and cyber warfare playing significant roles. Traditional battle lines are blurred as the conflict spills into cities, towns, and rural areas across the nation.

—BBC WORLD NEWS, DECEMBER 9, 2051

Day 5: December 15, 2126: Unknown Location
Ward

Ward roused to the sound of footsteps on the polished gray floor. Eyes slipping open, he stared at the nothingness in front of him. The floor reflected the dim half-light of his room. It was clean other than a sparse scattering of gray dust around his cot that he'd been noticing of late. It was barely perceptible, but when you stared at the floor long enough...dirt, he supposed. Maybe from the cleaning robot not being properly serviced. More likely from him. The thought made him shudder.

As far as he could see or tell from the supine position on his stomach, his room was windowless. It was evening, he supposed, because otherwise the artificial lights would be brighter, but he couldn't be sure.

It was hard keeping track of days, but Ward thought it had been at least three since Andromeda had come. He believed this because of three things. First, the light had gone through three cycles of brighter and darker. Then, there was the cleaning robot, which had come six times. At first, he was surprised that a place like ReInception wouldn't demonstrate its wealth and arrogance by employing Prole to clean, but as his mind cleared day by day, he realized—of course they wouldn't send Prole to clean the room of a Prole prisoner.

Also, the dressing on his wounds had been changed six times, and he suspected that was done twice a day. It was an agonizing ritual that dragged him out of the peaceful, pain-killer-induced slumber that had become his reality into the moments of clarity that he both craved and dreaded. Sometimes, he was yanked from dreams of his childhood with his sister, before everything had gone wrong, or from remembrances of the few, quiet moments he'd had with Leandrea. Often, he dreamed of new moments with her that they'd never had and probably never would. Dreams of them in the faraway places that Leandrea had said they could run off to together. He'd told her it was impossible. Now, he regretted that more than anything. He could have run away and saved them both. Instead, they'd stayed, hoping to save everyone else, and now they were all doomed.

Usually, the ministrations dragged him from nightmares, some of Lea being tortured or pursued by Officer Aisling down dark corridors and through flooded tunnels. Many of how helpless he'd felt as Ferryman choked him, and he'd had to watch as Lea sliced Ferryman's neck to save Ward's life. That empty look in her eyes that followed haunted him. Mostly, Ward dreamed of being strapped in a chair, a blue-lit ring encrusted with microscopic nodes being lowered down over his head, ready to take away everything that was him. When he had that dream, he was glad for the pain to wake him.

The last reason he suspected it had been about three days was because the pain was slightly less agonizing each time he woke. He was getting better, and that meant that his time was running out.

The footsteps moved across the room from the door toward his bed.

Ward ran his tongue along his top teeth and pressed his lips together, swallowing what small amount of saliva was in his mouth, trying to moisten his throat enough to speak. He hoped that the Med had come with water and ice. Ice was a rare luxury in The Catacombs and he couldn't get enough of it here—they gave it to him whenever he wanted it. It meant nothing to them, just as it had meant nothing to him when he was still Kallum Gordon. If he had to be here, he would enjoy this one small pleasure while he could.

Shifting on his cot, he moved his arms so his head rested on his hands. They felt like lead weights, constantly numb from hanging over the sides of the bed.

"Yeh think maybe I could try sitting up today?"

There was no answer.

"I'm getting awfully tired of layin' on my stomach."

Still no answer.

There were more footsteps and then the sound of someone lowering themselves into the chair near his bed. Ward's muscles tightened and his skin prickled. Admittedly, his experience was limited, but so far, the sound of someone settling into that chair never signaled something positive for him. Certainly, it was never the doctor.

Closing his eyes, Ward took a deep breath. Who was it this time? Andromeda? He didn't think so. The footsteps were too heavy. Kelvin again? He thought not, too. He had a feeling that next time he saw Kelvin, it would be from the vantage point of the ReInception machine. So who?

He inhaled again.

"Which ghost are you come to visit me today?"

"Beg ya?"

The voice sounded male. Softer than Dennison Kelvins and slightly higher. Also, like the voices of his other ghosts, vaguely familiar.

"Well, Kelvin was definitely Christmas Past. We needn't get into why but jes trust me on that. Andromeda, now she was Christmas Present, warning me about all the terrible things I'm to face if I don't fess up. So I'm figuring you must be Christmas Future."

There was a soft laugh. "Dickens?"

"Surprised a Prole would read, lah?"

"I've been told not to let anything about you surprise me."

"Yeah? And who told you that?"

No answer.

"You wouldn't've come here if you didn't want to talk, so yeh may's well."

"No, I'll talk. I was just thinking. I mean, if I'm Christmas Future, you must be Ebenezer Scrooge. Andromeda kind of implied that."

That made Ward laugh. The man laughed, too, soft and sad. It was the first laugh Ward had heard—or produced—since being captured. It made something tighten inside of him.

He knew that voice. He knew that laugh. Turning his head, he blinked a few times. His bed had been lowered so that all he could see were crossed legs and a torso. Uni silver. A little too slim for a healthy college-aged man.

Slowly, Ward pushed himself up onto his elbows. His arms shook and his back stung, but he found he could bear it. At least it didn't feel like he was tearing apart at the seams or as if someone was setting his back on fire.

Groaning, he rolled onto his side, so he was propped up slightly, weight resting on one arm. His hair hung over his face. It was too long, and it felt greasy. The Med kept his wound clean. He regularly put a machine on Ward that moved over his body, cleansing him...everywhere. It was humiliating, but better than being filthy. His hair had been rinsed with solutions, but not really washed in days. He couldn't imagine what he looked like—or smelled like. Chemicals and rot and funk. Pushing his hair out of his face, he tucked it behind his ear. The movement sent a pain shooting down his back, and he hissed. The room swayed. Maybe he wasn't all that well yet after all.

Finally, he lifted his eyes. When he saw the man in front of him, he sucked in a breath.

Leandrea's old boyfriend barely resembled the person Ward had first seen when he'd started watching Andromeda. That Hallyn had a light to him; a ready smile with bright blue eyes and shining black hair. At first, Ward had despised Hallyn simply because he was a privileged do-gooder Uni, like Lea. But also, as with Lea, he'd found he couldn't sustain his scorn. He'd spent a lot of time listening in on the conversations between the friends. Hallyn was a good man. He was kind. He stood up for people and beliefs. He didn't gossip, and he was never cruel. Maybe a little boring, but overall, the kind of person Ward might've been friends with had his life not gone sideways.

The man in front of him was wasting away. His cheeks had sunken in. He had deep blue circles under his eyes. His skin had a yellowish, jaundiced tint.

This was what ReInception hid from the world. When you modified someone for what they did, ReInception could be the promised miracle. It could cure addiction or obesity. It could help you exercise or stop smoking or drinking. ReInception saved countless lives.

But when ReInception was used to change who you were or against your will, this is what happened. You could see it in their faces. At best, they got sick—lost weight, lost interest in things they used to care about. At worst, they lost their minds. Ward knew because Hallyn looked just like Lucia Genesis, the head of ReInception, had looked in the secret vids that The Origins had—the ones that Iza had shown to Lea in order to convince her to join them. Ward knew because it's how Kitty looked after they'd modified her. This is why he'd testified against his parents and sent them to prison. This was what Kallum Gordon would have died to stop.He curled his hands into fists.

Ward wanted to hate this new version of Hallyn. All those terrible things he'd said to Lea, the way he'd succumbed to ReInception. Even though Ward knew it was something even the strongest of minds couldn't fight, he wanted to allow himself to believe it was weakness—maybe because he knew he was next.

And Ward had never been in love before. He'd been too busy staying alive. When he fell for Lea, the jealousy and insecurity that gripped Ward when he thought about Hallyn had taken him completely by surprise. Hallyn had loved Leandrea. He'd made love to her. He'd wanted to marry her. Hallyn could give Lea everything that Ward couldn't. A part of him would always wonder if ReInception could be reversed, whether Lea would go back to Hallyn.

But looking into those once-lively blue eyes, Ward's stomach dropped, and his gut twisted. Heat crawled up his body and, for the first time in days, he felt no pain at all. His muscles clenched and his jaw tightened. Everything in him vibrated with rage. Not at Hallyn, but for him. Suddenly, he felt exactly what Leandrea had felt that moment in the basement when she demanded to join The Origins. He wanted to get out of that bed and stalk across the building until he found Dennison Kelvin. Then, he wanted to put his hands around that man's throat and squeeze. Kallum had been a kind, innocent boy, but Ward had learned to be ruthless. He'd lost that edge since meeting Lea. Love had made him softer and more hopeful. Now that edge was coming back and he was thankful. That edge would keep him alive.

The truth was Kallum Gordon had died a long time ago. That boy had given up everything to save his sister. For that, he'd been beaten, starved, abandon, tortured and finally, had his identity erased until no one knew who he was anymore. Until Ward couldn't recognize his own face in the mirror. He wasn't Kallum Gordon anymore. But was he Ward? Someone anonymous; someone others had turned him into? A being meant only for the use of others. One of many called this designation, but with no name of his own.

Ward hadn't cared about the cause. He hadn't cared about stopping the corporation or about fighting for Prole rights. Ward just wanted to find his sister, or at least know for certain whether she was alive or dead. And then he wanted to disappear, never to be seen or heard from again.

Or at least that's what he used to want. Slowly, slowly, over the last two months, that had been changing. It had all been building up to this moment. It was the first time in years that he felt like Kallum Gordon again or, if not Kallum Gordon, at least someone who cared. Someone with something to fight for.

All of this went on in Ward's mind—Atom Bombs exploding inside of him, while Hallyn sat across from him, broken and unaware.

He stared at Ward, the pupils in those sky-blue eyes contracting to pinpoints.

"We met once before, you know."

Ward, of course, had seen Hallyn many times, but he was surprised that Hallyn remembered him.

"In a bar the night of the bombing. You weren't very nice to my girl—" Hallyn made a jerking movement, closing his eyes for a moment, shuddering his shoulders, and dipping his body forward. When he opened his eyes again, his pupils were wide, the blue barely a halo around a black void. "To Lea."

"You'd no business there. That's what I told her."

"But then you flirted with Andromeda. Why?"

"You know why."

Hallyn nodded at him, unblinking. "At the time, I thought it was because you were afraid not to. It didn't occur to me that you were trying to manipulate her."

"You mean it didn't occur to you that I might have a motivation of my own?" Ward heard the sharpness in his own voice and instantly regretted it. It was so easy to slip back into his old anger and assumptions.

Hallyn was quiet for a few moments. "No. That's fair, I guess. I try to be unbiased, but we all bring our prejudices with us whether or not we mean to."

Ward tipped his head, watching Hallyn carefully. What had they changed about Hallyn and what hadn't they? Lea said they'd programmed him to believe that ReInception was good and that being with someone who was anti-modification was unenlightened. That it made her a lesser person. Had they said nothing about Prole? Or was part of the problem that changing beliefs was so much more nuanced than changing habits? Perhaps that's part of what led to the conflicts and confusion such mods caused.

"In any event," Hallyn continued, "it's hard for me to understand how you went from that hostility you showed Lea at the bar to being—"

"With her."

"Are you?"

Ward said nothing.

"How? How are you with her?"

"That's not your business."

"Whatever is between you two, it convinced her to betray one of her closest friends—a friend who happens to be Dennison Kelvin's daughter. It might not make it my business, but it makes it his business."

"So now you're doing his bidding, too? How many of you ghosts will he send before he runs out of people he can bully?"

Hallyn shrugged narrow shoulders but didn't respond.

"If I didn't tell his daughter, what makes him think I'd tell you?"

"You'll tell one way or the other."

"So I've been told."

"Do you really care about Lea, or did you just use her to get information?"

Ward's back stiffened, and his eyes narrowed. "The more important question is whether you really care about Lea. Because you used to, you know. And not very long ago. Why is that, you think?"

Hallyn gave that strange shudder again, his pupils contracting and expanding. "Lea's a good person. She told me what you called her in that bar. All the things you said to her. Suddenly you're in love with her? It's just a little hard to believe."

Ward's face flushed, and his muscles twitched. "If I could get out of this bed, I'd…"

"You'd what? Hurt me for her? Defend her honor?"

Ward pushed air out of his nose, making a disgusted sound. "Why are you even standing up for her? You get sick at the very sight of her."

"Because regardless of what you believe, I still care about her."

The delivery was flat and lifeless. Almost rehearsed. Programmed even. Ward narrowed his eyes.

"You care about her, or you care about what she might know?"

Hallyn stared.

Ward shook his head, all the anger draining from him. "Oh, Hallyn. What have they done to you?"

"What have you done? That information could destroy everything."

Ward lay back down, all his anger suddenly depleted.

"You must've told her where to go. She wouldn't've known where to go on her own. She's never left here."

"Nor've I."

"Then you told her who'd get her out."

"I was going to get her out."

Hallyn nodded, looking down at his hands.

"I knew you'd be smart." The right side of his mouth tipped up into a slight smile. "Lea wouldn't be with you if you weren't smart."

Ward narrowed his eyes, his stomach twisting into that unfamiliar knot. But what was there to be jealous of from a man who literally couldn't love Lea? For whom appreciating her was now impossible?

"It actually sounds like you still care about her."

Hallyn winced, making Ward instantly regret the barb.

"Of course, I still care about her. You don't just stop caring about someone overnight."

"No?"

"It's not Lea that I have a problem with. It's her ideals."

"You sure about that? Because she told me that the very sight of her made you sick to your stomach."

Hallyn looked away, twisting his hands in his lap, his Adam's apple working as he swallowed.

Ward wondered if it was love at first sight, when Hallyn and Leandrea had met. It hadn't been for Ward. At first, he hadn't thought much about Lea at all other than to appreciate that her hair made her and her friends easy to locate in a crowd. His focus had been on Andromeda and how he might use her to get to her father. Lea only crossed his mind when he'd overheard her conversations; he'd found her do-goodyness insufferable. Her relationship with Hallyn had seemed dull and predictable. He wondered why he'd felt so uncharitable toward them. Of the group of friends, ironically, Andromeda was the only one he didn't find insufferable. At least she'd been what he'd expected of a Uni. At least she'd spoken her mind. He guessed he believed that deep down inside, they were all like that and the rest was window dressing and hypocrisy.

No. He hadn't thought much of Lea until that night at the bar. So small and irate. So unafraid. It was the first time he'd clearly seen her face—earnest and real. It was when he first learned that she wasn't modified.

There was another thing he and Hallyn had in common—they were both attracted to Lea's realness. He didn't know why it was so appealing to Hallyn, but he knew what it meant to him. Ward was modified. Not mind modification but changed from his head to his toes. The scars all over his body were proof of that. His sister, Hallyn, him—they were what ReInception was capable of. Someone like Lea—she was the only thing in this world he could trust.

When had he fallen in love with her? He didn't know, but once it happened, it had happened fast and hard. Maybe it was because she'd fought him with all her might and then trusted him with all her heart. Maybe it was the funny things that she blurted out or how she was afraid of the dark, yet fearless. Maybe it was how she was so small, yet she made him feel safe. She protected him. She saved his life. And even when she found out who he really was, he was still just Ward to her.

Whatever it was, it made him sad for Hallyn, because that's what he'd lost.

"I'm sorry, Hallyn, but I can't help you. I wish I could, but I can't."

And he did. He wished it so much that it squeezed his heart. That he could someday look Leandrea in the eyes and tell her he was the one who'd saved Hallyn; who'd made Hallyn himself again. Maybe then, he could be Kallum Gordon again. Maybe then he'd know for sure who Lea truly loved.

Nodding, Hallyn sighed. "I thought you'd say that. But I'll leave you with this, and I hope you'll think about it. You need to decide who you really are."

Ward blanched—could ReInception read minds now, too?

"What's that supposed to mean?"

"From the minute I saw you in the bar, I knew you were more than you were letting on. You say you are just an ordinary Prole. You try to look the part. You pretend you know nothing. But everything you do screams the opposite. From your instant ability to process who Andromeda was and find a way to use it to the big words that come out of your mouth, you wear that chip on your shoulder like it's a military medal."

Ward scowled. "What's your point?"

"Which one is it? Are you going to be the ordinary Prole and fade into the woodwork, or are you going to be whoever it is that is busting so hard to get out that it split you apart? You can't be both. And if you think it's the former, the only one you've fooled is yourself."

Ward snorted and then turned away. He was getting tired and so was Hallyn. He was slouching in his seat, eyes bloodshot and hands trembling on the chair's arms.

There was the whoosh of the door and Ward heard footsteps, light and quick on the tile. "That's enough, Hallyn. You have to rest."

The figure came into view, blurry at first as she approached Hallyn, and then coming into focus. A dark-skinned girl with dark eyes and hair.

Her mouth turned down in a frown.

"Kammeo." Ward pushed air from his nose. "I should have guessed you'd be in on this, too."

Kammeo stared at Ward, frozen for a moment behind Hallyn.

"How do you know my name?"

Ward shrugged. "I know lots of things."

Hallyn shook his head. "Don't let him bother you. Lea told him about you."

Kammeo's eyes narrowed, and she cocked her head slightly. "Is that right? Lea told you about me?"

Ward shrugged again. "Mayhap. Does it really matter?"

Kammeo stared at him for another few seconds and then put her hands on Hallyn's shoulders. "We should go. You need to rest."

Hallyn nodded, pushing himself up from the chair, listing slightly and letting out a soft moan. Kammeo put an arm around his waist and pulled his other arm over her shoulder. He leaned into her.

"This is what they do," Ward said. "This is what you've become. Hallyn. They don't care about you—they never did. They'll use you until there's nothing left."

Hallyn paused, breathing heavily just from the act of standing up. "You say that because you don't understand what it's really like—how important ReInception is for our health, our future."

"Yes. Look at how healthy you are. A month ago, you were playing wake ball and now, you can hardly walk."

"That's enough." Kammeo snapped.

Ward ignored her. "They won't stop until they've gotten what they need from me. They don't care what it does to you."

Hallyn stopped. "You're wrong. You don't know them like I do."

"I know them better than you think."

"I said enough!" Kammeo shouted. She stumbled sideways from Hallyn's weight. There were tears in her eyes. Suddenly, Ward felt ashamed.

Kammeo moved Hallyn toward the door until they were out of view and he could hear the whoosh of opening doors.

He knew that look in Kammeo's eyes just as well as he knew the one in Hallyn's. Ward called after her: "Maybe it's too late for Hallyn, Kammeo. But it's not too late to do something. It's not too late to stop this from happening to someone else."

Hallyn and Kammeo's footsteps receded. The door whooshed shut. All was quiet again.

CHAPTER TWELVE

The civil war rages on and the United States faces an uncertain future. The conflict has not only devastated the nation but also sent shockwaves around the world. The global order, long anchored by American stability, is now in flux, with new alliances forming and old ones being tested. As the United States grapples with its devastating civil war, the global balance of power is rapidly shifting. With the decline of American influence, several nations and alliances are poised to step into the role of world leader.

—WORLD NEWS FROM THE BBC, SEPTEMBER 3, 2051

Day 5: December 15, 2126: The Catacombs
Leandrea

"Absolutely not." Aisling crossed her arms. "It's dangerous enough with just two of us. And it's bad enough that I'm bringing back some stranger instead of Ward. The whereabouts of Katherine Vega must be kept secret."

"And how are ya' going to get out of here without me? Sure you wouldn'a be here if yeh had another way."

Aisling looked away without responding.

"I thought so."

Vella put their hands on their hips. "What you need?"

Aisling looked at Leandrea. Leandrea nodded her head. "Ward trusts Vella. So should we."

Aisling let out a long exhale, crossing her arms over her chest. "Fine. But it's on you if this blows up in our faces."

"Okay. It's on me. Just tell them."

"We need to get 12 nautical miles out to sea, into international waters. From there, I can get us to where Katherine is."

"And where's that?" Vella asked.

Aisling shook her head. "That I can't tell you. *You'll* have to trust *me*."

Vella pursed their lips and then, giving a small nod, strode toward the door. "Stay here. I'll be back."

Vella looked from side to side before stepping out of the building and slamming the door shut behind them.

Aisling rubbed her hand on her throat. A dark bruise was surfacing around the circumference of her neck. "Well, that went well."

"I'm sorry. I didn't expect them to react that way."

"Well, that makes one of us. That's exactly what I expected."

Reaching into her pack, Aisling pulled out a small metal object with a flat surface. Leandrea recognized it as a cellular repair wand used by meds. Activating the wand, Aisling smoothed it over the surface of her skin. Small scratches healed, and the bruising faded with each pass. "You're sure we can trust them?"

"Ward does and, like you said to me, what choice do we have?"

Aisling nodded, tucking the wand back into her pack.

Leandrea slid down to the floor, her back against the wall, as they waited for Vella's return. Outside the window, a pigeon perched on the sill, cooing and cocking its head from side to side.

"Have you ever met her?"

Aisling looked up. "Who, Kitty?"

Lea nodded.

"Yeah."

"What's she like?"

"Powerful. Angry. Brilliant."

"Sounds like her brother."

"Maybe. They don't look alike."

"Different dads."

"That and Kitty was too old for the physical mods. She still looks upper caste."

"Ward said she was non-comp from all the modding and remodding."

"Well, she's pretty sane now."

"How do you mean?"

Aisling shrugged. "She's just not non-comp."

Leandrea leaned forward, eyes widening. "Do you know how?" Her breath hitched. "Is there a cure?"

Aisling looked at her, body still and eyes blinking. She said nothing.

"What?" Leandrea scooted closer. "You have to tell me. If there's a way to reverse ReInception, it could change everything."

Aisling shook her head. "I don't really...It's—"

Leandrea put a hand on her arm. "Ash. Please."

Aisling shook her head again. "I'm sorry, Lea. I can't. Just by saying nothing, I'm...well, you'll need to ask Katherine."

"Ash..." Lea tried again. "Sirkka. If there's something, you can't keep that from the world."

There was the sound downstairs of a door opening and closing. Aisling grabbed Lea's forearm, leaning in to whisper. "Please, don't say anything in front of Vella. I'm sure Katherine will tell you once we get there—"

She stopped mid-sentence as Vella reentered the room, giving Leandrea one last wide-eyed glance. Biting her lip, Leandrea nodded slightly. She wasn't sure why, but Aisling was afraid of this...afraid that Leandrea had even guessed at there being a process to reverse ReInception.

Vella looked between the two of them. "I interrupt something?"

Rising from the floor and brushing the dirt from her pants, Lea shook her head. "No. Just trying to find out more about Katherine, but Aisling—" Aisling shook her head almost imperceptibly. "Well, Katherine's been guarding her secret just as hard as Ward. So we'll have to let her decide what to tell us."

Aisling exhaled, posture relaxing slightly. She looked up at Vella. "Can you help?"

Vella nodded. "Me and Sebs, we have a way. But the deal dinna' change. I go wit you."

"That's a terrible idea," Aisling said.

"I dinna' ask yer opinion. Yarn't leaving without me. This is too important for us. For the cause."

"You told Sebbe about Ward?" Lea asked.

Vella nodded her head.

"And?"

"He dinna' seem surprised. He'd had na' guessed, but I think he knew. If you understand me."

Leandrea nodded. She did understand. It didn't take much to know Ward was special. That terrible things had been done to him that made him so cautious. That he and Iza were hiding something big.

"He must've been very hurt."

Vella shook her head. "Nah. Sebbe'd die for dat boy. I would, too. Ward. Kallum. Does na' matter. We all know he's something remarkable."

Leandrea's eyes welled up. He was extraordinary. She'd known that from the start, too. You didn't have to know who he was to feel it—to feel this fierce loyalty toward him. As a boy, without even meaning to, he'd united people behind him. Brought them to a cause that threatened their society. Even now, after they'd done everything they could to subdue him, after they'd taken away his name and his face, even when he didn't want it, people rallied behind Ward.

At around one in the morning, they snuck out through a back window, dropping into an alleyway. They wound their way through the Catacombs, avoiding main thoroughfares, until they reached a portion of the levee system called the Harlem Gate, that was open during low tide. The NARI System was carefully protected. But the gates were all automated and the smaller ones often only had one or two guards.

The group hung back in the shadows as Sebbe approached. "Oi!" He called out, approaching the guards with his hands held up, where they could see them.

The guards turned. Both were taller than Leandrea, one narrow and the other broad shouldered. One lifted a weapon, pointing it at Sebbe. The other hung back as Sebbe came up to them, now too far for Leandrea to hear what he was saying.

Sebbe gestured out toward the water, pointing to an unseen object. They nodded at whatever Sebbe was telling them, one of them taking out a pair of binoculars while the other continued speaking to Sebbe.

Leandrea couldn't see what happened next from her vantage point, but she knew Sebbe was sneaking a derm patch with some sedative onto the skin of one of the guards. It was the same thing that Ward had done to Andromeda. The other guard, Vella and Sebbe had told them, was a sympathizer.

Seconds later, the thinner guard slid to the ground. Sebbe and the broad-shouldered guard caught them on the way down, dragging them into an observation booth and propping them in a chair.

Sebbe waved the group over and they ran forward, keeping low and to the shadows.

The broad-shouldered guard nodded, smiling at them widely. "Heya. Hi! Oi! I know you." He chucked Lea on the shoulder. "You didn't tell me I'd have a celebrity on the boat! I'd've rolled out the red carpet!" He laughed. He looked like he was having the greatest day of his life.

"Shouldn't we be worried about that guy?" Aisling gestured toward the guard on the ground.

The big guard laughed, waving off her concern with a few flips of the hands. "Them? Nah. Sleepin' on the job?" He made a tsking sound. "Frowned upon, that is. They'll be keepin' that to 'emselves."

The group followed him toward a small boat that was tethered to a floating dock. Putting an index finger to his lips, he activated his comm.

"Oi, Donato."

He listened for a second as someone responded.

"Yup. Yeah. Got a Proleo here say he saw something out in the water. I'm gonna' to check it out. Make sure it's nothing."

He was quiet again for a second.

"Yup. Yeah. Prezzie's in the booth keeping an eye on things." He winked at Lea, listening again.

"Yup. Yeah. All quiet otherwise."

He nodded. "Uh, huh. Yup. Me? Take a joy ride while I'm out? Never!"

He laughed at something the person on the other end said, this time winking at Vella.

"K.O. I'll be back at ya' as soon. Over."

He turned toward the group, the deuce-eating grin still on his face, eyes crinkled in the corner.

"Lez go!" Taking long strides, he moved toward the boat, arms swinging back and forth in the exaggerated fashion of a toddler.

Lea pulled on Sebbe's cloak. "Won't his comm be tracking him?" she whispered.

"Sure, sure. And it'll show him doin' jes what he said."

"But don't they have other surveillance on these things?"

"Not much." The guard answered instead of Sebbe. "These gates were built seventy-five years ago now. Don't get me wrong. They do the job great. Keep the city safe. But they haven't had much upgrades. On the big guys, they have cameras and other surveillance, seismic readers and so forth—the ones that if they failed or were sabotaged, the city would be in a shit storm—literally. But these little guys?" He shrugged. "Something goes wrong, they stick or break or whatever—and they do, all the time—don't make a big difference so long as they don't all fail at once. And for that to happen, you'd have to attack the central control system, not the gate. Now that's where they got the big surveillance guns...also literally."

Leandrea swallowed hard and started biting at her thumbnail. What the guard was saying made sense, but these gates kept everyone in the city safe. That the security around them, however small they were, was so lax gave her the jétons.

The guard herded them all into the boat, untying the line from a cleat on the dock and pushing them out into the water. A command to his comm started the engine and activated a light that scanned back and forth over the river. A small gull briefly alit onto the railing and then took off, swooping out into the darkness.

As he headed out to sea, the guard sang:

My father was the keeper of the Eddystone light
He married a mermaid one fine night!

Leandrea wondered if the guard was non-comp. It was a job they might give to an ex-crim, one who'd been through ReInception. Looking at Aisling, she saw the same look on the woman's face that she must have had on her own, wide eyed and slack jawed.

Aisling looked at Sebbe. "Is he out of his mind?"

The guard turned to look at Aisling, the smile still plastered on his face. "Want a little tip?"

Aisling nodded.

"Don't throw a guy's mama in the grid for deuce that weren't her fault and then pay him a menial wage to do an important job!"

The man cackled, pushing the boat faster.

Yo, ho, ho! The wind blows free
All for the life on a rolling sea!

The man's laughter trailed behind them as the boat moved through the darkness, out into the middle of the Hudson. He swung the craft left, pushing the boat even faster, speeding them downriver and toward the tip of the island—back past The Floods and Marshes that Lea and Aisling had just worked so hard to escape. And then, they were out in the open sea.

Aisling pulled her visor out of her pack, struggling with it against a powerful, salty wind that blew toward them. Turning her back toward the wind, hunched over, she put the visor on, engaging the sides with the implants in her temples. Her mouth moved, but Leandrea couldn't hear a word she said.

They were well past Manhattan, out in open water, the boat bouncing up and down on the choppy waves, when Aisling instructed the guard to slow his engine. The boat light scanned the water. Leandrea saw nothing but waves. Scanning the horizon, she saw no lights from other ships out on the water.

Suddenly, out of her peripheral vision, Leandrea saw an object surface, large and silent. It moved toward their boat.

"Cut the light," Aisling commanded.

The guard obeyed and suddenly, there was only darkness and the sounds of water hitting the sides of the boat.

Leandrea's eyes adjusted to the blackness. In the dim light of a quarter moon, she could barely make out the craft coming toward them, wide, black and silent, like something from another planet. It undulated, as if alive. Her stomach clenched, and she shuddered, taking an unconscious step back from the railing.

"What is it?" Sebbe asked, his voice full of awe.

"It's what the outside world holds for you," Aisling responded. "It's home."

The craft pulled up in front of them, and a portal opened, wide and glowing faintly, like an enormous mouth.

The Guard whistled. "Well, if this 'aint the best day of my life!"

"I'm sorry." Aisling turned toward Sebbe and the guard. "I wish I could explain more, show you around. But we can't wait. We have to go now."

Vella didn't hesitate. They looked at Sebbe, nodding at the man. "Yell be okay?"

Sebbe nodded. "Sure, sure." He pulled Vella into his arms. They were the same height, both broad in the shoulders, but something about Sebbe's grasp on Vella gave that sense of protectiveness.

Vella pushed away, tears in their eyes. "Dunna' worry. I'll be fine."

"Sure, sure," Sebbe nodded. "I know yeh will."

"Come on," Aisling pulled at Leandrea's sleeve.

"Just one sec." Leandrea stood in front of Sebbe, her heart suddenly high in her throat and fluttering so that she could barely breathe. This man had been everything to Ward and now she was leaving him here when all the rest of The Origins were being rounded up. Eventually, they'd give up the head of their underground and the whole of the Authority would be looking for him.

"Come with us," Lea pleaded.

Sebbe smiled, taking her chin in his fingers. "Yeh know I kent." He smiled, those gentle gray eyes damp with tears.

"But they'll come for you."

"I'll be okay. I always am."

Leandrea nodded, but she didn't believe it.

"That's my boy they have, you know." The tears slipped down his cheeks.

Leandrea nodded. She did know, just as she knew Sebbe was the closest thing Ward had to a father. If she left him here, if something happened to him, would Ward ever forgive her?

"Ward, Kallum, it dunna' matter to me. He's my boy and I'm going to get him. You hear?"

Leandrea nodded again. "You do what you need do from there. I do it from here. Between the two of us, we kenna' fail. Right?"

Lea tried to believe what he was saying was true.

"Someday soon, we'll be together again and you'll tell me all about the place that ship came from. Promise?"

Leandrea threw her arms around him, holding him tight. "Promise."

He rubbed her back. "I promise, too."

"Lea!" Aisling called. "Now!" She stood in the mouth of the craft. Vella already descending inside.

Sebbe smiled at her one last time. "Ward were right that first time. Yer a clady wee bird, but yeh can do whatever it is you set yer mind to, sure, sure. You jes have to believe it much as he does."

CHAPTER THIRTEEN

As ReInception technology continues to shape the dynamics of the civil war, its ultimate impact remains uncertain. The potential for profound psychological and societal changes is immense, complicating efforts for resolution and reconciliation. However, the misuse of such technology may also galvanize international and domestic efforts to end the conflict and establish stringent controls over its application.

—NBC VIDNEWS TONIGHT, JANUARY 17, 2052.

Day 5: December 15, 2126: Unknown Location
Ward

The day Ward and Kitty ran away, Kitty cut out his comms. His whole life had been a constant stream of input and suddenly, jarringly, it wasn't. The void was intense; he thought he'd lose his mind.

Then, he found a stack of books by some guy named Stephen King. They were yellowed, moldy, crumbly things left behind by some other fugitive or castoff. Some were too frightening, especially when you were stuck below ground in the dark. But others had spoken to him—ones of escape and fantasy, like the "Dark Tower," or "The Girl Who Loved Tom Gordon."

Hallyn's comment brought to mind one book in particular. It was about a writer—Paul, he thought? Paul had been in a car accident, back when there were such things, and a crazy woman named Annie found and imprisoned him. Annie was Paul's "biggest fan." She would not let him go until she extracted another story from him. The entire book took place with Paul, stuck in a room, trying to figure out how to get away from Annie. He'd been badly injured. He couldn't walk. Both characters were clever, but Annie held all the power. Yet somehow, in the end, Paul managed to escape. The question that Ward was trying to answer, the part of the story that he was trying to remember, was how, from a position of utter weakness, Paul had regained his power.

Hallyn was right. Ward had never been good at hiding his disdain for those who presumed he was stupid or lesser just because he was Prole. At the same time, he was trying to hide who he was, he also wanted to declare it to the world. When a member of the upper caste treated him like he was nothing, like he was no one, it made him angry. "Don't you know I was just like you?" He wanted to scream. "Do you even know who I am?"

His body and his understanding of the world may have changed, but his mind was the same mind as Kallum Gordon's, at least for now. Kallum Gordon and Ward were both survivors. The difference between them was that Kallum Gordon had been willing to fight for others. Ward had given up on the world—he was too busy trying to survive to worry about anyone else. Now, Ward had something to fight for again, people he cared for and needed to protect. He had something to live for. He couldn't keep lying in bed, doing nothing, awaiting his fate and what extracting information from him would mean. It wasn't about protecting The Origins—he was still ambivalent about "the cause." It was about the people in it—people who'd cared for and protected him. Vella with their strength and defiance. Sebbe—the closest thing he'd had to a father since his testimony had sent his own father to the grid. Even Izabelle—despite their differences and her ruthlessness, she'd kept her promise to keep his identity a secret when ransoming him would have made her a fortune that would have funded The Origins or elevated her from Prole.

But what could he do? He could barely move. He was Paul in a building full of Annies, all trying to extract information from him. Like Annie, they were going to get their story no matter what it took. How could he, like Paul, use that to his advantage?

Ward heard the familiar whirring as the cleaning robot got ready to pass under his cot. He watched with interest as it circled and polished all around and under his bed. About an hour earlier, the Med had changed Ward's dressing, smoothing the nanite-impregnated gauze over his wounds. The tiny doctors had gotten to work. His back started to itch as they healed him.

As always, shortly afterwards, the robot came to clean. Twice a day. Always after the Med changed his dressings. Any second now, it would pause next to one of the bed legs and stay there for a few moments, spraying its antiseptic and using its antimicrobial lights. Churning its brushes, but not moving. His back would begin to itch even more, then a faint, gray dust would fall all around him and the itching would stop.

At first, Ward hadn't been lucid enough to connect the robot to his wounds being dressed. He'd been in too much pain to care. Then, he'd just assumed he was dirty.

It was not dirt.

Ward wanted to ask the Med about it, but even through the fog of his pain meds, instinct warned him not to. Maybe it was the Med's own whispered words about Ward asking too many questions, and the way the man hardly spoke to him anymore. Maybe it was the fact that it only after the Med left that the robot came. No one would notice the dust if they weren't looking for it, or, like Ward, staring at the ground all the time with nothing else to see. The dust never accumulated enough for anyone else to take notice because the next time the little robot came around, he would clean it up before another round of grey dust fell.

Just the day before, he'd overheard Kelvin arguing with the doctor. "Why isn't he healing faster?"

The Med said he didn't know—agreed it was taking longer than normal. "Maybe it's something they did to him during the surgery that's preventing him from healing."

"What are we in, the dark ages?" Kelvin had shouted before stomping off. "Fix him!"

Ward had been wondering the same thing. Why wasn't he healing faster? There was nothing about the fact that Ward's surgery had been based on old medicine that would prevent current treatments from working as well on him as they did on everyone else. He'd seen it countless times as a Ward—runaway Prole children captured from their hiding places in the subway tunnels and in The Floods—sick, starving, wounded—brought in and treated. They all ended up just fine. He himself had been brought in half starved, malnourished and with festering wounds. Within days, he was completely healed. Within weeks, he was strong enough for them to put him through the body modifications that had made him Prole; the surgeries that turned him from Kallum to Ward. Could those mods be what prevented his healing? Possibly, but he didn't think so.

Right on schedule, the little bot whirred into view. Pausing just below him, the machine sprayed and brushed, over-shining that one spot of floor until his skin started to crawl. Then, the robot went on its way. The dust fell. The itching stopped.

Ward was beginning to understand.

Someone was buying him time, but he didn't know who, and it wouldn't help for long. Eventually, someone would find whatever was installed in the robot that was killing his nanites. Whoever had done that would pay for trying to help him.

Hallyn was right. Ward needed to decide who he wanted to be. Even with the interference, he was getting better. Not even close to being able to walk down the hall on his own two feet to attempt an escape, let alone help anyone else get out, but well enough to sit in a chair. Well enough to sit in *the* chair.

To take back his power from a position of weakness, Paul leveraged his story and then held it hostage.

An idea took shape. It could backfire on him completely, but it was the only option Ward had. His only chance to control the story.

He called for the Med and, a few moments later, heard the *swoosh* of the door opening and then footsteps.

Ward rolled onto his side, propping himself up on one hand so he could see the doctor's face, hoping it would tell him enough to confirm his suspicions.

His back burned, but it didn't hurt so much that he couldn't hold his position. He didn't feel any tearing or blood. Yes. His time was almost up.

"Everything okay?" The Med's brow furrowed. "You really shouldn't sit like that. You'll damage your new skin."

Ward stared at the man, wincing as he pushed himself further up.

"Tell them I'll talk."

The Med inhaled sharply and then paled. "You'll what?"

"You heard me. I'll talk. But only to Andromeda."

The Med froze, and Ward saw a slight tremor in the man's hands. "Are you—" he started. Then he stopped, opening his mouth as if about to say something, and then closing it again, like a landed fish.

It wasn't proof that the Med was the one helping him, but it was enough for him to be almost certain. Everything they were saying was being monitored and recorded. The Med couldn't risk saying more, but he wanted to.

"I'm sure."

The Med nodded. "As you wish." He walked away without another word.Ward woke to a foot tapping next to his bed. He didn't have to look to know who it was.

"You summoned me?"

He turned his head. Today, Andromeda's skin was dark, her hair a deep purple. Her eyes were a pretty, hazel green, orange spokes radiating from around her pupil. He thought they might actually be her real eyes and wondered why she was so eager to alter them. Mostly, he appreciated her shedding the disorienting imitation of Leandrea.

"Is the doctor here?"

Andromeda shrugged. "Why, you need a witness? I'm not going to hurt you—again."

"I just wanted to make sure we're alone."

She stared at him for a moment, unblinking, arms crossed over her chest and mouth pursed tight. "We're alone."

Grunting, he turned to his side. "Help me up."

She raised an eyebrow.

"I'm tired of staring at this floor and I..." he inhaled a shuddering breath. "I can't say what I want to say laying on that bed."

"You mean feeling weak."

He laughed. He didn't feel weak, he was weak. He hadn't sat up in days. His arms felt like lead weights. His back still burned with every move.

"Just help me."

She poked out her lower lip. "I don't think the doctor is going to like this."

"Well, I'm sure he's watching and listening to everything, so he can hear me now when I say I'm not talking until I'm sitting up in a chair."

Andromeda turned to face the door, pausing a moment, nodding, and then turning back to Ward. She shrugged. "It's your funeral."

She reached for him, wrapping her hands around his upper arm, pulling as he pushed. She was strong; he remembered the feel of hard muscles beneath smooth skin when he'd massaged her in her father's apartment—the first time, stalling to give Leandrea time to locate some of Kelvin's DNA. The second time, it had been to massage a transdermal sedative into her skin so that he could steal Kelvin's files. She had every right to hate him for what he'd done to her. He had no right to hate her other than for something that wasn't her fault. He wondered if she ever hated herself for who her parents were, the same way he had.

The feel of his skin stretching across his back as she pulled lit him on fire again, the fog of pain killers receding, clearing his mind as he'd hoped it would. The pain was there, but tolerable. Probably not a good thing for his overall situation, but it was what he needed at the moment.

Once he was sitting up, he looked around.

The room was small with bare, gray walls. The wall behind him was clear glass, and the Med stood outside, watching, his brow furrowed, and his mouth turned down. Kammeo stood behind him, staring at Ward. He wasn't sure why she was around so much. She must have been working for Kelvin. He'd recruited the whole gang. All of Lea's closest friends. All the people he thought could help find her. But from what little he knew of Kammeo from watching her all those months, he couldn't see what purpose she might serve.

Ward didn't see Kelvin, but he was sure the man was watching them and listening. He looked at the bed he'd been stuck in for all these days. It was a plain, clean bed with a thick mattress. Above him was a contraption with lights, jets and cameras. It wasn't something they had in The Origins med facility, but he knew it was a med rig. The device cleaned patients and allowed doctors to do much treatment remotely. There were disinfectants and light therapies. Nanobots could be programmed and released from the rigs for treatment. It could perform advanced first aid. It was first invented to treat patients after the Delhi Superbug made absolute sterilization so critical. It was improved for use by space travelers. Given Ward's fragile state and susceptibility to infection, it's what they should have been using on him were they not so eager to extract information from him. Next to the bed was the chair that all his Christmas ghosts had sat in as they visited him. Nearby was another chair. He pointed his chin toward it. "There."

Andromeda looked toward the Med and then back at Ward. "I'm not sure that's such a good—"

"I'm going there with or without your help."

Andromeda laughed. "Without my help, you're going to be a bleeding puddle on the floor."

"Then I guess you'd better help me because your father won't be happy if these wounds tear open again."

He started to push himself up, gritting his teeth and groaning at the pain.

Andromeda shook her head. "Fleshhead." But she took his arm, helping pull him to his feet, supporting his weight as he hobbled toward the chair. He wanted to quip something back at her, but it was all he could do not to cry out. He stumbled, nearly falling, but caught himself on the arm of the chair, Andromeda stumbling under the weight of him.

She grunted, helping him upright again. "What are you made of? Lead?"

Lowering himself into the chair, Ward breathed hard. "Something like that." Warm blood trickled down his back, his mind going from lucid to fuzzy around the edges as he swayed in his seat.

Andromeda caught him as he listed to the side. "This was a bad idea. I'll call for the Med."

Ward shook his head, putting his hand to his forehead. "Just give me a moment." He rubbed the side of his face, where his usual prickly stubble was turning into a full-on beard. Normally, the med rig would have taken care of it, but he'd been face down all this time.

"Floods you're stubborn." Andromeda walked across the room to a food reconstitutor, asking for juice.

"With ice." Ward rasped. "Please."

"With ice," Andromeda told the machine.

She handed Ward a cup, and he sipped, sugar and cold prickling at his throat. His heart still throbbed in his chest and his breathing was rapid, but at least he didn't feel like he was going to faint anymore.

Andromeda sat across from him. Christmas Present. "Okay. You got me here. What do you want to say?"

"Tell them to turn off the surveillance."

Andromeda laughed. "You think they'd leave me alone in a room with you without watching?"

"What could I possibly do to you in this condition?"

"What difference does it make if they turn it off anyhow? I have a comm. My whole body is a surveillance device."

"Maybe you don't want anyone else hearing what I have to say."

Andromeda narrowed her eyes, folding her arms across her chest.

"Fine. I'll tell them they can't listen, but you know they'll watch and my comm will record your every move. So unless you have a death wish—"

Ward leaned forward, elbows on his knees and hands hanging down between his thighs. He was breathing hard, his head swimming and his back burning. He wasn't sure how long he could stay conscious. "Please, Andromeda."

She paused another moment and then nodded. "Fine. Turn off the audio." Ward watched her as she listened to someone speak to her via her comm chip. She nodded. "Okay. Fine, just turn it off." She listened again, nodded again, and then looked at Ward.

"Okay. It's off. Say when you have to say."

It wasn't true; they were still listening. Maybe Andromeda believed it, or maybe she didn't. That didn't matter. What mattered was Andromeda believing he was trying to confide in her. She needed to believe that Ward thought they weren't listening.

Taking a deep breath, he nodded. He looked up at her, meeting her eyes, knowing, thanks to her father, that they wouldn't give him away.

"Your father's files were corrupted in the transfer. They didn't all make it to Lea before you came in."

Andromeda pursed her lips. "So, what did make it through?"

"I don't know. I handed the files off before my surgery. I never found out what was extracted." This part was mostly true, anyhow.

Andromeda laughed. "You want me to believe you didn't look at those files before giving them away? Do I look that LowQ to you?"

Ward shook his head. "There was no time. The files were on Lea's comm. It was too dangerous for her to keep them and we never got a chance to look before the Authority started pursuing us. My priority was getting them off her and getting the implant out of my back. I knew it would be several days before I'd be able to leave, and I had no time to waste. And I knew that the less Lea and I knew, the safer we'd be."

Andromeda laughed again. "Even if I believed you, which I don't, why do you want to talk to me if you didn't see anything?"

"I said that not all the files made it through the transfer and that I didn't see what was extracted. I didn't say I saw nothing."

Andromeda leaned back in her chair, crossing one leg over the other, and swinging it. "I'm listening."

"While the files were transferring, when I was at the apartment, I skimmed through some of them. One in particular caught my eye. It had your name on it."

Andromeda stiffened but didn't look away.

"I wondered why Dennison Kelvin would have a file about his daughter among his ReInception files."

Andromeda's mouth tightened. The leg stopped swinging. "I'm sure there are files on everyone who's been modified. Nothing strange about that."

"That's the thing, Andromeda. You aren't modified."

She stared at him a moment, blinked, and then laughed. "That's funny Ward."

He'd expected this reaction; her disbelief. He'd thought hard about how to tell her this story. He didn't need her to believe it right away. In fact, trying too hard to convince her would only push her away from the truth. He just needed the accusation to seep in enough for her to begin to wonder.

"I'm not kidding. Think about it. It makes perfect sense."

Andromeda laughed again. "Why are you wasting my time?"

"Haven't you ever compared yourself to your modified peers and wondered why you are so different? You can drink whenever you want when the mere thought of it makes your friend Kammeo gag. You sleep with whomever you want—not even consent protocols in place."

Andromeda shook her head and rolled her eyes. "Okay, Ward. This has been fun—"

"As soon as I told Lea, she knew it was true, too. You don't prioritize studying. When you're gaining weight, I bet it's not your mind that stops you from eating more. It's a pill, isn't it?"

Andromeda stopped laughing, her face reddening slightly. "That's none of your business."

"C'mon Andy," he needled her, using the nickname her friends called her. "Dig deep. Think about your friends who are modified and how they behave. Think about how your father feels about his precious girl. You sleep with people of every sex. You don't exercise. If you were modified, don't you think your parents would have changed all that?"

Andromeda's nostrils flared. She was breathing hard. He was getting to her.

"Maybe my doctors just did a better job." Shaking her head, she stood. "This is absurd. My father's the head of ReInception. It's an advantage that he wouldn't keep from me."

"But he did, and for good reason."

"Okay." She laughed, but this time, it was forced and humorless. "What's this good reason?"

"In the file, there was a communication between your father and someone else. You want to know what it said?"

Andromeda squeezed her arms tighter around herself.

Ward closed his eyes, scouring his perfect memory. He opened them.

"He said, 'Want to know something funny? My daughter isn't mod. We've told her she is, and the power of suggestion alone was enough. They're never touching my daughter with that machine. Not when I know what it can do to people.'"

Andromeda clenched her jaw, a vein throbbing in her temple. Her hands balled into fists. "Oh, and that you remember word for word? Come on, Ward."

"You know it's true."

"I'm done wasting my—"

The door whooshed open, and Dennison Kelvin walked in. His face was purple, and veins stood on his forehead. Ward grinned. Just in time.

"Enough of this!"

He grabbed Ward by the arm, yanking him to his feet. Ward screamed. Too heavy for Kelvin to hold up, he fell to the floor. Ward felt his back tearing and hot blood everywhere. The room started to spin. Kelvin grabbed his arm, trying to pull Ward to his feet again. Ward screamed again; spots swam before his eyes.

The Med ran in, grabbing Kelvin by the arm. "Stop this! You'll kill him."

Dennison Kelvin wheeled on the Med, eyes bulging. "I don't know what's going on here, but I've had enough of it. If he's strong enough to try to manipulate my daughter, he's strong enough for the chair."

Andromeda was sobbing and Kammeo ran in, putting her arm around her friend and ushering her out of the room.

Ward's back was on fire. Blood wet the floor around him. He started to laugh just as Kelvin pulled back a foot and then, swinging it forward, kicked him hard in the side.

Everything went black.

CHAPTER FOURTEEN

In the tumultuous aftermath of the United States' second civil war, a new controversy has emerged: soldiers are being interred and subjected to government-backed ReInception experiments.

According to reports, the program aims to "rehabilitate" former combatants by reprogramming their loyalty. Critics argue this amounts to a violation of human rights and bodily autonomy, sparking outrage among civil liberties groups and the international community.

"These soldiers have already endured the horrors of war," said Dr. Maria Thompson of the Human Rights Watch. "Now, they're being denied their basic rights and subjected to invasive and ethically dubious procedures."

The government defends the program, citing the need for national security and societal reintegration. "ReInception offers a pathway to healing and stability," stated Homeland Security Secretary James Walker. "Our goal is to ensure these individuals can return to society as productive and peaceful citizens."

—AUGUST 18, 2054: POST-CIVIL WAR U.S. FACES CONTROVERSY
OVER REINCEPTION EXPERIMENTS ON SOLDIERS

The Manta moved soundlessly, undulating through the water like the creature it was named for. Leandrea was strapped to a soft, white chair, the cushioning warming against her cold skin. Soon, she stopped shivering; it was the first time she'd been warm in days. Her chair and three others were oriented in a circle, feet facing inward, all slightly reclined with the ceiling inches above their heads to keep the profile of the craft low.

"Won't the government be able to see us?"

Aisling shook her head.

"This craft has the most advanced stealth tech in the world. U.S. surveillance will identify it as marine life. The shape, the temperature signature—everything matches the Manta ray that it mimics."

"Isn't this bigger than a Manta?"

Aisling shook her head again. "Mantas can get over thirty feet. We're smaller than that, but the signature of the craft appears smaller on most sensors anyhow. Besides, we're in international waters now. Even if they locate us, there's nothing they can do."

Vella laughed. "I'm sure yeh don't believe that would stop them."

Aisling sighed, further reclining her seat, relaxing deeper into the cushioning which now nearly engulfed her. "We have a few hours before we arrive. You should get some sleep."

Leandrea noticed she didn't respond to Vella's comment.

As exhausted as she was, Lea didn't think she could sleep. Her mind churned with thoughts and fears. What would happen when they arrived? When and how would she get the files to safety—who could she trust with them? What was happening to Ward?

Still, she settled into the embrace of the seat, which reminded her of the comfort of the bed in her dorm. It seemed like years since she'd been in a soft bed.

There were no windows or any way to see out. It was possible to make the front of the craft transparent, and there were goggles connected to sensors on the outside of the ship that Aisling said would allow them to observe the surrounding area, but they were 300 meters down—there was nothing to see, at least not if all went well.

Lea tried not to think about how deep down they were and how small the space was. How, if anything went wrong, they would die and no one would ever find them. But she couldn't stop herself. She'd never been in the ocean, let alone below it, and the water still terrified her.

She closed her eyes to the faint, pinkish cabin lights and tried to imagine a future where she and Ward weren't on the run. A future that she hoped Katherine Vega could give them. She only prayed it wasn't too late for Ward and, if it was, that Aisling was right. If Katherine had found a way to cure her confused mind of what ReInception had done to it, maybe she could cure others as well. At last, she fell asleep, praying that whatever process has unmodified Katherine could be replicated.

Leandrea woke to a slight shaking of her arm. The craft was angled upward, Leandrea's body now at a slight decline. She opened her eyes to find Aisling awake and in a seated position, now shaking Vella awake, too.

"We're ascending. Almost there."

Leandrea felt slightly sick to the stomach, holding it as she looked around.

Vella moved their seat into a more upright position, staring ahead and wringing their hands. Leandrea, too, felt nervous about what she'd find when they surfaced. Her sleep had been fitful and full of terrible dreams about what was being done to The Origins and especially to Ward. She was eager to meet Katherine; to formulate a plan. She was anxious to get out of this craft, which felt claustrophobic and stale, and breathe some fresh air.

As the ship leveled out, the front end of the Manta morphed from the smooth ivory of the interior to transparent. Leandrea gasped. She hadn't known there were things like this impossibly beautiful technology. The dark, greenish waters grew lighter as they neared the surface. They broke through to bright light and large, gentle waves. In front of them was a vast white wall, at least twelve feet high. A portal opened in the wall, allowing them to pass through.

Leandrea's mouth fell open and her eyes were wide. She'd seen vids of Seasteads—floating, self-ruled and self-sustaining colonies on the ocean. There were many places Leandrea had heard about, or seen vids of, but hadn't seen in person. A vast lunar colony that had started being constructed shortly before the civil war, and a smaller one on Mars that served as a launch point for further space exploration and as a mining colony. Earthscrapers that extended as deep into the ground as they did up into the sky; mag-lev trains that traveled faster than sound.

But the United States government closely controlled information about these places that had independent governments and their own rules about ReInception and other advanced technologies. They presented these options as anarchistic and backwards. What little else she knew was from her parents, telling her what they learned and saw when they were at international conferences. But when they traveled, their movements, too, were carefully controlled. They'd seen little of such societies either—just the edges of what was possible and how the technology they worked on was implemented in places that weren't limited by pre-existing infrastructure.

What was revealed to Leandrea didn't look like anarchy. It looked like heaven. The inside of the city wall was covered with plants of every imaginable variety—hanging gardens festooned the sea barrier as far as her eyes could see. Spread out in front of her were low profile, undulating buildings, also covered in plants and trees. Some structures were open to the air and others, dome-covered like the roof farms of Manhattan. Small craft moved about above and below the water in an organized ballet. People were transported through clear passageways, like the ones she used in The Above, and at intervals, massive tree-like towers rose into the sky, higher than the eye could see. Small, Zeppelin-like structures protruded from the trunks, and massive petal-like platforms radiated around the tower, casting parts of the city in shadow. From their low vantage point, she couldn't see how far the Seastead spanned, but it was surreally beautiful, like it had been painted in colors brighter than reality, teeming with people and life.

"Welcome to Tob Namara." Aisling smiled. "An independent Seastead governed by the people and overseen by Katarina Donovan—Formerly known as Katherine Vega."

Lea looked at her. "Kitty."

Aisling smiled as the Manta docked with a quiet "Click," the nose of the ship expanding to a wide, oval exit. The trio stepped out, squinting into the sudden bright light. The sky was slightly overcast, but bluer and brighter than anything Lea ever saw at home.

Standing a few yards ahead of them in the shade of a domed entrance was a woman with dark, olive skin, shoulder-length black hair, and crystal blue eyes. She wore loose-fitting, wide legged pants and a fitted jacket that crossed her waist in the front. She stood, feet evenly spread and her hands behind her back. With her high cheekbones, wide mouth and full lips, Leandrea knew who she was right away. This was Katherine Vega, Daughter of Dillon Vega and Veronique Gordon, Ward's missing half-sister.

Speeding up her pace, Aisling reached Katherine, putting her arms around the woman and embracing her. When she stepped back, Katherine stared at Aisling for a few moments, smiling and touching her hair.

"Sirkka, I'm so glad to have you back. I'm sorry it took so long."

Aisling nodded and swallowed, her eyes glassing over.

"I'm sorry, too. I'm sorry that I failed you."

Katherine squeezed Aisling's shoulders, looking her in the eyes. "It was not your fault. You found him for me. It's more than anyone else has ever done."

Aisling opened her mouth to say more, but Katherine shook her head. "We'll talk more later. For now, introduce me to the people you've brought."

Vella stepped forward, eyes wide and a tremor in their hands. "It's really you, isn't it?"

Katherine nodded and smiled, like it was a question she'd been asked dozens of times before. "It's really me."

"I kenna' believe it. How is it the whole world doesn't know you're alive?"

"Soon, I will explain everything, but for now, you are all to call me Katarina, " she looked at Lea, "or Kat." She smiled, knowing Lea would be in on the joke.

Stepping past Vella, Katherine stood in front of Leandrea. She was taller than Lea, but not by much. She was muscular, but like a fit upper caste, not like her Prole brother. She looked older than her twenty-seven years, but beautiful, with strong, chiseled features like Ward's.

"So, you're Leandrea." She looked Lea up and down, as if trying to determine what Ward might have seen in her. "You must be very special for Kallum to have fallen for you. He was never one to give his love easily."

Something about Katherine telling Lea what Ward might think or feel made her skin prickle and her stomach tighten into a knot. How much could Katherine really know her brother all these years later?

"He's the one who's special, not me."

Katherine gave her a small, tight smile. "He is very special. And very important."

"Implying what?"

Aisling took in a small hiss of air. "Careful how you speak."

Katherine smiled, squeezing Lea's shoulder. "It's okay Sirkka. I like a girl who'll defend my brother." Her eyes were warm and glassy. "I'm not implying anything. I'm stating a fact. And I'm glad he had you to love him."

"Has." Leandrea stared at the woman, wanting to say more. To ask why she'd abandoned her brother. She wanted to tell her how much it *still hurt* him and how he'd spent his whole life looking for her when his suffering had been unnecessary. If only she'd told the world who she was, Ward would have known she was alive—he would have known where to go to be reunited with her.

She bit back her lecture. There was time for all her questions. For now, all she needed to know was that this was Kallum's sister—the woman he'd been willing to give up everything to save, and anything to find. And apparently, she was as smart and clever as her brother to have risen to rule an entire city-state at such a young age. Katherine was her only chance of helping Ward now, and seeing this place and what it implied about her power gave Lea hope.

Leandrea forced a smile. "I'm sorry. It's been a long few days—I'm not myself, and it's gotten hard to know who to trust." She wrapped her arms around herself, subconsciously putting her fingers against the slight rise of skin below her left armpit, where Ward had secreted the chips. Her stomach churned again, and she felt like she was about to throw up. Sea travel didn't seem to suit her very well, but Tob Namara felt as firm as real ground; she'd feel better once she ate something and found out what Kitty—Kat had planned.

Katherine smiled. "I'm sorry, too. It's wise to be wary. But I hope you can understand that it was my brother who I'd hoped Sirkka would bring back to me, not two strangers."

Leandrea nodded. "I do understand. I wish he was here instead of me, too."

Katherine stared at her a moment, unblinking, and then squeezed her shoulder again. "Finding him was the hard part. Now that I know where he is, I'll get him back. Trust me."

Lea wasn't so sure. First, they didn't actually know where he was. They assumed he'd been taken to ReInception headquarters, but he could be anywhere. If he was there, extracting him would be near impossible without help on the inside. Leandrea could only hope that there were a lot more people like Aisling out there—working for Katherine and already in place. It was probably Ward's only hope. In his current condition, he certainly couldn't help himself.

Katherine signaled for Lea, Vella and Aisling to follow her, proceeding up a walkway and into a domed structure. A flock of seagulls cawed, swooping over them and looping around, landing on a nearby parapet. Their small, black eyes followed the group as they walked past. Birds were infrequent in New York City, and Leandrea stared back at them, uneasy with their attentiveness.

"Only a few of my closest, most trusted advisors know who I really am. They, of course, helped get me here, helped to install me in the government, taught me about politics and diplomacy."

"Why you?" Leandrea asked.

"For the same reason that The Origins wanted Ward. My name, once we reveal it, will have power. But it also turns out that I have an aptitude for it. I'm more than my name now, and the people who want me in power know that."

Leandrea wondered if the people around Katherine believed that, or it was just what they told her. Only time would tell.

"And this place?" Vella asked.

"Construction began on Tob Namara before the War of Coastal Incursion. It was founded by people who wanted to escape the conflict in the United States and govern under their own rule. It started on a ship and grew over the last century to this self-sustaining, self-sufficient community. The structure allows us to grow or contract the city depending on current population. We have the most advanced technology in the world."

Katherine led them into a clear pod that rose through the center of the dome, letting them out onto a lookout atop the structure. Spread out before Leandrea was a vast complex of interconnected disks of varying sizes and configurations. They were arranged in concentric circles around a massive algae farm at the center of the city.

"Our city extends above and below the surface of the water. What you see here is only half of what we are made of. Below the surface are just as many structures that are functional, but also stabilize the city. They house our schools, businesses, homes, research facilities and fisheries."

She gestured upwards, pointing to the massive petals sprouting from the tree-like towers. "Those petals aren't just decorative or shade-providing, they are also—"

Leandrea gasped. "Skybergs!"

Katherine laughed. "Yes. Of course you know. These are the most advanced in the world. The petals can be articulated to provide shade to the city or to let sun in depending on the ultra-violet and radiation values. Thousands of small panels on the top can be repositioned to absorb sun and produce energy for the city, or to refract light from the sun and back into space. They deflect heat from entering into the atmosphere, like glaciers and icebergs once did."

Tears stung Leandrea's eyes. "My parents helped develop those, but I never thought I'd see them in person."

"Your parents' invention has become standard for seasteads. They protect the city, generate power, and help heal the planet." She turned to look at Leandrea. "Your parents are great people. Later, I can show you where we store, repair and build the panels. Would you like that?"

A lump formed in Leandrea's throat and she nodded, swallowing hard. She began chewing on a nail. "My parents...Are they...Do you know if..."

"They're still in New Zealand, but the pressure for them to return to the U.S. and surrender themselves is contributing to a growing global political crisis. You haven't seen the vids in the last few days, I'm sure."

Leandrea and Aisling shook their heads, but Vella nodded. They opened their mouth to say something, but Katherine cut them off.

"We'll get to that. I promise. First, you need to understand more about us and what we are or are not capable of. We are an elected oligarchy with certain socialistic influences. Everyone must do their part if they want to be a part of the community, but no one is forced to be here or to stay. Everyone has a job, and everyone serves in our military."

Katherine pointed toward a domed-in structure nearby; a group of children sat at desks wearing visors and staring at invisible screens while another group ran outside, chasing a flying disk. "Here, we've brought back a sense of community; children learn together in groups and play outside. Until the age of fifteen, the only embedded technology allowed is med-tech to identify and repair mutations or illness. Of course, we use the most modern methods to educate, but they are independent of the body, rather than implanted. This way, we are raising the next generation to think independently before we augment their intelligence. At fifteen, we begin to introduce technology and military training. By sixteen, we are all netted."

Vella and Leandrea glanced at each other. Augmentation and modification were part and parcel of life in the U.S., but Augmented Intelligence, or "Augintel," which involved embedding AI into the brain to bolster intelligence or "netting" was considered too dangerous for the public. It was permitted only for the most senior leadership and important thinkers in the government. Even her parents, who were trying to repair the climate, were not permitted Augintel.

Vella gripped the rail, staring down at the children. "You mean everyone here in netted?"

Katherine smiled, clasping her hands in front of her. "The world needs not only the intelligence of machines, but the empathy of humans to survive and thrive, to repair what has been damaged. Why would we deny ourselves the ability to be the best of both? Do you think we'd be solving the problems and making the technological leaps we've made in the last twenty-five years without it?"

Leandrea wasn't sure what leaps Katherine was referring to, but the idea of everyone's minds netted to computers frightened her. Her whole purpose for running away with Ward, for taking the risks she'd taken, was to stop ReInception. That was just habit modification. What Katherine was talking about was actually computerizing the brain. Leandrea shuddered.

They continued walking as Katherine kept explaining. "At sixteen, our citizens receive their first netting. The computer assesses the brain's potential, helping us identify optimal careers and what further netting can help them realize their potential. It's also when they begin military training."

"Is netting how you fixed yourself?" Lea asked.

Aisling drew in a breath, her body going rigid, but Katherine laughed. "It's okay, Sirkka. Are you asking how I reversed my ReInception?"

Leandrea nodded, her pulse quickening and butterflies in her stomach.

"Yes and no." Katherine turned her back to the railing, leaning against it as she faced Leandrea. "It's true, what they say; ReInception is permanent. It creates neural pathways that are deep, that our brains cling to. We can't undo that, but we can block the pathways and reroute the impulses through new pathways, or even back to original pathways."

Leandrea's brow furrowed. "I don't understand."

"We use Augintel nanites to reroute the impulses. Think of them like traffic officers, programmed to block certain entries and exits and to redirect traffic to a detour. Over time, we believe the pathways formed by ReInception will fade; that the new pathways will take precedence and the nanites will no longer be needed. We haven't tried to remove them—they do no harm, sitting there in the brain, redirecting traffic to where it belonged in the first place. I don't see the point of risking taking them out to find out if modification will reassert itself, but that's what we believe."

"But can't you just put them back in if you take them out and the programming reverts?"

Katherine turned her hand from side to side. "Augintels can revert the programming, but they can't cure psychosis. We already know that too much routing and rerouting can damage the psyche in other ways—conflicting pathways assert themselves; the brain can't reconcile it."

At this, Katherine smiled at Aisling, squeezing the woman's arm. Aisling had tears in her eyes, staring at Katherine with clear adoration. Leandrea finally caught on. Aisling wasn't just working for Katherine, she was in love with the woman. Did Katherine—could she—love her back? If she'd truly "cured" herself, then she could.

"Could you deploy it on a large scale? Could you use the reversal on people who go non-comp or have ReInception imposed on them against their wills?"

"It's a delicate process. As with ReInception, each person must be diagnosed and reprogrammed individually. You can't know how to redirect the traffic if you don't know where it's headed."

Leandrea nodded her understanding but didn't share what she knew about mass ReInception—not yet. They would mass program Prole with certain directives. It didn't matter to them that it would cause mental conflict. The goal was to weaponise the Prole and cause chaos. Then, it could only be undone one by one. A whole segment of society was at risk of going non-comp with no quick fix.

Leandrea was exhausted. She had to get the files to the right people, and fast. There were only three people in the world who she trusted with the files, and one of them might be in a ReInception machine himself right at that moment. The other two, as far as she knew, were still in New Zealand.

"Katherine, I know you've already risked so much to get us here, but I need you to do one more thing for me."

Katherine turned toward her, brows raised.

"I need you to bring my parents here."

CHAPTER FIFTEEN

New Delhi, India — A medical crisis is sweeping through India as a highly resistant bacteria, dubbed the Delhi Super Bug (DSB), wreaks havoc on the nation's newborns. The bacteria, which mothers acquire during childbirth in hospitals, has proven lethal, causing a catastrophic spike in infant mortality rates. DSB's resistance to all known antibiotics has left healthcare professionals scrambling for solutions. Hospitals are overwhelmed, and the country's healthcare system is on the brink of collapse. The government has declared a national emergency, urging international medical organizations to provide immediate assistance.

—REUTERS, MARCH 13, 2056

Day 6: December 16, 2126: Tob Namara
Leandrea

K itty exhaled. "I don't know, Lea. That's a tall order."

"You got us here. It can't be harder than that."

A small bird landed on a railing outside the glass. Cocking its head from side to side, it watched them a moment, and then lifted off, swooping through the sky and away. Kitty followed its path with her eyes. "I think you need to see the Vids."

"What Vids?" Leandrea asked.

"The ones about you. You need to know what's been happening the last few days."

They exited the domed building and took a moving platform to one of the towers. As they traveled between buildings, they were halted momentarily as a door opened to their right and a group of people poured out, jogging past them. They all wore uniforms of a gray mesh and had visors over their eyes. As they passed Kitty, they tapped their visors. "Sir!" each said as they passed.

Katherine kept her hands clasped in front of her, smiling slightly as the group moved past, sprinting around a corner and out of sight.

"Cadets," Katherine said, "newly minted according to their uniforms. The uniforms work together with the netting and Augintel to stimulate muscle growth, drive to achieve, if needed, aggression."

Leandrea shuddered, unsure if this was any better than the augmentation and modification they used in the U.S. or just a horse of another color. She wondered if it was voluntary or if everyone in Tob had to go through the process no matter what. Katherine had already said they all served in the military. Leandrea held her tongue, not wanting to offend Katherine or sound accusatory. Later, once she got her parents here, there'd be time for mildly accusatory questions.

They entered a pod inside one of the support structures that looked like a twisting vine. Leandrea heard the pop and hiss of the pod pressurizing with their rapid ascent. She looked out over Tob Namara. The group of cadets moved quickly down a path. Ahead of them was another unit, these in similar uniforms but with colored bands on the shoulders, Leandrea assumed to designate rank. They headed toward a structure with dozens more soldiers already inside.

Katherine turned around to face her, back to the clear glass.

"Our military is the most advanced in the world." The illusion of Kitty, unmoving in front of her, and the city sliding rapidly past and below them, gave Leandrea vertigo.

"Why do yeh need such a military?" Vella asked. "What are yeh preparing for?"

It was a good question. As far as Leandrea knew, as far as the U.S. government told them, there was relative peace in the world for the first time in decades. The U.S. had scaled its own military back to focus on climate repair and rebuilding after the war. Then again, did you need a military if you had a whole caste you could reprogram? She wondered, suddenly, whether more could be done with those chips. She shuddered, wrapping her arms around herself.

Katherine looked at Vella, still in that relaxed pose of hands in front of her. It felt practiced, like someone had told her any other pose could have meaning read into it—arms crossed were defensive, hands moving around too much, aggressive. Katherine's mien was a study in neutrality. In fact, everything about her was carefully neutral—like her benign half smiles.

"Tob is the most advanced city in the world. Building from the ground up, so to speak, allowed us that luxury. We had no dated infrastructure to contend with. No pre-existing political in-fighting. No one lives here under duress—we all want to be here. This allowed us to progress far past what established cities are capable of. Our augmented intelligence permits us to think beyond what the average human believes possible. With it, we take the collective ideas of society and make vast leaps and improvements. It is the way we're finally making the advances that mankind only dreamed until now."

They exited into an office complex so high up that all Lea could see when she looked out the windows were clouds and the tops of the Skybergs. Here and there, office workers sat or stood, gesturing through the air in a way that reminded Leandrea of Ward's deft hands, hacking their way through the computer systems at Uni. These stations were more advanced, each worker wearing a visor that Lea assumed connected the Augintel to the corporate systems. They could see something in front of them, but no one else could.

Vella caught up with Kitty, keeping pace as they moved down a hallway. "Why not share such knowledge?"

"We do; much of it. We just don't want it forcibly taken from us."

"Is there such a threat?" Vella seemed more than curious.

"There are many threats in this world. And the relative peace is only as good as the stability of any other nation at a given moment. We share much, but we also have much to protect. Also, building Tob Namara was not cheap. We have debts to pay and leveraging our advanced tech is how we'll do that. Soon, Tob will be the world's only debt free, profitable nation states."

Turning toward Vella, Katherine put a hand on their arm. "Our military is a defensive force, only to keep us safe in the event we need it. Never to aggress." She smiled, giving Vella's arm a small squeeze.

She led them into an office, gesturing for them to sit around an oblong table. On the table were visors. Katherine gestured to Leandrea and Vella. "Put them on. They'll have limitations since you aren't netted, but you'll still find them useful."

Facing the front wall, Katherine commanded: "Play yesterday's U.S. News vids about Leandrea Justus."

Leandrea placed the visor over her eyes. In front of her, a person with hair of deep purples, blacks and blues that looked like an oil slick appeared; Leandrea jumped. The holographic tech was far superior to what she was used to—the person seemed to be in the room with her. They had deep blue eyes that matched their hair and pale skin, with a complex swirling pattern like Andromeda favored. Leandrea swallowed hard. Seeing the newscaster made her miss her friend. She wondered how furious Andromeda was with her and Ward for how they'd used her. She hoped, but didn't believe, that her friend would someday understand why she'd done it.

"In the United States, a hunt continues for the fugitive known as Leandrea Justus." A 3D projection of Leandrea appeared next to that of the newscaster. The image, from the waist up, hovered to the newscaster's left, slightly above their shoulder and smaller than life, rotating around. Her curly, red hair completely covered her back and Lea reached up, touching the locks that, just a few days earlier, Aisling had hacked off with a knife. Her image blurred as she swished her hands through it. Stepping back, she watched as the broadcast continued.

"Although the government and ReInception will not comment, it is believed that Ms. Justus, with the assistance of someone inside of the Authority, may have escaped the city."

The image morphed into the scene that Leandrea had witnessed from the building window when Ward was taken by the Authority.

"In further news, recently detained members of The Origins have been taken to an undisclosed ReInception location for 'debriefing.'" The newscaster made air quotes, "But we all know what that is code for in the United States."

The camera zoomed in on Ward on the stretcher, blood staining his back. "VBS News, Reykjavik has learned that among those captured was the fugitive Ward 17,362 Bedford, the man who Ms. Justus was last seen with. The Ward appears to be in critical medical condition." The woman swung around so that she faced the vid, gesturing to it.

"This leaked footage shows The Origins being herded into waiting hovercraft. Sympathy for The Origins has grown after Ward Bedford was seen being mistreated by The Authority."

Leandrea inhaled sharply as she watched a replay of Ward falling to the ground; Amie trying to rush to his side but being held back by Authority. Footage of large O's splattered in red paint on walls across the city appeared and vanished in quick succession.

"In a transparent effort to flush out Ms. Justus, ReInception released the following video."

Leandrea froze as the figure of the newscaster faded and was replaced by Hallyn. He stood in the middle of the room, his familiar bright blue eyes staring right at her. He was thin and looked tired, the once glossy black hair that always hung in his eyes, cropped short.

"Leandrea." She held her breath, squeezing the seat arms. "It's me. Hallyn." He gave a small chuckle. "Yeah, I guess you know that. Why am I acting like we're strangers? I'm sorry for what I said to you. All those terrible things. You know I didn't mean it." His pupils dilated and then contracted. His breath caught as he inhaled, like he was about to cry. He swallowed hard, wiping sweat off his forehead with the back of his hand. "Please come back. If you come back, all of this will stop." Tears stung Leandrea's eyes as another image appeared, this time of someone she didn't recognize inside of the ReInception machine. When the camera was back on Hallyn, he was looking to the side, like he was seeing what she was seeing.

When he said this will all stop, did he mean whatever they were doing to the person in the chair, or whatever they were doing to him?

Facing the camera again, Hallyn stepped forward, putting his hand on a table. "They are only trying to protect us. If you come back, if you tell them what you know about The Origins, none of this will be necessary. Lea." His using her nickname made her heart skip a beat. That deep love she'd felt for him knotted in her chest. It was not the same passionate longing she had for Ward. Not the willingness to burn down the planet to save him that Ward inspired in her. It was a calmer kind of love that she'd had for Hallyn. The love you give to the few pure souls you come across in life. Ward's love made her angry—spurred her to action. Hallyn's love had always made her want to be better. Was he still in there, thinking he could help, even from inside of ReInception? Despite all they'd done to him, that was Hallyn to his core. Maybe ReInception couldn't take that away, at least not entirely. At least not without destroying him completely.

Leandrea wiped her tears away with the heel of her hand, pressing on her eyes to try to stop herself.

Hallyn faded and was replaced again by the news reporter. They leaned in. "Leandrea Justus, if you are watching this, don't fall for it. There are places that will give you sanctuary."

"Stop vid," Katherine commanded. The newscaster faded away, and there was just an empty space at the end of the table again. "Play today's news about Storm and Serafin Justus."

A vid of Lea's parents being herded into a hovercraft appeared. Leandrea's mother huddled against her father. Their hair whipped in the wind, and they covered their faces with their hands as they approached the waiting transport.

"Pressure from the U.S. mounts for New Zealand to send home the parents of Leandrea Justus. Speaking on behalf of the renowned climatologists, the prime minister of New Zealand has released the following statement on behalf of the couple."

Before stepping into the craft, her mother briefly turned her face. Her brow had that familiar, worried furrow that made Lea's stomach drop like a heavy stone.

"Leandrea is a kind, hardworking young woman. She has never been in trouble with the Authority or with anyone else. We've not had any contact with our daughter since before the raid on The Origins, but we're certain that she's not a part of any terrorist organization. There's a reasonable explanation for all of this. We don't believe reports that she stole anything from Dennison Kelvin, but if she had anything to do with stealing his files, she'd've had a good reason for it. She'd only do it because she'd no other choice."

Leandrea put her face in her hands, trying to stifle a sob. She was exhausted. She'd barely slept in days. Everyone she loved was under attack. It was all too much.

"That's enough," Vella snapped. "She gets the point."

The newscaster faded, and Katherine turned toward them.

"That's just a couple. There are hundreds of reports like these, and you can imagine what the ones in the U.S. are like—making sure that you and The Origins look like the villains."

"This is only more proof that we have to get my parents here."

"And risk the weight of international pressure coming down on us? Tell us what you found out, tell us where the files are, and we can use that as a bargaining chip. We can—"

There was a tapping on the glass and Leandrea looked over. A girl, maybe eleven or twelve, stood outside. As soon as Lea saw her, her skin went cold.

"Ah!" Kitty smiled. "Here's someone I want you to meet."

She gestured for the girl to come in. The girl hesitated for a moment, eyes locking with Leandrea's. They were wide and sky blue. She had broad, full lips and high cheekbones. There was no mistaking the resemblance to the vids Leandrea had seen of Kallum as a young boy. She swallowed, watching the girl make her way hesitantly across the room until she stood in front of Katherine. She was just a couple of inches shorter than Katherine, and had that unblinking, steady stare Leandrea had seen on Ward's face so many times.

Katherine smiled, cupping a hand around the back of the girl's neck.

"I'd like you to meet my daughter, Dillon."

The girl looked first at Lea, then at Vella. When she spotted Aisling, her eyes widened and her mouth spread into a wide, familiar smile. "Sirkka!"

She ran over to Aisling, throwing herself into the woman's arms. Aisling smiled, squeezing the girl and kissing her on the cheek. "I can't believe how much you've grown!"

"It took you forever! Mom said you found my uncle but…"

Aisling squeezed her again. "I'll tell you all about it later, but don't worry, we're going to get him out of there."

Leandrea and Vella looked at each other, eyes wide, and then turned back toward the girl.

"You've a child?" Vella asked.

Katherine laughed. "I do. Dillon, I'm pleased for you to meet Vella. They are one of the leaders of The Origins."

Dillon nodded, looking Vella up and down and then shifting her eyes toward Leandrea.

"And this is—" Katherine began.

"Leandrea Justus. I saw her in the vids." The girl turned her eyes on Lea.

Her voice was deeper than Leandrea would have expected from such a young girl, her tone even and serious.

Leandrea tried forcing a smile, but she couldn't get over the fact that Ward had a niece—one who looked exactly like Ward had as a child.

If Leandrea had guessed the girl's age correctly, it would have meant that she was born shortly after Katherine had disappeared from Ward's life.

Katherine patted her daughter on the shoulder and kissed her on top of the head.

"I'll be out in a few moments, and then you can ask all your questions. For now, please give us a few minutes more."

Dillon nodded, pausing a moment to look around the room again before stepping out the door.

No one spoke for a few seconds, Vella twisting her hands and Aisling clearing her throat.

Leandrea crossed her arms over her chest, inhaling a deep breath. It wasn't hard to do the math, but it was hard to meet Katherine's eyes; she forced herself to.

"Is that why you left him?"

Katherine shook her head.

"No. When Kallum and I were hiding in the tunnels, there were things I had to do to keep us alive. I felt a lot of shame about many things that happened to me after I was modified, even when I couldn't control them, but I feel no shame about the sacrifices I made for my brother. Dillon resulted from my doing what I had to for us. I didn't even know I could get pregnant when it happened. When I pulled out my comm, resumption of my regular ovulation cycle was a consequence I didn't think of. But no. That's not why I left Kallum. I never would have left him if I'd had a choice."

Leandrea shifted her weight, biting her lip. Her sudden anger at Katherine surprised her. Thinking of Kallum so young and alone in those tunnels...But this was the explanation Kallum had been seeking for years; it was a reason that his sister left him that he could live with—to save his niece.

"The last time I saw Kallum, I'd left him in a hiding place in the tunnels and told him to wait for me. I was in The Floods, scrounging for food, when a member of The Authority spotted and arrested me. Of course, they knew who I was. The Origins were a fledgling organization at the time, but they had people on the inside in the Authority and ReInception. When I was being transported from the grid to ReInception, the Origins intercepted the transport. They extracted me and brought me to Izabelle. It had already been almost a week, and I was desperate to go back for Kallum, but they told me it was too dangerous. If they didn't get me out right away, I'd never escape. By the time The Origins went back for him, he was gone."

Katherine paused, closing her eyes and rubbing her forehead. Tears poured down her cheeks and her voice shook.

"He was so smart. So brave. I was sure he made it. I had to leave the city, but Iza promised me she'd never stop looking for Kal. I didn't find out I was pregnant until I was already out of the country."

Lea felt like she'd been slapped in the face. Her gut clenched and her breath stopped. In her peripheral vision, she saw Vella stiffen and her eyes narrow.

They took a step toward Katherine, body angled forward, muscles tensed."Yer sayin' Iza knows you're alive?"

Katherine tilted her head. "Of course she knows I'm alive. The Origins are the ones that got me out. Didn't you...Didn't she..." Her eyes shifted back and forth between Leandrea and Vella. Her mouth fell open and her hand went to her neck. Leandrea could see her throat moving as she swallowed. "She never told you? Never told him?"

Leandrea shook her head. "No. The whole reason Ward was with The Origins was because Iza promised to help him find you."

Katherine's eyes shifted toward Vella. "Is this true?"

Vella's nodded their head. "I dinna' know who he was til two days ago."

"I don't understand this." Leandrea felt dizzy. She rested a hand on the table, steadying herself. "Were you and Izabelle in touch?"

Katherine nodded. Her skin had gone pale and her hands trembled as she stared down at them. "She never told me she found him. When Sirkka finally determined for sure who he was, she was sure that no one else had figured it out."

Vella cocked their head. "And you thought it was jes coincidence Ward worked for Iza?"

Katherine nodded. "I did. I mean, it wasn't surprising that Kallum would have found his way to The Origins. Given how smart he is, what had happened to us, I just assumed he'd made his way into Izabelle's confidence on his merit, not because of his name. I could understand why he'd hide his identity from her, and he'd been missing for so many years—he looks so different..."

Blood rushed through Leandrea's veins. Her face went hot. She balled her hands into shaking fists. "Well, Izabelle knew. She's known who he was since he was released from the facility when he was sixteen."

Katherine shook her head. "I can't understand. Why wouldn't she tell him? Tell me?"

Leandrea thought she knew, but she didn't want to speculate and she was still unsure how much she should reveal to Kitty. Ward had trusted and loved his sister more than anyone in the world, but that was someone he'd known a long time ago, with the innocence of childhood and the devotion of a younger sibling. A lot had happened to both of them in between.

Aisling stepped forward. "We won't know until we can contact Iza. Do you still have a way to reach her?"

Katherine shook her head again. "Since the raid, all channels to The Origins have gone silent. Anskot hër," she muttered, putting a hand on Lea's upper arm, squeezing gently. "Lea. We're running out of time. You must tell us what you know."

Leandrea's eyes shifted around the room. Her breathing quickened as she chewed on a thumbnail. Her other arm was wrapped around her middle. Unconsciously, she stroked the tiny lump where the chips were glued inside her skin. She didn't know what the next right move was, but she had to make one. Floods, she wished she had someone to confide in; someone who could give her advice. But Ward had warned her not to tell anyone where the chips were, not even Sebbe or Vella. He'd told her they were her bargaining chip. She wouldn't squander the leverage Ward had given her.

She dropped her hand from her mouth.

"I know where the files are and I can get them to you."

Katherine's eyes widened. She stepped closer to Leandrea, squeezing her arm a little tighter. "Where? Tell me?"

Leandrea looked at her. "Here's how this is going to work."

CHAPTER SIXTEEN

Lucia:

I wanted to bring to your immediate attention a deeply concerning issue that has come to light regarding the use of our technology. It has been reported that there is unauthorized use of our ReInception technology on prisoners of war in the Lexington, Kentucky camps.

Details are still emerging, but initial findings suggest that our technology is being applied without proper oversight and consent. This is not only against company policy, but also poses significant ethical and legal risks. This misuse of our technology could potentially lead to severe consequences for both the individuals involved and our company's reputation.

My sources say that there are individuals inside of ReInception who are complicit. We need to act swiftly and decisively.

Beryl Alemi, CCO

—TRANSCRIPT FROM THE FILES OF DENNISON KELVIN

Day 5: December 13, 2126: Unknown Location
Ward

When Ward came to, he was back on his cot, the med rig blasting his back with a cold solution that blissfully numbed his skin. There was shouting in the background.

"What was he talking about?"

"He was talking nonsense, and you know it."

"That's what I thought until you busted in."

"Stop this, Andromeda."

The Med approached the gurney, laying strips of cloth across Ward's back. "That was truly LowQ."

The cloth was so soothing. The pain was gone. "Was it?" Darkness creeped into Ward's vision. He shook his head. He needed to stay awake.

"Tell me! What are you trying to hide?"

"This is not the time or place for this, Andy."

"This is the perfect time—"

The Med pressed something against Ward's upper arm. "No!" But it was too late. Ward felt the prickle of the NFiT and the tingling of the pain meds moving up his arm and through his system.

"We are going, Andromeda. Right now."

"I'm not—"

"Really, really LowQ," The Med whispered.

"Maybe helping me was LowQ," Ward mumbled. He wasn't thinking clearly.

"Helping you? I'm a doctor, of course I'm helping you."

"That's not what I mean." Ward's eyes slid shut. "The bot."

"What bot?"

"The..." He couldn't think clearly. "You know. The bot."

Ward closed his eyes. The Med shook his arm and Ward's eyes slipped back open. "What bot, Ward?"

Ward tried shaking his head clear, but his brain felt like a stone, knocking into the sides of his skull each time he moved his head. His mouth filled with cotton. "The bot." Of course, the doctor knew about the bot. Who else would have sent it?

"Dammit," the Med let go of Ward's arm.

He'd warned Ward not to talk so much...

For days and days, the tunnels went from dark to the dim light of sun seeping in through the grates and back to darkness. Kallum wasn't sure how long Kitty had been gone, but his OLED lamp had degraded to where it barely emitted enough light to see five feet around him. He'd long since passed hunger and had become cold and lethargic despite the warmth and dampness of the tunnels. He'd long passed the constant feeling of terror and crossed into the realm of numb, sleeping most of the time and waking at small noises, hoping his sister had returned. More than once, the feel of small sharp teeth breaking through his skin had roused him. The first few times, he'd try to catch the rats, hoping that if he killed one, he might find a way to cook and eat it. But even if he was healthy, the little survivors would have been too fast for him. Now, he could barely move enough to shoo them away. The wounds were seeping and infected, and he was out of medspray. If he didn't leave now, he'd never leave at all.

He'd known for a while that if Kitty could return, she would have already. He kept hoping there was something that had delayed her—maybe she'd been injured and needed to heal enough to get to him. Maybe she'd been caught and, just now, was plotting her way to get free and back to him. If she came back and he was gone, they might never find each other again.

But Kitty would also know her brother was running out of time. She'd worked too hard to keep him alive for him to just die here, waiting. All those vids they'd watched together about survival. All the techniques they'd practiced together to prepare them for the day they'd escape the borders and into the wild were about survival—foraging and building shelters. Hunting and starting fires. None of them had prepared him for surviving alone, underground—in the dark, damp of the abandoned subways tunnels of an old, forgotten New York.

He had to decide whether he was going to die waiting for someone he knew deep down wouldn't return or try to live. He was only seven, but he was smart enough to know that couldn't survive on his own, at least not here. Not in his current condition.

He waited until the half-light poured through the grates and then slid his thin frame underneath the row of pipes that concealed his hiding place. Looking around, he made sure no one else was nearby and then pushed himself to his feet. The tunnel swayed and contracted around him. He stumbled, leaning against the slick, damp wall for support. Like that, half leaning against the slime-coated walls, slipping and pulling himself back up with the sounds of rushing water and chittering creatures all around him, he made his way toward the distant lights that meant the tunnel's opening into an old, abandoned station. From there, he'd climb the steps and hope that the exit wasn't blocked. If it was, he wasn't sure he could make it to the next station.

There was a sting on his arm. Ward's eyes flew open, suddenly completely alert. He was strapped to a chair. He started pulling against the restraints. They were so tight around his wrists and ankles that he could hardly move. Eyes wide and darting from place to place, he struggled to decipher the dark shapes around him. Straining his neck, he looked over his head, dreading the halo that would tell him he was out of time. Nothing was there. Where was he? He was sitting under a dim light that faded into blackness. The sounds of his thrashing echoed around him. His back didn't hurt, but he felt blood, wet and warm, behind him.

"Bring up the lights." Kelvin's voice echoed in the darkness.

Lights burst on, blinding and harsh. Ward flinched, squinting against the sudden assault. A couple of yards in front of him, he could make out a shape. It was blurred—outside the range of where his vision was clear, but right away, he could tell what it was. It was *The* chair, but he wasn't in it. Not yet. He thrashed wildly, not caring that more and more blood poured down his back. It was starting to drip onto the floor.

"Calm down," the voice said. "You're going to kill yourself acting like that."

Kelvin's voice, placid and patronizing.

"Where am I? What is this?"

"Well, isn't that obvious?"

Ward didn't want to give Kelvin the satisfaction of knowing how frightened he was. The last time he was strapped in a chair like this...the last time...*Stop thinking about it!* He admonished himself. But the feel of the chair and the straps was too familiar. The sound of that voice...

"Please, don't do this."

Kelvin laughed. "I'm not doing this. You did this. I'm done trying to be nice; to negotiate with you."

Ward took a deep breath, trying to slow his breathing, calm his panic. These could be his last moments as himself. Was hysterical and weak how he wanted to be remembered? *Control the story*, he reminded himself.

Remembering that how he spoke had tipped Lea off to the fact that he was hiding something, Ward leaned heavily into his accent. "I'm jus Ward. I dunna' know anything."

"I doubt that, but don't worry, I'm not putting *you* in the machine. Not yet."

Ward's brow furrowed, his heart speeding up. What kind of trick was this? He hated himself for the hope that shivered in his chest. But if Kelvin wanted him to watch this, it could only mean that someone more important than him to the cause, or more important to him than himself, was going in there. Dread closed his throat and sent hope fleeing.

"Den why m'I here?"

"The doctor tells me that the chair will kill you. But now that I know someone was helping you, I thought some motivation was in order. If you are as loyal as they tell me, we might not even need to put you in the chair. A win-win, don't you think?"

Ward didn't understand. Who was "they?" How many of his friends were already gone? Ward's breath came in short bursts. He couldn't get enough air.

"I tell yeh, true, true. Em jes Ward. I jes do what told. Deh girl, Lea, she sorry fer me. Dey jes use her, sure, sure."

Kelvin snorted. "We'll see."

To Ward's left, a door opened, light seeping in from a hallway. No, not a doorway, something smaller; rounded. A portal? He tried to take in his surroundings. Low ceilings. Gray walls. He squinted, trying to bring the portal into focus, but all he could see was the haze of light. Then there was a noise. Footsteps coming closer. The scrapes and grunts of a struggle, garbled, distant, shouting. A woman? A shiver ran up Ward's body, a lump rising in his throat. Lea? He gripped the chair arms so hard that his hands ached.

"Ah. Here we are."

Someone approached the ReInception chair, sitting down next to it. Ward could make out the white jumpsuit of a Med. Short, dark hair.

Tall and lean. But the features wouldn't come into focus. His Med? He didn't know. The person moved their hands through the air. An arced holoscreen lit up, forming a translucent barrier in front of the chair.

The struggle grew closer. "Stop fighting! I don't want to hurt you!"

"Buhay! Hum Ji!"

Ice froze Ward's gut. He knew that voice.

"Yell ney get nutt—"

There was a *shhhzzzp*, and a shriek. The voice cut off.

Ward's breath came in short bursts, body shivering. The room swayed. Please, no, he thought, but he bit his lip, resisting the urge to call out to her. To scream at Kelvin. Yelling would only tell them what they wanted to know about his relationship with the woman.

A small figure was dragged into the room, arms gripped on each side by Golds. Despite her advanced years, Iza bucked and twisted, feet scrabbling on the ground.

"Know each other?" Kelvin's smug voice echoed around the chamber.

Iza's head lifted, the blur of her face swinging in Ward's direction. She froze, and Ward knew his presence surprised her. He'd never known Iza to even miss a beat before. The diminutive, unassuming, unsuspected old woman who'd pretended for years to be a weak, old librarian, but, behind the scenes, was not only the founder of The Origins, she was The Original. And the only person besides Lea who knew his secret.

His body shook. He gripped tighter to the chair. No, *no, no.*

Iza huffed. "Sure, I know him." Her voice was calm and level. Too calm given the fight she'd just been putting up. "He de Ward yeh been searching."

"The Ward *you* sent to steal my files."

"I dinna' have nuttin' to do wit dat. Nor wit dem terrorists."

Kelvin laughed, a quiet, deep sound. "We already know that's not true, otherwise you wouldn't be here. Put her in the chair."

They dragged Iza toward the chair again. Grunting, she twisted her body from side to side, fighting even though she must have known it was useless. Ward heard that *shhzzp* again, and she cried out in pain.

"Iza!" The scream came out before Ward could stop himself.

Kelvin laughed. "See. I knew you knew each other."

Iza was shoved into the chair, arms held down by Golds as straps constricted around her wrists. Still, she kicked and bucked as they grabbed her legs, holding them down as the lower restraints engaged. Next came a strap across her waist. She thrashed her head from side to side until they shoved her back by the forehead, locking in the head restraint. Slowly, the silver halo descended until it surrounded her.

She could no longer move. There was just the sound of her breath coming in quick gasps.

"You'll kill her." It came out of Ward in a sob. He knew it gave him away, but he couldn't stop himself. He and Iza had their differences. They knew each other for what each was. Despite that, she was the closest thing he'd had to a mother since his own mother had gone to the grid. Maybe ever.

The Med seated next to her gestured across the air. The holoscreen lit up, showing panels and images. Ward couldn't make them out, but he knew they'd be instructions and vitals. For a willing participant, this would be the stim grid that would help the Med identify brain patterns of habit and how to override and redirect them. What this looked like for an unwilling conscript, Ward didn't know.

The halo illuminated, blue and silver, casting Iza's face in a spectral glow.

A low, bestial moan emanated from deep in Ward's throat.

"Do you know how this works?" The Med's voice was calm. Not the voice of Ward's Med, which meant that the man was still out there somewhere. That if he had been helping Ward, then maybe...

Iza didn't respond. Ward wished he could make out her expression. Tell if her eyes were locked on his. Whether she was frightened or defiant. Likely, she was both. The minutes were numbered for both of them. He'd known from the first that his dreams and plans were half fantasy, but it was a hope he'd clung to. It had given him the fight he needed to stay alive. Like the blood from his back, the fight was draining from him.

"I'll ask you a series of questions," the Med continued. "First, about the things that are most important to you, that trigger your pleasure receptors. If you cooperate and tell me what these things are, I can more accurately capture the data."

Iza gave a small, high-pitched laugh.

"If you won't answer my questions, I will have to guess based on your brain's response. It's not as accurate as if you give me your answers. It will get the job done, but not well."

"Yell ney get nicht frem me."

The Med sighed. "Izabelle. Understand this. The reason people go non-comp from this process is not because there's a problem with the technology. It's because we can't get accurate reads."

"Which'a ney happen if yeh dun force people."

"Perhaps right. But for you, as for them, this is happening whether or not you want it to. It's in your personal best interest to do whatever you can to improve the outcome."

Iza spit. "My best interest. Hum ji."

The Med shook his head. "It's always this way with you people. You think you can fight it and you think that gets the best of us, but you only hurt yourself."

Iza spat again.

"Okay then." The Med gestured in the air. "Let's begin"

The halo's glow intensified and there was a low humming that Ward felt deep in his chest. An oval image floated in front of the Med. Ward couldn't see it clearly, but he could tell it was a scan of Iza's brain. Ripples of light crackled across the surface like a lightning storm.

"Your name is Izabelle—I-Z-A-B-E-L-L-E, correct?"

Iza didn't respond, but there was a snap of bright light across the brain image. The Med tapped on it.

"You are a librarian."

Another bolt ran across the image.

"You work at Butler Library, Columbia University."

There was a quiet crackling sound. A *Shhhhzip!* from the machine.

"Ah, good. I see it's a place you love."

Iza grunted but refused to respond.

"You are part of The Origins."

Shhhhzip!

⁕

It went on for a long time, longer than it would have taken had Iza told the Med what to ask. He proceeded methodically, first through questions that he knew the answers to and then to others that he didn't, mapping responses to see what triggered a positive or negative response. Do you like dogs? Cats? Babies. Garlic.

Ward had never been through the process, but he knew it was usually quick and targeted, replacing one pleasure for another. This was not about that. It was about using the machine for interrogation by changing Iza's mind.

The Med stood, going over to a cabinet and removing something. He approached Iza with it. For the first time since they put her in the chair, she spoke.

"What dat? What you give me?"

Ward heard the familiar click of an NFiT.

It won't hurt you. It's just a solution we've developed that will make you more receptive."

"What you mean? What you—"

"It's okay. You're going to be able to relax now. We are getting to the part where I overwrite certain of your impulses. Just listen to my voice and stay calm. I'll remind you that outcomes will improve if you are responsive. But we'll get what we need either way."

The pale orb of Iza's face turned in Ward's direction. If only he could see her.

"Iza…" He wanted to reach for her. Hold her as he never had. Tell her not that he loved her, he did and he didn't, but that he was grateful. That he knew what she would tell them soon, and it was not her fault."

"Ward. I should have told you…"

Shhhzip! Iza screamed. "Now, now. None of that."

The Med moved his chair in front of the screen. "The medication should be kicking in now. We can begin."

"What is your role with the Origins?"

Iza didn't respond; there was a flicker on the scan, lower on the brain image, and less intense than most other responses.

"Still not answering," the Med mumbled.

"Are you the leader of The Origins."

A bright flash.

"Did you found it?"

Another bright flash.

Iza began to sob. Ward had never heard her cry. He'd hardly ever seen her show any emotions other than excitement and anger—the two spectrums of the world he existed in. Was this another act? Another ruse? He didn't think so. It was over. She had lost, and she knew it. Which meant *they* had both lost.

CHAPTER SEVENTEEN

In the aftermath of the War of Coastal Incursion, the United States faces unprecedented economic and social turmoil. The conflict has depleted our workforce and created a climate of widespread unwillingness to engage in essential labor. To ensure national stability and rebuild our infrastructure, it is imperative to explore unconventional solutions. I propose the establishment of a caste system with forced labor as a temporary measure to address our current challenges.

—FROM THE DECLASSIFIED FILES OF THE WHITE HOUSE; SECRETARY OF WAR ARHAN SINGH'S PROPOSAL TO THE CABINET FOR OPERATION PROLE, AUGUST 18, 2056.

Day 6: December 16, 2126: Tob Namara
Leandrea

"This is no time for games." Katherine turned toward Ashling. "Do you know? Did she tell you?"

Aisling's skin paled. She shook her head. "Not a word."

She stepped toward Leandrea, her eyes so wide that the whites showed all the way around her irises. She grabbed Lea's arm tighter, giving it a small, sharp shake. "You have to tell me. Now."

Leandrea stepped back, yanking her arm from the woman's grip. "You'll get them when you do what I tell you."

"This isn't a game. It's a matter of—"

"Those files are the only chance I have of getting my parents here instead of them being shipped back to the U.S. You know what will happen to them, there. I've already lost Ward. They'll use him to get to me, to the files, and to The Origins. I won't let them use my parents, too. Tell New Zealand I know where the files are. I'll tell you where they are once my parents arrive safely."

Katherine stepped in toward her, face so close Lea could smell her breath. "We don't have the luxury of waiting. Do you know what they could be doing to The Origins right now? To my brother, who you say you love?"

Swallowing hard, Lea stepped back. Katherine thought she knew Ward, but the boy she knew was not the man Lea knew. If Lea didn't use the files to keep herself safe, he'd never forgive her no matter what they were doing to him right then. And if she didn't use them to save the Prole, she'd never forgive herself. There was nothing she could do to guarantee that the information would be used to that end. She didn't even know what was in the files. But her parents were the only people she trusted to help her try.

"Then you'd better work quickly."

"I don't even know if N.Z. will agree to that—that they'd start an international incident without even knowing what you have. What proof is there that you even got any of the files to safety? If you tell me what's on there, perhaps I can persuade them, but short of that…"

"You'll just have to trust me."

"Why would I do that? Why would they?"

"Because, like you said, I love your brother. I wouldn't risk his life for something that he's willing to die for. New Zealand knows who I am. By now, the whole world does."

Katherine gave a growl of frustration. "This is not how diplomacy works, Leandrea. You are a naive girl who led a sheltered existence. And much as I love my brother and would do anything for him, larger things are at stake here."

Leandrea dropped her arms and straightened her back, trying to look more confident than she felt. "Nothing larger is at stake. Your brother knows everything. He is everything. Every person in the world wants to know what happened to Kallum Gordon. Right now, he's in the hands of ReInception where they are doing Floods knows what to him. Your brother is the one everyone cared about. That sweet boy with the big blue eyes..."

Katherine's face reddened, and she inhaled sharply through her nose, mouth pinched tight.

"You may be Katherine Vega, but even that won't be enough if people find out you sacrificed your brother. Again."

Katherine's face turned a darker shade of red. She clenched her jaw. Turning toward Vella and Aisling, she said. "Talk some sense into her before I do something she'll regret."

Vella shook her head. "Shell ney do nuthin' she don wan to. Jes give her what she wants, sure."

Aisling crossed her arms over her chest, staring at Lea, head slightly cocked. "She's been with me for days and said nothing. Perhaps if she knew—"

Katherine cut her off. "Absolutely not."

"If I knew what?"

Katherine stepped close to Lea, face still red, cheeks quivering. Like her brother, her anger came quick, but it was more contained and less calculated.

"You aren't a politician, Lea. You aren't even part of this community. You know what my brother and I went through. You know how far he was willing to go to escape. Think about what I was willing to do to get where I am, and what I might do to make sure no one threatens me or this society that I help build. Do not test me."

Lea crossed her arms, mirroring Aisling's defensive posture. Could

Katherine do something to her that she wasn't aware of? They had tech here that Leandrea hadn't even known existed until an hour ago. If ReInception could change Leandrea's mind simply by triggering her pleasure centers, what might netting her do?

But she had no other plan; no other bargaining chip. She had to take the risk that even if Katherine could force her to give up the information, she'd be unwilling to do that to her in front of witnesses.

"I know what he went through. And I know what you are to him. But I don't know *who* you are at all. Don't test me, either. If you think I'm doing this just to save your brother, then you don't know me...or him."

Watching Lea, Katherine drummed her fingers on the table for a few moments. The color faded from her face and cheeks, draining down into splotchy blotches on her neck.

"Okay," she finally said. "And if I talk to them—if they won't send your parents here anyhow..."

"There's no reason to start an international incident. They don't have to tell the U.S. what they've done. They can say my parents have escaped; gone missing."

"Your parents are still chipped. And in any event, no one would believe that. Your parents are the most watched people on Earth right now."

"So were you when The Origins extracted you, yet here you are."

Katherine's eyes narrowed, foot tapping on the floor, finger clicking rhythmically on the table, again and again. "There are ways to get you to talk that are not so friendly as my asking."

"So you'd force it out of me? You think your brother would ever forgive you?"

"Yes, I do. He'd understand that some things are more important than any one person. Some things are life and death."

"Katherine—" Aisling stepped forward, but Katherine held up a hand. "Leave it, Sirkka." She turned back toward Lea. "Lucky for you, I'm no monster like Dennison Kelvin. I'll get your parents, but I have conditions."

"Go ahead." Lea crossed her arms over her chest.

"First, I get access to the files and the information on them before anyone else. You and your parents don't leave here until that happens."

"Agreed."

"Second, you tell no one who I am or who my brother is. I get to decide when that happens."

Leandrea thought about arguing this point with her. That was also Ward's choice to make for himself. But she hadn't had the power to stop Katherine from revealing her brother to the world before they met. She had no more power to do so now.

"Okay." Leandrea offered her hand to shake. Ignoring the gesture,Katherine gave her one more look and walked out of the room.

——— ◄O► ———

Day 7: December 17, 2126: Tob Namara

At dusk two days later, a craft swooped down from the sky, skimming across the water and coming to a stop at the entrance to Tob Namara. The vessel bobbed in the water, moving forward and then docking. A wide portal telescoped open and two armed guards wearing burgundy and black uniforms emerged, ion weapons at the ready. The portal closed behind them as one approached Katherine.

It had taken extensive promises to New Zealand by Tob to secure her parent's release—promises that started with Lea and her parents being sent back to New Zealand once Katherine had the files. Other agreements that Lea was not privy to had also been made. Whatever they were, they left Katherine in a sour mood. Leandrea didn't care. She bounced up and down on her toes, eager to see her parents at last.

"Where are the Justuses?" Katherine asked the guards.

"They're on board, your honor. Sorry, we can't let them off the craft until we've searched everyone. "

Katherine reddened, but said nothing, raising her arms over her head. A small bird with a cap of red feathers alit on the ground near her, chirping and cocking its head.

The guard scanned each of them before signaling to his companion. He touched his ear, lips moving as he spoke into a comm device. Moments later, the craft opened again and Lea's parents emerged, holding hands. There was this cliche about how stress aged people, but it had. Lea had never seen her parents looking so worn out. Her mother's hair was loose and tangled, whipping around her face in the sea's wind. Her father had bags under his eyes and he'd lost so much weight. But when they saw Lea, they dropped hands, running towards her and pulling her into an embrace. Leandrea grasped them so hard, she thought her fingers would break. Her chest was tight, all the emotion she'd been suppressing bubbling up into crushing sobs.

"I'm sorry. I'm so sorry!"

They stroked her short hair, shook their heads and told her that, "No, it was okay."

She was twenty years old, but in their arms, she was five again, feeling safe for the first time in weeks.

Breaking the embrace, her mother leaned back, cupping her cheeks and looking her in the eyes. She touched Lea's hair. "Oh, Lea."

"It's okay, mom. I'm okay. But I have so much to tell you. There's so much to do."

Her father squeezed her hand. "We're together now. We'll figure it out, okay?"

Leandrea nodded, biting her lip. She was so relieved not to have to be brave; not to have to make all the decisions. For so many weeks, there had been no one she could trust, no one to talk to. And just as soon as she and Ward had found that in each other, he'd been taken away from her.

She sobbed again, leaning against her parents, letting the tears fall.

When they finally broke their embrace, Katherine approached, reaching out her hand. "Storm. Serafin." They shook her hand. "I'm—"

"Katarina Donovan," Lea's father interrupted. "Of course, we know who you are. You were the first to implement the Skybergs. We've been wanting to see them for years."

"As I've wanted to meet you for years. Your designs will save the world."

Lea's father smiled, glancing at his daughter, and pulling her close. "Thank you. Thank you for arranging for us to get here. I can't tell you—" his voice hitched "—I can't tell you how much it means to us. How worried we were. I can't imagine what this has cost you."

Katherine smiled, the expression not reaching her eyes. "Much as I'm glad you're here, you understand, of course, that this was not an entirely altruistic exchange.

Leandrea's mother kept an arm tight around her, turning to face Kitty. "We'd assumed, but we can't imagine what we have to offer."

"Not you." Katherine pointed her chin toward Lea. "Your daughter. We made a bargain. I'll expect her to uphold it. Soon."

Squeezing her mother's hand, Leandrea faced Kitty. "Is there somewhere I can speak with my parents alone?"

Katherine's mouth turned down in the corners, but she nodded. "I'll give you some more time, but then—"

"I'll keep my promise. Just please—there is so much I need to explain to my parents first."

Katherine stared at her, unblinking. There was so much of Ward in that stare. What would he make of his sister if he could see her now? She thought he would be proud. Unsurprised to see the person he thought so much of rise to such status. But Lea had none of Ward's adoration for Katherine; she wasn't sure what to make of the woman; whether to trust her. Ward was a cynic, eyes more than open to the faults of the world and the people in it. But would he be able to see Kitty clearly? She didn't think so.

"I'll give you a half hour." Katherine turned toward Aisling. "Take them to the gardens."

Aisling hesitated. "Maybe somewhere more—"

"The gardens, Sirkka. They need their privacy."

Aisling drew in a deep breath. "Your honor."

⸺◆⸺

The park was unlike anything Lea'd seen before, even within the domes. Colorful, waxy tropical blooms surrounded fountains and boulders carved into benches. Small pools were filled with tiny neon fish darting in and out through a vibrant coral nursery. Pink flamingoes stood on one leg in ponds, watching them pass with small, black eyes, while bright yellow birds chirped in trees that cast the pathways in shadow. As they passed the pond, turtles slid off branches and into the water, heads peaking just out of the surface and turning to watch them pass.

Aisling led them through the park. "This is a nursery for endangered plants, reefs, and animals. We grow and breed them here and then release or plant them in environments where they can survive."

"Part of your Neo-environmental program," Lea's father said. "I've read about it."

"Controversial," her mother added.

"We understand environmentalists are concerned about releasing species into habitats that aren't native to them, but when their native environments can no longer sustain them, it's that or extinction."

Storm angled his body toward Aisling. "If history has told us nothing else, it's that fooling with mother nature's plans has unforeseen consequences. History is replete with the results of species crossing into new territory and usually, it upsets the balance."

Aisling shrugged. "Your area of expertise, not mine. But our conservationists here would say that the balance is already upset. If we change a species' environment so significantly that they can no longer survive in it, then we have a moral obligation to move them to a place where they can survive."

Leandrea's mother opened her mouth to frame the next part of her retort, but Lea placed a hand on her arm. "There'll be time for this later, but for now—"

"Right, I'm sorry." Lea's mother smiled. "You know how we get."

Leandrea smiled back. It was one of the things she loved most about her parents. Their passion for the environment, their endless energy to try to repair and restore the planet. Growing up, the preaching and arguing was often too much, but in that moment, Lea wished she could listen to it all day. It was hard to believe she'd ever taken these amazing people for granted.

Aisling stopped, gesturing toward a shady area with some benches. A peacock strutted by, trailed by a parade of peachicks. "I'll leave you here for now. I'll be back in a half hour. By then, I suggest you be ready to tell Katherine where the files are."

Leandrea nodded. "I will."

Lea and her parents watched as Aisling disappeared around the bend before leaning toward each other.

"Tell us everything," her mother said.

CHAPTER EIGHTEEN

The working caste will be comprised primarily of soldiers from the losing side of the war who have been subdued through the use of ReInception. This advanced psychological conditioning ensures compliance and reduces the risk of rebellion.

—FROM THE DECLASSIFIED FILES OF THE WHITE HOUSE; SECRETARY OF WAR ARHAN SINGH'S PROPOSAL TO THE CABINET FOR OPERATION PROLE, AUGUST 18, 2056.

Day 6: December 16, 2126: Unknown Location
Ward

The interrogation was wearing them both down. Ward felt it in himself and saw it in Iza. For a while, she'd shown tremendous strength, but hours later, she was doing no better than Ward. She was strong, but she was also old and with all the trauma being a Prole caused a person, but none of the strength that DNA modifications granted younger Prole.

One hour, then two. Then, he lost track. Long enough that he was listing in his seat, and Izabelle barely conscious. Slowly, subtly at first, and then in bigger and bigger strides, the shift took place. Ward didn't even notice it was happening until Izabelle started answering their questions. She started to change her mind.

"Iza, how do you feel about ReInception?"

Ward stirred, lifting his head.

There was a faint brightness in the lower, left-hand part of Iza's brain, and a blinding *zap!* in the top right. Iza twitched.

"I feel..." she hesitated... "I guess I feel good about it?"

The Med moved his hands across the screen. Made an adjustment. Asked again.

"How do you feel about ReInception?"

The brightness in the left corner had faded. Fireworks exploded in the top right.

"It's good. I can see that now."

"And The Origins?"

This time, fireworks on the left.

"I thought it was the right thing to do. Now I see...It was only hurting us."

"Us who?"

"Us The Origins. Us, you. All of us."

"Can you tell me about The Origins? About why you joined?"

Ward straightened in his seat, hands gripping tight at the chair arms, alert now. If being Kallum was Ward's greatest secret, this was Iza's. And in one session, they were extracting it from her. They didn't stand a chance. They never had. His heart throbbed in his back. His muscles tensed.

Izabelle shuttered. "I...I don't..."

The Med made more gestures. The center of Iza's brain lit up.

"Get it off your shoulders, Izabelle. It's such a burden to bear alone. You'll feel so much better."

Iza twitched again. "It's just not something..." She trailed off, her voice monotone, her speech slurred.

The portal telescoped open, and Kelvin walked in, striding toward the Med. "This has taken long enough."

"It's a delicate process. These are the most important things to her. The most private and therefore, buried the deepest. It takes—"

"Yes. It takes time. We've been at this for hours."

"She's strong. Maybe if we continue tom—"

"I'm running out of patience. For both of you. Amp up the pleasure and pain receptors if you have to."

"She's strong, but she's old. I'm not sure what that would do to her."

"Amp them up!" Kelvin smacked his hand on the table. "You think what happens next matters? No! What matters is knowing how much has gotten out there. We are out of time. Do you understand?"

The Med nodded.

"You have ten more minutes and then I'm taking over. You know I'll not be as kind."

The Med nodded again, turning his head to watch as Kelvin stalked out of the room.

Gesturing across the screen, the Med made adjustments. Amping up the feedback, Ward supposed. Izabelle said nothing. Even strapped in, even with his terrible vision, Ward could see how she slumped in the chair.

"Please," he begged, "you'll kill her."

The Med looked at him. "Then tell her to cooperate. If she'll listen to you, tell her that."

Ward swallowed hard, biting at his lip, his heart beating so hard that it hurt to breathe. It wouldn't have mattered what he said to Izabelle a few hours ago, but this weakened version might listen to him. He might be able to convince her to save her life, if not her sanity. But the Izabelle he knew would never forgive him for such weakness. If the roles were reversed, he'd never forgive Izabelle. No. That wasn't true. Izabelle would know better. She'd never relent. Yes, their relationship had been strained. Yes, it had been based on their respective desires and selfishness. But respect was love between them. Respect for each other's strength and mission. Iza would want to fight to her very last breath. Ward would not take that away from her.

He turned away.

"Have it your way." The Med gestured on the screen again. He asked no questions, but snaps and fireworks of light went off all over the image of Iza's brain. She shuddered in her seat. Small moans and gasps came from her. Biting his lip, Ward squeezed his eyes tight. His tears burned like acid.

"Why did you join The Origins?"

Iza groaned. There was a loud "snap!" and she gasped.

Ward looked toward Iza again, hot tears spilling down his face, making his blurry world smear and warp.

"Why did you join The Origins?"

"I dinna' join The Origins."

"She's lying," Kelvin shouted over a speaker. "How is she lying?"

"Please, sir." The Med's voice quavered. "A moment." He cleared his throat. "What do you mean, Izabelle? We've already established that you are a part of it."

"Dinna' join it. Started it."

When Ward and Kitty were living in the tunnels, they would make paper boats out of ancient newspapers or pages of old books they'd found. Sometimes, the boats would float away, downstream and disappear into darkness. Ward would imagine them traveling out of the tunnels and into the ocean. All the way across the world to places where people were kind and parents loved their children just the way they were. But sometimes, the boats didn't make it. They'd fold in on themselves, sinking below the surface and into darkness.

"Explain."

"When I was small, my family was in an internment camp. Me dah was a soldier. They experimented on him…"

Ward crumpled. He sank, all the airing leaving his body. All the fight. His head drooped forward. Iza's voice faded into the background, garbled and droning, her story, The Origins' story, unfolding. A story that she'd told to no one except to him. In the darkness of the library stacks so that they'd share a great secret, she'd taught him about the hidden history of his country, about all the lies he'd been told. About how the world had arrived at a place where there were Prole and parents who changed their children.

It was a gift she'd given him so that he would tell her his story. So that he would tell her what she'd already guessed.

His back was hot and sticky. The pain was returning. It was only a matter of time, and all he wanted to do was sleep.

With Kelvin listening, Iza told the Med how she'd been imprisoned and starved as ReInception honed its technology on POWs on the losing side of the U.S.'s second civil war. How, by the time her father was released, she couldn't even recognize him. Even worse, he didn't recognize her. How the resolve had built in her to do something about it, to form a resistance. She didn't join The Origins; she was The Original.

Finally, they got to the files. To Ward. He raised his head. The tears long gone. Iza long gone.

"What was in the files, Iza?"

She shook her head. "I don't know. I never went to HQ. You can understand why." Her heavy accent had slipped. Faded into the common tongue that she'd been raised with. That she spoke to her college students. The voice of her facade, now her only voice.

The Med turned, looking up toward the observation window where several figures stood. One Ward knew to be Kelvin's. But there were several others: blacks, golds and whites, and three silvers. He wished he could see their faces as they'd listened to Iza's story. He wondered if they'd even known things like that happened; hearing it for the first time, knowing it was a truth that had been hidden from them. To him, it had been a revelation. It had turned his understanding of his world upside down. Them? He wondered if they even cared.

Kelvin's voice came over the speaker. "That can't be right. Press her harder."

The Med didn't even have to prompt her. He didn't even have to use his machine anymore. Iza was theirs.

"I never went to HQ. It would have risked my cover. And we couldn't use any tech to get the information back and forth and risk interception. I know the chips made it to HQ, but I don't know what was recovered. And I don't know where they are. With you after the raid, I'd think."

Kelvin cursed. "Ask her who knows. Ask her where the chips are!"

"You can ask her," the Med said. "She's not going to fight you anymore."

The speaker clicked off, and a gold moved through the observation booth—Kelvin, vanishing from sight, reemerging a few moments later into the room. He stood in front of Iza, arms crossed over his chest.

"Where are the chips? Who knows what's on them?"

Iza shrugged. "I don't know who knows what was on them. You took down the operation before any information got to me."

Kelvin growled in frustration, swinging his hand across a table. Knocking objects off of it and onto the ground.

"After all this time! You know nothing?"

Iza didn't respond.

"Then who does? Who knows?"

Iza's face turned toward Ward. He was drained. Emotionless. A tiny spark in him hoped it was some kind of ruse. Iza knew how to put on a show. Knew how to make people believe her. Maybe this had all been an act, so they'd believe her when these questions finally came. Maybe she was still in there.

His hope crumbled as Iza lifted a finger, pointing at him. "Ward knows."

"How? How does he know? Why him?" Kelvin was shouting now, leaning on Iza's chair, his face just inches from hers.

"Well, he's not just a Ward."

"What do you mean? What do you mean he's not just a Ward?"

"He's a genius." Iza's mouth stretched into that prideful smile of hers. The grandmotherly one that snuck out once in a while when she told people about her boy genius. Like the smile she'd given to Lea the first time they'd all been together.

"Iza. No," Ward whispered.

"He's got as much reason as I to want ReInception gone. Maybe even more."

"Iza, please." But Ward knew it was no good.

"What do you mean? What reason?" Kelvin shook her chair, shouting.

"Well, surely you've figured it out by now, haven't you?"

Kelvin screamed, spit flying from his mouth. "Figured out what? What haven't we figured out?"

"Silly man. It's so obvious. He's Kallum Gordon."

Everything in the room stopped. No one moved. Every face in the room, in the observation window, turned to look at Ward. Instantly, the fatigue was gone. The pain was gone. Blood rushed through his body like a tidal wave, filling his muscles and his veins. It throbbed in his temple. His groin. His back. He was frozen like the rest of them, but not in shock. In the way of a big cat, waiting to pounce. Every fiber in him thrummed, ready.

Kelvin wheeled, striding toward Ward. Grabbing Ward by the chin, he looked at him. Turning his face from side to side. Ward yanked his head away. He shook at his restraints, screaming.

"Meet your monster, Frankenstein!"

Kelvin let go, instinctively stepping back, even with Ward still strapped down. Little Kallum Gordon stood no chance against Dennison Kelvin, but thanks to Kelvin, Ward could snap his neck.

"Impossible." Kelvin squinted at him. Ward was grateful that the man was close enough for Ward to see his face. How the color drained from his skin. The way his hands trembled.

"Remember me?" Ward grinned.

Kelvin's eyes narrowed, nostrils flaring.

Ward remembered that look; this face. Remembered how Kelvin, then a mid-level med tech, had made making Kallum Gordon unrecognizable his pet project. Every time he attached the electrodes that stimulated Kallum's muscle growth so that he'd be turned into a Prole, every operation to scar his fingertips and retinas, to change his eyes color, came with a reminder that no one would ever know who he was again. That everything he'd done, everything he'd lost, was for nothing. Yet here they were.

"What did you think would happen after you discarded me? You changed more than my appearance—you changed me. Really, I should thank you."

Kelvin laughed. "Thank me? Look at you. Your testimony set this company back for decades. *You* almost ruined us, so I ruined you."

"That's what you think, but you didn't!" Ward spat. "And want to know the best part? I wasn't a threat to you at all until you did this to me!" Ward flexed his muscles; shook at his restraints. "Now I'm going to finish what I started. I'm going to take you down."

Ward looked up at the observation room. He couldn't make out her features, but he could see the outline of her purple hair, a hazy cloud around her dark skin. All that mattered was that she was listening...that his assumptions about her were right.

"Did your daughter know what you were doing to a small boy when she was home playing with her toys? Did you think about her while you tortured me?"

Kelvin slapped him, but Ward was beyond feeling. "Was that when you decided, Kelvin? Was that when you decided that you'd never let

ReInception get their hands on her?"

"Get him in the chair!" Kelvin shouted.

Ward leaned forward, veins pulsing in his forehead and arms, teeth gritted. "You can't win. Don't you know that? No matter what you do to me, I win. I get out of here—I take ReInception down—Kallum Gordon did that. You reprogram me? Alter and alter and alter my mind until there's nothing left of me, I still win, because you're the guy who destroyed Kallum Gordon because you were afraid of him—of me. Kill me, you make me a martyr. I win. Every time."

The portal opened and four Prole marched in, wearing the red. No, not Prole. Modified Authority. The kind that showed up in Prole places, lying and trying to blend in. The Prole always knew. It was the way they cut their hair, looked you right in the eyes, rolled up a sleeve. The way, no matter how they looked, they still didn't want to look Prole.

They strode toward Ward, undoing his restraints and yanking him from his chair.

The Med who'd been treating Ward raced over, trying to push the Authority away. "He's not ready! He won't make it."

Kelvin shoved him to the side. "I don't care anymore. Put him in the machine."

Ward kicked, trashing back and forth. "That's your solution for everything, isn't it? Tell her! Tell Andromeda that she's not modified because you know this thing is poison!"

Kelvin punched Ward hard across the jaw. Iron filled his mouth as he laughed, happy for the pain keeping him lucid.

"Have you used it on yourself, Kelvin? Before you knew what it really did, did they use it? Do you stay awake at night wondering when you'll go insane?"

Kelvin spun on his heels, face right in Wards. Spit flying. "The truth—*Ward*—you are going to die the way you lived, with everyone wondering what happened to Kallum Gordon and no one giving a deuce about some anonymous Ward." He turned back toward the authority. "Get her out of the chair. Put him in."

The Authority hesitated, looking at each other. At Ward. "That's right," Ward looked at them. "Kallum Gordon. Make sure you tell all your friends. Or are you going to kill them, too, Kelvin? Because you know you'll have to if you want to keep this silent. You'll have to kill everyone in this room because none of them will be able to resist the urge to tell people what happened to Kallum Gordon. That I was right here, all along. That—"

"No!" Kelvin shouted, smacking Ward across the face again. It only made Ward want to fight harder. He laughed, knowing he was getting to the man. Knowing he was right and that before the day was done, he'd be all over the news again.

The Authority dragged Ward toward Iza, her face finally coming into focus. Tears poured down her cheeks. He'd never seen her cry, and the sight of it was ice in his blood.

The work on her mind, done, they released her restraints. She was pushing herself out of the chair that they were about to force Ward into.

"Stop, please, stop." She reached for Ward. "Please. You don't need to hurt him." They released her other arm, and she stretched toward him, thin, strong muscles like metal cable under paper-thin skin. "Please. Don't hurt him. I know how to get him to cooperate."

She walked toward Kelvin in choppy, unsteady steps.

His face was red, eyes bulging, pulse throbbing in his temple. She smiled up at him, like she couldn't even see it. She put a hand on his arm. Squeezed and patted like he was a beloved grandson.

"You don't need to do this at all. Just give him what he wants."

Kelvin's eyes didn't leave Ward's. "And what's that? What does he want?"

"That's easy. He wants his sister."

CHAPTER NINETEEN

Psychological Warfare in the War of Coastal Incursion and the Rise of The Origins

Disinformation Campaigns: Both factions used ReInception to spread disinformation, creating false memories of enemy atrocities and undermining trust. This lead to increased paranoia and hostility between communities.

De-radicalization: Attempts were made to capture and reprogram enemy combatants and sympathizers. The hope was that by erasing extremist views and implanting more moderate perspectives, the opposing side's resolve would weaken.

The unpredictable outcomes from ReInception's use at that time had unforseen consequences not just to POWs, but also to their surviving family members.

—EXCERPT OF SENIOR THESIS BY AMALIE THAKOR,
UNIVERSITY OF DELHI

Day 7: December 17, 2126: Tob Namara
Leandrea

Leandrea scanned her surroundings, looking for hidden surveillance devices. The U.S. didn't need outside surveillance—the technology was embedded in its entire population. For so long, Leandrea had trusted that the government only used that technology to surveil its population when they had reasonable cause—in accordance with the law—but now she knew better. It was remarkable how quickly and completely she'd become a suspicious person.

Lea's comm chip was no longer active, and she wasn't netted, but there were thousands of ways Katherine could eavesdrop on Lea's discussion with her parents. The bench, the rock, the trees, satellites...this park was a false narrative intended to make Lea believe she had privacy. She knew better.

Apparently, so did her parents. Her mother followed her, "Tell us everything," with a finger to her lips that she attempted to disguise by scratching her face. Lea gave a small nod. They could be seen, too—cameras as small as flower stamen could be all around them, zooming in to watch their every move. Leandrea would share nothing with her parents that she didn't also want Katherine to know. But now that they were here, she wasn't sure she still needed to hide much from Katherine. She and Ward's sister had the same goal—eliminate ReInception. She'd let Katherine use her connections to share the information with the outside world. Smarter people than her, people with power, would decide what to do next. So long as rescuing Ward and the other Origins was part of what Katherine bargained for, Leandrea would know she'd done everything she could.

Leandrea sat between her parents, one of their hands clasped in each of hers. Staring down at her lap, she squeezed, trying to think of where to begin.

She closed her eyes and took several deep breaths. "So much has happened in the last few weeks. I'm not sure where to begin. There was a bombing. We ran. We got separated in the crowd. Ward helped me when I was lost—kept me safe until the freeze was lifted, and then walked me back to a pod. Just as we were parting ways, he told me that The Origins would be blamed for the bombing and that they didn't do it. That they were being framed by ReInception. For some reason, I believed him."

Lea continued her story, telling them again about how Hallyn had been modified by his parents; how they took away his beliefs. She told them how, in desperation, she sought Ward. How that led her down the path to learning more about The Origins, to feeling like she had to help them. So she conspired with Ward to use Andromeda to get to Dennison Kelvin's files.

She explained how Aisling was pursuing them and they had to run. When she got to the part about Ward almost dying at the hands of Ferryman and how she saved him, her mother gasped, covering her face and her father sobbed. But they didn't interrupt. They didn't stop her until she reached the end of her story...well, almost the end.

"There's something else you need to know."

Leandrea's parents were pale. They looked worn and exhausted. Not knowing what had happened to her had aged them in the previous few weeks. Knowing was breaking them.

"Just before the raid on The Origins, right before Ward underwent surgery, he told me something. He told me he's Kallum Gordon."

Her parents froze. "What?" Her mother covered her mouth with a shaking hand. "But how?"

Her father moved closer to her. "Are you sure?"

Lea told Ward's story. How Aisling had been looking for him all along.

Lea's father shook his head. "This is just incredible. I understand why Ward...Kallum...hid who he was. But why would Katherine keep it a secret from the world all these years?"

Leandrea shook her head. "I don't know. Maybe she doesn't want that pressure. Maybe she wants the anonymity."

"But that doesn't make sense." Storm scratched his chin. "Her name has power. She could have used it for—"

"Political gain? Clearly she has." Leandrea gestured around her. "You don't think she built all this without leveraging her name?"

"But she could have done so much more—"

"Tried to free her brother, for starters," Lea's mother added.

"I don't know. All questions I haven't had a chance to ask her yet."

"Well, based on her reputation, I'm sure it's intentional and I'm sure she has a plan," Lea's mother said.

Leandrea nodded. "I'm sure she does. Which is why we need a plan, too. These files are the most valuable thing on the planet right now. I'm not giving them up without knowing what she'll do with them and without my own demands being met."

Lea's father narrowed his eyes and pursed his lips, shaking his head slightly. Leandrea knew he was trying to warn her not to say too much, but did it matter whether she said it now, under surveillance, or later, to Katherine's face? The demands would be the same. Her parents could help her with the nuances and details, with things she might not be thinking about, but the big picture was clear. It would not surprise a shrewd politician like Katherine.

"Okay," her mother said. "So what is it you expect her to do?"

"Tob Namara is a sea city—it's powerful for its size, but it's too small to tip the scales. First, we need alignment on where the files will be shared. We need to make sure there's a plan for the release that will ensure the safety of the Prole.

"Second, we need assurances that any bargains made with the U.S. government and ReInception include the safe release of The Origins and Ward."

Leandrea's mother opened her mouth to speak, but Lea held a hand up.

"It's not just because of how I feel about him. That's Kallum Gordon they are holding captive. That name is power. He can't be modified and then used for the ReInception cause."

Her parents glanced at each other but said nothing. A small bird chirped in a tree.

"Which brings me to my third requirement. Katherine's government has developed the technology to reverse ReInception. I will not tell her anything about the contents or whereabouts of the files until she has given us that technology."

Leandrea's mother had taken a sustenance bar from a pocket and was breaking it into small pieces, popping some in her mouth and dropping other bits to the ground. The small bird swooped down, hopping around the crumbs and pecking at them, but not eating.

Tossing another crumb to the ground, her mother said, "You know she has ways to get you to tell her without your agreement."

"Of course, but I'm Leandrea Justus. That name has power now, too. And you're here, and Vella and Aisling. Is she going to coerce me in front of all of you?"

"If she has to, yes." her mother said.

Leandrea turned toward her mother. "She won't have to. What am I going to do with this information? She's right about me. I'm naïve. I've no experience in politics. Someone like her must ensure that these files get into the right hands. All I'm asking is for some concessions in return."

Leandrea's father nodded. "Well, let's just hope she's as rational as she paints herself to be."

There was a distant sound of feet crunching on gravel. A few moments later, Aisling and Vella approached. Vella had changed into one of the loose, flowing costumes preferred by Tob Namarans. The style was similar across the population, signaling sustainability requirements, but it came in every color imaginable. There were no rules about who could wear which. Vella looked cool and comfortable in a pale turquoise that complimented their purple hair.

Seeing Leandrea look at the clothing, Vella gave a half-grin. "You kenna' imagine how good it feels to be out of that jumpsuit."

Leandrea smiled. She'd worn more than a few Prole jumpsuits in the last few weeks. They looked the same as what the upper caste wore, but the fabric was heavier and it wasn't temperature regulated like the upper caste version. She had only worn it in winter, but imagined in summer, it was stifling.

"Well, it suits you." Lea reached out, touching the fabric and running it between her fingers. It was soft and light, perfect for the tropical climate.

"Feels like freedom." Vella turned toward Leandrea's parents. "I'm Vella. Leandrea's..." Vella paused, her eyes meeting Leandrea's for a moment and then turning back toward Storm and Serafin. "Lea's friend."

It would have been an overstatement a couple of weeks earlier. They were barely acquaintances and Lea had been a massive nuisance to Vella. But after what they'd been through together, after all the risks Vella had taken to save her and Ward...

"More than a friend," Leandrea finished. "Vella saved my life—more than once."

Vella blushed. "May be that's a scanty overstatement—"

"It's not." Leandrea turned toward her parents and Aisling. "When Ward and I were fleeing from..." Leandrea glanced at Aisling. She'd just explained to her parents everything that had happened and that she'd thought Aisling was her tormentor. She'd told them about Ferryman, but not that Vella had given her the knife she'd used to kill him. The speed at which the pendulum of her life had swung back and forth the last few weeks, how her relationships to people had shifted—it was beyond chaotic. It was disorienting. Her most trusted companion, Hallyn, was someone who she could no longer trust. Aisling, who'd been pursuing her mercilessly, had rescued her from capture. Vella, who'd seen her as nothing but a spoiled Uni inconvenience, helped her escape capture not once, but twice.

"Well, it's more complicated than I can sum up. But it's not an overstatement." She looked between Aisling and Vella. "Both of you. Both of you saved me. And I can't thank you enough."

Aisling bit her lip, twisting her mouth into an expression that Leandrea couldn't quite read. She glanced away and Leandrea thought she was fighting back tears.

Vella, still blushing, patted Leandrea's arm awkwardly. "Well then. That's enough of that. You saved my boy. I saved you. I guess that makes us all family."

"I guess it does," Leandrea smiled at Vella—so strong, so beautiful. At home, Vella was persecuted as a Prole. An outlier for being agendered—not forbidden to non-Prole, but something she'd always thought was uncommon to the upper caste. Something she now understood many upper caste parents were programming out of their children. Here, Vella was free for the first time in their life. She couldn't imagine what it must feel like.

Aisling ran a hand through her short, black hair, still refusing to meet Lea's eyes. "We have to go back now. Kat's waiting."

Leandrea nodded, grabbing her parents by the hands. "Let's do this."

CHAPTER TWENTY

WHEREAS, *the caste system was established as a means of reallocating resources and responsibilities to United States Citizens in accordance with affiliation during the War of Coastal Incursion, and*

WHEREAS, *convicted felons of any caste pose a significant risk to the stability of society, and*

WHEREAS, *the Prole system provides a means for those who have behaved or acted in a manner detrimental to society to make amends for their transgressions,*

NOW, THEREFORE, *the Prole Reassignment Act will be adopted into the laws of the United States, and all non-Prole felony offenders convicted from this date forward will be subject to its rule whereby, upon conviction, they will be recategorized as "Fallen," and recast as Prole.*

—THE PROLE REASSIGNMENT ACT OF 2075

S lowly, eyes turning before chin, Kelvin rotated his head toward Iza.

"What did you say?"

"If you just tell him where his sister is, he'll cooperate and we can all go home."

"What are you talking about?"

"She's alive."

Energy, like electricity, surged through Ward. His mind prickled as he looked toward Iza, too. What trick was this? Had the ReInception not worked on her? Was she trying to buy time?

Kelvin cocked his head to the side. His face was expressionless and placid, his voice, too calm. Ward shivered; the small boy inside him whimpered. He knew that voice. He knew that look. It's how Kelvin behaved when the worst was about to come. "Where?"

Iza looked, not at Kelvin, but at Ward. Her voice, usually sharp as a pin, was soft and grandmotherly. "I'm sorry I didn't tell you. I thought it was for your own good."

Ward slid his jaw forward, bottom teeth over top, jaw muscles flexing. This couldn't be real. "Iza. What are you talking about?" he echoed Kelvin's words.

Izabelle took small, stuttering steps toward Ward, holding onto the arm of one of the Authority to steady herself until she stood in front of him. Authority still held him by the arms, but their grips had loosened. Like everyone else in the room, they were frozen, breaths held as shocking revelation after revelation was made.

Standing in front of Ward, Izabelle grabbed both his arms, looking up at him. With her head tipped back and her eyes wide, Ward saw in her the girl she'd once been, like they'd not simply changed her mind, but regressed it so she was now a child stuck in an old woman's body.

"What are you talking about?" he asked again.

Again, the tears in her always-before dry eyes. "She's not who you think, Kallum. She's not the sister you knew anymore."

Ward stared, trying to see into Iza's soul. He'd been with her so long, knew how to read her signs and hints. The silent communication between them had always been seamless, but now...She wasn't his Iza anymore. He couldn't read her. He knew he should stop asking questions, but what did it matter? She'd say what she wanted to say. And he had to know.

"Iza. Tell me what you mean."

Iza turned toward Kelvin. "I need to sit. Can I sit?"

Kelvin snapped his fingers at one of the Authority, gesturing toward a chair. The man stepped away from Ward to get it and then carried it to Izabelle. She lowered herself down, letting out a small moan. Shaking her head, she looked down at her hands. "I'm so tired. Too old for this."

Ward still couldn't understand. Was this a ruse? No. It wasn't. He'd watched what they'd done to her. Watched her change. He had to let go of that hope.

Sighing, Iza squeezed her hands together. Her knuckles were thick and knotted. Painful in a way that wasn't necessary. They wouldn't be like that if she weren't Prole. They'd had the medical technology to cure all her ailments for decades, fixes that cost the government next to nothing, but that they withheld from the Prole—because they could. Just so the Prole would suffer, die, recycle.

"The day your sister left you in the tunnels to get food, the Authority captured her. The Origins were a fledgling organization, but already, we'd infiltrated the Authority. When we found out they had Katherine, and when they were taking her from the grid to ReInception, we intercepted the transport and took her."

Ward's heart pounded in his temples, his eyes. He clasped his hands together, squeezing so tight, his knuckles cracked.

"She begged to go back for you." Iza nodded to herself. "Yes, back then, it was all she wanted. You should know that. I know it's all you ever wanted to hear, and it's true. She was desperate to get back to you. You were young. Alone. Afraid. Sick with hunger. But we couldn't risk losing her—so we promised her we'd find you."

Ward had always known Iza had been hiding things from him, just as he'd been hiding things from her. But he'd never imagined that all this time, she'd hidden from him the one thing he'd wanted to know. He'd given everything to her and she'd kept this from him. Why?

"We did go back for you, but it'd been five days from when she was captured to when we were able to get her. Another two to convince her to tell us where you were and that we'd find you. By the time we got to the tunnel, you were gone. When I found you again—" Iza took a shuddering breath "—when you came to me saying you wanted to join The Origins, at first, I didn't know it was you, of course."

For a moment, Iza's eyes closed, and she swayed in her seat. Kelvin patted her face sharply. "Izabelle. Where is Katherine?"

Ignoring Kelvin, Iza looked at Ward. Her eyes were red and swollen. They had a far-away, foggy look. "My boy. My sweet boy. The years were not good to her. What they did didn't just affect her mind, it affected her soul. There are things she's planning—"

Izabelle shuddered, inhaling sharply. Her hand went to her chest. "There are things, Ward, that I would break your heart to tell you. I was waiting until..." she trailed off "...until..."

Kelvin grabbed her arm, shaking. "Where is she Izabelle?"

Izabelle froze, staring at Ward. Her mouth hung open, but no words came out. Her left hand tightened on her jumpsuit, scrunching the fabric. Her eyelids fluttered and her body convulsed.

The Med ran over, scanning her. "She's having a stroke." He looked up at the Authority standing next to Ward. "Help me lay her down!"

The Authority looked to the Med. Looked to Kelvin.

Izabelle entire body shook, arms and legs kicking, eyes rolling back in her head.

"Help me," the Med shouted. "Now, or she'll die!"

They let go of Ward's arms, racing to help the Med, each grabbing one of Izabelle's limbs and holding her down while the Med scanned her.

Wards looked at Kelvin and their eyes met. Ward watching his face transform—the slackening of jaw, the widening of eyes, as Kelvin realized the mistake.

"No!" Kelvin lurched forward. "Don't take your hands off him!"

But it was too late.

Ward grinned.

The lights went out.

Ward leapt toward Kelvin, but the space in front of him was empty.

"Coward!" Ward shouted. "Where are you?"

Hands grabbed at Ward, but he roared, shaking them off.

Shouts came from every direction. The sounds of running feet. And then hands were around his biceps. Small, weak, hands. Ward shook them off, but they just grabbed at him again.

"Get off of me," he bellowed. Then, a voice in his ear. A hot, harsh whisper. "Stop fighting me, Gondu. I'm getting you out of here."

Ward froze. "Andromeda?"

"Do you want to die you fleshhead? Now!"

She clasped Ward's hand and pulled. He followed, trying to process what was happening. It was either another trick or she was helping him. He thought it was the latter—he must have gotten through to her. It was a chance, his only chance. He was Paul and the cops were outside Annie's house...he just had to stay alive long enough for them to help him.

Andromeda pushed Ward against a wall. "Don't move," she hissed.

He heard her tapping something. A control box lit up. The portal began to open, letting light in. Kelvin's voice came from across the room. "Andromeda? What are you doing?"

"Now!" Andromeda shouted, grabbing Ward's hand and pulling him toward the opening. The panels were still moving apart. She squeezed past, but Ward was too big to get through the small space.

"Hurry!" she pulled at him.

He waited another second as the doors continued to move apart. The Authority and Kelvin were running toward him. They were almost there. Taking a deep breath, he forced himself through the door, his back scraping against the metal, skin tearing again. Slick blood lubricated the passage and Ward slipped through. As soon as he was clear, Andromeda started tapping at the control pad. Shapes moved toward them, coming into focus as they came closer. Kelvin was screaming at the Authority: "Stop them!"

A small figure with long black hair and wearing the silver, moved in front of Ward, blocking the entrance.

Legs braced, arm stretched out in front of her, weapon at the ready, she looked fearsome despite her small size. "Go!" she shouted, "I'll cover."

Kammeo? Ward had believed he had a chance of swaying Andromeda, but not her friend. Kammeo was a ReInception zealot. Why was she helping him?

The portal began closing again as Kammeo pointed her pulse gun toward the approaching figures and fired. Light zigzagged out of the weapon, spreading to hit the approaching Authority and Kelvin, dropping them to their knees.

"Let's go!"

Ward glanced at Andromeda. There were goggles over her eyes.

Kammeo wore them, too—something that had allowed them to see in the dark. Andromeda grabbed Ward's arm, pulling him down the hallway. He slipped, almost losing his footing. Looking down, he saw blood. Felt the dampness on his back. His vision contracted.

Andromeda followed his gaze. "Later. Got it?"

Ward nodded but felt his mind getting fuzzy. He'd been bedridden for days. He'd lost weight. Muscle. Blood faster than it could be replaced. He'd been awake for hours and hours. Maybe days. He wasn't sure how far he had to go to escape; how long he could hang on.

Andromeda pulled him along as the door closed behind them. He heard Kammeo's footsteps behind them as they hurried down the narrow, rounded corridor.

"What is this place?" he asked.

Andromeda kept moving. "You'll see soon enough."

Reaching the end of the corridor, they turned left, ducking through another low, narrow opening.

They encountered no one else—no other Authority, medics or ReInception workers. It didn't make sense.

The walls were a dark gray metal. Everything was low and narrow. Ward was beginning to understand. They reached the end of the corridor. In front of them was a narrow ladder. Andromeda climbed, Ward following close behind. Above her, there was a panel in the ceiling. She knocked on it several times and then Ward heard a creaking, groaning sound.

There was noise down the hallway. The sounds of running feet.

"Hurry!" Kammeo urged. "They're coming."

Andromeda was breathing hard. "Almost there. Hold them off if you have to."

The panel above them opened, and Ward saw the orb of a face appear and vanish. "Hup! Hup!"

"Sebbe?" Could it possibly be him? Hope, fleeting and unfamiliar, thumped in Ward's chest.

Andromeda climbed the ladder the rest of the way and then vanished over the edge. Ward followed, his head spinning, his grip slipping. Kammeo pushed him upwards; her hands, tiny and weak on his once-strong muscles. Still, the small boost helped. They were risking their lives for him. He had to get them out of here. Cresting the top, he again squeezed through an opening too small for him, gritting his teeth and stifling a scream as his raw back, slick with blood, scraped against metal again. And then he was free, over the edge and in a set of strong, familiar arms.

Sebbe's cheeks were damp with tears. "I got you m'boy."

Ward collapsed against Sebbe, the large man wrapping an arm around Ward's shoulders. Andromeda reached a hand down, hoisting Kammeo out of the opening. The two women heaved the porthole door, closing it, clamping it shut. They wedged a bar into the handle just in time to stop the men below from opening it again. There was banging on the door, muffled shouts.

Ward looked around him. He was on the deck of a boat. Something old and steel. Surrounding him were dark, choppy waters.

Andromeda pulled up her visor, so it rested on top of her head. She squinted against the water's spray.

"It won't hold them long. We've got to go."

Sebbe gestured toward the side of the ship where a ladder swung and shifted.

Andromeda held a hand up to her forehead, looking down over the edge, then back at Ward, brow furrowed. "I don't think he can make it."

"He'll make it, sure, sure." Sebbe looked at Ward, brows drawn together in concern. "Won't you m'boy?"

Ward nodded. "I'll make it."

Andromeda looked at him once more and then nodded. "You first," she told Sebbe. "You're the strongest. You help him. Kam and I will follow."

Sebbe nodded, letting Andromeda move in to support Ward as he stepped away, throwing a leg over the railing, catching the ladder and climbing down.

Ward leaned hard against Andromeda, feeling her sag momentarily under his weight and then straighten back up. She was strong, stronger than Lea. And maybe almost as brave.

Ward looked at her and Kammeo. "Thank you."

The pounding on the hatch got louder, and then there was the whir of a machine. A bright red line started to glow in the metal.

Kammeo's eyes widened. "Don't thank us yet."

Letting go of Andromeda, Ward moved toward the railing. Lifting his leg to get over the side, he let out a muffled cry.

"You're sure you can do this?"

Looking up at Andromeda, Ward nodded. "Not much choice, is there?"

Andromeda shook her head. "Just hang on. Just a while longer."

Ward nodded and began to descend. Each movement of his arms was agony. Every pull on his back sent the darkness in closer around him. Then, he felt strong hands on his feet, then his calves, around his knees. He reached the bottom and collapsed just as the darkness closed in and the world and the pain vanished.

CHAPTER TWENTY-ONE

While the rest of the world competes for resources and fights the uphill battle to repair damage already done, Tob Namara will be a model for how floating nations can restore the environment, enrich, rather than exploit, its populations, be havens from disease, and free humanity from politicians.

—VIVIAN WILSON, FOUNDER OF
THE TOB NAMARA PROJECT, 2091

Day 7 - 8: December 17 - 18, 2126: Tob Namara
Leandrea

Katherine sat at one end of a long, oval table, a visored security guard behind her. Five other people who Lea didn't recognize flanked Katherine, with Aisling taking the empty seat to her left.

The translucent glass behind Katherine revealed a kelp forest; caustic light dappled on seaweed. Leandrea stared past fish darting in and out of coral and clusters of mussels in nurseries, into the blackness of the sea beyond. The sun had long since set, but this wonder was lit with ambient lights shining down from the city. Leandrea couldn't take her eyes off of it.

The thick glass aquarium walls were built to impress, and they did. Aisling assured Leandrea that there was little to see from the rest of the sub-surface structures that extended below them for over 300 meters—submerged hanging skyscrapers made of pressure-resistant metals and cement descending deep into the blackness—but Leandrea still wished she could explore the whole thing. To be underwater, yet unable to drown...

Her mom squeezed her arm. "You okay?"

Leandrea nodded. The water she knew was impenetrably dark—oceans choked with noxious seaweed and lakes, over-warm and algae-coated. This water was clear and alive; more shades of blue than she could possibly have imagined, with phosphorescent pools glowing all around the city at night.

Tob Namara was a wonder.

"It could all be like this," her mother whispered. "It would be so easy."

"Sit, please." Katherine gestured toward the empty chairs. She smiled at Lea and her parents. "If you wish, you can stay for the rest of your lives. Help us realize this city's full potential. Let it continue to serve as a model for peace and progress."

Leandrea settled in next to her parents, Vella sitting to her right. She imagined what it would be like to live here, to bring Ward here with her to this place without Prole. It was not so long ago that he'd told her they could never be. That life for them would be a life of fugitives. A place like this had seemed impossible—one that made its own rules, that made the world better instead of worse. If he wasn't back there, captured and with who knows what being done to him, the temptation to abandon the fight and stay here might be too much to resist.

Katherine gestured to the room.

"This is my cabinet—all my trusted advisors. They know everything."

Vella raised an eyebrow. "Everything."

Katherine nodded. "You can say anything in front of them—I'd be sharing it with them anyhow."

Leandrea looked at the group. They all looked older than Katherine, even if they didn't have to. It was a purposeful decision about physical modification. A decision to look more mature; one that made people feel more comfortable and secure in their leadership.

"These are the people who founded and built Tob." Katherine looked at them, smiling. "They are the true leaders of this place. They trust me to put a face on it—to let the world know what progress looks like and how the world could be, but they and not I are the true geniuses behind Tob."

The cabinet acknowledged her speech with tight smiles and nods—their faces frustratingly inscrutable.

Katherine tapped the table with her index finger. "Okay then. To business now. You have demands?"

Swallowing, Leandrea nodded. The word made her squirm. She'd never been in the position to demand much of anything. But Ward's life was on the line because of the files. She wouldn't squander them.

"I do. But I'm sure you'll find them acceptable."

Katherine made a "go on" gesture with a hand and then crossed her arms in front of her on the table.

"First, I need to know where you intend to share the files. I need to be sure that they will go to a government that is anti-ReInception and sympathetic to the Prole, but not against the populace. This is about equity, not overturn."

Leandrea waited for a response. Hearing none, she continued.

"Next, part of any negotiation for the files must include the release of Ward and any other Origins held captive. Before the files are released, they must be freed to a neutral zone—here, Iceland, New Zealand, I don't care. So long as it's a place where Prole are illegal and they'll be protected. You cannot reveal Ward's identity—not without his permission. He wouldn't want that."

Katherine's mouth tightened, and her eye twitched, but she said nothing.

"My parents and I will be sent to New Zealand. You will retain the original files, but you will provide us with a full copy, and we will verify you've done so before we leave."

One of Katherine's advisors opened their mouth to object, but Katherine put a hand on theirs, stopping them.

"Continue."

"My last demand is that you will provide me with your process for reversing ReInception. The process, the technology, all of it. You will share it with the world, and you will not charge for or profit from sharing that information. You will do it for free—as a service to the greater good."

Another of Katherine's advisors started to speak. Again, Katherine stopped them.

"Your terms are acceptable."

"What?" A man to Katherine's right stood up, his face turning red. "Kata—"

"I said the terms are acceptable." Katherine spoke through clenched teeth. "Sit down."

The color on the man's face deepened, but he sat.

Leandrea looked at her parents and then back at Katherine. "Really? Just like that?"

"Just like that." Katherine smiled. "Your demands are more than reasonable, and mostly what I would have done regardless."

"Okay." Leandrea felt uncertain. Something seemed unfinished. Should she have asked for more? But no, her demands were reasonable, and they wanted to accomplish the same things. Why shouldn't it be this easy? For the first time in weeks, she felt hopeful. She smiled. "Okay! We'll work out the details—"

"The details are simple. I'll review the content of the files and then broadcast them, first to the leaders of all mod-free countries and then to the world. I will reveal who I am. I will demand the release of my brother and the other captives—"

Leandrea's father gave a light snort. "You don't actually believe it will be that easy, do you?"

"Easy?" Katherine raised an eyebrow. "No. Not easy. But we have the technology to broadcast directly to the American people. They will know who I am. They will hear what the government is doing. From there, negotiations will begin because the U.S. will have no choice. They will start with the release of the Origins. It will take time, diplomacy. Change cannot happen overnight. But it will be a start."

Her instinct was to go back to New York. To do something brave and epic like a hero in the storybooks to save the Origins and the Prole. But what could she really do? She wasn't a soldier or a politician. She hadn't even studied politics in school. She was an art history major for flood's sake.

The sooner things moved ahead, the sooner Ward would be freed. The sooner change could begin. She had to leave the negotiations to the professionals. She'd go with her parents to New Zealand. Kitty would negotiate for the release of Ward and the rest of the Origins and if she didn't, then Leandrea would take matters into her own hands. What that meant, she wasn't sure, but she had faith that Kitty would use her power to free her brother. If she had half the devotion to Ward that Ward had for her...

"Mom? Dad?" Leandrea's parents looked worried. Their matching furrowed brows told her they weren't sure what to make of this quick concession, either. Her father gave her a slight shrug. Her mother put a hand on her shoulder.

"Before we go, we want to understand what the files reveal and what that means to you. Not just your basic plan, but your plan with that knowledge in mind—"

"Agreed," Katherine smiled again. "Besides, you have worked for the government your entire adult lives. I could use your counsel. And we'll begin right now." Leaning forward, she reached across the table for Leandrea's hand and shook it. "You should be proud of yourself, Leandrea. You've shown bravery and compassion beyond what anyone could have possibly expected. I've got this now. Okay?"

Leandrea watched the woman for any signs of deceit, but she held Lea's gaze. The world had hardened Katherine Vega. She was strong. She had an army—small, but the most advanced in the world—and a small but powerful and progressive nation behind her. As soon as she announced herself, the whole world would be behind her and her brother. This was the right thing to do.

Withdrawing her hand, Leandrea rubbed her side in the place where Ward had hidden the chips. She'd guarded this secret with everything—she would have died for it. Tob Namara was a city that stood for everything the world could be. It was repairing the environment. Its citizens had equality—they were peaceful and industrious. If not here, with these people, if not with Ward's sister, then where?

Leandrea nodded. She raised the hem of her ivory blouse. It was light as air. Turning sideways, she touched the tiny red mark where Ward had made his incision. "Here they are. They were here all along."

As Katherine inserted the chips into a data hub, Leandrea's stomach clenched. She clasped her hands in front of her on the table, squeezing. She and Ward hadn't had a chance to see what the files contained before they had to flee. They only knew what little Ward was able to view as the files transferred, like that Andromeda was not modified.

This wouldn't have made Kelvin look very good, but it wasn't the explosive smoking gun they needed to topple an entire social structure. Lea was about to find out if everything they'd sacrificed was worth it.

Katherine put on her visor, netting herself into the computer, and began scanning the files. Katherine's embedded tech allowed her to review the thousands of documents that Leandrea and Ward had stolen, scanning for the relevant information. Katherine's team waited patiently, used to this technology and methodology, but Leandrea looked at her parents, worried. It would have taken days, maybe even weeks, for them to go through everything that was there. It would take Katherine only minutes, but that also meant that Katherine could pick and choose what she wanted the rest of them to see. It wasn't lost on Lea that the rest of Katherine's advisors also waited when they could have been reviewing the files simultaneously.

She had to stop second-guessing everything. They'd have a copy of the files; that was the agreement. They'd be able to review everything at their own pace later on. Yet that would be too late to have a meaningful say in whatever Katherine was planning.

The flashing images on the screen paused on a boy strapped to a chair, probes inserted into his muscles. Leandrea recognized him immediately; Kallum, when he was young. He looked much the way he had in the famous vids of him at the trial. Thinner and maybe a little taller, but there was no mistaking who he was. To his right was the man performing the procedure. He looked familiar. Leandrea squinted and then her eyes went wide as recognition dawned. It was Andromeda's father, Dennison Kelvin. He was younger, but Leandrea was certain it was him. There was no audio, but there was no mistaking what these were: these were recordings of Kelvin turning Ward into a Prole. Leandrea glanced at

Katherine. She was trembling, her mouth tight and her hands gripping the table. And then the image vanished from the screen.

Leandrea's eyes shifted from side to side as she tried to process what she'd just seen. Kelvin had modified Ward? And then, years later, Ward had pursued Kelvin to extract this data. It couldn't be a coincidence. Ward must have known. Yet he'd never mentioned it. He'd always made it seem like encountering Andromeda at the bar the night they'd met was a coincidence that he'd capitalized on. Maybe that was true. But why hadn't he told her about Kelvin? Was it possible that Ward hadn't connected the powerful head of Prole modification with the man who'd tortured him? If it was anyone but Ward, she'd think it was possible. He'd been young and afraid; on the verge of starvation. Alone. Maybe Kelvin hadn't identified himself at the time or had used a different name. Yes, anyone but Ward might have failed to make the connection, but this wasn't someone else. It was him. Ward had eidetic memory....

Katherine was frozen in her seat, no images scanning across the vid screen—just blank, white space. Aisling reached over, touching her arm, but Katherine shook her off. As shocking as this had been for Leandrea to see, she could only imagine what it was like for Katherine. How guilty she must feel. What an invasion of privacy it must have felt like to have everyone witness her brother's torture and modification at the same time she did. This is what leaving him behind had cost him. Even if it wasn't her fault, it must have felt like it.

For a moment, the room was still and there was only the sound of Katherine's breathing, fast and urgent. Then, the images and documents began flashing past again.

Leandrea continued watching, but too shocked to focus on anything but what she'd seen. Ward had targeted Kelvin long before that day at the West End; Leandrea was sure of it. Why hadn't he told her? Why hold this back?

The images froze again. This time on something labeled "Canis Fidelis." Leandrea could only pick up bits and pieces as Katherine skimmed through. She flashed by images Lea recognized as related to the chips the government had begun implanting in Prole about ten years earlier. Ward's was inserted when he became a ward—after his identity as Kallum Gordon was erased, when ReInception no longer knew who he was. It was the thing they'd just removed from him before he was captured.

"Stop!" Leandrea said. "What is this?"

Katherine paused, the image on the screen freezing. She pursed her lips. "It's..." she hesitated, files moving past again and then back to the image; a blueprint for the device.

"The device. What are their plans for it?"

There was quiet again for a few moments and then Katherine removed her visor, placing it on the table in front of her. She looked at Leandrea.

"Some of these files are incomplete, but what you and Kallum managed to extract is priceless. You're heroes. It will take a long time to fully analyze what we have here, but I've tagged and highlighted several items that I want my cabinet to focus on first. This will be enough—enough for us to expose ReInception and the U.S. Government. Enough, maybe, to free the Prole."

A cheer went up in the room, but Katherine had ignored her question.

"But this last piece...the device. Your brother almost died getting that removed. For all we know..." Leandrea inhaled a shaking breath. "For all we know...." She couldn't finish.

Katherine blinked a few times, but her face remained carefully neutral. Leandrea thought she would have had some reaction to the implication, but she was more than just a big sister now; she was a politician. It behooved Lea to remember that.

"There is much we'll need to analyze, but as far as I can tell, it's a device they can use for remote activation."

"We knew that already. Ward...Kallum had seen as much when he did the transfer. Does this tell you more? The what? The when?"

Katherine held her gaze. "No. No specifics. At least not that I absorbed this quickly."

"But 'Canis Fidelis'...faithful dog. What do they mean by that?"

"Kallum didn't tell you anything about it?"

"I don't think Kallum knew about it. I don't think he saw it. Like I said, he was in a rush."

"Or maybe he just didn't want you to know about it."

Leandrea thought about everything Ward had told her...all the intimate details of their lives that they'd shared. Then she thought about all the things he hadn't told her, like about Dennison Kelvin. Was he embarrassed? Did he think it showed weakness? Was he hiding more than she knew?

Katherine sighed, looking sympathetic. "I'm sure it's nothing. I'm sure it's just that he was embarrassed for you to know what ReInception had planned for him. It doesn't matter, really. It didn't happen."

"What didn't happen?"

"They didn't turn him into the faithful dog. This was about him, Leandrea. Their plans to turn Kallum Gordon into their faithful dog. Their mouthpiece."

Lea shook her head. "I don't understand. Kelvin erased his identity. The plan was that no one ever know who he was."

Katherine shrugged. "Maybe the explanation is in the lost data. Maybe they changed their plans or Kelvin went rogue. I don't know. All I know is that they'd intended to mod Kallum, like they did to Lucia, and instead, they took him out of the equation. I guess the reasons don't matter anymore. All that matters is that if...when we free Kallum and he comes here, what he says will be of his own free will."

CHAPTER TWENTY-TWO

The concept for Skybergs was sparked by a simple idea seventy-five years ago. Scientist created a paint so white that it reflected over 98 percent of the sun's rays. It didn't take a huge leap to start thinking about how we could utilize this technology on structures. The trick is being able to manipulate the reflection—it's something we want going back up into space, but not blinding us down here on the surface. Seasteads have been the perfect partners. They are building from the ground up, so we can be mindful about placement and implementation. Plus, they are out at sea, so we can pick and choose where we implement. We anticipate this collaboration even allowing us to create microclimates that will cool some of the most vulnerable areas of our oceans.

—DR. SERAPHIN JUSTUS IN HER ADDRESS TO
THE UNITED NATIONS COUNCIL FOR CLIMATE CHANGE, 2100

Day 10: December 13, 2126: Upstate New York
Ward

Ward jolted awake. He lay on his stomach, on a too-small bed, arms and feet hanging over the edges. The mattress sagged in the middle and smelled of mildew. He shuddered. For a moment, he thought he was back at ReInception—back in his medbed. But the covers over him were warm and heavy, the air in the room hot and damp. There were no rails on the sides. No tubes or equipment. No small robot passing by to kill his nanites. He'd been so sure the Med had programmed the robot to buy him time, but he'd been wrong. So who'd been programming those bots?

Turning his head, Ward saw a bedside table, a metal lamp with a dimly lit bulb. Everything looked small and ancient. Not made for Prole. Made before Prole.

Groaning, Ward rolled onto his side. There were heavy bandages wrapped around him. His back ached, but the pain was tolerable. His tongue felt thick and dry. He was hot and sweaty; damp hair clung to his forehead. The stiffness in his muscles told him he'd been in one position for too long. The shivering told him he had a fever, but nothing too bad. Nothing he couldn't push through.

"Hello?" It came out faint and raspy. "Hello!" he called louder. There was nothing except clicking noises from a panel along the bottom of the wall. A slight burning smell.

Holding his side, Ward pushed himself up to a seated position. He wore a pair of shorts that looked...he didn't know what they looked like. Not something cut from an old jumpsuit or made from the material all their clothing was made from. Like the table, they looked ancient—bright blue with two white stripes on each side, shiny and smooth.

The room was small, with wood-paneled walls painted once-white, now gone a dull yellow. Black mold creeped up a corner. There was a small, woven rug on the floor next to the bed, scratchy under his feet—yellow, orange and red spiraling inward. Paintings on the wall depicted scenes of the forest and animals. The floors, table and bed were clean, but the tops of picture frames and the lamp had a thick layer of dust on them, like someone had tidied up, but not very well.

Ward forced himself to his feet, swaying a bit and steadying himself on the headboard. The shorts slid down to his hips and when he tried to pull them up, the waistband snapped, crumbling in his fingers, the shorts falling to the ground. He tried bending to pick them up, but the raw skin on his back protested. He was finally healing, his skin tight and itchy, but not hot or painful. His surroundings were bizarre and confusing, but he had no sense of any immediate danger. Kicking the shorts out of the way, he grabbed the blanket off the bed, wrapping it around his chest and shuffling toward the door.

The door opened into a narrow hallway. This, too, with wood paneling, but dark and unpainted. Family photographs hung crooked and cracked, old and faded. Ward scanned them. There was an Asian man with black hair and dark eyes fishing from a dock. A white woman with long blond hair sat on a beach with two black-haired children. No one looked familiar, but the adults depicted would be long dead by now, and the children grown old and probably modified beyond recognition.

At the end of the corridor, light spilled in from another room, and there were the sounds of talking and laughing. There was a smell, too. Sweet and yeasty. His mouth watered and his stomach groaned. He felt like he was in a dream and touched the wall just to be sure this was all real. The wood was rough under his palm, both assuring and confusing.

He moved toward the voices.

"Ney, ney. You'll not get nuthin' from me with all dat flattery."

Sebbe's voice.

"Sebbe," he tried to call, but it came out as a raspy whisper. He picked up his pace. He was thirsty and hungry, his legs weak and heavy beneath him. But he felt better than he could have imagined would ever have been possible again; against all odds, his mind was still his own. He was out of ReInception—where almost didn't matter. Sebbe was here and laughing. For a moment, he froze, putting his fist to his mouth and biting his knuckles, pushing back an emotion he no longer quite recognized. Something that fluttered in his stomach and tingled in his chest.

As he moved toward the end of the hall, he tried to remember what had happened. How he'd gotten wherever he was. He recalled Iza's words about Kitty and how she'd clutched at her heart. Swaying, he squeezed his eyes shut for a moment, resting against the wall, breathing hard. Andromeda and Kammeo had saved him. Sebbe came for him. Iza was gone. After that, he remembered nothing.

He started walking again.

"Aw, just one more, please?' Andromeda's voice. Light and laughing.

"Ah. Alright. Jes a skootch." Sebbe again.

Ward stepped into the room. It was a kitchen, small but bright and airy. Curtains blew inward from an open window over a large white sink. Sebbe stood in front of a black stove wearing shorts and his government issued gray tank, stained with sweat spreading from the armpits. In the center of the room was a small, round table covered in a bright yellow tablecloth with white flowers, surrounded by four wooden chairs. At the table sat Andromeda and Kammeo, both wearing their jumpsuits pulled down and tied around their waists. Their white tanks were stained and dirty, too. Ward squinted, trying to focus on them better as he moved closer.

Andromeda's hair was the same bright purple it had been last time he'd seen her; no time to change it in the rush to escape, he guessed. But unmaintained, the patterning on her skin was fading, her true color, a light, golden brown, like an almond shell, emerging. Next to her sat Kammeo, smiling for the first time he could remember. She was pretty—he'd never realized it—with very black eyes and eyelashes, and very black hair, her skin a warm, dark brown the color of the black walnut dining room table in his childhood home. It had been his mother's prized possession. Something made by a famous artist, by then, long dead.

Kammeo glowed the way the wood did after his mother carefully applied lemon oil. Ward remembered the warmth of it, and the swirling gradations of color—the natural material, something rare and precious in a world that no longer cut down trees. Maybe some of Kammeo's ancestors had been South American or African—he wondered if she even knew. It was something you didn't ask people about and many people no longer knew. For most, it was enough to know which side of the war they'd fought on, and the rest didn't matter. It had mattered to his mother. She'd babied her inherited Moroccan antiquities with greater care than her own children. He'd never thought about those things until just now. The hand-woven rugs and perforated brass lamps. Where had they all gone?

Andromeda turned her head, spotting him in the doorway. She smiled at him, and he was struck by how young she looked without all the beauty mods. How tired. It was in the slump of her posture, the set of her mouth, the puffy darkness beneath her eyes. Something of the spark had gone out of her. It caused a pit in his stomach emptier than the hunger—he'd done this to her. He'd told her what her father really was. He knew what it was like to find out that your parents were capable of cruelty. He knew what that did to a person.

"He has risen!" She said with a forced brightness.

Kammeo and Sebbe turned to look at him, Sebbe's face breaking into a wide grin. He dropped whatever he was using to cook and crossed the room in three long strides, taking Ward by the shoulders. "M'boy. At last. Come! Sit! Sit! You'd be hungry."

Taking Ward by the elbow, Sebbe led him to an empty seat. Ward lowered himself slowly, wincing at the aches in his muscles and his tightness of his skin. The old chair groaned beneath him but held.

"How long was I out?"

"Three days." Kammeo lifted a cup to her mouth, sipping at a steaming drink.

Staring at it, Ward licked his lips. His mouth tasted like he'd been eating sand.

Andromeda rose, collecting a mug from a cabinet and pouring a hot liquid into it, placing it in front of Ward.

"Thank you," he mumbled. The cup was bright yellow and had a drawing on it of a little white dog with a little yellow bird flitting around his head. The dog was smiling and wore a red scarf.

It was surreal and bewildering, this retro-domestic setting with Andromeda serving him a drink like they were from a different century—or friends. He wasn't sure which was more unlikely.

Lifting the cup to his lips, he sipped the hot liquid. It was tea, stale and tasteless, but warm enough that he didn't care. As it went down, it washed away some of the sandpaper, reminding him of his small room in the dorms and his burner and herbs. He never thought he'd miss that lonely place—it had always felt so temporary. But compared to what he'd been through in the past few days, it was paradise. It had been safe, at least for a while, and there'd been his books—and Lea.

"Just take it slow," Kammeo told him. "We tried to get some water into you the past few days, but not much luck. You don't want to get sick." She didn't meet his eyes, but stared at her hands, wrapped around her own mug of tea.

The room had gone strained and quiet. Ward felt like he was in an alternate universe. His enemies were here with his closest friend. Sitting in an old room eating pancakes and drinking tea like nothing was wrong.

Kallum Gordon had eaten pancakes. He'd eaten them all the time—dripping with hot butter and sweet jam made of real crushed fruits or studded with chocolate chips. Kallum Gordon had taken pancakes for granted. Ward 17,362 Bedford had never had a pancake. Never had strawberry jam or maple syrup. It was like his alternate realities were colliding.

Ward took another sip of tea and then put the mug down. He didn't want to. He wanted to gulp the whole thing, even if it scalded him from muzzle to tail. He wanted to do anything possible to freeze this moment and never move past it. He wanted to live in this lie forever.

Clearing his throat, he tried to steady the tremor in his vocal cords. If he opened his mouth, whose voice would come out, Ward's or Kallum's?

"Can someone tell me what the Floods is going on here?"

Sebbe put a platter on the table stacked high with fluffy, golden disks. Sliding an empty plate in front of Ward, he put one of the pancakes on it. Ward picked it up with his fingers. It was soft and spongy, like their Prole cook's had been when he was small. Taking a small bite, he chewed carefully. The sweet, fluffy dough melted on his tongue, his tastebuds prickling. He resisted the urge to moan.

Reaching across, Andromeda took two pancakes off the stack and started eating with gusto. Kammeo kept staring at her mug.

Settling in across from Ward, Sebbe took a pancake as well. Ward's stomach growled, and he took another bite. It was so good, and not just because he hadn't eaten in days, but because it was real food instead of the meal bars he was used to. It was the best thing he could remember eating since before he fell. He wanted to inhale the whole thing in two bites and then grab the rest of the stack and eat that, too, shoving it into his face in giant fistfuls. Instead, he took another small bite.

"Where should we start?" Andromeda asked.

There was only a tiny bite left in his hands. How was it all gone so fast? Ward popped the last bite in his mouth. "I guess we can start with where are we?"

CHAPTER TWENTY-THREE

Katherine's Law is the informal name for a U.S. regulation passed in 2113 calling for two-parent consent in certain situations for ReInception.

The law is named for Katherine Vega, a teenager who was put through ReInception by her mother and stepfather in order to suppress her homosexuality after her father had gone to court and successfully obtained an injunction against the modification. The case was the first of its kind, both for the ruling originally prohibiting Katherine's mother from modifying her without her father's consent, and then for its decision to allow Katherine's father to attempt to have the procedure reversed.

The matter ended in tragedy when Katherine's father was killed by her stepfather and mother. They were convicted on the testimony of her younger half-brother, Kallum Gordon. The whereabouts of both Katherine and Kallum are unknown; they are presumed dead. Conspiracy theorists claim they were murdered by ReInception. Others maintain that they are being sheltered in a country where ReInception is illegal. Sightings of the siblings have become the thing of Urban Legend.

—KATHERINE'S LAW OR THE TWO PARENT RULE

"We're in Hallyn's family hunting cabin." Kammeo still wouldn't meet his eyes.

Ward sent a sharp puff of air out of his nose. "Of course they'd have a hunting cabin."

Kammeo scowled, finally looking at him. "This cabin is saving your life right now, so maybe reserve your judgment."

Reaching across the table, Andromeda squeezed her arm. "It's ok, Kam. People don't change overnight. Once a Gondu..."

Sebbe snorted. "Yer right there."

Ward narrowed his eyes at the man. "Really?"

"Yar a grouchy thing anyhow, true, true."

Andromeda laughed and Ward saw the corner of Kammeo's mouth tremble into what almost might have been a smile.

Ward exhaled. "I'm sorry. Yer right. I've no right after all you've done for me. Tell me, then. I'll keep my mouth clammed."

Kammeo glanced at him as if to see if he could be trusted. He could—so long as he could trust her, anyhow. Despite what she'd done for him, he didn't yet. None of this made sense. It felt like a trap or a dream—that hypnagogic state he'd been in and out of for the past weeks with its too-bright colors and too-crisp edges.

"They've had this property for over a century. His grands bought it during the great pandemic a hundred years ago. He says they never used it much after that, and they never hunted. But it's been in his family since. His grand thought that the whole world would fall apart. Built a bunker for food stores and everything. That's why we have all this." She gestured to the pancakes. "He brought Lea here once." She glanced at Ward, catching him wince. The idea of Lea there with Hallyn in such a quiet, out of the way place... The only thing that made him feel better was knowing that the idea was as painful to Kammeo as it was to him—at least they had their respective jealousy in common. "Anyhow, Andy was able to pull the records and find out where it was. They'll never come looking here. I don't think Hallyn even knows I know about it.

"They'll track yer comms," Ward said.

Lifting her hair, Andromeda turned her right ear toward Ward. Where her comm should have been was only the smallest red scar.

"We removed them two days before we broke you out. Ever since the media got wind of Lea removing hers, people all over the country have been doing it. They're calling it the 'No Justus, Just Us,' movement. My father wasn't happy, but he chalked it up to me hopping on another trend. He figured as soon as it got inconvenient, I'd replace mine."

"No Justus..." Ward trailed off, shaking his head.

Andromeda shrugged. "Your girl's a trendsetter. Who would've thought."

Ward looked at her. She smiled, but her mouth was turned down in the corners and her eyes, glassy.

Ward shook his head. "For everything I done to you, I'm sorry. It was for—"

"Yeah, yeah. A greater cause. I know." She tossed her hair over her shoulder.

He continued to stare at her. Her mouth trembled. The tears hung suspended on the rims of her eyes and then she blinked and they spilled over the edge. She turned her face away.

Sniffling, she wiped the back of her hand across her nose.

"Sorry. I didn't mean it that way. I mean, not my tone." She stared up at the ceiling, patting away the tears from under her eyes with her fingertips. "I meant it *was* for a greater cause."

Ward nodded. "It was, but I'm sorry just the same."

Staring down at her hands, she nodded. "Thank you."

"What was it convinced you?"

She continued to look at her hands, picking at an invisible hangnail. "It wasn't really any one thing. Mostly, it was overhearing what my dad said to you when he thought I wasn't listening."

Ward nodded.

"Which I know you did on purpose."

Ward nodded again. "Yes."

"I mean, first it was figuring out you were telling the truth...about my dad...about me not being modified. That was a hard one. I mean, he was protecting me because he loves me. But, you know. Hypocrisy and all that. I thought I could live with it. Tried to convince myself that even if it wasn't the safest choice for me, it was still the *safer* choice for others. You know...lesser of two evils. But then when I found out who you are...what he did to you…"

She glanced up at him, tears now flowing freely down her cheeks. "Is it true?"

Ward shrugged, looking away. It was hard to look her in the eyes and not see himself—what the truth had done to him—what he'd done because of it.

Andromeda shook her head. "I keep making excuses for him, like that he was young at the time. He thought he was doing the right thing. But he—" She let out a small hiccup. "He tortured you. You were just a kid." She shook her head. "Lea was right all along."

Putting her face in her hands, she sobbed. "I mean, it's my dad. How could he do all those things to protect me and then do that to you?"

Sebbe put a hand on her arm and squeezed. "Someday, maybe you kin ask him. But fer now, it's okay to mourn. He's yer da. Yeh love 'em."

She sobbed harder. "How? How can I love him?"

"Same way I still love my mother, I guess," Ward said.

Andromeda looked up, her eyes bloodshot and red-rimmed. This was the woman Lea called friend. Ward had always been so sure this was who she'd be when it came down to it, otherwise Leandrea wouldn't have been so loyal to her; wouldn't have been so hurt when they betrayed her. He was glad he was right, but he, more than anyone, was also profoundly sad about it.

"Did Lea know already…when she came to the apartment with you to help you steal the files? Did she know?"

Ward furrowed his brow. "Which part? About you? About me? About your dah?"

Sniffling, Andromeda shrugged.

"She didn't know who I was yet. She knew I was hiding something, but I wouldn't tell her what. She didn't find out until we'd already run away. I hadn't planned on telling her at all. I hadn't planned on her going through any of this. Once I knew there was no going back, I dinna' want to hide it from her anymore."

"Let me guess," Andromeda smiled. "She insisted."

Ward nodded.

"Yeah, stubborn that one. But she always knew you'd suffered, and I was…" She looked away. "I'm ashamed of how I treated you."

Ward let out a heavy sigh. He wasn't sure whether he was ready to forgive her or just too exhausted to stay angry. "I think you more than made up for it, getting me out of there. That was brave. Siao, lah! But brave."

Andromeda sniffled and laughed.

"And you?" Ward looked at Kammeo. "Her, I can understand. But you? Why?"

Kammeo's eyes were dry. Her hands were steady. "Because of what they did to Hallyn."

Ward stared at her. "And jes like that, you're a non-believer?" His lip curled. "You. Modified within an inch of yer life."

"Ward," Sebbe warned.

"No." Kammeo nodded. "I'll answer that. I am modified within an inch of my life, and I still believe in it. It's made me better. Healthier. A smarter student."

"Not a better friend, though." Ward huffed out of his nose again.

Kammeo pursed her lips. "I regret if I hurt Lea, but I don't regret loving Hallyn."

"Course you don't." Ward took another pancake, chomping off a big bite. The discussion made him uncomfortable. Of course, he was glad Lea wasn't with Hallyn anymore, but he also hated how it happened. He hated that it hurt her. How she'd felt betrayed by, but sympathetic to Kammeo. Lea always had space in her heart for forgiveness. It was something he admired about her. Something he hoped to emulate. But he wasn't sure he had space in his heart for that kind of absolution.

"If she loved him so much, she wouldn't've ended up with you so fast. Would she?"

Ward scratched his cheek. "Then why'd you help me—If Lea's so fickle. If I'm so bad. If ReInception is so good."

She cocked her head, staring at him, considering her answer. "It can be good. But not the way they used it on Hallyn. Not the way they plan to use it on your kind."

"Our kind." Ward nodded, not looking away. "We're human, too, you know. I used to be just like you. We all did." He was about to say more, but Sebbe put a steadying hand on his shoulder.

"She been through lots, meh boy. She comin' round. Don't happen overnight, lah."

Kammeo's relationship with Hallyn had been hard on Leandrea.

Leandrea knew Kammeo had been in love with Hallyn all along. Lea also knew Hallyn had only stopped loving her because his parents had illegally reprogrammed him; she suspected some of that programming had been about her specifically. But she'd also been sad for Kammeo, who would have known on some level that Hallyn was only with her because of that programming.

"And I didn't do it just out of the goodness of my heart."

Ward raised an eyebrow.

"You'll go back. You'll try to save the rest of The Origins. And when you do, you'll save Hallyn, too."

Both of Ward's brows rose. "I'm sorry, Kammeo. But he dinna' want to be saved."

"You're going to do it anyhow."

"Am I, now? And why's that?"

"Because you owe me."

"Yeh—you helped get me out. You—"

"I did more than that."

Ward turned his body in her direction, giving his full attention. Her lips were set in a thin, hard line and her arms crossed over her chest.

"Why exactly do you think you weren't healing?"

It took Ward a moment to process what she was implying. His mouth fell open, and his eyes went wide. "You did that? That was you?"

"What's he talking about?" Andromeda asked at the same time Sebbe said, "What's this now?"

Ward ignored them, shaking his head. "I can't believe it. How?"

"What is this?" Andromeda hit a hand on the table.

Kammeo twisted in her chair to face Andromeda. "There's a med bot that cleaned Ward's room. I programmed it to come through twice a day, after his bandages were changed."

Andromeda stared at her, Sebbe looking back and forth between them, confused.

"You mean the nanite impregnated cloths?" Andromeda asked.

Kammeo nodded, and Ward swore he saw the slightest smirk of satisfaction on her lips.

"Floods, Kammeo! My father practically went non-comp trying to figure that out. He started suspecting that the Med and that man has been like a loyal dog. If he'd found out—"

"He didn't."

Sebbe threw his hands up. "Kenna' someone explain to me what in frinn is going on here?"

"The cleaning bot," Kammeo said. "I rigged it with a small EMP device. Just enough to kill the nanites." She turned towards Ward. "How'd you figure it out?"

"It took a few days. I was so wrecked. But every time the bot came by, I itched so bad I wanted to tear my skin off. Then a dust would fall to the ground."

"The dying nanobots," Andromeda said.

Ward nodded. "I thought it was the Med. Almost said as much to him."

Kammeo watched him, her black eyes unnerving. "So now you understand. If it weren't for me, you wouldn't be you anymore. You owe me."

Ward nodded, closing his eyes. He was so tired. There was a fight ahead of him, he knew. This moment of false peace in this strange, off the map place wouldn't last. Right now, these were his only allies. Finding out he was Kallum Gordon made them see him differently; opened a window into his world and what he'd gone through. Maybe made them think he was capable of more than he really was. He wouldn't be the one to let them down...

"She wanted you both to be happy, Lea did," Ward said. "Know that."

"Did she?" Kammeo asked.

Ward tried to read her tone—whether she meant it sarcastically, or it was an honest question. Kammeo had earned the benefit of the doubt from him, and more.

"She did. I won't tell you she wasn't hurt, but she was gettin' past it. She always knew how much yeh loved him. She loved him, too, but not the way you did. She wanted that for both of you. It's what you do for people you love. You come round."

"Do you?" Andromeda asked. Certainly, she meant her father. She was asking him about his mother.

Ward turned his mug in his hands. The dog, with his scarf flying behind him. The bird, flipping through the air. He thought about his mother. The truth was, she'd never been a very nice person. Reprogramming his sister hadn't been about her concern for Kitty. It had been about herself—she was worried about what people would think. She was always worried about other people's opinions. Did Ward love her? He knew you should love your mother no matter what, but when he thought of his own, he felt a cold nothingness. He'd loved his father, despite what he'd done. He loved his sister's father—the man that his mother and father killed. He loved that man very much. How broken he must be to not love his own mother.

"I guess it's complicated."

Andromeda nodded. "I guess it is."

Taking a deep breath, Ward looked out the window. It was snowing again. It was so hot inside the house, even with the window open and flakes coming through the blowing curtains. The world had gotten warm...so warm...yet it snowed more and more in these parts. Had been for a century. In the summer, it was so hot, the air so thick you could barely breathe; thick like soup. Prole down in the Catacombs died from it, alone in their room in the half-abandoned buildings. In the winter, the air was dry and burned your lungs, like every molecule had fled south for warmth. Prole died from that, too, in the street and in the tunnels. Down in the Floods, they froze to death in the half-drowned buildings.

Inside here, it was warm. Ward wasn't sure how. Somehow it was on the grid, or there was a generator and available fuel. He didn't know. He didn't care. Outside, leaves hung heavy on trees and icicles as long as his arms were suspended from the eaves. He wished Lea was here with him. He'd build a fire and they'd curl up together on the old sofa. He could stay here with her forever, pretending that the rest of the world didn't exist. That its problems were not his own.

He turned back to look at his saviors. An unlikely trio as there'd ever been. The rich, spoiled daughter of one of the most important men in the world; a man who'd tortured and tried to erase him from existence. A man who'd lied to the world—and to his daughter—to protect her. The sullen zealot who loved someone she'd had no right to love. That love had opened her eyes. Made her do something impossibly brave to save a man who represented everything she neither liked nor trusted. A pockmarked Prole who by day ran a bar and by night, the underground. A man who'd loved him like a son when he no longer had a father.

And him. Prole. Savior. Hero. Traitor. Ward. Kallum. Frankenstein's monster. He no longer knew who he was or what he stood for. It was time to find out.

CHAPTER TWENTY-FOUR

"If anyone believes birds aren't real, we're the last of their concerns, because then there's probably no conspiracy they don't believe."

—NEW YORK TIMES, JULY 7, 2023,
"BIRDS AREN'T REAL, OR ARE THEY?
INSIDE A GEN Z CONSPIRACY THEORY."

Day 10: December 20, 2126: Tob Namara
Leandrea

Leandrea climbed into the back of a four-person transport, two armed guards in the front. Another transport in front of her held her parents and two more guards. Tob Namara was as secure a place as any in the world, but the N.Z. government wasn't taking any chances with Lea, her parents or the data.

The small pods took off, skimming low over the ground just inside the seastead's walls. Leandrea stared out the window as they passed through and then outside the city, leaving behind the tall structures and carefully planned urban landscape for the farms and fisheries on its outskirts.

For the first time, Leandrea got a sense of the scale and ambition that had gone into creating Tob Namara. It was hard to believe that humans built something so large and complex out in the middle of the ocean—an Island nation already so vast in scale that, when complete, Kitty said would rival pre-sea-rise Fiji in its size and scope. Seasteads also had the benefit of not being fixed and, therefore able to rise with sea levels. They could grow faster and better handle flooding as the decades-long work of restoring ice masses and re-lowering sea levels was done.

The transport flew low to the ground, within the protective canopy of Tob Namara's vast system of suspended panels that created the skybergs. Leandrea had already known that the Bergs screened and controlled the nation's sun exposure, deflecting unwanted rays back into space, and collecting solar energy to power the city. What she hadn't known was that they also screened the nation from outside surveillance. Katherine didn't want anyone to know that Leandrea had been in Tob Namara. As part of the trade deal, New Zealand would take the heat for that one.

The transports banked left in a gentle arc, following the landscape of the island, past the farms and smaller, suburban structures, and then turning into a young forest. The craft moved deftly between densely planted pine trees. Endangered animals that had been brought to Tob and seeded into the habitat turned at the soft thrum, and then bounded away, disappearing into the thick cover. Ahead, Leandrea could see the sun penetrating through at the edge of the forest. They were nearing the end when a bright flare deep in the woods caught Leandrea's attention. It grew closer and before Leandrea could process what it was, crashed into her parent's craft, exploding on impact.

Leandrea screamed as her parent's transport spun out of control, smashing against a tree.

"What the—" one of her guards began as another flare came from her right, hitting her transport. The blast shattered the canopy, the guard on the right side taking a direct hit, his face exploding in a spray of red. They whirled in space, bodies thrown against the side from centrifugal force, the other guard shouting to whomever was monitoring them, "We've been hit! We're going down!"

For a moment, they spun through empty air, and then they crashed to the ground, the vessel landing nose down. Leandrea was flung forward against her restraints and then whiplashed backwards. For a moment, she blacked out. When she came to, she was pressed forward, against her restraints, facing downward so that if she released her harness, she'd fall forward and into the cockpit. Below her, both guards were covered in blood and unmoving.

Moaning, Leandrea put her hand to her head. Blood dripped from a wound on her scalp and onto the dead pilots. Turning her head to look around her, she could see a few yards away that her parents' craft was on fire.

Adrenaline pulsed through her, clearing her mind and turning her muscles into coiled springs. Screaming for her parents, she struggled to release herself, fumbling with the harness clips and, at last, freeing herself. She fell forward, onto the bodies of the guards. The one who had been calling for help moaned softly—not dead yet, but he would be soon if she didn't get help.

"Sorry." Leandrea sobbed. "Sorry," trying not to do more damage as she crawled over him and toward a shattered opening in the canopy. Grabbing the visor off the dead guard, she pulled herself through. She didn't know if it would connect to anything—she wasn't netted and she was uncertain if that's how the N.Z. tech worked, but she had no other way to contact anyone. She could only hope that Katherine had been tracking the transport while it was still in Tob Namara and would send help.

Crawling forward over the front of the craft, Leandrea tumbled to the ground. Hot, thick blood oozed down her face, obscuring her vision. She couldn't move her right arm.

Pulling herself up, she lurched toward her parents. They were inside, unmoving, as the fire spread from the front of the transport, catching the ground below and beginning to move outward.

"Mom! Dad!" She screamed and then choked as the wet forest floor started throwing up thick smoke.

Coughing, she screamed again. "Mom! Dad!"

Still, they didn't move. She was just a few yards away.

The fire crackled and popped.

The craft exploded, a ball of fire shooting up through the sky. Leandrea was thrown backwards and to the ground. Debris rained around her, bits of shrapnel slicing her skin.

"No!" She screamed, pushing herself back to her feet, ears ringing, the ground swaying around her.

Another bright flare cut through the woods. Leandrea threw herself back down to the ground, curling up in a ball and covering her head as the flare hit the transport she'd been in, exploding it, too. She could hear nothing but a loud ringing in her ears. Holding her head, she rocked herself, the ground spinning and tilting around her.

She felt the heat against her skin, increasing as the fire moved toward her. She had to get out of there. Pushing herself to her feet, she stumbled, looking at the charred ruin of the craft that her parents had been in. She saw nothing but flames. Everything dipped and shifted. The fire closed in. She turned, still gripping the guard's visor as she stumbled toward the woods, away from the flames.

She was disoriented, unsure whether she was heading deeper into the forest or out of it; unsure of where the flares had come from. She might be walking toward her attackers, but she had to get away from the fire.

Looking up through the smoke, she saw movement in the trees. Someone running toward her. She turned, stumbled, crying out as her foot caught on something and she fell. She pushed herself to her feet, attempting again to run away. The smoke grew thicker. She could barely breathe. She could still hear nothing but the ringing in her ears.

Hands grabbed her from behind. She thought she screamed but couldn't hear the sound of it in her own head. And then the person was in front of her, dressed all in black, a mask over her face. Aisling. She was saying something, but Leandrea could only see her mouth moving.

Aisling held her shoulders, shaking her. She was repeating something. The sound penetrated the ringing. "Where are the files? Where are the files!"

Coughing, Leandrea tried to clear her mind. The files, she had them. She tapped the pocket on her chest. "Here. I have them. Here."

"And the process for DeInception?"

"It's on here, too. Aisling...what's going on?"

Aisling's mouth was against Lea's ear, shouting so that Lea could hear her through the ringing. "We have to get out of here!"

"My parents!" Leandrea shouted back.

Aisling shook her head, confirming what Leandrea already knew.

Aisling slid a mask over Leandrea's face. Lea inhaled deeply, choking again as fresh air filled her lungs. It had an odd scent to it, some kind of palliative, medicated aerosol. As it moved through her, the pain numbed, her airways opening back up. Aisling moved in front of Leandrea, shaking her again. Making sure they had eye contact.

"Okay?"

Leandrea nodded. She was not okay, but the fire was burning hot, moving rapidly toward them.

"We can't stay here."

Leandrea nodded again. In one hand, Aisling gripped a weapon, aiming it forward as, with the other hand, she pulled Lea away from the fire and into the woods. Two figures came at them from the right side, weapons lifting. Aisling blasted both of them with a wide, blue hot beam that incinerated them. She kept moving, not looking back.

They ran until they reached the edge of the forest.

"Stay close!" Aisling shouted, her voice still muffled and staticky. They raced across a clearing and toward the city walls. Aisling shouted something into a communicator on her wrist and the wall opened, revealing a craft bobbing on the water. Leandrea wondered for a moment why Aisling was contacting someone through a wrist comm. She was netted. If she'd been wearing her visor, should could have tapped into the system, getting help that way. For that matter, they were under attack. Why wasn't she in military uniform? It would have allowed her to deploy integrated weapons with thought and eye movement, better protecting them against their attackers.

Something wasn't right but Lea couldn't think straight.

The hatch portaled open, and Vella stepped out, waving them forward. They reached the craft, and Aisling stepped through the opening, pulling Leandrea in with her.

"Okay," she shouted toward someone outside Leandrea's field of vision. "Let's go."

Vella stepped back, outside of the craft and onto the deck.

"What are you doing?" Aisling asked. "We've no time. We have to get out of here."

Vella shook their head. "I'm not going. I kenna."

"What do you mean, you're not going?"

"I kenna' go back." There were tears in Vella's eyes. "I kenna' go back and live that life again."

"You can't stay here. When Kitty finds out you helped us…"

"She won't find out. I'll tell her I tried to stop you."

Aisling shook her head, pulling on Vella's arm. "No, Vella, she's lost it. You don't know the extent of her plans. What she's going to do."

Vella pushed Aisling away. "I know. I know everyting. I'm gonna' help her. I'm only helping you out of loyalty to the people I love, so you can give dem chance. But I want teh fight."

Aisling's mouth fell open. "What are you talking about?"

"She told me everything." Vella's face was grim. "Desperate times and all, lah."

"Thousands will die."

Leandrea looked back and forth between the two. Blood ran down her cheeks and her hands shook. She couldn't process what was happening. They'd been attacked. Her parents were dead. Aisling was talking about other people dying.

"Katherine? Katherine did this?"

Aisling ignored her. "Don't do this, Vella. She's going to start a war."

"You dinna know what it's like. Living like that. No better than slave. An experiment."

"And the Prole? What about them? They'll die, too."

"You think dey any better? Only reason people like me exist wit the Prole is 'cause Prole kenna afford to change us. Here, you start all over. You make the rules. Katherine promised…"

"Katherine promised." Aisling spat. "Katherine promises a lot of things. She says what she needs to say to get what she wants."

Vella shrugged. "What other choice do I have? If we dinna take down ReInception, we'll have no life. Never 'ave. Never will. Sometimes, yeh need a war and if I'm here on the inside. If she trusts me—"

"I thought the same thing." Aisling shook her head. "Vella, she'll let all of them die, including Ward."

Vella gave a sad smile. "Well, den you'd better get to 'em." They stepped back off the wing of the ship and onto the sand.

Aisling tried one more time, but Vella shook their head, lifting a device to their mouth.

"In two minutes, I'm calling dis in. If you dinna' want Kat to fry yeh for traitor, best be on way."

Tears filled Aisling's eyes as she shook her head. "How could you?"

"If you'd 'ave lived my life, you'd do the same."

Shaking her head, tears rolling down her cheeks, Aisling walked backwards down the ramp and into the craft, pulling Leandrea in with her.

The portal began to close, shrinking Vella to a tiny dot. "Save meh boy," Vella called to them, just as the last dot of light still shone through. "He the only one worth it."

⁕

As soon as the exit sealed, the craft dipped below the water. They were just beginning their descent when there was a pounding on the outside of the vessel.

The voice was muffled, but audible. "Don't leave me! Don't leave me!"

"Who is that?" Aisling shouted to someone else on the ship who Lea couldn't see.

"A girl. She's on the platform. Should we go?"

"Gondu," Aisling cursed. "Open it."

The exit portaled open again and a petite figure, holding a backpack to her chest, came into view.

"Dillon!" Aisling ran toward the girl, grabbing her by the shoulders. "You can't be here, Dillon. Go back!"

The girl shook her head. "You promised you'd take me with you."

"When it was safe."

"I can't stay with her. I have to help. We have to get my uncle."

"Sirkka! We have to go!" The voice came from inside the ship. "Craft are taking off from the city. Vella must have called it."

Aisling cursed. "Dillon, go back, now!"

"I won't." The girl's lip trembled, but she didn't move. "I can help you. I've been learning things while you were away. I know things. Her plans."

"Sirkka!" It was the voice inside the ship again. "We're going down, now. Get in or get out, but we can't wait anymore."

Aisling cursed, grabbing Dillon's arm and pulling her into the ship. The door closed again and the ship dove.

CHAPTER TWENTY-FIVE

Our brightest and most talented engineers and scientists have reimagined marine combat vessels. It is this kind of innovation that will make Tob Namara the world leader in cutting edge defense. Our crewed mother-ships shaped like Mantarays and Whale Sharks will be virtually undetectable by enemy forces. Built from pressure and temperature resistant alloys, the Manta's surfaces can morph in shape. Additionally, our first of its kind hybrid algae-electric power and propulsion technology relies entirely on renewable resources. Propelled by tunnel drives, Mantas will be able to travel at speeds of up to 150 knots.

—PRESENTATION OF DEFENSE MINISTER NATALIA PORTMAN TO THE TOB NAMARA EXECUTIVE CABINET, 2110

Day 10: December 15, 2126: Tob Namara
Leandrea

"What were you thinking?" Aisling shook Dillon by the shoulders. "You shouldn't be here. It's too dangerous."

"Too dangerous! You know what she has planned."

"Whatever else she might do, she'd never hurt you."

"Do you really believe that anymore?"

Leandrea blinked, looking between Aisling and the girl, trying to process what was happening, why the girl was there. "What's she talking about?"

Aisling turned to face Lea, a look of frustration dissolving into horror. "Oh, floods!" Concern furrowed her brow and her shoulders sagged. "We have to get that cut taken care of."

Lea shook. Sweat and blood ran down her face. Her mouth was dry and all she could see was her parents' transport going up in flames. "Who was Dillon talking about? Ash, you have to tell me." Her words were slow and slurred, like something inside of her had broken.

Taking her by the shoulders, Aisling guided Lea the rest of the way down the ramp and into a chair.

It was another sea vessel, but larger than the one they'd taken to Tob Namara. The walls were smooth and ivory, with dim lightings. Openings lead to other places in the vessel. A figure in a dark maroon jumpsuit sat at a console, a visor down over his eyes. He didn't acknowledge them, but stared straight ahead, unmoving other than small finger twitches.

"Ash—"

"Shh. Let's get you fixed up and then I'll explain." She turned toward the girl, who'd followed them into the room. "Dillon, get Leandrea something to drink. Juice...something with sugar."

She pointed toward one of the openings and Dillon nodded, vanishing down the ramp.

Aisling approached a wall, pressing a symbol to reveal a compartment. She removed a small case, then returned to Leandrea, kneeling by her side. She took a cloth from a package. Leandrea winced as Aisling gently wiped her face and then sprayed her wound. It tingled and then instantly went numb.

Aisling scanned Leandrea's body with a medwand, watching the readout.

"Other than some cuts, bruises, and minor burns, you seem to be okay."

Leandrea didn't feel okay. She felt nothing but a strange emptiness deep inside her. Her parents. All she'd wanted for months was to see them. Katherine had warned her it was a bad idea, but she'd insisted. Now they were gone, and it was her fault.

Aisling sorted through the contents of the bag and removed an NFiT. She brought it toward Lea's arm, and Lea cringed away.

"Your vitals are all too low. You're going into shock. This will help."

Leandrea wanted to resist, but she had nothing left in her.

Aisling pressed the tube against Leandrea's arm. A warm, tingling sensation spread through her, her shivering slowing to barely a tremble.

"Better?"

Leandrea nodded, the image of the burning craft fading slightly.

"What else was in there?"

"A sedative."

Her emotions began feeling as numb as her forehead. Part of her wanted to push the fog away. To be aware and take action. The other part wanted oblivion. She wanted everything to go back to the way it had been a month earlier, before the rally. She'd decide not to go to The West End. Not to go to the protest. She'd stay in her little bubble with her friends, letting other people try and fail to fix the world's problems. She'd stay there, where her parents were still alive and trying to make the world a better place. "*Even if it means never meeting Ward? Even if it means living in the dark, never knowing the truth?*" she asked herself. She wasn't sure. In that moment, the pain was so intolerable she believed she'd give up all of it just to have her parents back.

But that was fantasy, and this was reality. She needed to know who'd done this.

"Who attacked us? Was it ReInception? Did they find us?"

Aisling bit her lip and twisted her hands. "Maybe rest a while and then I'll explain."

Leandrea shook her head, the movement causing her head to swim. Her skin was clammy and damp. Her vision came in and out of focus.

Aisling's mouth twisted, and her brows pulled together. Leandrea looked at her carefully for the first time since Aisling had rescued her—again. Her eyes were red and puffy. A dark bruise was forming on her cheek.

Dillon came back with the drink, and Leandrea took a sip. It was cold and sweet, like nothing she'd ever tasted before. In other circumstances, it would have seemed miraculous. Now, it was just juice. But it did make her feel a bit better.

"My parents. Is there any chance?" She knew the answer, but she asked anyhow.

Aisling shook her head. "I'm so sorry, Lea. I checked. There's no way."

Leandrea felt hollow and numb. She tilted her chin upwards. "Who hurt you?"

Reaching up a hand, Aisling touched her cheek. "Katherine and I had a fight."

"And she hit you?"

Aisling sighed, looking down at her lap. "She's not the person she was when I met her."

"And who was she when you met her?"

Aisling shook her head again. "I don't know any more."

Leandrea looked around the vessel. "Where are we?"

"That's complicated." Aisling lowered herself into a seat opposite Lea. Dillon stood off to the side, hands clasped in front of her in that same practiced pose as her mother.

"Try me."

Aisling twisted her hands. "You sure you're ready for this?"

Leandrea nodded. She wasn't, not really. But she didn't see how waiting would help. The meds were working. Her head was clear and the ringing in her ears had stopped. The narcotics were keeping her calm. She needed to understand what had happened. Who had attacked them.

"The chips," Aisling pushed. "You're sure the data is on them. The DeInception process."

Leandrea nodded. "I'm sure."

"No. Really sure. Not just that Katherine told you it was there."

Leandrea nodded again. "Yes. My parents and I demanded to review the transfer—to make sure we had everything before we left, including the tech for DeInception."

Aisling looked away for a moment, her face pinched and pained. "Okay," she whispered to herself. "Okay. At least there's that." She looked at Dillon and then back toward Leandrea. Her hands were in her lap and those fingers kept twisting. She took a deep breath. "Katherine is the one who attacked your transport. She killed your parents."

Leandrea stared at her, feeling a blank nothingness. "What?"

Aisling nodded. "I'm sorry. It's true."

Lea looked at Dillon, but the girl looked away, eyes damp, refusing to meet Leandrea's gaze. Leandrea felt confused. Disbelieving. She could tell Katherine hadn't liked her very much, but she thought it was her lack of willingness to just accept the woman's orders, or perhaps her relationship with Ward. "I don't understand."

"I swear, Lea. If I'd known, I never would have brought you here. She's been looking for her brother for so long, I couldn't imagine—"

The wound on Lea's forehead throbbed. Her stomach made a fist. "Explain."

Aisling rubbed her face with her hands. She looked exhausted and ten years older than when they'd arrived less than a week earlier. She looked how Leandrea felt.

Aisling looked at Dillon again, her eyes downturned and sad.

Dillon shrugged. "It's okay. Just tell her."

"I don't know where to start." Aisling paused, staring at her hands. "When The Origins extracted Katherine, she was borderline catatonic. Her programming and reprogramming, everything that had happened to her and Ward, finding out she was pregnant—she was on the verge of collapse. She was brought here because The Origins knew Tob was pioneering a technology that could block the programming, something they were calling "DeInception." Once perfected, it was implemented, not just on Katherine, but on others who'd been brought here over the years. On this, they have built a society of people who are not only loyal to Tob, but militantly anti-ReInception.

"As those people got older, they took roles in government. They formed our politics and policies. A small few knew who Katherine was. She was smart and ambitious. Just as Iza knew the power of Kallum's name, they knew the power of Katherine's and that, revealed at the right moment, it would be a rallying cry. The whole world watched Katherine's brother testify about how ReInception had destroyed her life, taken her sanity. Showing the world that DeInception restored not only her mind, but her identity will not only make Katherine one of the most powerful people in the world, it will make Tob one of the richest countries. It will allow them to expand their borders. Build other seasteads under their governance."

"But why attack my parents? Me? What do I have to do with any of that?"

Aisling adjusted herself in her seat, taking a deep breath.

"Katherine has no intention of sharing what's in those files with the world."

Leandrea cocked her head. "I don't understand. She wanted them so badly."

"She wants to control the content. She didn't want you able to release it when you discovered she was not. She won't share that information unless she thinks it will further plans for Tob. No. Let me correct that. Unless it will benefit her."

Leandrea shook her head. "But why?"

"ReInception isn't weaponizing the Prole, they are deploying a program that will domesticate them."

Leandrea narrowed her eyes. "Canis Fidelis. But Katherine said that was about Ward. About Kelvin reprogramming him."

"It's not about Ward."

"So what is it? What did she find that would be worth killing..." Leandrea gasped, choking back a sob. "Killing my parents? Trying to kill me?"

Aisling adjusted herself in her seat, crossing her legs and leaning in toward Lea. "We've known about the barcodes on the Prole since they started embedding them, but we didn't know what they were for, either. What Katherine expected to find in those files was proof that ReInception was going to weaponize the Prole. That they were going to use mass ReInception to deploy them as a militant force—have them rise against the upper caste so that the upper caste would support mass ReInception. The technology is there, but the government has to support it. Until now, they weren't willing to go so far. They want to maintain their self-deception that the Prole are free people. She thought that was ReInception's plan. Have the Prole attack the upper caste so that the upper caste would agree to mass ReInception to subdue the Prole. But an uprising would terrify the upper caste and many on both sides might fall in the process. What's in the files? Well, the plan is much more clever than that. They will use the device to subdue the Prole population. They will use mass ReInception to make them what they've been treating them as; faithful dogs. The upper caste already fear the Prole. They fear their strength and growing numbers. Docile Prole will be too appealing for them to worry about the ethics of it."

"But why would Katherine want to hide that? I mean, it's terrible, but why not expose that plan to the world? Get them to intervene?"

"Because she doesn't want anyone to intervene. She wants another civil war. She doesn't want a docile Prole population with outside governments fighting for their freedom. She wants a bloodbath."

Leandrea's mouth fell open. She shook her head. "Why? Why would she want that?"

"So she can seize power. Tob has an advanced and powerful military, but it's small. Why risk her military when a civil war can do the dirty work for her?" Aisling leaned in. "She lied to you, Lea. Our army is powerful, but it can't rival one the size of the United States. Not at full capacity, anyhow. Tob is running out of space and out of money. A power grab and a land grab. A chance to expand Tob's borders through what seems like a seizure of power for the greater good."

Leandrea let this sink in. She felt the blood draining from her face, her body going cold. She felt numb, raw, and powerless against competing, conniving forces.

Aisling nodded. "While the castes are fighting, she means to go in, topple ReInception and the government, and take over."

Leandrea shook. Even with the sedatives in her system, it was all too much.

"How?"

Aisling shook her head. "Something she didn't even tell me."

"What are we going to do? We're on her ship. She'll find us."

Aisling shook her head. "They can't find us. This ship is utterly stealth. I helped design and build this for Katherine to avoid our own advanced detection tech. It was meant for her to travel without anyone being able to follow her, including her own government. Now, I'm using it against her."

"So, where will we go next? Still New Zealand?"

"Nope." For the first time in days, Aisling smiled. "We going to get our greatest weapon against her."

"And what's that?"
"We're going to get Kallum Gordon."

CHAPTER TWENTY-SIX

Simply changing Kallum Gordon's appearance is insufficient. He must be undetectable by modern technology. Retinal scans, prints, DNA...anything that can link this boy to that name must be purged from government records. The Secretary of Privacy will be coming to ReInception next week to learn about our privacy practices and experience the machine for himself. He considers personal experience of the machine to be critical to his ability to adequately execute his job. We'll be modifying him to improve his eating and exercise habits, something he considers low risk. While he's in the machine, we'll convince him that Kallum Gordon is a danger to the government—a risk whose duty it is for him to mitigate. His entire job is risk and mitigation. It will be easy.

—FROM THE FILES OF DENNISON KELVIN

Day 11: December 21, 2126: Somewhere in the Atlantic
Leandrea

"Ward?" Lea's heart beat faster.

"About a week ago, Ward escaped ReInception custody."

Something inside of Lea's chest loosened and expanded. Energy surged through her limbs.

"What? How?"

"Your friends."

Leandrea shook her head, trying to figure out what Aisling meant by her "friends." "Hallyn?" It was the only option that came to mind. But that was pre-ReInception Hallyn.

Aisling pulled in her lips, for a moment, frozen, and then shook her head again. Leandrea wasn't sure what the look meant.

"No. Your other friends. Andromeda and Kammeo."

Leandrea cocked her head. "Kammeo. And Andromeda? Helped Ward escape. You're sure?"

Aisling nodded her head.

"That makes no sense."

Aisling shrugged. "We don't know the details. We just know they were working with Sebbe, the barman, and the three took him to a safe place upstate."

Lea shook her head again. "It can't be right."

"It is."

Lea had so many questions that she didn't know where to begin. Bird wings flapped in her chest. "Working with Sebbe? Why? How? How do you know where they are?"

Aisling held up her hands. "One thing at a time. All we know right now is where they are and that we need to get to them before Katherine does."

"Katherine knows where they are, too?"

Aisling nodded. "Ever since I identified Ward, we've been keeping track of his whereabouts. We use the faunabots."

"Faunabots?"

Aisling nodded again. "Birds, mice, rats."

Leandrea rested her forehead in her hands. Her head was starting to throb. Everything was moving too fast. She held up a hand.

"Okay. Slow down. Tell me what you mean."

Aisling gestured around them. "This ship, the one you came in on, these are highly advanced machines designed to avoid detection by mimicking other lifeforms."

"Right. Like the Ray."

Aisling nodded. "They should avoid detection all together, but if they don't for some reason, if someone notices them, they look like something else. Something innocuous."

"Okay. But how did that help you track Ward?"

"The sea craft are just one example of the spy tech Tob produces. We can do this with anything. A dog. A cat. A rat. A—"

"Birds."

Aisling nodded.

Leandrea had noticed them all over Tob Namara. There were fewer birds in the world than at any previous time in human history. For decades, they'd been succumbing to human forces—pesticides, domestic cats, skyscraper windows. All the birds she'd seen around Tob had seemed like part of the place's magic. Part of how they were repairing the world. They were on the dock when she landed. In the gardens, when she was with her parents—a place she intuitively understood was designed to give her a false sense of privacy, but she hadn't been able to locate the spy tech. She put her face in her hands.

"I'm such a simp. How could I not have seen it?"

"No one sees it. That's the whole point. They are all over the world. If anyone questions their origins, we take credit for helping bring back dying species. We breed them, we release them. Repair the world."

Leandrea laughed. "Repairing the world."

"But really, rats are the most common. Everyone has rats. Everyone ignores them."

Leandrea had a sudden flash of memory. That first time she'd been alone with Ward, after the bombing at the rally. He'd been guiding her up the dark emergency stairs to his room—that scampering and twittering in the darkness.

"How long have you been following Ward?"

Aisling pondered this for a moment, twisting her lips and staring at the low ceiling above them. "I started watching him maybe a month before you first met him. First, there were those rumors. Then there was his behavior—the way he was following you and your friends. After that—"

Leandrea froze, eyes darting up to meet Aisling's. "Following my friends?"

"Mostly, Andromeda, but yeah, he was tracking you guys."

"You mean after the bombing? After that night he found me and helped me, right?"

It's what Ward had told her. He'd overhead Andromeda in the bar, bragging about who her father was, and had seized the opportunity and followed them. It had explained the coincidence of him finding Leandrea after she'd only seen him for the first time earlier that day.

Aisling shook her head. "Uh uh. Before that. Not sure for how long, but by the time I was watching him, he was already watching you."

"That can't be right." Lea felt confused. She thought Ward had told her everything. After all, he'd told her his biggest secret, hadn't he?

Aisling cocked her head to the side. "He didn't tell you that?"

Leandrea rubbed her cheek. She didn't want Aisling to know Ward had lied to her, but her face started to heat up, betraying her.

Aisling's lips were pinched, and she poked her tongue around inside her cheek. When she opened her mouth, it made a small, popping sound. "I'm sure he had a good reason." Aisling's tone said she didn't believe it any more than Leandrea should.

Leandrea didn't answer. Her eyes burned. Her parents were gone. Her friends were on the side of ReInception, yet they had saved her...her what? What were she and Ward, really? She felt she knew him, but did she? All along, he'd been keeping secrets; he'd told her that. But she thought they were done with secrets the night he told her who he was. The night they'd—she shook her head. Ward was all she had left and now, she wasn't even sure about that.

Aisling touched her arm. "Look. You'll see him soon enough. You'll ask. I never got to speak to Kallum, but I was watching him for long enough to know that he's a decent person. If he didn't tell you, he had a good reason. I know he really cared about you."

Staring down at her hands, Leandrea nodded. "How much did you see? Of us, I mean."

Aisling inhaled a deep breath and then blew it out. "More than you'd like, but less than I could have."

"They were there that first day, when he carried me up to his room, weren't they? The rats."

Aisling nodded.

Leandrea thought back to Aisling's interrogation of her. How strange the woman had behaved. All the cruel and pointed questions she'd asked about Hallyn and Ward.

"So, that day I went to Hallyn's apartment, you'd didn't know all those things because Hallyn's mom told you, you knew because you were monitoring me."

Aisling nodded again, refusing to meet her eyes.

"But you let me believe that it was Hallyn's mom."

"Lea—"

"How much? How much did you already know? What did you see?"

"I gave you your privacy when I could, if that's what you mean."

"Yeah, but you decided when that was."

Aisling shrugged. "I'm sorry. It wasn't personal."

"Right." Leandrea closed her eyes and exhaled. She was so tired.

"Why ask me all those questions if you knew the answers?"

"Sometimes, so you wouldn't know how much I knew. So you wouldn't know I was watching. Other times, because I hadn't been able to monitor what happened. When you were in Ward's room, there was only so much the bot could survey without you noticing. A big rat in the room is a bit of a conversation killer. And in the library, the lower floors are secure. There's no way to get anything down there unnoticed."

"Right." Leandrea laughed. "Right."

"Look, Lea—"

Leandrea held up a hand. "Enough. I get it. You were doing your job."

"My uncle is a good man."

Leandrea and Aisling looked up. Dillon stood in the entryway, arms crossed over her chest.

Leandrea's chest felt tight, her eyes heavy. All she wanted was to curl up in a ball and sleep. "I know he is, Dillon. But he's also someone who spent a lot of years hiding things from people."

"He had his reasons."

"Yes." Leandrea nodded. "He did."

But what was his reason for not telling her the whole truth about how long he'd been watching Andromeda? That the first time she'd seen him in the bar was not the first time he'd seen her. She couldn't help but remember that searing judgment he'd lobbed at her the first time they spoke. He'd been watching her, and he hadn't liked what he'd seen.

"Lea—" Aisling tried again.

"I don't want to talk about it anymore. Just tell me what happens next."

Leandrea could tell Aisling wanted to say more, but she nodded. "Okay. As you know, we tracked you and Ward to The Origins. I was to contact him there. Extract him and the files and bring them back to Tob."

"But the raid happened."

"Yes. I was only able to help you escape, but we've kept track of him since. We followed the hovercraft. It took him to a ReInception facility that's off the grid; highly surveilled. Intense security. All we could do was wait and watch."

"But you know where he is?"

Aisling nodded, risking a small smile. "He's at a cabin upstate. I don't know exactly what it is or why they went there, but we'll dock as close as we can get to it. Once we do that, we'll have to move fast to rendezvous with them before Katherine can find us or get to them. And we have to get to them before they leave, otherwise we'll lose them."

"You don't have eyes on them anymore?"

Aisling shook her head. "I didn't have time to take the right equipment with me. And besides, as soon as Katherine realizes what happened, where I am, she'll cut off all my access. I'm sure it's happened already."

"So, once we dock, what next?"

Aisling shook her head. "I don't know, Lea. I vaguely know where they are, but without my equipment, I can't pinpoint it. We'll have to try to reach someone else in The Origins and hope that Sebbe—"

Leandrea's eyes went wide. Her heart sped up. She held up her hand, quieting Aisling. "Wait. You said they are in a cabin in upstate New York?"

Aisling nodded.

Leandrea smiled, feeling hopeful again for the first time since she'd lost her parents. "I think I know where they are."

CHAPTER TWENTY-SEVEN

The whale shark-shaped mothership is built from some of the world's strongest alloys. With surfaces that can morph in shape and resistant to pressures at depth of 7 miles or more, there is almost nowhere that the Whaleship can't go or hide.

—PRESENTATION TO KATARINA DONOVAN
AT THE MAIDEN VOYAGE OF THE WHALESHIP PEQUOT.

Day 11: December 21, 2126: Upstate New York
Ward

"Where's Lea? Where's my sister?" Ward leaned against the table, hands on the edges, as if about to throw the whole thing over. His three companions froze, each in a different phase of pancake consumption: Andromeda's piece was halfway to her mouth, Kammeo, mid-chew, and Sebbe reaching for another. The entire scene was absurd, like something from a twisted, post-apocalypse, bucolic still life.

"We kenna' just sit here eating through the stores of Hallyn's paranoid grandfather while the rest of the world falls apart."

Andromeda put her fork down, raising an eyebrow at him. "You weren't exactly in the condition to dive into battle. And besides, weren't you ready to run just a few days ago?"

Ward glowered, but Andromeda just rolled her eyes. "I'm not scared of you. Never have been."

"I was going to leave with Lea when I thought my people were safe. Before I knew my sister has been out there all along and no one was telling me."

"Yeah," Andromeda snorted. "I guess that's a lot."

Ward felt his face getting hot. "What is your problem with me?"

"My problem is that you," Andromeda jabbed the fork in his direction, "are absurdly mercurial. Not only are you being irrational, but also an ingrate. Do you know what we risked to drag your unconscious and ridiculously deucing heavy, useless self here? We were almost killed."

Ward pinched his lips together, trying to let his anger subside.

Kammeo watched him out of the corners of her eyes and slowly started chewing the remaining bite in her mouth. Sebbe looked about to laugh.

Ward glowered. "Dat fin-doh?"

Sebbe snorted. "Et fin-doh when yeh catch no ball, yah." Sebbe laughed harder. "Yer all riled, but useless, sure, sure."

"Em no hum ji. We kenna' jes set here do nitch. Iza mort. Ami mort."

Sebbe put up his hand, trying to calm Ward. "Para para."

Kammeo was looking back and forth between the two men. "Would you speak English, please?"

Andromeda waved her fork in the air. "You can barely walk. What kind of help are you going to be?"

Ward slammed the table. "I can't just sit here while everyone I care about is in danger. How can you?"

"We aren't just sitting here," Andromeda said. "Just because you were getting a few days of beauty sleep doesn't mean we were doing nothing."

"What do you mean?" Ward asked.

"Should we show him?" Andromeda looked at the other three.

Kammeo shrugged. "May's well—if he can get down the stairs on his own, because I'm never carrying him again."

"Para, para," Sebbe said again. "Wash. Dress. Den we show you."

"Showers can wait," Ward said. "Show me."

Andromeda raised an eyebrow again. "No, seriously. You need to take a shower, if not for the sake of our poor olfactory bulbs, then at least for the sake of your skin not getting infected. If that doesn't heal, we have no way to help you out here. No nanites. Any meds here expired five decades ago."

"Fine," Ward pushed himself to standing, a groan escaping despite his best efforts. "I'll go, but after that, you show me everything."

Ward couldn't remember the last time he'd been in a real shower. Not a prole cleansing pod with its harsh chemical and hissing jets, but an actual shower, with soap and water.

Anything hotter than lukewarm set his new skin screaming, but it felt divine anyhow. There was a bar of soap so old it had cracked and yellowed, but wet, it foamed up and gave off a faint floral scent. As he rubbed it over his arms and legs, dirt came loose, his skin turning a whole shade lighter, gray water running down the drain.

He ran his hands over his body. He'd lost a lot of weight, his stomach now slightly concave, the ridges of his ribs apparent beneath his fingers. There was only so much muscle he could lose—he'd been so heavily engineered—but what remained felt rubbery and useless, stiff and cramped. He stretched as best he could without overtaxing his new skin, interlacing his fingers and reaching his arms up over his head, touching the ceiling. His joints popped and crackled as he bent from side to side.

He rubbed soap onto his face and into his hair, stooping down under the shower head to rinse off. "Floods these people were small," he muttered.

Rubbing his hands over his face, he felt the thick beard that had grown. Prole were required to keep clean shaven, he guessed so that their faces were easily seen and identified. The depilatory gel that would get sprayed on his face was part of the cleansing cycle in the pods. Here, he'd probably have to use something like a razor to get the hair off. He'd seen them in vids, but never used one. He touched his face again. The thick, black hair was coarse, yet somehow soft. It made him feel safer, less recognizable. He decided he'd keep it, at least for the time-being.

Reluctantly, he turned the water off, stepping out of the shower and onto the old rug. Kammeo had dug up another set of ancient clothing, pants with a soft, thick-ish material and a drawstring at the waist. He pulled them on. They were snug and at least a couple of inches too short, but they were warm and, pushed down to his hips and left loose, didn't chaff his sensitive lower back. He pulled a sweatshirt over his head, looking down at the logo on the front. It said, "Renegades," and there was a cartoon raccoon holding a bat. Before they left here, somehow, they'd have to find him some Prole clothing. He never thought he'd miss the stiff, identical uniform, but at least he didn't feel ridiculous in it.

"Really small," he muttered again.

Ward padded down the hallway, back into the kitchen.

"Well, that's better!" Andromeda chirped. "I mean, you look absurd, but at least you smell half human."

"Thanks," Ward said, but he smiled a little. "Now, can you show me this big surprise?"

His three companions stood, Kammeo walking over to a small door. She opened it and Ward peered inside. It was a small closet with shelves and some canned goods stacked along them. Reaching in, Kammeo turned on a light.

"See that panel back there?" Kammeo pointed behind a few boxes and Ward looked. There was a small plate with a button on it. "Press the button and step back."

Ward pressed the button. There was a clicking sound and Kammeo stepped forward, sliding one of the shelving units to the left, revealing a staircase leading down. She started descending and Ward followed, Andromeda and Sebbe behind them.

"After the pandemic and before the war, it became more and more common for wealthy people to build survival bunkers. They figured that if there was a nuclear war or something, they'd be able to ride out the attack in places like this. There's an independent power source, enough shelf-stable food and water to last for months."

They reached the bottom and Kammeo flicked a switch, the room lighting up. In front of them was a space as large as the cabin above, and certainly more modern. There were two massive, comfortable-looking sofas. In the open rooms to either side, Ward saw bunk beds with blankets neatly folded at the base. A good-sized kitchen stood against the right wall and there were shelves and shelves of books, games and other items that Ward assumed were for entertainment or education if stuck there for a long time. Kammeo flicked another switch and in a room toward the back, screens came to life.

Kammeo headed in that direction.

"Back here are the comms and surveillance equipment." Kammeo walked into the room, sitting in front of the large desk on one of the two chairs. There were computers, screens, radios, headsets—more equipment than Ward had ever seen in one room. Much of it was similar to, but more advanced than, the historic computers he'd repaired at Butler Library—the ones he and Iza used to access old data and information about the U.S. before the second civil war—information that the government tried to keep from the population. Ward judged this equipment to be newer than that, but at least a few of decades older than what was used now.

Kammeo pointed at the various devices. "Computers, radios. This stuff is old, but it all still works. There is also access to information outside the U.S. I think that's why they didn't replace with newer equipment."

Ward sat next to her, looking at the different screens and panels. "How do you know so much about all this?"

Kammeo shrugged. "My family has a bunker, too."

"Of course they do."

She turned a flat stare at him. "You Fell, right? Bet your family had one of these."

He stared back at her, thinking. Had they? The more time passed, the less he thought about his life before—the more surreal it all seemed. He didn't recall anything like this, but he was seven when he Fell and his mother had been over-protective of him. She'd thought that her lack of supervision and her ex-husband's liberal sharing of information with Katherine had led to her "problems." Now, he took that to mean Katherine being queer, but back then, he wasn't sure what it had meant. His sister had been eight years older than him. Where Kallum was cautious, Katherine had been adventurous. Kallum had learned from books, vids and tutoring to augment what he learned in school. Kitty had learned in the world. Book smarts versus street smarts is how he thought about it now, but back then, he'd thought Kitty was some kind of anomalous miracle. This smart, fearless being that he hoped he could be like when he grew up. Another time. Another life. Someone who wasn't him anymore.

"Well?" Kammeo cocked her head to the side.

Kallum's father had been part of ReInception. They'd been wealthy. If everyone else had them, even people who didn't work for ReInception, like Hallyn and Kammeo's parents, probably they did, too. Likely, his mother hadn't told him about it because she didn't want to scare him. Had Kitty known about it? Could they have hidden there all those years ago?

"I'm...I'm not sure. Maybe."

"Where would it have been?"

Ward shook his head. "I don't know. We didn't have summer houses or cabins...not that I recall. Where was yours?"

"At our building, in a complex below the basement. But there was another one at my aunt's house in South Carolina. A third at an uncle's. The whole family had them."

Ward nodded slowly. There had been aunts and uncles and cousins. Grandparents. He hadn't thought about that for so long. Now, he assumed they'd all shun him as Prole, but back then, what would they have done? Would they have helped him and Kitty or turned them in? Memories of them had faded to fuzzy snapshots of people with blurry faces. People you saw every year or so on holiday. They gave you gifts and told your mom how big you'd gotten. When both your parents went to prison and both Fell for their crimes, the children Fell, too. There was no option of an upper caste relative taking them in and raising them. Only Prole could raise Prole. He'd forgotten he even had other family out there somewhere. He forgot that there were people out there who might have wanted him. Or not.

He blinked a couple of times. "Huh."

Kammeo tilted her head the other way, like a puppy trying to understand. "What?"

"Nothing, I just...nothing."

Kammeo shrugged, turning back toward the screens. "If you say so."

He liked this girl. When he'd been watching the group of friends, trying to find a way to have contact with Andromeda, Kammeo was the one he'd learned the least about. She was quiet and solemn. She spoke little, and when she did, it was always in hushed tones. Andromeda was all lightness, joking, and laughter. Kammeo was the serious one in the group, always seeming slightly put off about where they were or what they were doing. Maybe a little sad. Lea…she'd been somewhere in the middle, joking with Andromeda, taking Kammeo seriously, but trying to pull her out of her shell. Leandrea was a connector. The type of person who brought people together. He'd liked that about her, the way she drew him out without being too pushy. With Lea, he remembered what it was like to be happy. But he had a feeling that he was most similar to this girl.

There was a loud beep, and a light started blinking. All four of them turned to look at the monitors.

Flashing on the screen over and over again were the following words: "Intruder! Intruder! Intruder!"

CHAPTER TWENTY-EIGHT

<u>Summary of The Physical Modification of Kallum Gordon</u>
The process of modifying Kallum Gordon took approximately three months to complete. The boy's body responded well to muscle and growth stimulation as well as hormone treatments. Other than being an inch or two shorter than the average male Prole, I believe that, as he grows, his physicality will be indistinguishable from Prole born.

—FROM THE FILES OF DENNISON KELVIN

Day 12: December 22, 2126: Upstate New York
Ward

Six figures, all in dark clothing, all non-Prole, moved through the woods at a rapid pace. The cameras moved with them, covering from the sides and from above. Three of the people were larger, two more slight and one, smaller than the rest. One moved at the front, weapon trained ahead, while another covered their rear.

Sebbe watched the group advancing across the screen. "Trained. Least some of 'em."

"Authority?" Kammeo asked.

Sebbe shook his head. "I dinna' think so. Military, sure."

Ward narrowed his eyes, trying to focus better. "Is this one a child?" He tapped at the smallest figure on the screen.

"Kenna' tell." Sebbe rubbed at his nose. "T'be odd. Way they move seems trained, too. Jes small, mebbe."

"Have you seen anyone else in the area since we got here?" Ward asked.

Andromeda shook her head. "Not a soul. Town's been abandoned for years, ever since an attack at a power plant upriver contaminated the water."

Kammeo tapped through the screens, switching views. "They're headed this way."

Ward turned to face her. "Does anyone else know about this place? Could anyone have guessed you'd come here?"

Kammeo shook her head. "No way. Like I said, no one comes up here anymore. Not just Hallyn's family. No one. Hallyn never took me here."

The group was closing in, now less than a quarter mile away. Proximity alerts flashed, lights strobing across the entire room.

"Well, obviously someone knowsi." Ward hit the table. "Gondu. Ney a skootch pachem."

Kammeo was breathing faster. "Should we secure the room? The entrance is hidden. If they don't know to look here—"

"En be sittin' ducks?" Sebbe made a sharp sound, sucking air in through his teeth.

Andromeda stood, moving quickly toward a closet. "I say we lock down. Arm ourselves. Hopefully, they'll take what they need and move on. If not..." She threw open the door, revealing a stockpile of weapons.

"They won't leave. Not if they're looking for trouble or, worse, for us. The place is full of our stuff. Clearly occupied. I'm mean," Ward laughed angrily, "we left bedang pancakes on the table."

"Gondu," Sebbe hissed. "How ken we be such sallop!"

On the cameras, they watched the group pause, looking around. They were close enough, now, to see the house.

"Plan!" Andromeda shouted. "Like now?"

Sebbe hissed through his teeth again. "Arm yerselves. Lock de room. They canna' come down faster en one ta' time."

Andromeda started handing out weapons, but Ward didn't move from the screen.

"Wait." He held up a hand. "They're stopping again."

One of the smaller figures looked around, scanning the forest.

"They're looking for the cameras."

"Of course they're looking for the cameras. So what?" Andromeda grabbed another weapon, throwing it toward Kammeo.

Ward held up a hand, staring at the screen. "Just...just wait."

A figure moved toward the trees, still looking around. The cameras would be impossible to spot. They'd be barely the size of fingertips, hidden in tree knots and camouflaged by bark, but that didn't matter. What mattered is that this person knew they'd be there. Not a revelation—any house with a survival bunker would have surveillance. But this was a small, unassuming old house in the middle of nowhere. This person knew *this* house—knew there was a bunker.

"Hallyn?" Ward turned to look at Kammeo. "Could he be one of them?"

"No. He was..." She drew in a shuddering breath. "He was barely coherent when I left."

Ward's heart sped up. "If it's not Hallyn..."

The figure stopped, facing the woods, angled toward but not looking exactly at the cameras, like they knew they were there somewhere, just not exactly where.

They lifted a hand toward their head.

Ward's hands shook, his heart beating harder in his chest. He leaned in closer, bringing the figure into the best focus his damaged eyes would allow.

The figure pulled a cover off of their head and, staring toward the camera, smiled.

A small pale face. Hair cut short, but deep red, like fields of poppies he'd seen in books.

"Lea!" Ward jumped out of his seat and ran for the stairs.

Sebbe tried grabbing for him but missed. "Stop! It kenna' be a trap."

Ward barely heard him. It wasn't a trap. He knew it. Her smile. *Her* smile. He'd thought he'd never see it again.

He burst through the front door, running toward the woods. He didn't know which direction to go; he just ran, ignoring the frozen ground under his bare feet. Ignoring the angry protest from his just-healed back.

"Lea!" He screamed. Stopping in a clearing, he turned in a circle. "Lea!"

A figure separated itself from the trees. Fair skin stark against dark clothing. The bright red hair, cropped and chaotic.

She ran for him, throwing herself into his arms. "You're here! Oh, God. I thought I'd never see you again!"

She wrapped her arms around his waist, squeezing. He wanted to scream in pain. For joy. "Is it really you?" Ward's face was wet with tears. He pushed her away for a moment so he could see her face. Skin sallow. Dark circles under her eyes. So thin. But his Lea.

Ignoring the pain and the cold, he lifted her, holding her against him as tight as he could, sobbing so hard that he couldn't speak. He felt her body shaking against his. Her tears wetting his neck. He held her closer, never wanting to let go ever again.

"I thought you'd been captured. I saw you pulled into the building and—"

Hearing a sound, he glanced up to see five other figures emerging from woods. They all unmasked. All approached except for the smallest person, who held back. From this distance, Ward couldn't make out their features, but one came closer to them, moving faster. Black hair. Slight, muscular build. Something about the way she moved... His eyes narrowed and then went wide. The hair had changed. The clothing wasn't red. But he knew the face of his tormentor.

Dropping Lea, he pushed her behind him, holding up a hand. "Stay back! Stay back!"

He cursed. Why hadn't he brought a weapon? Sebbe had warned him it could be a trap. Lea must be their hostage. He growled, crouching slightly, fists raised, ready to pounce before the woman could get a stun or shot off.

Aisling held up a hand. Slowed her approach. "Calm down. I'm not who you think."

Ward's muscles tightened, ready to spring. Glancing toward the house, he saw Sebba and Andromeda out on the porch, weapons trained on the approaching group.

"Not another step," Ward hissed. "We'll take you all down."

"Stop!" Lea grabbed his arm. "Stop. Ward. It's okay. She's with me. She got me here."

"She…" He looked at Lea and then back at Aisling, who'd done as he said, stopping a few feet away. The other people in her group had all lowered their weapons.

Lea pulled at his arm. "It's okay. Let's go inside. We'll explain everything. Just trust me, okay?"

He looked at Lea. Trust me. Every instinct he had told him not to. After all these years of running, after being captured by the enemy and then escaping, here, again, the enemy was at his door. *Kill her. Grab Lea. Run.* It was all his mind could process.

Lea shook his arm again, eyes wide and earnest. "Trust me."

He stared at her a moment, mouth dry, body shaking.

He lowered his arms.

⁓❖⁓

Ward stared at the girl sitting opposite him. His wide lips quivered on her face. His wide blue eyes…or the wide blue eyes he used to have, stared back at him.

"My niece?" Something was stuck in his throat. In his chest.

Leandrea squeezed his hand.

"Dillon." The girl was trembling and biting at her lips as she stared back at him, looked away, and then stared again.

"Dillon," he repeated. He couldn't get his head around it. "Like—"

"Like my grandfather." The girl blinked again with his eyes."

Ward turned to look at Lea. "How…how old is she?"

"She's right there." Lea smiled, tears in her eyes. "Why don't you ask her?"

He was trying. It was hard to look at the girl. He didn't know why. It made him feel disoriented and strangely shy. Dillon. Like Kitty's father. He'd loved the man. He'd watched him die. He'd given up everything in his honor.

"Dillon." The name stuck to his tongue, cramped his throat.

"I just turned twelve," the girl said.

Her voice was small and light, but he could see his sister's strength and defiance in her eyes.

"Twelve." He looked from side to side. The number cramped his stomach. Twelve years. He was seven then. Alone in the subway tunnels. Starving and waiting for his sister to return.

"So you were...so Kitty was..." The cogs in his brain clicked so fast that he couldn't quite keep up. He felt dizzy. He looked at Lea.

"Is that why..."

"Why your sister didn't come back?"

Swallowing, he nodded. He wanted her to say yes so badly. For this to be the answer. His sister had given him up to save her. That was something he could understand. It was something he could live with.

"No, but that's a long story, too."

"So. But..." He didn't even know where to start. "She's alive?"

Leandrea nodded. "Very much."

He swallowed hard. His hands shook. Alive, but not here. But her daughter was. Her *daughter*.

"You saw her?"

Leandrea nodded again. She held his hand, her palm so small and cold. "Do you want me to start at the beginning?"

Ward nodded.

Andromeda brought over two cups of hot tea, placing them in front of Ward and Lea as Lea began her story, starting from the moment Aisling had contacted her when he was in recovery. Telling him how the woman had helped her escape. He thought of that moment, seeing Leandrea pulled back into the window and how helpless he'd felt. He'd thought for sure that she's been taken into custody. Reprogrammed.

Lea kept talking as Kammeo wrapped a blanket around his back. He realized he'd been shivering. There was sweat on his brow.

He whispered, "Thank you," as Lea told him about crossing the ocean. Meeting his sister and Dillon. The city that Kitty ruled and the years she'd spent looking for him. It was like hearing that all his dreams had come true. His sister, not just alive, but thriving, leading. She hadn't wanted to give him up. She'd never stopped trying to find him. Aisling, not his tormentor, but the person who'd been trying to save him.

Lea told him how her parents had arrived. About the information on the chips. About the plans they'd all made together to save him, to stop the war, to save the Prole.

Joy tingled across his skin and up his spine. Hope prickled his scalp and behind his eyes. She'd never given up on him. She was never going to stop fighting for him. And now, there was a plan to save the rest of The Origins. To stop ReInception. His sister was a part of it! He had a niece. It was more than he could ever have possibly hoped for or dreamed of.

And then Leandrea stopped, tears filling her eyes. She looked at Aisling.

"Please. I can't tell him the rest."

The tingle of joy turned into a ripple of fear. Ward looked between Lea and Aisling. "Can't tell me what?"

Aisling stood behind Lea, squeezing her shoulders as Ward looked up at the woman. He understood mentally that she'd been looking for him all along, trying to find and save him. But his body, unable to reconcile this with what his brain knew, prickled with the desire the rip her hands off Lea's shoulders and throw her across the room.

He breathed in deeply. Exhaled slowly. Something terrible was coming. Something terrible was always coming.

"Jes tell me."

CHAPTER TWENTY-NINE

<u>**Summary of Modification of the Genetic Material of Kallum Gordon**</u> *Synthetic biology was deployed, enabling the creation of entirely artificial genomes designed to resist profiling. These were inserted into Kallum's cells to produce a genetic identity that does not match any known human sequence.*

—FROM THE FILES OF DENNISON KELVIN

Day 12: December 22, 2126: Upstate New York
Ward

W ard pushed himself to stand. He felt like he weighed a thousand pounds; like he was a thousand years old. But his eyes were dry and his hands steady.

He turned to look at the woman he loved. Her face was swollen and blotchy, her eyes a network of red lines. How had he not seen it the moment he saw her? The deep circles under her eyes. The slump in her posture. How thin and frail she'd become in just a couple of weeks. How had he not recognized grief?

"I'm sorry for your loss."

The words came out hollow. He knew somewhere deep inside, that he meant them. But he didn't feel them. He didn't feel anything.

Turning away from the table, he walked down the hallway toward his room.

He heard the scrape of chair legs and then Andromeda's voice. "Give him some time, Lea. He needs to be alone."

"We can't stay here." Aishling's voice. "Katherine knows where you are, too. She could send people here at any moment."

"He's in no condition to travel." Andromeda said. "And we don't have anywhere else to go."

"We'll leave first thing in the morning, when we've time to pack supplies, prepare a plan. Sure." Sebbe said.

He shuffled down the hall and into his small room, closing the door quietly behind him. They'd figure out what to do next without him. But if his sister could track them anyhow, what was the point of running?

He sat on the edge of the bed, the mattress sagging under his weight, sitting there in his too-small clothing—a ridiculous monstrosity perched on a too-small bed. A ridiculous waste of life. He was not the same person his sister had left in those tunnels. What self-delusion had led him to believe that the sister who left him would have been the same? Even then, she hadn't been the same person he'd worshipped as a small boy—not since before he went to court—not since before his mother reprogrammed her. His entire life, he'd yearned for a mirage.

He put his face in his hands, wanting to feel something, wishing for anger or tears…anything. Instead, there was just this hollowness, like he'd been scraped out with a scalpel, like his gut was a sinkhole. Swinging his legs up, he lay in the bed on top of the covers, staring at the cracks in the ceiling. His feet hung over the end, and the bed groaned and sagged beneath him as if to mock how grown and huge he was, and how, like the bed, his dreams had been small, juvenile and stuck in the past.

Footsteps approached from down the hallway. Lea, coming to console him. He was ashamed of the dread he felt. She'd just lost her parents, while he'd lost something that hadn't even been real. He should console her—isn't that what you did when you loved someone? Yet he couldn't muster up the emotional energy to even sit up in the bed.

The door creaked open. "Uncle?"

He blinked. Something stirred in his chest. This girl had known about him her whole life, while the idea of her had never even crossed his mind. Who did she think he was? Probably also someone who was long gone—some sweet, innocent, idealistic boy who would do anything for his big sister.

"Dillon." He pushed himself to sitting, the name familiar and warm in his mouth. He didn't know why she was here instead of home with her mother. Why Leandrea or Aisling would have let her endanger herself by coming to this place. But he was glad that she was—it was the only thing he was glad for.

Standing in the doorway, she looked around the room.

She'd grown up in a place that had been built from the ground up only a couple of decades before she was born. It sounded both miraculous and surreal—to be in a place with no history, no rotting infrastructure. Nowhere to hide.

"This place must seem so strange to you."

Wide eyed, the girl nodded.

"Have you ever left Tob Namara before?"

She shook her head.

"Ever seen a place like this?"

"In vids, I guess."

"Me too," he smiled. "I mean, not like where I live is pretty, but this place is stuck in the far past." He pointed to his feet hanging over the edge of the bed. "Before Prole, as you can tell."

She fidgeted, stepping from foot to foot.

"Are you Prole?"

He considered. "I think so. At least that's what they've been tellin' me all these years."

She stared at her feet. "I guess I never thought of you that way."

"I guess you wouldn't. I imagine if you don't grow up with Prole, you jes don't think that way at all. I wouldn't know, but maybe you can tell me."

She twisted her hands, refusing to meet his eyes.

"You can come in if yeh want. I'm not as mean as I look."

She glanced up at him, a red blush creeping up her neck and onto her face. "I...I don't think you look mean."

This time, he shrugged. "It's okay. I know how I look. Sometimes, it comes in handy, but I sure dunna' want to scare you." The Prole accent came heavier when he was tired—when Kallum slipped further away from him and Ward took over. He wasn't sure who to be for this girl...his niece...Kallum or Ward? Upper caste or Prole? Probably, she just wanted her uncle. He could try to be that—like he'd been so many other things when his survival necessitated it—if only he knew what it was to be "uncle."

Her smile, that oddly familiar smile, quivered as she walked into the room, looking first at the bed and then at an old wooden chair with chipping paint that sat in front of a desk, trying to decide where to sit. She opted for the chair, turning it to face him. She sat stiffly, probably unaccustomed to a seat so rigid and unforgiving.

Ward pushed himself further up on the bed. "Want to know something?"

She nodded.

"There's a secret bunker under the house and everything there is much more comfortable."

"Then why are you here and not there?"

"I was just wonderin' that meh self." He smiled at her, and she laughed, a small, girlish giggle. It was funny to feel so shy and awkward around your own blood, but she was a stranger.

"You don't sound like the rest of them. Not even like Sebbe, but you're both Prole."

"I was part of the upper caste until I was seven, remember? I guess some of that stuck with me. But I'm good at sounding how I need to, depending on who I'm with."

"So this is how you think I need you to sound?"

Ward thought about this a moment, feeling that odd flicker in his chest again, the heaviness lifting ever so slightly. "This is just how I sound. I don't feel like I should sound like anyone but myself with you."

That made her smile again. Ward had never been good at saying the right thing just because it was expected of him. With Dillon, he felt like the right thing to say was what he actually felt.

The girl's shoulders relaxed a little, her mouth slightly open. Her wide blue eyes studied him in a way that felt curious and non-judgmental. He wasn't sure what he felt...gladness, maybe? It wasn't a feeling he was accustomed to. And it was a selfish feeling; with him was about the least safe place on earth.

He stopped smiling and shifted, wincing and pushing the pillow further behind him. The exertion of running out to Lea, the cold on his fragile skin, the surge and then drop of adrenaline—it had all left him feeling sore and raw.

"Why are you here, Dillon? If yer mom's been telling you about me, then you know that being here is dangerous."

Clearing her throat, she stared up at the ceiling. "My whole life, my mom's been telling me about you. How sweet you were. What you did for her. I watched all the vids of you in the courtroom."

She glanced at him, eyes damp, and then looked away again, twisting her hands in her lap.

"She told me all those things, and I couldn't stand not knowing what happened to you. I started guessing what they might have done, that you might not even be alive. She never gave up hope you were out here somewhere. If nothing else, then because you could be leverage someday—for either side."

Glancing at him, she blushed again. "I'm sorry. That was..."

"Honest?"

She nodded.

"It's okay, Dillon. I'm pretty tough, as you might imagine. I've been wondering the same things about Kitty all these years. Finally knowing the truth...it's a big burden off my shoulders."

The girl gave him another tentative smile. "My mom isn't..." Dillon looked up at the ceiling, searching for the right words. "She's...well, it's been hard. DeInception was still being studied when I was a baby. My mom wasn't so good back then. While the scientists were working on helping her, other people mostly looked after me, like Sirkka."

"You love her very much, don't you?"

Dillon nodded. "She was always there for me until she went to find you."

Ward winced. "I'm so sorry, Dillon."

The girl shook her head. "No, I mean, I was happy she went to look for you. But my mom was better when she was around."

"How do you mean?"

"As they perfected DeInception, my mom started getting more stable. It takes a long time, especially when someone has been programmed and reprogrammed like she has. There were a lot of sessions, and then a lot of therapy. Improvements in Netting helped speed it up for new patients—"

"Netting?"

"Netting."

Ward shook his head.

"It's like comms, but more...like wired right to the brain."

Ward shuddered. Augintel. He'd asked Aisling more about that later. For now, he wanted to know about his sister and his niece.

"Once she improved, she started getting involved in politics. She became obsessed with finding you, but instead of it being about helping you, it was in the context of how important finding you was. How having you by her side would foment her cause. I know..." she glanced at him.

"It okay. Jes say what you mean. I'm not that little boy anymore."

"I mean, I'm sure she still loves you, but she's not—"

"Not a very nice person?"

Dillon shook her head. "I try to understand why, what her life was like, how she's trying to do this to make the world a better place. Well, that's what she says. And maybe she used to mean it..."

"But you don't think she does anymore."

Dillon shook her head again.

"And you thought I'd be different?"

Dillon nodded. "You were so brave."

"I'm not that person anymore either."

The girl's lip wobbled, and tears rolled down her cheeks. "I try to be like you. Brave and kind."

Brave and kind. Was he? Had he ever been? He guessed that Kallum was a brave boy. And he'd been kind to his sister. But was what he'd done to his own parents kind? He wasn't sure. He wasn't even sure if it was right anymore. He'd been held up as this epitome of loyalty, but that loyalty had been to his sister. What he'd done to his parents was decidedly unloyal. People always saw him as one thing or another, but he knew that he'd always been both sides of the coin. Ruthless and loving. Kind and cruel. Loyal and disloyal.

The girl looked so wide-eyed and hopeful. He thought of how his sister had become after she was modified: Unstable. Prone to sudden fits of rage. There was a lot more he needed to understand about DeInception before he believed it was the miracle it sounded like. Maybe it could undo programming, but could it undo the psychosis it had caused? He didn't see how.

"The truth is, I guess I'm brave when I need to be—for the people I need to be brave for. But you can't always do what you need to do *and* be kind. Do you know what I mean?"

The girl nodded, wiping her nose with the back of her hand. Ward looked around for something, some paper or cloth for the girl. Rooting through a drawer in a bedside table, he found a sock. It was old but looked clean.

"Sorry. Best I can do." He tossed her the sock, and she laughed, wiping her nose with it.

"I'm glad you're here, Dillon. I'm so pleased to meet you." And he was. He'd walked in here feeling empty and hopeless, but now his chest felt full, like it was filled with light. "But it's not safe for you here. It's not safe to be near me."

"It's not safe at home, either."

Ward narrowed his eyes, furrowing his brow.

"What do you mean?"

"It's going to get bad, uncle. Very bad. I came because I had to tell you. I had to warn you. And had to get away from her so that we could have a chance to stop her."

"You know her plans?"

Dillon nodded.

"Can you tell me them?"

She nodded again.

CHAPTER THIRTY

Long Term Outcomes: *Genetic modifications could have unpredictable effects on Kallum's health and development. The complexity of the human genome means that unintended mutations could lead to serious medical issues or unanticipated outcomes as the boy matures.*

—FROM THE FILES OF DENNISON KELVIN

Day 13: December 23, 2126: Upstate New York
Leandrea

Leandrea lay on a bed in the bunker, staring up at the ceiling, chewing on a thumbnail. She felt fractured and separated from her old life, with Ward, Andromeda, Sebbe and Kammeo upstairs and she, down here, with Aisling, Dillon and Aisling's loyal men in the bunk rooms. When she and Hallyn had come here, they'd slept in this room. It had felt like an adventure, hiding down here in the safe room, in this warm, cozy bed, with the facade of an innocent old house above them. Hallyn, who fit against her like a piece of a puzzle, curled around her back.

She loved Ward in a way she hadn't known it was possible to love someone, a deep, gut twisting yearning. Until a couple of days ago, she'd regretted nothing. When Ward was in danger and she was making a plan, when she had hope and allies, it all seemed worth it, and everything seemed possible. Now? She couldn't deny that her life was less painful without him. Her parents would be alive. She would still be passively fighting for the Prole, Hallyn by her side, as blissfully ignorant as the rest of the world about Kallum Gordon's fate. Could you love someone truly yet wish you'd never met them? If Hallyn had fit like a puzzle piece, Ward engulfed her, consumed her, set everything in her world on fire. And the most heartbreaking part, he hadn't meant to. If he could take it all back, he would. Would she? She wanted to say she'd do anything to bring her parents back but wishes didn't work that way. Wishing didn't work at all.

She felt alone and unmoored. The people she used to talk to, her parents, Hallyn, were lost to her. Ward, upon learning that his sister had killed her parents, had shut down.

She wanted to be angry at him, but she understood he must be in shock. After weeks with ReInception doing who knows what to him, after all those years of trying to find his sister only to discover she'd become just as ruthless as the people they'd been trying to escape. All those days thinking that either something terrible had happened to her or that, like everyone else, she'd abandoned him.

She rolled over in the bed, facing the wall. The bunker was full of paintings of bucolic landscapes—green pastures and dark forests, beaches with empty vistas and blue waters. She supposed they were meant to soothe people trapped in there for a long period of time, bringing the outside world inside. But none of those landscapes were real—at least not anymore. They were images of a past she couldn't imagine and a future that seemed impossible.

When she'd been here with Hallyn, they'd just wanted to sneak away and have an adventure—somewhere away from prying eyes. Somewhere private. They'd dipped into the stash of carefully inventoried supplies for popcorn and sat on the sofa watching vids. They hadn't thought about or cared that, sealed, the safe room blocked all signals from reaching the outside world, including their comm signals. By the time they emerged a day later, their parents had been in a panic, both their children having suddenly gone dark. Was that when Hallyn's parents started hating her? When their son, for the first time, defied them?

After Ward had left the room, Andromeda and Kammeo had filled Leandrea in as best they could on Ward's story—what had happened to him after he was captured, how he'd opened Andromeda's eyes to what her father was really like, and how watching Hallyn deteriorate had similarly opened Kammeo's eyes. It broke Lea's heart thinking about Hallyn that way, so frail and confused. Now that they had the tech for DeInception, she hoped she'd be able to help him some day—heal him. But the process would be long and hard, and Hallyn would have to be willing.

This room was filled with Hallyn's smiles and laughter, his kindness and humor. His ghost.

Grabbing the blanket and a pillow, Leandrea tiptoed into the common area, nesting in the corner of the massive sofa that sat in front of the vid screens. Resting her head against the side, she closed her eyes.

She heard the soft sound of footsteps coming down the stairs and the door to the room she'd just left creaking open.

"Lea?"

She sat up, squinting at the large shadow filling the doorway.

"Ward? Over here."

He walked toward her, sitting on the ell-shaped part of the sofa perpendicular to hers, his shoulder just inches from her head. She felt that wall back between them, like the one that had been there when she'd first realized she cared for him, and he'd rebuffed her. Now, she didn't know who had erected that wall—him, because his sister had killed her parents or her, for breaking his heart by telling him. It didn't matter that it was neither their fault.

He reached for her hand, and she let him take it, but the wall did not waver.

"I'm so sorry, Lea. I'm so sorry about your parents. I'm sorry that I couldn't give you what you needed earlier."

"I understand."

And she did, but it didn't make her feel better.

"They sounded like wonderful people."

"They were." Using the past tense still didn't feel real.

"I'd hoped to meet them someday. I'd hoped they'd find room for me in their hearts the way you did."

Sitting up, she turned toward him. Letting go of his hand, she pulled her legs in close to her chest, hugging them.

"Before they died, I told them about you. I mean, they'd seen you on the vids, so they knew there was something between us, but I told them everything."

Ward shifted to look at her. In the dark, his face was shadowed and unreadable. "You told them who I am?"

"Yes."

"And?"

"I mean, they were surprised."

Ward gave a small huffing laugh. "No doubt."

"I think it helped them understand...understand why I was doing what I was doing. Why I'd fallen in love with you so fast."

He shifted his body so that he was facing her, too, brushing her hair off her face. He took a lock between his fingers, twisting it.

"Not much of a disguise, is it?"

Ward laughed. "Not at all. But I like it. It suits you."

She could hear the smile in his voice. "And the beard suits you." She put her hand to his face, stroking his cheek.

"Does it?"

"It makes you look softer, somehow. Your outsides match your insides."

"Well, I guess that's ok—specially since I don't know how to shave."

At this, they both laughed then went quiet again.

"Andy and Kam told me a bit about how you got here, but there were a lot of gaps."

"It's quite a story, Bird. So many strange things happened."

Something shivered through her middle and quavered between them when he called her by his pet name for her. At first, it had been an insult, but quickly, it had become affectionate; something only he called her.

"I bet."

"If you can stand it, maybe I can tell you in the morning. It's been a long day, and I haven't been well."

"Your back?"

He nodded. "For starters."

Leandrea understood, but she dreaded him leaving her side. The wall was there, but it was shimmering now, less solid. They needed more time.

He inched closer to her. "Can I ask you something?"

She nodded. "Of course."

"Is gondu, gondu."

Lea laughed. "Now I really want to know."

"Kammeo told me you came here with Hallyn. When you did, you stay in that room with him?" He jutted his chin toward the closed door.

He couldn't see it, but she blushed anyhow. "I'm sorry."

"Is that why you're out here?"

She nodded. "Too many feelings in that room."

Ward nodded. "I ken understand you're sad about him. I am, too. He's a good man."

"He is."

Ward squeezed her hand. "We'll get him out of there, Bird. We'll help him."

"You think we can?"

"We can try. We have to. We have to save all of them." Ward went quiet, breathing faintly in and out.

"Can I ask you something?"

"Sure."

"Andromeda told me you convinced her about ReInception. She said she overheard you and her father talking about how she hadn't been reprogrammed, so she knew her father was lying, and you were telling the truth."

"Yes."

"But that wouldn't have been enough. I know Andromeda. She's a lot of things, but disloyal isn't one of them. She worships her father. Something else happened, didn't it?"

Ward nodded.

"What?"

Ward sighed, leaning back against the sofa and taking her hand again. He squeezed it, staring down at her, his eyes shadowed. His hand trembled slightly in hers, the pause drawing out, a dark and heavy presence in the room.

"Kelvin is the one who did this to me. He was the one who took me when I was a boy. He was trying to make his name with ReInception, trying to prove that modification didn't have to stop with Prole infants. He was the one who took my identity away and threw me back into the tunnels to live or to die—he didn't care—so long as no one would believe who I really was."

Leandrea nodded slowly, more pieces of the puzzle clicking together. "So, when you told me you overheard Andy in the bar, bragging about who her father was, and you saw an opportunity—"

"That was true, but it wasn't the first time I'd seen her. I'd been following you all for months, trying to find a way to make contact."

"I see." Leandrea ran a thumb along the back of Ward's hand, feeling bone and sinew.

"So, Andromeda found out that her father did this to you."

"She did."

"And so she helped save you."

"She did."

Leandrea was quiet, staring down at their hands, trying to process everything Ward was telling her.

"Are you angry?"

"Angry?" Leandrea searched herself, trying to determine what she felt. "No. I just don't understand why you didn't tell me in the first place."

"Because if you'd known I was after Kelvin all along—if you knew that what I really wanted was—"

"Revenge?"

Ward shifted in his seat, thinking about this. "Revenge. No. I don't think I wanted revenge. I wanted to expose him. To expose all of them. There was nothing to stop me from doing what I needed to do until you came along."

"And you think I would have tried to stop you?"

"If you'd known everything? Yes. I think you would have."

"Would you have stopped if I asked you to?"

Ward stared at her for a few moments. "No. I would not have."

Maybe she should have felt angry about this, but she didn't. Not about the lie he told then, or the truth he told now. She understood why he'd done it. Why he'd picked and chosen his truths. She rested her head on his shoulder. She was so tired. She'd been traveling for three days, non-stop, with no sleep other than what Aisling induced with drugs to keep her in one piece. There'd be more time for this tomorrow. More time to talk and figure out what had happened to both of them, who they were now, and what was next.

"Will you stay with me?" The question came out small and timid. She was so afraid that he'd say no, but she couldn't bear the thought of him leaving again.

Ward laughed. "Like you have any other choice." He put his arm around her and pulled her in close. "For two weeks, all I could think about was, were you alive? What were they doing to you? You think I'll let you be more than fifty feet from me ever again?"

Leandrea took his hand, pressing it against her cheek. "Me too."

"Plus, the bed upstairs makes my cot in the dorm seem luxurious."

She laughed. "Hang on."

Running to the supply room, she grabbed more pillows and blankets, bringing them back to the sofa and setting up the other side for him. They lay perpendicular to each other, heads touching, hands held. For the first time in weeks, a peaceful sleep took them both.

They woke to the sounds of an alert blaring, both of them jumping up and throwing back their covers. Aisling and her people poured out of the rooms, Sebbe, Kammeo and Andromeda racing down the stairs.

"What the Floods is that?" Ward's eyes were wide.

"It's an emergency alert." Leandrea raced to the control panel at the end of the room. "It means there's going to be a government broadcast."

The screens came to life, an alert symbol showing. The text scrolling below announced that, at any moment, the president would make a statement. Leandrea bit her nails as they crowded around the screen, waiting.

An image materialized on the screen, not of the Oval Office, but of another familiar place. It was a dais in front of a tall building—a large treelike structure with massive, blinding white leaves radiating around it. Katherine Donovan stood in front of a crowd, a mask over her eyes. Next to her stood Vella, wearing flowing peach robes, their hair now a natural brown and a pin designating some kind of official status pinned on their chest.

"What the Floods?" Aisling pushed her way closer, Dillon by her side.

"I don't understand. Who is it?" Asked Ward.

Leandrea looked at him. "It's your sister."

CHAPTER THIRTY-ONE

Unfortunately, the retinal modification created permanent scarring and damage to the boy's eyes. Only a transplant will restore his vision. As an aside, I would note the boy's incredibly high tolerance for pain and a tendency toward martyrdom. Even when told that expressing his pain levels would help reduce his suffering, the boy refused to cooperate.

—FROM THE FILES OF DENNISON KELVIN

Day 14: December 24, 2126: Upstate New York & Tob Namara
Ward

A dark, olive-skinned woman with shoulder-length black hair and crystal blue eyes stood in front of a lectern. Squinting, Ward moved closer to the screen, trying to get a clearer view of his sister. She was unmistakable with her sharp cheekbones and the wide full mouth they shared—his mother's mouth. He wanted to reach for the screen and touch it, as if that would assure him she was real, but in the room full of people, of strangers, he restrained himself. She was smaller than he remembered, thin and sharp, but straight-backed and sure. That confidence he'd remembered from their childhood radiated from her.

He felt a hand squeeze his own, and he looked down at it. Dillon. The girl looked up at him. She was terrified, eyes wide and lips trembling. The smile he didn't know had formed on his face until now fell away.

"It's okay," he assured her.

Dillon, skin waxy with fear, shook her head.

Katherine had assassinated Lea's parents and attempted to kill Lea, too. If Lea hadn't insisted on keeping that copy of the files, maybe Katherine would have let them go. He wanted to believe that she couldn't be so ruthless. He wanted to make excuses for his sister, like that she was sacrificing them for what she believed was the greater good, even if it was misguided. Rulers had to make hard decisions all the time. If he convinced himself that Lea keeping the files was the reason the Justuses were dead, then it was his fault. He told Lea to never let those files fall into someone else's hands. He was the one who'd told her they were her lifeline, so it was his fault, not Kitty's.

Dillon had told him of a different plan. Concepts scraped together into a less than full picture from bits of discussions she'd overheard. A plan to share the contents of the files publicly in order to encourage the Prole to revolt with the promise of support from Tob Namara. Their military was small—far smaller than the U.S., but also far more technologically advanced. Decades of the U.S. creating barriers against the rest of the world, both political and real, had left it behind as the rest of the world moved forward, Tob leading the charge.

The crowd quieted down, and Ward's sister spoke.

"The world knows me as Katarina Donovan, but before I was Katarina Donovan, I was someone else. Someone you all know. My name was Katherine Vega."

There was a long silence and then cries of surprise from the audience. People began shouting questions.

Kitty put up her hand. "Please, let me finish and then I'll take your questions." She took a deep breath. "After my brother, Kallum, and I ran away, we were in hiding. The Authority caught me, and then I was rescued by The Origins. I was brought here under a false identity. Raised by the people of Tob Namara, I rose in a position of government. Only the most trusted members of the Cabinet knew who I was."

"Where's Kallum Gordon?" Someone in the audience shouted. There was muttering and people nodded. "Yes! Where is he?"

Kitty raised her hand again. "I'm getting to that." She looked at Vella and then back toward the audience. "Several years ago, a member of our military was sent to the United States and embedded herself within the Authority. Her goal was to find my brother. A couple of months ago, she succeeded."

There were gasps. "Where is he? Where's Kallum Gordon?"

"My brother is a Prole. This was achieved through cruel torture inflicted upon him when he was just seven years old. Other measures were taken to obscure his identity. They were equally cruel. As suspected, he was raised as a Ward. When he was released to work and pay back his societal dues," her lip curled as she said this, "we were able to put together clues that helped locate him."

Kitty produced a small cloth and dabbed at her eyes. Wiped her nose.

"How do you know all of this?" Someone asked from the audience.

Katherine cleared her throat and adjusted her jacket. "My brother is a member of a group of freedom fighters known as 'The Origins.'"

"The ones that bombed the rally?" Someone shouted.

"One thing at a time, please. There will be plenty of opportunity for questions. But no, The Origins are not responsible for the bombing. Nevertheless, about two weeks ago, my brother was taken into custody by ReInception. You have all seen the vids of a Ward and a brave young woman, Leandrea Justus, fleeing from capture."

Ward squeezed his niece's hand. His body, rigid. "No, Kitty," he thought. "Please, no."

"That Ward, who was fleeing from capture, was my brother, Kallum Gordon."

Around Ward, the room tilted, his knees gave way.

From far away, he heard his niece call "Help!" as he crumpled against her. Strong arms caught and held him, lowering him gently into a chair. On the screen, the crowd erupted, everyone shouting at once. Again, Katherine held up her hand.

"Our operative was able to help Ms. Justus escape, but my brother was removed by The Origins and taken to a highly classified ReInception facility. We know that, when he was taken, Kallum was in dire medical condition. For weeks, we were unable to determine anything about his health or his whereabouts."

Ward had been told. The animals. Mice. Birds. They hadn't been able to penetrate the ReInception facility; they hadn't been able to actually see how Ward had been treated. But they knew he was there. They'd waited for him to emerge and then...

"Oh no." Ward muttered. How had they not seen it? "Oh no!"

Everyone in the room turned to look at him. Leandrea grabbed his arm. "What is it?"

She wouldn't. She couldn't.

"Ms. Justus and our operative returned to the U.S. to assist my brother and his allies and ensure their safety in the battle to come."

"Liar!" Dillon screamed, tears flowing down her cheeks. "You liar!"

Proximity alerts started to blare, screens lighting up all over the room. They looked toward the monitors and saw a swarm of birds descending toward the house, landing in the trees all around them. From the forest, deer, coyote, mice and rabbits emerged, closing in on the house, surrounding it.

"No." Aisling muttered. "No, no, no. Why would she do this?"

"Gondu!" Sebbe cursed. "She's trying to flush us out!"

"I'm happy to report that Ms. Justus and our operative, Officer Sirkka Aisling, have rendezvoused with my brother, Kallum Gordon, along with a surviving and brave leader of The Origins, who we have been only able to identify as 'Sebbe.' With them are—"

"What the Floods!" Andromeda screamed. "Arschlog!"

"Andromeda Kelvin, daughter of Dennison Kelvin, Kammeo Te Awa, whose parents are also active supporters of ReInception."

Kammeo covered her face.

"What the floods is she doing?" Andromeda looked at Aisling.

Aisling shook her head. "Trying to flush us out, like Sebbe said."

"But why?"

Aisling shook her head again. "I don't know. I swear. I don't know."

Kitty looked right into the cameras. "Even they know that ReInception is evil. And what I'm about to tell you will convince you, too."

Aisling had told Ward that Tob Namara had the tech to hack into the U.S. systems and broadcast. If Aisling was correct, then right now, Kitty's face would be on holoscreens all over the U.S., the ways his and Lea's images had been when they were fleeing. Prole all over—everyone in the U.S—would see her face...and what? Did she really think they'd just rise up? Katherine hadn't lived amongst the Prole. She'd been part of the upper caste. She didn't know how Prole thought or felt. Getting them to revolt would not be as easy as making speeches and promising support. All she'd succeed in doing was expediting Kelvin's plan to use mass-ReInception to subdue them, getting many of them killed along the way. Ward's sister was playing right into Kelvin's hands.

Kitty raised a fist into the air. "Prole! Heed me, Prole! The device that ReInception has implanted in your back can be used for mass ReInception. We have the proof, right here on the files that Leandrea Justus and my brother, Kallum Gordon, so bravely stole from Dennison Kelvin. You need to fight back before it's too late. My army—"

The camera panned toward rows of people in military uniforms, visors on their heads, futuristic-looking weapons at the ready—

"Will be there with you unless ReInception stands down."

Suddenly, an image appeared on the screen of a small yellow house in the woods.

"And my brother, Kallum Gordon, and his brave friends will be there to fight with you, too. Just like he fought for me."

The birds and the animals closed in, moving toward the house, landing on the roof and pecking at the windows upstairs so that it sounded like a hailstorm.

"Rise Up, Prole! Rise up and fight! I, Katherine Vega, am with you. Kallum Gordon is with you!"

Upstairs, glass broke. Everywhere was the sound of beating wings. On the cameras, they could see them swooping through the kitchen and bedrooms, searching the house.

"Tell me you closed the doors!" Leandrea screamed.

"We did!" Dillon cowered against her uncle. "I did!"

The birds tapped and pecked, knocking over objects and bashing into walls, banging against the pantry door.

Ward wheeled to face Leandrea, Kammeo and Andromeda. "Can they break in? Tell me they can't get into this thing!"

Leandrea shook her head. "It's a blast door. It's meant to withstand a nuclear event. But they know where we are, Ward. We can't hide here forever."

The birds beat against the walls and the floor. On the vid screen, displayed to the whole world by his sister, the image zoomed out, the house further and further away, showing first the village, then the mountains, then the river.

"Gondu!" Sebbe cursed. "She's showing them just where to find us."

"Come out, Kallum Gordon! Come out and show the world your face. Show the world who Kallum Gordon really is! I'm here for you, Prole. I'm here for you, my brother, like you were there for me. Rise up, my brother! Rise Kallum Gordon and fight!"

CHAPTER THIRTY-TWO

Kallum's extensive genetic modifications could have unpredictable health consequences, potentially leading to serious medical conditions or unanticipated side effects.

—FROM THE FILES OF DENNISON KELVIN

Day 14: December 24, 2126: New York City
The Doctor

"Why didn't you shut down the transmission?" Kelvin screamed at the President.

On the screen, the President, sitting at a long, oval table with whichever chiefs of her staff had been onsite when Katarina Donovan, aka Katherine Vega's transmission, went live, looked grim.

"If we could do that, don't you think we would have?"

The Med stayed in the back of the room, hands clasped in front of him, along with the rest of Kelvin's most trusted employees.

"How can you not be able to block transmissions from outside the country? How LowQ are you?"

Kelvin paced the room, shaking his head and waving his arms through the air, face red and spit flying, like a rabid dog.

The President's mouth turned down. "Calm down Dennison."

"Calm down! Do you actually understand what just happened?"

The Secretary of War stood up, holding a finger toward the camera. "Mind your tone when speaking to the leader of our country! Don't think you are—"

"Calm down? The Origins have my daughter! That...woman...can say whatever she wants to anyone in this country. She's been spying on us with fucking mice!"

The President crossed her arms on the desk. "We are putting together a plan—"

"A plan? To do what?"

"To destroy their spy tech. To take down their transmission capability."

"That could take months. We need to execute the protocol."

"Are we sure we want to do that? There's no taking it back." This to her cabinet, and not to Kelvin. Kelvin responded anyhow.

"Are we sure!" His face turned maroon, and he sputtered. "She just potentially sparked the revolution. Are you going to take your chances on the Prole population rebelling? They are in our homes. Our businesses. They put our food on our tables, for floods sake! Subdue them! Now!"

The Secretary of War hit his hand on the table twice, commanding attention. "Subdue a third of them, you mean. What about the others?"

The Secretary was calm in this storm, as he was in all storms. The Med's programming made sure of that. His programming made sure that all of them walked a line. Except, of course, Kelvin, who had never let anyone touch his mind.

"A third is better than none," the President said.

The Vice President clicked on his mic. Per protocol, he was not in the war room. He and the president could never be in the same place at the same time—not after what happened during the War of Coastal Incursion. "We need time to talk this through. We can't make this decision rashly."

"We don't have time to talk this through," the Secretary of Defense said. "Look what's already happening!"

Screens around the room lit up, showing Prole pouring into the streets in major cities all over the country: New York, Chicago, Austin.

"With a third of them controlled, we have a chance. It will frighten the rest and we can at least contain things while we formulate a long-term plan. If we need to, we can round up those who continue to protest and modify them.

The President looked at the Secretary, her mouth grim. "Take a vote."

"All in favor?" The Secretary raised a hand. Everyone else in the room followed. "Aye."

The President sighed. "The motion is passed. Dennison. Execute Canis Fidelis."

Dennison turned to face the Med. "Execute the protocol."

Nodding his head, the Med turned and left the room, walking down a hallway and into a control center. Being by Dennison's side all these years, working with him to implant the devices into the Prole, to test them—it had been hard doing that to all those Prole, ever reminding himself that it was for the greater good. Now, he would find out if he'd been telling himself the truth, or swallowing lies.

He sat down in front of the computer as it interfaced with his comm. He rattled off a series of commands that only he knew, which, in turn, opened the Canis Fidelis protocol. From there, he used manual inputs to enter a subroutine.

There was a squeak as a small mouse scrambled across the floor, climbing up his chair and then his desk. Sitting next to him, it faced the screen.

"Are we sure about this?"

Turning its small head to face him, nose twitching, the tiny creature nodded its head.

"Okay then." The Med nodded. "Override Protocol Canis Fidelis."

Override accepted, his comm responded.

"Execute Protocol Cave Canem."

Are you certain you want to execute Protocol Cave Canem? His comm asked.

"Execute Protocol Cave Canem," he repeated.

Protocol executed, his comm told him.

He turned back to face the mouse. "It is done," he told Katherine, via the tiny spy. "God help us, it's done."

In the hallway, he heard screams. Placing the mouse on his shoulder, the Med exited the room. At the end of the hall, a Prole lifted a Gold by the neck, slamming the man against the wall again and again until the screaming stopped and the body went limp. Calmly, the Med walked past, the Prole ignoring him as he dropped the body and went after the next Gold. Every Prole in ReInception had the implant; Kelvin had seen to that. Insurance against a rebellion by his workforce should this day come, turned as a weapon against him.

The Med continued down the hallway, sounds of violence reverberating through the corridors—screams, the pounding of bodies against floors and walls, cracking bones and sickening squelches.

To the right, from the control room, the Med heard Kelvin screaming orders at the Authority: "What the hell is happening here! Shoot them!" Turning left, the Med winced at the sounds of gunfire and falling bodies behind him, the Prole that he'd weaponized instead of subduing, unwilling martyrs to a cause that had been chosen not by them, but for them. Three blue-clad Prole ran past him and toward the control room, ignoring his White, as they'd been programmed to do.

He went through an exit door, into a stairwell, running up several flights of stairs to the ground level. The lobby was empty except for the two dead Authority, laying on the ground, blood still pouring from crushed skulls.

He continued past the bodies, pushing through the blood-slick turnstiles, through the glass doors and out into the streets.

He froze. Unchipped Prole shook in horror, backs against walls and cowering on the ground with their heads covered as their chipped brethren attacked anyone in gold, black or red.

Armed Authority gunned down activated and non-activate Prole alike, shooting anything in Blue that moved. Non-Prole ran screaming in every direction, trying to escape the chaos. It was only the first five minutes and, already, the streets were covered in blood.

Throughout the city, the voice of Katarina Donovan echoed between buildings, her voice deafening over the sounds of sirens and shouts.

"Rise up, my brother! Rise Kallum Gordon and fight!"

Falling to his knees, the Med put his face in his hands. "What have we done, Katarina? What have we done?"

The tiny mouse opened its mouth exposing razor-sharp teeth. It turned its head so that it faced the Med's neck and bit.

GLOSSARY OF TERMS

<u>Common Language</u>

Arschloch = Asshole
Augintel = Augmented intelligence
BCI = Brain Computer Interface
Brute/Bruto = Brainless or stupid
Cage = Jail
Non-comp = Crazy (as in non compos mentis)
Deuce = Shit—as in "full of deuce"
Flesh heads = Idiots
Flood/floods = Fuck—as in, 'what the floods' or "flood 'em"
Folken = F'ing
Grid = Jail
Having a dip = Fooling around/ having sex
Ill Penny = Bad luck or a bad omen. Something unwanted that continuously
    turns up
Ivory = Snobbish
Jetons = Jitters or heebie-jeebies
Keep = A bartender or barkeep
Ken sai = Prole Patois for bullshit that made it into common usage
Lo sento = Slang/sarcastic "I'm sorry."
LowQ = Stupid
Lowered = A term used for people who lose their upper caste status and
    become Prole, but it can also be used as an expletive, such as "I'd rather
    be lowered than show my fear," like "I'd rather be damned."
MDR = Multidrug Resistant
Meshing = The process of implanting technology into the brain to
    seamlessly integrate humans and technology
Mod = Modified—as in having gone through ReInception
Narrow = Small minded
Netting; Netted = The process of enmeshing the brain with computer
    technology

NFiT = *Needle Free Injection Technology*

Delhi Super Bug ("DSB") = *An MDR resistant bacteria that caused massive infant mortalities in the mid 2020s. It began in India and spread throughout Asia*

Pod = *Elevator*

Simp = *Stupid*

Storming = *An expletive, such as "fucking gorgeous," would be "storming gorgeous."*

Tapang = *Courage*

Thaw out = *Take a chill*

Tweak = *Reprogramming when ReInception is failing or faltering*

Uni = *University student*

Ward = *Pylon wards of the state, usually orphans or children whose parents are in prison or executed.*

Wrecked = *Ruined. Caught.*

Yala = *Okay or let's go*

Yellowed = *Frightened or cowed*

Prole Patois: Patois is a clipped version of English with expressions from other language thrown in, reflecting its multicultural influence.

Anxious = *Kan-chee*

Bang = *Exciting*

Bedang = *Stupid/ridiculous*

Beatha = *Whiskey or hard alcohol*

Bring down storm = *Get us in trouble/get the authority called*

Buhay = *Lowlife*

Canary/Bird = *Derogatory Prole term for the upper caste*

Catch no ball = *Unable to understand something*

Chavlaz! = *That was awesome, that was great*

Clady = *A problem as in "non she wee clady, she fierce," means she won't be a small problem, she'll be a big one*

Clam = *Close your mouth or shut up*

Cor = *Heart*

Fin-doh = *Funny*

Gold = *ReInception employee*

Gondu = *Idiot*

Hum Ji = *Coward*

In Frinn = *"In hell," or "in the hell"*
Jadab = *Cute (sarcastic)*
Kang = *Smart*
Ken sai = *Bullshit*
Lah = *An exclamation or emphasis, as in "Rude, lah!" means that's so rude.*
Mort = *Die/dead/dies*
Nitch = *Nothing or never*
Pachem = *Peace*
Pakshet = *Shit, fuck, or goddamit*
Para para = *One at a time or first things first*
Pro a Pro = *Prole to Prole as in "trust me."*
Pune yer Cara = *Punch your face/ punch you in the face*
Red = *Authority*
Relak = *Relax*
Sabo = *Sabotage or saboteur*
Sallop = *Sloppy/lax*
Sian = *Fed up*
Siao = *(See-ow) crazy*
Shell = *She will or she'll*
Skootch = *Pinch or small amount*
Uzhe = *The Usual or The same?*
Yell = *You'll or you will*
Yo = *Me or I*
Your grandfather own this place? = *Call someone out on obnoxious behavior*

Seasteader/Tob Namara Slang
Anskot Hër = *Damn her*

ACKNOWLEDGMENTS

It took a year longer than I'd hoped to get this sequel out into the world—sometimes, life gets in the way of progress.

Thank you to Michael Dolan for having faith that book two would be worth the wait and for being the ultimate optimist, muse and connector. You are everything that is right in the publishing world. Thanks also to my Winding Roads Family—what a blessing to be part of such a supportive, collaborative and optimistic group of authors. Special thanks to N.J. Gallegos and Alexander Nader for reading drafts of this book and providing me with feedback. To Charleigh Frederick, thank you not only for your thoughtful and often hilarious feedback, but for your unceasing support of me and other authors on social media and for being my Geek Girl buddy.

To my friends—I am so lucky to have such good ones. Especially to Maria, Janet, and to Heather, Heather and Heather—I will always be your Veronica. Thank you all for being my cheerleaders and muses—shoulders on a rough day and laugher every day.

To my husband, thank you for making my home a place of peace and sanctuary and for handling all of the madness when I trot off to many conferences, bookish events and retreats.

To my children for encouraging me, making me laugh and correcting my slang. Every book gets a dedication, but in the end, it's all for you. Words cannot express what a joy it is to be a part of your lives every day.

ABOUT THE AUTHOR

Sarena Straus is the multi-award-winning author of the REINCEPTION Trilogy and of BRONX DA: TRUE STORIES FROM THE SEX CRIMES AND DOMESTIC VIOLENCE UNIT. In 2010, BRONX DA sold as a TV pilot to CBS/Paramount. Sarena went on to spend a decade commenting on TV, Radio and Podcasts about criminal cases and law. She lives in the Hudson Valley, NY with her husband, two children, two dogs and a barn cat. When not writing or practicing law, you can find her traveling off the beaten path and scuba diving whenever and wherever she can.

Learn more about Sarena at www.sarenastraus.com and on Substack at https://sarenastraus.substack.com.